SUSAN WIGGS

HALFWAY TO HEAVEN

MIRA®

ISBN 0-7394-2146-8

HALFWAY TO HEAVEN

Printed in U.S.A.

To Alice Borchardt,
dear friend and gifted writer

ACKNOWLEDGMENT

This novel's journey from writer to reader made a lot of stops along the way. A number of truly generous people took the time and care to read over the manuscript, and I thank them from the bottom of my heart: Barb and Joyce, of course, and my Port Orchard pals, Anjali, Kate, Janine, Lois, Rose Marie and PJ. My editor, Martha Keenan, offered many sharp insights, and my agent, Meg Ruley, added that crucial element of fun along with her valuable opinions regarding book titles.

Special thanks to Phil Plait, the original Bad Astronomer, for technical information. Any astronomical badness contained herein is my own.

Part One

A lady should always have an easy, becoming and graceful movement while engaged in a quadrille or promenade. It is more pleasing to the gentleman.

—Lucien O. Carpenter,
The Universal Dancing Master, 1880

One

The bridal bouquet sailed past a dozen outstretched arms, hitting Abigail Beatrice Cabot smack in the face before it dropped into her unsuspecting hands. Just for a moment she saw stars; her eyes watered and her nose stung from the cloying sweetness of gardenias. She blinked twice, then exploded with a terrific sneeze.

First, a deathlike pall fell over the boisterous crowd of well-wishers. Then titters rose from the young ladies nearby, and a flurry of whispers erupted from the wedding guests gathered in the East Room of the White House.

"I'm allergic to gardenias," Abigail muttered in an agony of humiliation. Tattered petals drifted down her face and over the front of her dress, leaving behind a powdery yellow residue. A comb dislodged from her hair, and she felt her braid coming undone.

Dropping the bouquet, she didn't look to see where it landed, but sought escape, shedding the occasional torn flower as she went. A rustle of speculation stalked her across the polished marquetry floor. With each painful step, she tried not to hear the whispers, but couldn't avoid catching a few all-too-familiar phrases: *What a disgrace to Senator Cabot. His daughter's always been a little odd, hasn't she? Must be such a trial to him....*

At the moment, her father stood to one side of the room, regarding her with a crushing look of disappointment. Instead of enhancing his image as the senior senator from Virginia, she'd managed to remind everyone in the room that all of his money and power could not buy him a proper daughter. Suddenly, she wanted to die. His expression, the snickering of the guests nearby—it was all too much. In her haste, she nearly stumbled and fell, lurching a little and further undermining the stability of her coiffure.

Everyone passed in a blur: the strapping bridegroom in his military dress uniform and the dainty bride in her pearl-encrusted gown, trying to see what had become of her bouquet; the cluster of gentlemen gathered around the president, vying for his attention; the first lady and her bevy of gossips, avidly discussing the latest disgrace of Senator Cabot's daughter.

Although the guests parted like the Red Sea before her, Abigail couldn't avoid the impression that they had all gathered for the sole purpose of witnessing her faux pas. Feeling the darts of a dozen pairs of eyes, she wove an awkward path across the ballroom, hoping to reach the glass doors at the northeast gate before she sneezed again.

She was appalled at making such a spectacle of herself at her friend's wedding. She hadn't wanted to be here in the first place, and had raised all the usual protests—she was too plain, too awkward in company, too inept on the dance floor.

But, of course, Father's insistence had prevailed.

Senator Franklin Rush Cabot always got his way, particularly with his younger daughter, who wanted so desperately to please him.

Abigail kept her head down and concentrated on making her escape, navigating a crooked path around wedding guests, potted plants, passing waiters. Feeling another sneeze coming on, she yanked a lacy handkerchief from her sleeve and jammed it against her nose. She managed to stifle the explosion, but nearly blew her ears deaf in the process.

Though not deaf enough to avoid the snippets of gossip, which went from group to group like a contagion. *Scandalous, isn't it? She should have been married off by now. If her mother had lived to see this, she would have been devastated....*

This was a White House wedding, Abigail thought, sneaking a glance at her critics. Beautifully dressed, their manners as finely honed as their tongues, they were the elite hostesses of the capital, the wives of senators, cabinet secretaries and industrialists. Couldn't they find something more interesting than Abigail Cabot for amusement?

She kept her gaze fastened on her goal: escape. The door to the northeast gate stood open to the autumn night, framing a sky as black and deep as eternity, spangled with an endless arch of stars.

She hurried as fast as she dared, but her shuffling pace was too slow. It always was. She didn't push herself for fear of yet another disgrace, although by now she should be resigned to the prospect. From the time she was very small, she had known she was different. She couldn't run and skip and play as other children did. But at night, when Abigail swept the sky in search of the stars, she could soar.

The safe emptiness of the east veranda beckoned. She was almost there. Almost free.

At last she ducked out the French doors and found herself on a blissfully deserted patio. Black shadows shrouded the flagstones and walkways. A late-autumn chill sharpened the air. Letting out a long, tense breath she hadn't known she was holding, Abigail pressed her hands against the figured concrete rail. She was probably soiling her gloves, but that didn't matter now. She'd be hard-pressed to find a dance partner or anyone else to hold her hand tonight.

As she had on so many other previous occasions, Abigail had tucked her pathetically empty dance program into her sash and forgotten about it. She had never filled one, nor could ever hope to.

Plucking the loose comb from her hair, she used it to re-anchor her coiled braid. Then she moved along the rail, her petticoats making a discontented *swish* around her legs. The breeze cooled her throat, and the night sky worked its calming effect on her. Often, the sea fog and city lights interfered with the view, but tonight was unusually clear. There was Andromeda, the Chained Princess, suspended in eternal captivity. The great winged horse, Pegasus, rode high in the south. Saturn was on the rise; a month from now it would be Jupiter's turn. The slow, infinite spinning of the stars swept Abigail away from her moment of ignominy. The sky in all its glory never glared down in judgment at insignificant, earthbound creatures who made a habit of disgracing themselves.

But then, inevitably, pedestrian concerns intruded. She was neglecting her duties, hiding out here like a coward. This was not just any wedding. It was a wedding hosted by the president and first lady. She and the bride, Nancy Kerry Wilkes, had attended Miss Blanding's Lyceum together.

She had come with such high hopes of pleasing Father. So far, all she'd done was get hit with a bouquet and suffer a very public attack of allergies. But the night was still young, Abigail reminded herself, stiffening her spine and squaring her shoulders. Like a prisoner about to face a firing squad, she turned back to the ballroom and advanced toward the French doors.

Velvet draperies with gold cords and tassels framed the glittering reception. Refracted gaslight turned the crystal shades of the sconces to diamonds. During his administration, President Grant had done up the room like a ghastly gothic steamboat. Not to be outdone, President Arthur had hired Louis Comfort Tiffany to cover the ceiling in silver and create jungles of palm plants in each quadrant. She couldn't imagine what the current administration would come up with.

In the forgiving light of the Baccarat chandeliers, the scene resembled a beautiful painting come to life. Ladies spun like ballerinas in their pastel gowns, contrasting with the gentlemen in their fine black tuxedos. The military men were even more impressive in full dress uniform—deep navy for the Annapolis men, crisp dress greys for West Pointers, military blue for the corps de garde. Everyone looked so polished as they wove through the kaleidoscope pattern of the dance set, glittering parts of a grand design. All were satellites to the incandescent bride and groom, who moved with joyous precision through the steps of a lively waltz. Everything kept turning, cogs in a greased wheel. Mercifully, the world had forgotten Abigail.

Like a fairy-tale princess, Nancy Kerry had married a handsome West Point graduate whose pedigree was as impeccable as his military manners. The glowing couple made it look so easy to be perfect. They made it look so easy to be happy.

Abigail's father stood near the punch buffet, deep in conversation with Vice President Butler. In their swallowtail frock coats and gleaming spats, they resembled a pair of large, earnest beetles.

She searched for her sister, but Helena was nowhere to be found. She was probably off somewhere being gorgeous and outrageous. Those were the two things Helena did best. At any rate, it was just as well Helena had made herself scarce for the time being. It was bad form at a wedding to outshine the bride.

As usual, it was left to Abigail to do what was right, what was expected. Never mind that she wasn't any good at it. Being the best person for the job was less important than actually doing the job.

As the elder sister by three years, Helena should be the one playing the dutiful daughter, Abigail thought with a twinge of resentment. But that, of course, would require Helena to care about propriety.

No one cared more than Abigail. She gave herself a stern, silent lecture—she was a grown woman now. She must push past her paralyzing reluctance, go back into the ballroom and redeem herself.

But just as she closed her fingers around the door handle, a flicker of movement caught her eye.

She peered into the shadows at the edge of the patio. A gravel path, flanked by stone benches, meandered into the darkness of the White House gardens. And upon one of the benches, surrounded by fall-flowering spider lilies and autumn crocus, sat an embracing couple.

Abigail pressed the handkerchief to her mouth to stifle a gasp. Oblivious to her presence, the couple had their arms wound around one another, their mouths glued together in a passionate kiss. Some perverse impulse drew Abigail across the patio and into the shadows so she could get a closer look.

Sweet heaven, he had his hand all the way up the woman's skirt. Her leg lay draped across his lap, revealing the dark ribbon of a garter banded around her thigh. Abigail's fascination rose as the woman moaned and dropped her head back, exposing her décolletage, her breasts as pale and smooth as twin moons. The man kissed the shadowy cleft between them, and Abigail felt a terrible tug of heat she had no name for.

Sagging against the rail, she imagined what it would be like to have a man kiss her like that, touch her the way the bold stranger was touching the woman, hold her in a way that suggested he'd never let her go.

"Oh..." The woman moaned again, her voice rich with passion. "Oh, Jamie, Jamie..." Leaning back even more, she turned slightly, so that the faint starlight outlined her face.

Abigail edged forward, riveted by the scene. A pale branch of autumn trumpet lily brushed across her face, and she pushed it out of the way for a better view of the woman who now lay with her head dropped back, her eyes closed, her mouth half-open in ecstasy. She had slender hands and a pale, beguiling—and exceedingly familiar—face. Recognizing her, Abigail nearly choked. Heaven above, it was

Mrs. Caroline Fortenay, the president's sister. His widowed sister.

An ominous tickle stung Abigail's nose. No, oh, please, no, she thought, holding the handkerchief to her nose and moving away from the floral hedge. But despite her terrified efforts, she could not quite manage to stifle the next giant sneeze. It erupted with volcanic force, racking her whole body.

The couple on the bench broke apart. The man said a word Abigail had never heard before, though his furious tone made her blush.

With less than a second to act, she pushed away from the wall and crossed the patio, heading for the doorway. The handkerchief flew from her hand and drifted to the ground. Without stopping to pick it up, she ducked into the ballroom.

Praying no one had seen her hasty entrance, she smashed herself against the wall, shut her eyes and tried to catch her breath. When she opened her eyes, the party went on uninterrupted. Glassware clinked in accompaniment to laughter and conversation, and no one seemed to mark her presence. She let out a long, slow sigh of relief. Heavens, who would have thought a sneeze could get her in so much trouble?

Perhaps something to drink would calm her nerves. As she wandered toward the refreshments table, she brushed her gloved hands over her skirts. She wished she'd listened to Helena and ordered a new gown rather than adding a bit of tired lace to her one good dress. She'd always found better uses for her money and her time, and had no head for fashion. But now that she was in the midst of the social whirl, she knew she'd been mistaken. She looked like someone's poor relation—a spinster aunt from the country.

"Miss, you dropped something."

The resonant male voice froze Abigail in her tracks. Her shoulders tensed, and a terrible heat prickled the back of her neck. Slowly, her chest filling with dread, she turned.

She found herself facing a very tall stranger. A humiliated glance at his face gave her a swift impression of ice-gray eyes, sun-gold hair, a face shaped by hard experience and a mouth lifted in the most mocking grin she had ever seen.

It was him. The man from the garden. *Oh, Jamie, Jamie...* The man who had seduced the president's sister was holding out Abigail's handkerchief as though it were a dead bird.

Flushing to the roots of her ruthlessly ironed and lacquered hair, Abigail snatched the wisp of fabric. "Thank you," she muttered, wishing she could hide.

"You're quite welcome," he replied in a deep, easy voice, so rich it lulled her senses.

Oh, Jamie, Jamie...

"Indeed," she said, her mouth dry, her cheeks on fire. Casual conversation was hard enough with a stranger, let alone a stranger she'd just seen making love to the president's sister. "I, um, I'd wondered where that had gone."

"Well, now you know." A dazzling and insolent smile lit his face, and his cold eyes clearly reflected the knowledge of who she was and what she had seen.

And what she'd felt while watching it.

"And I have you to thank for it," she blurted out. "And now that I have, I must be going."

He cleared his throat. "Miss, you might want to use that hankie to..." With his index finger, he indicated the upper ridge of her cheekbone.

Oh, no. She brushed at the area, then checked the handkerchief, finding a bright smear of yellow powder from the bouquet. She forced herself to look up at him. ''Anywhere else?''

Nodding, he angled his body so that she was shielded from the crowd. Raising a discreet finger to his own face, he indicated two more places. Abigail brushed quickly, until he nodded in approval. ''You show a great deal of promise,'' he remarked.

''So,'' she said, bobbing an awkward curtsy. ''Goodbye.'' This man, she realized, had managed to reduce her to a blithering idiot in mere moments. She had to get away from him before the gossips got wind of it. Stuffing the handkerchief into her sash, she walked away. She was still struggling to compose her nerves when she found herself face-to-face with the only object she liked looking at more than the stars.

Lieutenant Boyd Butler III.

The first time she had seen him, he'd been a lad with skinny limbs poking out of short pants, clammy hands gripping her as they suffered together through dancing lessons. And even then, she'd thought him marvelous and gallant. Then he had gone away to school and they'd lost touch. Now he was back, transformed by the years and by the naval academy into a glorious man. This was her first time to see him socially, and her senses shrilled at the prospect.

''Miss Cabot.'' The vice president's son bowed from the waist. ''I confess, you startled me.''

''Good evening, Lieutenant Butler.'' She cut a glance over her shoulder to see if the stranger had followed her, but mercifully, he had melted into the crowd.

Because it was expected, she offered her right hand

to Boyd Butler. Too late, she remembered that she had soiled her gloves on the concrete railing outside. She couldn't decide whether to snatch her hand away or to brazen it out, and while she dithered, he took her fingers and raised the back of her hand to his lips, focusing only briefly on the black streaks that marred her white gloves.

Their fathers found Abigail and Lieutenant Butler in this position as they strolled past, making a turn around the periphery of the room.

"I say," the elder Mr. Butler exclaimed. "Can this be our progeny, making friends with one another?"

"We're already acquainted, sir," the lieutenant pointed out. "Miss Cabot was kind enough to renew our friendship when I happened to be on duty at the Naval Observatory."

Abigail's long-held admiration of him soared, for the truth was, she'd been refused access to the observatory, and she was so determined to gain entry that night that she'd threatened to report the incident to the president himself. Boyd had stepped in, seeing no harm in letting a woman use the observatory. How kind of him to avoid pointing out how belligerent she'd been that night.

"In fact," Lieutenant Butler continued, "I was about to ask Miss Cabot for a dance."

A dance. Dear heaven. She cast a desperate look at her father. His perfectly groomed side-whiskers framed a face wrought of ambition and determination. Deep in his fiercely intelligent eyes glowed a promise, but a promise withheld. It was not that her father didn't love her; he simply wasn't the sort of man to give out his affection with blind abandon like the sun on a cloudless day. He expected something in return, something as simple as it was impossible.

But she would try. Holding on to the promise she saw in her father's eyes, she tried to behave in the charming, ladylike fashion that seemed to come so naturally to other young women. Turning slightly toward Boyd Butler III, she smiled up at him. He was quite a distance away—not due to any particularly prodigious height, but due to her small stature. Abigail viewed her shortness as one of far too many personal failings.

Still, her father and the vice president were watching. "I daresay, I have never met a kinder soul than I did that night at the observatory," she declared.

Her father favored her with a tight, controlled smile. "Mr. Butler, your son is to be commended, then. For it takes a special tolerance to abide my daughter's unusual enthusiasm for stargazing."

A sting of defensiveness touched her spine. She kept watching the lieutenant. Oh, if he would defend her right this instant, she would love him forever.

He grinned broadly at her father. "Sir, I find a lady's interest in science little different from her interest in embroidery. Both are equally baffling to me."

As the three men laughed, Abigail tried to decide whether or not Lieutenant Butler had put up enough of a defense on her behalf. He was so incredibly good-looking that she decided to give him the benefit of the doubt. Yes, as politely as possible, he'd managed to contradict her father without offending the senator. Genius. The man was a genius.

"Miss Cabot, may I have the honor of this dance?" asked Lieutenant Butler.

She felt like a rabbit aware of a wolf nearby and safety far away. On the outside, she stood frozen, incapable of movement. On the inside, her heart beat so fast that her chest hurt. Her father stood watching, waiting. The promise in those eyes moved slowly, like moonset at midnight, soon to disappear altogether. She couldn't let his esteem slip away. She mustn't. She'd already disgraced herself once this evening in the matter of the bride's bouquet. If she refused to dance with the son of the vice president, she would never endure her father's disappointment.

The prospect burned her with the heat of mortal fear. She felt herself turn to her partner with the wooden, jerky movements of a marionette. "It would be my pleasure, Lieutenant Butler," she said.

Her reply had the desired reaction all the way around. Boyd the younger smiled and offered his hand. Boyd the elder nodded his head in approval. And her father's eyes filled with pride and affection, warming her through to her soul.

Now all that remained was to get through the dance without another mishap.

Concealing anxiety behind a smile, she put her hand in Lieutenant Butler's and accompanied him to the dance floor to await the next set. Please be something slow, she prayed. A stately couples dance— even she could navigate that.

The strains of a violin's high whine poured like liquid silver through the room. Lieutenant Butler executed a perfect formal bow and Abigail answered with a brief curtsy. Then he cupped one hand at her waist while the other cradled her palm. His unfailing precision and courtesy gave her confidence as the first beats of the dance sounded.

The rhythm was mercifully slow. Her knees went weak with relief, but she steeled herself against sagging. The dance steps were familiar to her, for she often lay awake at night and pictured herself dancing, always with flawless grace. Reality was a different thing altogether. As they moved off to begin their orbit of the dance floor, she clutched his upper arm in a death grip and scowled in concentration. Lieutenant Butler could not know it, but to Abigail it was a journey fraught with peril. He mustn't guess she was mere inches from collapsing like a broken doll.

But oh, Lord. Oh moons of Venus. He was talking to her, asking her something. "...quite an alliance, wouldn't you say?"

"Yes, indeed," she said quickly. "Quite an alliance."

"I can't say it surprises me." Lieutenant Butler seemed totally unaware of his impact on the female wedding guests. Each time he passed, painted silken fans appeared like umbrellas in a rainstorm, fluttering in front of pretty faces that blushed at the very sight of him. With his every dark hair plastered in place with Macassar oil and every seam of his uniform ironed to knife-blade crispness, he was the American dream personified.

She found herself studying his wonderful mouth, shadowed by a perfectly waxed mustache. If she were to kiss that mouth, what would happen to the mustache? Would the wax break? Would it be crushed by her ardor?

Flushing with her brazen thoughts, Abigail took pride in the fact that he had chosen her. She was not nearly as pretty as the Parks girls of Albemarle County, not nearly as witty as the visiting New York heiresses, not nearly as graceful as the bride's Baltimore cousins.

But she was smarter than all of them.

Not that this was any great virtue.

"Why are you not surprised?" she asked, concentrating on the simple dance steps. She was still not sure what he was talking about, but he hadn't noticed that yet.

"Because my father is the presiding officer of the Senate and yours is chairman of the railroad committee. Between the two of them, they essentially control the entire Congress."

She nodded, frowning as she narrowly missed swirling into a passing couple. She recognized Mrs. Fortenay, now put together and gliding regally across the floor. To Abigail's consternation, she recognized Mrs. Fortenay's partner, too. He was the same one she had encountered on the veranda.

Unbidden, a thrill of illicit heat curled through Abigail, and she caught her breath.

"Does that trouble you?" asked Lieutenant Butler.

"Of course not," she hastened to say. "Our legislature could be in no better hands than our fathers', wouldn't you agree?"

The stranger caught her staring at him over Lieutenant Butler's shoulder. He winked. *Winked.*

A shiver passed over her. At first she thought she had imagined it, but the broad, teasing wink had been unmistakable. So had her alarming physical reaction to him.

"Who is that man?" she blurted out before she could stop herself. "The insolent one we just passed."

Butler turned slightly and looked beyond her. "Oh.
Him."

"I take it you know him." When they rotated
again, the motion nearly threw her off balance, but
she got a better look. He was remarkably tall, well
over six feet. His suit fit with tailored perfection. He
wore his light-colored hair too long, and unlike most
fashionable gentleman did not sport a thickly waxed
mustache or side-whiskers.

"I know of him," Lieutenant Butler corrected.
"James Calhoun. He's a freshman congressman from
Virginia. Has a reputation for being wild and ruth-
less."

"James Calhoun." She tasted the staid, almost conventional name, but in her mind she could hear the
president's sister crying out, "Oh, Jamie, Jamie..."
He definitely looked more like a Jamie than a James.

"He went to university in Europe, I'm told. I understand it was over the protests of his parents, who
believe every proper Virginia gentleman should attend Old Dominion."

Abigail tried to imagine parents being disappointed
in a son educated on the Continent. "And who are
they?" she asked. "The Calhouns."

"His father, Charles Calhoun, raises racehorses,
and I've heard the son has an eye for buying Arab
stock, and has traveled to dangerous places in order
to acquire horses." Butler chuckled. "And now he's
become a congressman." The lieutenant's smile disappeared, eclipsed by a shadow of discontent.

"What is the matter?" she asked, dragging her
foot. He no doubt found her a tedious and inept partner.

"I am reminded of my own duties," he explained.

"Sometimes I feel that the eyes of the world are on me."

She thought he handled public attention exceedingly well, but said nothing. It was no secret that his father's party was grooming Lieutenant Butler for a stellar political career. Perhaps even the presidency one day.

"I do understand that I'm needed," he assured her without vanity. "I understand the need for leadership, but it's a heavy burden. Sometimes even I have a need for…" His voice trailed off.

"For what, Lieutenant Butler?" Oh please, she thought. Whatever he yearns for, let me be the one to give it to him.

"Never mind. You will think me entirely daft."

"No, I won't. Please tell me."

His gaze shifted to the floor. "Every so often I wish there could be nothing but romance and poetry in my life."

Abigail nearly lost her balance, and only by gritting her teeth through the pain did she manage to keep from falling. Why did the female partner always have to dance backward? she wondered. It wasn't fair, and for someone like her, it was downright hazardous.

"That is a noble human need," she told him. Oh Boyd, Boyd, her heart sang. I'll give you romance and poetry. Every minute of every day. Never mind that she hadn't the least idea how to achieve that, but for his sake, she would find a way.

"You are easy to talk to, Miss Cabot," he said. "I feel such comfort in your presence. The pressures of my station lighten when you are around."

If Abigail were not hopelessly earthbound, she would have soared at that moment. Without the steady anchor of her dancing partner, she would have floated halfway to heaven by now.

Here was her chance. This was the moment to tell him what had been in her heart since they were gawky adolescents. Taking a deep breath, she teetered on the precipice, then plunged over the edge. "Lieutenant Butler, I daresay I feel the same."

"Sweet mercy," he said suddenly, staring at something over her shoulder. He nearly let go of her. Only by tightening her own grasp could Abigail stay anchored to him.

"Is something wrong?" she asked, terrified that she'd offended him with her bold declaration.

"Who is that creature?" He asked the question without looking at her; indeed, he seemed to have forgotten her existence. "She's a goddess."

Abigail craned her neck, following his gaze. The earth seemed to stop spinning, and her clumsy feet were planted firmly on the ground of reality. Lieutenant Butler, and every other male in the East Room— the bridegroom included—stared gape-mouthed at the arched entranceway. Abigail did not have to wonder whose arrival had created such a stir. This had happened dozens of times before.

When every male eye turned, when every male head emptied of all thought save one, it could only mean one thing.

Her sister, Helena, had arrived.

Like Venus on the half shell, borne to the shore on the foamy crest of a wave, she glided into the East Room and stood beneath the doorway from the entrance and cross halls. As always, she eschewed the fussy fashions of the day in favor of a flowing, apple-green sheath of a gown that accentuated the virtues of her perfect figure. A glorious swirl of copper-colored waves crowned her head and framed a face so beautiful that the sight of it drew attention from even the most jaded of men.

Abigail glanced up at her partner, who had all but forgotten her, and who clearly hadn't heard her heart-felt declaration. She tried to let her hopes deflate slowly. For five minutes, she had felt genuinely happy dancing in Lieutenant Butler's arms. She'd dared to hope he was attracted to her, and perhaps he had been for those few moments.

Now, of course, he was lost to her.

"That is my sister, Helena," she informed him, unwilling to put off the inevitable. "Fashionably late as usual."

She braced herself, knowing what would come next. He would politely remark that Abigail looked flushed and overexerted; surely he'd taxed her strength to its limit and was duty-bound to deliver her to a chaise by the refreshments table. He would try his best not to be entirely transparent as he begged for an introduction to Helena.

And Abigail, for her part, would try not to feel crushed as she did so with a smile on her face, then stepped out of his way while he fell head over heels in love with her sister.

Through no fault of her own, Helena had upset the pattern of the dance set. Too late, Abigail realized that Boyd had inadvertently moved her backward to the edge of the slick, polished dance floor.

And then it happened. She stepped wrong, felt a shooting pain up her leg. She clutched him wildly but lost her grip and stumbled back. Over her shoulder, she could see the table laden with a towering wedding cake, priceless presidential china, Dolly Madison's silver service, a pyramid of Irish-crystal champagne glasses. And she was falling straight toward it all, arms windmilling desperately, finding nothing to hold on to.

Lieutenant Butler's face registered pure horror. He lunged to stop her fall, but missed.

Then a miracle occurred. A pair of strong arms caught her from behind and propped her against a massive, broad chest.

"Easy now, miss." The now-familiar voice was honeyed with a Virginia drawl. "You don't want to become the main dish at the banquet."

It was the stranger, Jamie Calhoun. The warmth and firmness of his body startled her; it was a solid wall between her and disaster.

Taking her hand, he casually brushed a smudge of dirt from her glove. "I do like a girl who's not afraid to get her hands dirty in the line of duty," he said, laughter edging his words.

Awash in humiliation, she pulled her hand away. "Thank you for your assistance, sir. Now I wish—"

"Hasn't anyone ever told you to be careful what you wish for? Come along, my dear. The dance isn't over yet." Leading her as though she were a wayward child, he delivered her safely back to Lieutenant Butler.

"Sir," he said, "in the future I'd advise you to keep a closer bridle on your partner."

Jamie Calhoun stood to one side, hovering to make certain he'd linked them together and Abigail was steady on her feet once again.

"You know what they say about fast women and blooded mares," he added with the same wicked wink he had given her earlier. "Give them free rein, and they'll trample you every time."

Chuckling with inappropriate amusement at his own witticism, he strolled away.

Abigail burned with mortification. She was sure Lieutenant Butler could feel the heat like a fever.

She despised James Calhoun, despised his crude wit and cynicism with the fire of a thousand suns. Yet even as she did, there was one key fact she was forced to acknowledge. When every other man in the room had been staring at Helena, Mr. James Calhoun had been watching *her*.

Two

What a pathetic creature, thought Jamie Calhoun, studying the brown-haired girl in Butler's arms. When the set ended, the lieutenant's face reflected the relief of a witness to a mercy killing.

Observing the incident from a distance, with one shoulder propped against a gilt and fluted column, Jamie decided that the party had gone on far too long for his taste. The president and first lady had retired, but the bride and groom and their guests seemed determined to carry on the tedious celebration into the wee hours. Caroline Fortenay had her charms, but after that rude interruption in the garden, she had been avoiding him.

Politics, and a loose association with the groom, had brought Jamie to the White House for the occasion. Newly elected to Congress, he needed to form alliances and this reception afforded the greatest concentration of political influence in the Potomac watershed.

He wouldn't have noticed the small, intense woman at all, but he'd been tracking Lieutenant Butler. An Annapolis man, dense as an andiron, but he had his uses. His father presided over the Senate, and therefore an association with the Butlers must be cultivated.

This evening, little business was getting done, save, apparently, between Senator Cabot and Vice President Butler. Seated at a round table, the two of them conspired like a pair of old pirates. They were the only males in the room who did not seem completely distracted by the arrival of the redheaded goddess.

The other women attempted to take the new arrival in stride, congregating at the buffet table so recently imperiled by the clumsy female dancing with Butler. The goddess had not been able to move far beyond the grand entrance, for a legion of male guests had made their way toward her, supplicants paying homage to a queen.

She was beautiful, Jamie acknowledged, looking over the heads of the crowd to study her. She was, in fact, quite flawless, with a lithe, willowy body and a face right out of a Renaissance painting. Of course, beauty had its limits, unless it was accompanied by more useful attributes. Jamie admired her as one might admire a piece of fine art, in a remote cerebral fashion that excited nothing inside him except a vague aesthetic appreciation. Yet the baser part of him assessed her with a crude lust.

He was about to go looking for Timothy Doyle, a reporter for the *Washington Post* who could always be counted on to fill him in on Capitol Hill gossip, when a movement caught his eye.

It was the other one, the little wren of a woman, cutting through the crowd with Butler in tow. Intrigued, Jamie helped himself to a flute of champagne and edged in closer.

"...my sister, Miss Helena Cabot," the brown wren was saying.

Jamie came to full attention. Two important facts struck him. First, their name was Cabot. And second, the goddess and the wren were sisters.

They must be Franklin Cabot's daughters.

Intrigued, he found Doyle at the fringes of a group of congressmen, eavesdropping on their conversation. Grabbing Doyle's arm, he pulled him aside.

"Tell me about the Cabot sisters," he said without preamble.

Doyle rolled back his lips in a wolfish grin. "A mismatched pair, wouldn't you say? They've been gossip fodder for years, if you must know."

"I must."

"Honestly, it's not that meaty. Rumor has it that he's given the command. He wants to see them married, and married soon. Miss Helena will have no problem in that department, you'll notice." He nodded in her direction. "But the younger daughter? Abigail's her name."

"Abigail," Jamie repeated, tasting the three syllables. Yes, she looked like an Abigail, watchful and earnest in her drab, old-fashioned gown, probably more at home with books and quiet, solitary pursuits.

"Yes, poor Abigail. An odd bird, always dithering around at the university. They say she's some sort of genius—though clearly not on the dance floor." He snickered. "I swear, seeing Butler leading her around was like watching a buyer with a cow at the stockyards."

"That's harsh, Doyle."

"The capital's a harsh place, especially for a spinster with an odd bent. I'm told Cabot would give anything to see them married off.''

''Anything?'' Jamie's interest sharpened. ''His support in Congress?''

Doyle tucked a thumb into his tight cummerbund. ''Give it a try, Calhoun. But be warned. Better men than you have attempted, and failed.''

''I'm not looking to marry,'' Jamie said, his voice hard and flat. Given his history, a wife was the last thing he wanted, or needed. Or deserved.

''See that fellow there?'' Doyle indicated a heavy-jowled older man speaking with Senator Cabot. ''That's Horace Riordan, the railroad millionaire. He's been trying to influence the railroad bill for months. But it's a funny thing about Cabot. It takes more than money to get his attention.''

''His daughters' favor?''

Doyle winked. ''Maybe.''

The beauteous Helena smiled and flirted with Butler, who lapped up her attention like a thirsty hound dog. The lieutenant probably didn't intend to be rude, but the angle of his stance cut the lesser sister completely out of the conversation. Neither he nor Helena saw the woman's face grow pale, then fill up with color. No one but Jamie saw the fragile tremor of her mouth, nor the way she conquered it by momentarily sinking determined teeth into her lower lip. An expression of weary resignation indicated that she had endured this before.

Jamie Calhoun had never been known for his chivalrous behavior; quite the opposite. But this vulnerable creature was Franklin Cabot's daughter, and he was going to rescue her. In her undying gratitude, perhaps she'd give him access to her father.

Tossing back the last of his champagne, he handed the glass to a passing waiter and excused himself from Doyle.

"Miss Cabot," he said, approaching them. "I'd be honored to make your acquaintance."

Both women turned toward him, Helena with artless expectation and her sister with mingled distrust and annoyance. Butler narrowed his eyes, assuming a territorial stance in front of Helena.

Jamie sketched a bow. "How do you do? Lieutenant Butler, I remember you from the dedication ceremony for the Union Hall monument. You did a fine job standing behind your father on the podium, looking regimental."

"Thank you, Mr. Calhoun." Butler didn't seem to catch the sarcasm. With practiced manners, he made the introductions. Helena greeted Jamie with the confidence of a queen, her emerald eyes sweeping over him in flattering appreciation. Gawky, blushing Abigail had eyes he could only describe as remarkable. Those eyes had been the first thing he'd noticed about her, after the sneeze. They were wide and clear, of a blue so intense it made him think of rich velvet. At the moment, her keen eyes regarded him with a deep and abiding suspicion. The goose. Didn't she realize he had come to rescue her?

"Mr. Calhoun is newly elected to the House," Butler explained to the ladies. "I'm pleased to say he's a member of the right party."

Jamie made himself look appropriately grateful. The fact was, he'd chosen the party based on their need for a candidate to fill a key seat in Congress. None of his constituents knew much about him. If they did, they'd probably run him out on a rail, decked in tar and feathers.

"And where is your home district, Mr. Calhoun?" Miss Helena's voice was as attractive as the rest of her, so soothing it was almost bland.

"I'm a Chesapeake boy, ma'am. Born and raised at Albion Plantation on Mockjack Bay."

"And how are you finding life in the capital?" asked Miss Helena.

"I like it fine, ma'am, though I fear I'll soon be homeless. I've been living at a boardinghouse near Snow's Park, but the place has been sold and must be vacated. I despair of finding new lodgings."

Miss Helena's face lit up, radiant as a Raphael Madonna. "You should come to Georgetown, then. Our neighbor, Dr. Rowan, lives alone in a large town house and, well, you know it's just a crime what they pay even the most gifted professor. I'm certain he would welcome a boarder."

"Helena," Miss Abigail said, her voice harsher than her sister's, her diction more clipped, "surely Mr. Calhoun doesn't need our help in finding lodgings."

"On the contrary," he said, pleased to see opportunity opening with such ease. "I'd be grateful for any help." He grinned down at her, pretending to have no notion at all that he'd displeased Miss Abigail.

The orchestra broke in with a long, tuning A. Butler snapped to attention like a guard on duty. "The 'Emperor Waltz,'" he announced. "Miss Cabot, if you would do me the honor." He held out his hand to Helena.

Jamie should have given Abigail time to compose

herself, but he didn't. He turned to her too quickly
and saw something he wasn't supposed to see. Naked
yearning and inconsolable heartbreak, coupled with a
strange, almost weary joy. Her hands, clad in soiled
gloves, knotted nervously together. She was the very
picture of misery. He wasn't doing a very good job
of playing the hero.

"Miss Cabot, may I have the pleasure of this
dance?" he asked, favoring her with a practiced bow
and a smile that had worked on more women than he
cared to remember.

She glared up at him, face pinched, eyes narrowed.
"No, I think not, but thank you for asking."

At first, the rejection didn't even sink in. Only once
in his life had Jamie been rejected by a woman. Of
course, that episode had been eclipsed by the ensuing
events. Since that day, he'd always believed being
turned down by that woman had been both the best
and the worst thing ever to happen to him. But he
had never forgotten the brief, vicious sting of that
feminine *no.*

"You don't care to dance?"

"No, thank you. I've never been fond of going in
backward circles. In fact, I'm quite weary of it."

"Very well. Then I'll let you lead."

She blinked in surprise. Her extremely blue eyes—
surely her best feature—studied him with new curiosity. "That would be unorthodox."

"It would. Do you disapprove?"

"No." She craned her neck to search past him.
"However, my father would."

Jamie decided not to press his cause. Franklin Cabot was the whole reason for this tiresome game in
the first place. "In that case," he said, "I insist you

mollify my bruised affections with a stroll in the gardens.''

She laughed aloud, a startling burst of merry sound. "I'm not like your other women. I think you would survive without mollification, Mr. Calhoun.''

"Why do you say that? I might be very fragile," he pointed out.

She laughed again, even louder this time, drawing a few stares but seeming not to notice. "In that case," she said, "I shall cruelly leave your shattered heart to be swept up with tomorrow's ashes.'' With that, she walked away. She had a curious gait, quick but uneven. Now she was fleeing again, but this time he wouldn't let her go, couldn't afford to.

"Please stop following me," she said without slowing her pace or looking at him.

"I can't help myself. You're the most interesting person I've met all night."

Another laugh, this one curt and bitter. "Then you'd best introduce yourself to more people,'' she advised. "I warrant you can do better."

He placed his hand beneath her elbow and steered her toward the French doors. "Your modesty is becoming, but unnecessary.''

At her pull of resistance, a surprising heat stirred between them, and he held her elbow more firmly. He hadn't been expecting to feel genuine curiosity about her. Normally he preferred his women beautiful and brainless. They posed no challenge. No threat.

Abigail Cabot was not beautiful and she was far from brainless. She was short both of stature and of temper. Yet he found himself intrigued by her. He wondered what it would be like to explore the thoughts behind those vaguely unsettling, midnight-blue eyes.

"Believe me," she said, "I'm not being modest."

He guided her toward the northeast gate. "It's an overrated virtue anyway."

"I'm not going outside with you," she said, trying to disengage her elbow from his grip.

He could tell by the flaming color in her cheeks that she was thinking of the private liaison she'd interrupted earlier in the evening. "Miss Cabot, your virtue is safe, I promise."

"Why should I trust you? I don't even know you."

"Trust yourself, then. A man can't take a woman's virtue unless she surrenders it. You don't appear to be the surrendering type."

To his relief, she seemed satisfied with the comment. Dropping her resistance, she accompanied him out to the shadowy patio.

"Beautiful night," he commented.

"Not really." She angled her face to the night sky. "It's only slightly above average."

"Are you always this argumentative?"

"Just objective." She pointed at a broad constellation. "The North American Nebula is barely visible tonight, the Double Cluster in Perseus is unimpressive and we can only see a glimmer of Barnard's Loop."

In most women, a smattering of knowledge was charming, but Abigail did not offer the explanation in order to charm him, he could tell. Nor did she possess only a smattering of education. She probably had an encyclopedic knowledge of the night sky, and God knew what else. The woman was beyond irritating— she was literal, contentious and prickly.

"Fine," he said. "It is an average night. What of the wedding? Was it an average wedding?"

She pushed her finger absently at her lower lip, showing no comprehension of the fact that he was teasing. "Heavens, no. It was distinctly above average."

"And why is that?"

"Because it was a love match."

"Now, *that*," he said with a chuckle, "is overrated."

"Love?"

"Indeed." He couldn't begin to tell her how deeply he believed that.

"Then obviously you have never been in love, or you wouldn't say that."

If only she knew. But of course, she never would. "And you. You've fallen in love?"

She held his gaze with hers. "With every bit of my heart."

Her absence of coyness and stark honesty inspired a stir of feeling that took him by surprise. And she was so completely misguided that he felt compelled to point out her error. "Lieutenant Boyd Butler," he said, playing a hunch.

She ducked her head and shifted her gaze away.

"Then why is he dancing with your sister?"

"I know you're from the coast country, sir, but you don't appear to be stupid. My sister cannot enter a room without causing half a dozen men to fall in love with her. Mr. Butler is no different."

"So you claim to love him, but he is smitten with your sister."

"This is really none of your affair."

"But I feel compelled to point out something you

don't realize,'' Jamie said. ''You're not in love with Boyd Butler. You never were.''

She bristled and scowled at him. ''I most certainly am. How would you know, anyway?''

He ignored the question. ''When did this epiphany happen?''

''I've known him since we were children. Our fathers are friends. It was no epiphany, sir. It's something that has been building for years. But tonight...'' Her voice trailed off, and her pointy, intense face turned sweet and soft, startling him. ''Tonight we shared a special moment.''

A rather one-sided moment, but he didn't call attention to that. ''And what does it feel like, your great love for the lieutenant?''

She frowned. ''Like...finding the solution to a mathematical problem simply by inspection and intuition. Even though he doesn't reciprocate my feelings, simply knowing that I love him makes me happy.''

''There,'' he said. ''That proves you don't love him.''

''What? The fact that he makes me happy?''

''Yes.'' He took her hand, feeling its small warm shape inside the snug glove. ''Falling in love does not make a person happy. Tell me, have you ever fallen on your face?''

She frowned at him in suspicion. ''Yes.''

''Did it hurt?''

''Yes.''

''Why do you think they call it *falling* in love? When you truly fall in love, you'll know it. You will weep with the knowledge.''

''Nonsense. Why would I weep?''

Ignoring propriety, he brought up his hand, grazing his knuckles along her cheekbone. She seemed so shocked by his boldness that she didn't move or speak. Her skin was silken and fragile beneath his touch. He heard the breath catch in her throat, and suddenly he wanted to push her, to tempt her. But he didn't, because her odd, prickly attitude shook him. He dropped his hand.

"Because, my dear Miss Cabot, it will hurt so much."

Three

At Number 32, Dumbarton Street in Georgetown, Abigail nearly stumbled in her haste to reach her chamber. She, Helena and her father had arrived home late, and by that time her discomfort was extreme. She managed a cordial good-night to her sister and father, then retreated to the privacy of her third-floor room. The narrow stairwell of the Georgian-style town house never seemed steeper than it did after a night of dancing and engaging in pointless conversation.

Before retiring, she and Helena had unfastened each other's bodices and corsets so as not to wake Dolly. Many ladies of quality thought nothing of rousing their personal servants at all hours, but Helena and Abigail would never dream of doing so. The housekeeper had left a ewer of hot water on the wash-stand, and it was still lukewarm. Abigail threw a handful of Epsom salts into the basin, set it on the floor and poured in the water. Then, issuing a sigh of relief, she untied and removed her shoe. With an even deeper sigh, she sank her right foot into the water and shut her eyes. The sharp pains that arched through her foot were as intimately familiar as the loneliness that crept upon her at odd moments.

She leaned back in the chair, glowering at the discarded prisonlike boot she had worn for as long as she could remember, day in and day out. When she was small, she used to pray for the ugly, twisted limb to grow into a dainty well-shaped foot that matched the left one.

Now that she was grown, she had given up praying for the impossible. She'd been born with the affliction and she would die this way. In between, she would stumble through dances and promenades with her secret concealed beneath the hem of her gown. That was to be her lot in life, and she was determined to accept it. With weary eyes, she stared at her bad foot in the water.

Her mother had died moments after giving birth to Abigail—an undersize newborn with a deformed foot. What a terrible curse that must have been to Beatrice Gavin Cabot, renowned for her fortune, her pride in being married to an ambitious young senator and her joy in her first daughter, Helena. What grief Abigail's mother must have suffered, holding her malformed second baby while bleeding to death. In Abigail's mind, the tragedy was always and inexorably linked to her imperfection. It was something she lived with every day, a shadow that moved beside her with every crooked step she took.

But maudlin thoughts were as annoying as they were pointless, so she pushed aside her bleak reflections and lifted her foot from the warm water.

She shed her gown and undergarments, hanging them in the dressing room and putting on a floor-length nightgown and robe. Donning a pair of carpet slippers, she left the room as quietly as she could. The slippers did not correct her limp as well as the specially made shoe did, but she had only a short way to go. Opening a low, narrow doorway at the end of the hall, she climbed the stairs to the roof.

The midnight sanctuary welcomed her. It was the one place she always belonged, because it belonged wholly to her. Ever since she was very young, Abigail had harbored an intense fascination with the night sky. At the age of five, she suffered terrible troubles in her sleep, and took to creeping to the window at night and sitting for hours, staring up at the stars. As her schooling progressed, she used to devil her tutors with questions about the vast universe until she exhausted their knowledge. Finally her father had engaged an impoverished mathematics student at Georgetown who'd given her a map of the stars and a folio of photographs made of the stars and planets.

She'd saved her clothing allowance for years in order to build her rooftop sanctuary—Abigail's folly, her father and sister called it—but they had learned long ago not to argue with her about her abiding passion. And so Abigail Cabot became the only woman in the capital to own an observatory.

It was not ideal, for the thick atmospheric conditions at sea level often interfered with her stargazing. Still, she made do, only occasionally yearning for clearer, brighter skies.

The swiveling domed structure was patterned after the private observatory of Maria Mitchell, the most eminent astronomer in the country, now retired and living on her pension from Vassar Female College. But Abigail had a gift even the great Professor Mitchell lacked. She could see sharper and farther with her naked eye than anyone on record.

She had always been blessed, or cursed, depending on how one looked at it, with almost inhumanly acute vision, always the first to see a ship on the horizon, or a flock of migrating geese overhead. Her strong perception of color showed her springtimes so green her eyes smarted, and autumns so intensely orange and gold that her heart ached. Struck by the beauty around her, she often felt twinges of sentiment she didn't understand.

When she picked out constellations others couldn't see without a telescope, people used to think she was playing a hoax, but a series of tests at the university and the Naval Observatory proved her claim. Perhaps this was how nature had compensated Abigail for her damaged foot.

The moon had set, creating a better field for naked-eye viewing. For a few moments, she forgot her ennui about earthly matters, sat down on a low stool and lost herself among the stars. Although the sensation was decidedly unscientific, she felt herself moving beyond the earth, beyond the known world into something infinite and mysterious.

Drawing in a breath of crisp autumn air scented by wood smoke and drying leaves, she swept the sky with her gaze.

"Hello, Mother," she whispered to the woman she had never known. "I danced tonight. With Lieutenant Boyd Butler. It was so wonderful. You would have been proud of me—" She broke off, her musings rudely invaded by the image of her nearly falling, then finding herself caught in the arms of the insolent Jamie Calhoun.

She scowled away the memory and continued. "The vice president's son. Can you imagine, Mother? Of course you can. Father was a politician's son, too. Perhaps it's in our blood to love men who govern. Mr. Calhoun—another man I met tonight, but he's quite a different sort than Lieutenant Butler—claims it is not love at all because it doesn't make me want to weep and rage and pound the floor and tear my hair out. Of course, none of it matters, anyway. Boyd Butler will never know what is in my heart, and it will be another of my secrets. So. I just thought you'd want to know that. Good night, Mother. I love you."

Abigail's whisper faded into the chill air. She came up here every night not just to engage in fanciful one-sided conversations with a ghost, but to study the sky. And not just because it was beautiful and vast and mysterious, though it was all of those things. She was looking for something.

She was looking for a comet.

When she told this to people, they often looked baffled and shook their heads. "Wouldn't it be easier to find a needle in a haystack?" they would ask.

Abigail never expected it to be easy. She didn't ever expect to give up, either. Helena might sort through their mother's jewels and pictures, looking for her in old keepsakes, but Abigail knew better. If she were ever to find her mother, it would be up in the vast night sky, hidden among the stars.

"Good morning, Papa dearest." Bursting into the dining room, Helena sang the greeting off-key, causing him and Abigail to wince. "Good morning, sister dearest." Leaning down, she kissed each of them. "And what a beautiful day it is."

Their father smiled indulgently and set aside his *Washington Post,* which he had been studying with deep absorption. Removing his silver-rimmed spectacles from their perch on his nose, he stood to hold out Helena's chair for her. "Indeed it is."

Abigail had supplied him with the same information a few minutes before, but he must have forgotten. She smiled at Helena, too; she couldn't help it. Someone as comely as her sister should be an object of flaming envy, but the fact was, Helena's looks were no more her fault than Abigail's foot was hers.

Their father offered Helena a basket of biscuits and jam, and she thanked him with a smile. "Coffee?" he offered.

"Yes, please."

A maid stepped forward to fill her cup.

"Abigail?" their father asked, "would you like some coffee?"

"I drink tea, Father. Thank you, though." She drank tea at breakfast every single morning.

Abigail loved the mornings when the three of them had breakfast together. Franklin Rush Cabot was not a demonstrative father, and time spent with him was precious. Sometimes she thought Helena avoided serious talk of marriage because she did not wish to leave their father. He was the only constant in their lives, the sun around which they orbited.

"Have you plans for the day?" he asked Helena.

She nodded, her coppery curls erupting with the motion. "I have a dress fitting with Miss Finch. She's apprenticed to Madame Broussard, you know." Helena propped her elbow on the table, cupped her chin in her hand. "I would so love to have a gown designed by Madame herself, but they say her waiting list is over a year long.''

He lifted a bristly eyebrow. ''Is that so? I'll see what I can do.''

Helena beamed. ''Thank you, Papa. Oh, I am so lucky to be your daughter.''

He pushed the spectacles up his nose and returned to his perusal of the paper. ''The luck is mine, I assure you,'' he said. ''What about you, Abigail? You could do with a new frock, couldn't you?''

She flushed. ''My plans for the day are a bit different. I must go to Foggy Bottom to help Mr. Hockett calibrate his ship's chronometer.''

''Perhaps Hockett's the lucky one, then,'' her father murmured without looking up.

Abigail smiled at him, but he didn't see. Charismatic and brilliant, he took obvious pride in Helena's looks and in Abigail's accomplishments, yet he always seemed to expect more than either sister could give.

She studied her father, the lines etched in his sternly handsome face, the precise creases of his boiled collar stark against his ruddy skin, the lambent eyes concealing a world of thoughts. A wave of yearning swept over her. She wanted to take his hand, to ask him what he was thinking, but she didn't dare. He withheld something of himself; Abigail couldn't put her finger on it, but she sensed that he wanted just one more elusive thing, and if she could give it to him, his happiness would be complete.

He had the subtle, wounded reserve of a longtime widower who had never found the heart to remarry. That quality alone caused female hopes to rise, and over the years a parade of ladies had vied for his attention, but he'd never chosen another wife. That made the sisters feel even more responsible for his happiness.

"Mr. Hockett insisted on my help," Abigail explained, although neither Father nor Helena had asked. "He used another calibrator last time and was more than a second off."

"Is that so?" His tone indicated a decided lack of interest. Then he motioned with his hand, and the maid came forward to pour more coffee.

Abigail knew her father loved her, but he didn't *see* her. She kept thinking that if she did the right thing—discovered her comet, found support for his issues in the legislature, married the right man—her father would finally open all of his heart to her. Then again, she was probably dissecting the situation with too much thought—a habit of hers.

"If I needed something calibrated, I would certainly pick you to do it," Helena declared loyally, then turned to her father. "Is there an account of the wedding?"

"Indeed there is." He pushed a folded section of the *Post* toward her. "A long column by Timothy Doyle. Read the last bit. You're mentioned several times."

"I cannot possibly read a word until I've had my coffee," Helena declared, swirling a spoonful of sugar into her cup. She slid the paper over the table to Abigail. "Read me the important parts."

Abigail folded back the thin broadsheets. This was yet another reason she could never resent her sister. Helena needed her too much. In a far less obvious way, Helena was as damaged as Abigail.

"Ah, here you are. 'Miss Helena Cabot was resplendent in a gown from La Maison d'Or of New York, and was seen to dance with Mr. Troy Barnes on two occasions, and Lieutenant Boyd Butler once.''' Abigail's voice thickened as she read his name; she prayed her father and sister hadn't noticed.

"Resplendent," Helena repeated, clasping her hands. "Such a lovely word. Equal parts splendid and..." She thought for a moment, then inspiration flashed. "Redundant."

"I'm very pleased with your conduct last night, my dear. Both Barnes and Butler are extremely suitable." Father set aside his coffee cup and gave Helena his full attention. She fairly blossomed under his regard, a rose turning its center to the sunlight. "As you know, your future is of paramount concern to me. Lieutenant Butler in particular would make a remarkable catch. It would not displease me if you were to encourage his suit."

"Then of course I shall," Helena said with a breezy wave of her hand. "If Lieutenant Barnes—"

"Butler," he corrected.

"If Lieutenant Butler meets with your approval, Father, then I'm sure he's entirely suitable," Helena said.

With clinical attention to detail, Abigail measured sugar for her tea. She estimated the weight of the sugar crystals to be six grams, and she was probably not far off the mark. Yet the measuring failed to distance her from the conversation. She couldn't believe what she was hearing. Of all the men scrambling to court her sister, their father had chosen Lieutenant Boyd Butler.

For perhaps a tenth of a second Abigail considered mounting an objection. But even before the thought was fully formed, she crushed it. Admitting her feelings for the lieutenant would only confuse a simple matter. And it *was* simple. Butler's heart belonged to Helena; Father's expectations had been raised for a suitable marriage. He always got his way—eventually.

Abigail had taught herself long ago to confine her yearnings to things she could control, like her star charts and astronomical observations.

"You must have business with the vice president, then," she said, her voice neutral.

He pressed his hands against the tabletop. "I'm a believer in making the most of my advantages. My dear, I've been a senator longer than you and your sister have been alive. I love my country and have dedicated my life to making it the finest nation in the world. Currently, there is a movement afoot to hobble the railroad expansion right here in Virginia. My task is to win the support of the vice president."

Abigail couldn't help wondering what lay at the heart of her father's desire—a wish for Helena's happiness, or his need for a political alliance? With the merest hint of censure in her voice, she asked, "Is it possible to do that without sending Helena off to marry a man she's just met, a man she hardly knows?"

"Anything is possible."

"Don't you want me to get married, Abigail?" Helena asked, picking at the biscuit crumbs on her plate.

Abigail measured her reply with the same precision she measured her sugar. "I want you to do whatever makes you happy."

"Pleasing Papa makes me happy." Helena covered the biscuit with jam and handed it to him.

"Young Butler is smitten, Abigail," Father said, taking the biscuit. "Everyone saw that last night. Your sister is in need of a husband. Why not bring the two needs together?"

Because I am in love with Lieutenant Butler, Abigail thought, pressing her teeth into her lip to keep from saying it. She scanned the rest of the newspaper column, noting that the disreputable James Calhoun merited a respectable few inches of gossip. He'd portrayed himself as a country gentleman, but the paper focused on his golden good looks, his suave continental manners, his reputation on the horse-racing circuit. And, of course, on his deliciously unmarried status.

The report made his status as a newly elected congressman seem far less important than his mysterious charm. Lost in thought, Abigail folded the paper exactly down the middle, then folded it again, running her thumb along the crease. She lined up the corner of the paper with the corner of the table. Then she moved the saltcellar to the precise middle of the lace cloth.

Helena observed her with baffled affection. "How on earth did you get so fussy, Abigail?"

Abigail didn't know, and so she said nothing. In addition to her freakishly sharp vision, she had a keen sense of spatial relations, knowing when she entered her room if some object was the least little bit out of place. A mysterious idiosyncrasy within her demanded order and precision whether it be a folded paper, a saltcellar, books on a shelf or even a floral arrangement. It was one of her many unattractive foibles.

Her father pushed back from the table. "I must be

off,'' he announced. "I have nothing but committee meetings until the Senate convenes.'' He kissed his daughters in distracted fashion, then went to gather his papers for a day of planning for the new legislative session.

"Well,'' said Abigail in the wake of his departure. "It seems you're going into politics.''

"Or perhaps politics will be going into me.'' Helena stared at the shock on Abigail's face, then burst into laughter. "Am I too bawdy for you? Have you never felt the stirrings of desire for a man?''

Abigail could think of no reply, so she said simply, "Really, Helena,'' and added another two grams of sugar to her tea.

As Helena nattered away about the wedding reception, Abigail felt a bittersweet ache rise in her chest. How wonderful it would be to fit into the world as her sister did, blithely certain of people's love, acceptance and esteem.

"...and so I invited him to call on us,'' Helena was saying.

Abigail snapped to attention, and her heart lurched. "Lieutenant Butler?''

"Who? Oh, him. No. I was speaking of Mr. Calhoun. If you'd been listening, you would have heard me say that.''

"So you want Mr. Calhoun to court you, too?''

"Didn't you see the man? Every young lady in the room last night wanted him.''

"Not this young lady.'' Abigail pictured the golden hair, the blatantly sensual features, the icy gray eyes that could slice a person to ribbons with nothing more than a look. There was something dangerous, possibly predatory about the man. He seemed to find the world entirely too amusing, yet at the heart of his mirth was a chill, shadowy darkness. He didn't seem to her to be a man capable of being happy.

"Well, of course I didn't invite him to come courting," Helena went on, her conversation flitting madly, a hummingbird in search of nectar. "He's coming to board with Professor Rowan." Helena folded her dainty hands beneath her chin, framing a slightly mysterious smile. "You see, it's too perfect. Poor Professor Rowan is rattling around in that huge old house next door. He has all the room in the world and no one to share it with."

Abigail felt a surge of affection for her sister. Dear Helena, always trying to manage people, to weave them together like threads in a tapestry. "And have you informed Professor Rowan that he's about to become host to a freshman congressman?"

"I sent Dolly over to set his house in order first thing this morning," Helena said. "Professor Rowan will be ever so grateful, won't he?"

Probably not, but like everyone else in the world, he was biologically incapable of saying *no* to Helena.

"About the courting," Abigail said, keeping her voice casual. "Do you mean to let Lieutenant Butler pursue you, or were you only saying that to please Father?" She held her breath, waiting for her sister's answer.

"He asked permission to write me from Annapolis, and of course I agreed." Helena sighed. "He pleases me, too."

"But do you love the man?"

Helena added an extra dollop of cream to her coffee. "I haven't decided yet. I just met him."

Abigail's secret desires pressed at her, seeking escape like bubbles in a bottle. With a stern will, she kept them inside. Yes, she loved Lieutenant Butler. Her heart told her that. Yet her far more reliable mind convinced her that Boyd Butler was out of reach. She loved navel oranges from Jaffa, too, but that didn't mean she could have them anytime she wanted. They simply weren't available.

Abigail would never tell Helena how she felt about Boyd Butler. She would never make Helena feel guilty simply for being Helena. It wasn't her fault for being what she was, no more than it was the fault of a perfect magnolia blossom for attracting bees.

Last night the lieutenant had confessed his yearning for romance and poetry, but what he really wanted was Helena, and who could blame him? She was beautiful and charming. She had her secrets, but so did everyone.

"I don't have to decide today, do I?" Helena asked with a brilliant smile.

"Of course not."

"I abhor making decisions," Helena said, using the tip of her finger to gather up the crumbs on her plate. "Don't you?"

Abigail couldn't help laughing. "Actually, no. I like deciding what's to come next, and then making it happen."

"I don't," Helena declared. "How tedious. If I never make up my mind about anything, then every day comes as a surprise."

Shaking her head, Abigail finished her tea. She wished she'd planned a busier day to keep herself occupied. But it was not to be; the calibration would not take place until late afternoon. She had no proper occupation, although astronomy was her vocation.

Three days a week, she worked for Professor Drabble at the university, computing star charts and studying astronomy.

She was content with the work, and preferred a classroom to a ballroom. For her, a gala party was rife with lethal hazards—flying bouquets, fast dance sets, breakable objects placed in the path of a clumsy woman.

By contrast, no one at the university seemed to know or care that she was different. In the laboratory or observatory, she was known for her keen mind and sharp eye, not criticized for her unkempt looks and argumentative manner. She dreamed of mountaintops under crystal skies, islands in the middle of vast oceans—places far from the crowded fishbowl of the capital city and the insular snobbishness of Georgetown.

As she and Helena prepared to go their separate ways, Dolly came in with a printed card on a silver tray. "A gentleman has come to call, miss." The housekeeper set the tray in front of Helena.

"Goodness," Helena exclaimed, not even looking at the card. "He wasted no time getting here. Please show him to the front parlor."

"Yes, miss."

Helena beamed across the table. "Oh, this is going to be fun, isn't it, Abigail dear?"

Of course it wasn't going to be fun. Not for Abigail. Helena loved to play with people as though they were fashion dolls, dressing them up, sending them out on adventures together and watching what happened. Perhaps social meddling was a science of sorts, but quite a different science from astronomy.

When they descended to the parlor, their visitor

stood with his back to them, hands on his slim hips as he looked out the window. Filling the tidy, well-appointed parlor with his assertive presence, he stood one hundred ninety centimeters tall in his polished fashionable shoes. He was exactly five centimeters taller than Lieutenant Butler, Abigail noted.

"Good morning, Mr. Calhoun," Helena said, gliding across the room as though she wore ice skates. "How good of you to come."

Abigail approached him more slowly. She could not have glided unless she was in a gondola on a calm sea.

He turned, sending her a dazzling smile that did odd and unexpected things inside Abigail. "On the contrary, it's good of you to have me. You both look quite recovered from last night's festivities."

"We mustn't waste a minute," Helena said. "I cannot wait for you to meet Professor Rowan."

"Your father's not at home?"

Abigail felt a sting of suspicion. Typical politician. Always looking for the advantage. "If you meant to call on our father, you should have arrived earlier," she said.

"What, and rob myself of the charm of your company?" He lifted an eyebrow, mocking her.

"Something tells me you don't need any more women in your life." Abigail couldn't resist the veiled reminder of what she'd witnessed in the White House garden.

"My dear, any man will tell you, there's no such thing as having too many women in one's life."

"Never bicker with my sister," Helena broke in.

"Why not?"

"Because you'll lose." She took Abigail's hand. "My sister can outbicker anyone."

His grin was devilish, yet seemed filled with unfeigned delight. "Perhaps she's met her match."

"Doubtful. You don't know Abigail, Mr. Calhoun."

"Helena, please." Abigail squeezed her hand. Perhaps her sister was right, but Abigail's argumentative nature was a defense. She kept the hard shell of her intellect in place to cover the softer underbelly of her vulnerability. "Mr. Calhoun didn't come all the way across the city to hear about me."

"She's a first-order scholar at the university," Helena said, ignoring Abigail's discomfiture. "My sister is the most distinguished student in the department of mathematics, and one of her specialties is in deductive logic. She has a deadly way of arguing. The wise man gives in without a fight."

He gave a low whistle, and his gaze feathered over Abigail with a subtle insolence. "I'll keep that in mind. But you understand, I've never been one to shy away from a good fight."

"That attitude will stand you in good stead in Congress," Abigail said, hoping to change the subject. This man disturbed her. Memories of his garden seduction kept flashing through her mind. If she didn't know better, she might mistake curiosity for attraction.

But no, she thought. That was what she felt for Lieutenant Butler. Mr. Calhoun inspired a different sort of fascination. He was a sight to look at, his shadowy gray eyes burning deep, his body honed like an athlete's, his hands looking less pampered than they should for a gentleman. When she studied James Calhoun, she had an overwhelming perception of danger. He didn't threaten her in any physical way, but in a deeper sense. He challenged and provoked her, and outside of academia, she disliked being challenged and provoked. It made her uncomfortable.

"Let's go, then," Helena said, leading the way into the light-filled stairway that angled up through the tall, narrow town house. It was one of the finest features of the house, open from top to bottom with oriel windows at each landing.

Abigail fetched her latest batch of notes and calculations to show the professor. Then they descended to street level, pausing at the cloakroom to don fringed shawls and bonnets. Professor Rowan lived next door, but the autumn air was brisk, and manners in Georgetown restrained. No lady ever left the house without a wrap and hat. Even the Cabot sisters had not excused themselves from that rule. So far.

As they stepped outside, Abigail stole a look at Mr. Calhoun. The breeze toyed with his too-long hair, and the sunshine glinted in his mirrorlike eyes. What would it mean to have this handsome devil living right next door to them? And what on earth would he think of Professor Rowan?

Four

A derelict, half-dressed servant answered the door. Jamie had a swift impression of dark hair in need of barbering, distracted eyes behind thick-lensed spectacles and a mouth pulled down in annoyance. The man was not elderly; in fact, he was a strapping young specimen, yet he shuffled along slowly as though in no hurry to do anyone's bidding. Jamie wondered what sort of gentleman would allow a servant to comport himself in such a manner.

"Honestly, Professor Rowan, what can you be thinking? It's eleven o'clock in the morning and you're not dressed," Helena Cabot scolded.

"I am dressed," the man said, rubbing the shadow of a beard on his cheeks. He brushed at the crumbs littering the front of his gaping robe. "Not dressed means naked. I am not naked. But if you prefer—" His ink-smudged hand went to the front of the threadbare robe.

"You wouldn't dare." Abigail pushed past him into the house. "We've brought your new lodger to meet you, and you mustn't frighten him off."

Jamie stepped into the foyer. So the derelict was

the eminent Professor Michael Rowan, one of the noted intellectual treasures of Georgetown University. For no particular reason, Jamie had expected a pale, subdued bachelor scholar in his twilight years. Instead, his clearly reluctant host was a husky man who didn't look a day over twenty-five.

"Not to worry," Jamie said. "I've never been frightened by the sight of a naked man." He extended his hand to the professor. "How do you do. James Calhoun. Miss Cabot was kind enough to offer an introduction."

Professor Rowan shook hands cordially enough, leaving only a small ink stain on Jamie's palm. "Which Miss Cabot?"

"The kind one." Jamie couldn't resist saying it.

Abigail sniffed and poked her nose into the air.

"Refresh my memory," said Rowan, scratching his head. "Was I expecting a guest?"

"Mr. Calhoun isn't exactly a guest," Helena explained. She favored the professor with a look any other man would have walked across hot coals for, but Rowan didn't notice. "He's your new lodger."

"When did I agree to take in a lodger?"

"Right this instant, you great fool. You're rattling around in this house all alone, and you can barely afford it, so you really must take in a lodger." Helena clasped her hands. "You and Mr. Calhoun will get along just famously."

"I don't get along with anyone."

"Then it doesn't matter who your lodger is," Helena pointed out.

"True." Rowan nodded and led the way to a parlor cluttered with wires and magnets, stacks of papers and books, a machine with cylinders on the wall. In-

trigued, Jamie scanned the room. He considered himself an educated man, but the contraptions that littered
the place baffled him. He thought he recognized a
pressure gauge hooked up to beakers and glass tubing,
and the oak plaque and brass paddle of a disassem-
bled telegraph transmitter. An oblong wooden box
spewing wires and horns dominated one wall. A fire
alarm system, perhaps?

"Mind the gyroscope," Rowan mumbled, brushing
past Helena, completely missing her worshipful look.

"Why do you have a gyroscope?" Jamie asked.
"Do you go to sea?"

"This instrument has a number of useful applica-
tions," Abigail said. She and Rowan elbowed each
other like a pair of naughty schoolchildren. Jamie
Calhoun had seen many places, met many people, experienced many adventures, but he still thought the
present company strange indeed.

The rest of the house was nearly as cluttered as the
parlor. The old residence had tall-ceilinged, narrow
rooms and floors that creaked. Rowan explained that
he conducted many of his experiments at home because they required constant monitoring.

"I used to sleep in the Laboratory of Applied Sciences," he said, "but some of the other faculty members objected, so I had to find a place of my own."
He smiled distractedly. "There is much to be said for
making work into one's life, isn't there, Miss Abigail?"

"Indeed, I have found it so."

"My sister is a great astrologer," Helena explained.

"Astronomer," Rowan corrected.

She waved a hand. "The distinction isn't important."

"It's as different as a man from a woman." Despite the spectacles, his stare sent out undercurrents of meaning.

Helena caught her breath with an audible gasp before turning away. "What's important is that she is going to be famous. Tell him, Abigail. Tell him how you're going to be famous."

"Helena, that's not the reason—"

"She's going to sight a comet with her telephone on the roof."

"Telescope."

"Didn't I say that? And the president will strike a gold medal in her name. I declare, it's all too exciting."

"I'm all aquiver just thinking about it," Jamie muttered.

"No need to be sarcastic," Abigail said.

"There are easier ways to strike gold."

"It's not about the medal." Abigail handed Rowan a file of notes covered in mysterious mathematical symbols. "More work on my comet calculations."

"A parabolic orbit," he said. "Well done."

"Is it?" Her face lit up, and for the first time since he'd met her, Jamie realized she was almost pretty. "The more I learn, the less I trust myself. And the more I compute, the deeper the mystery seems."

No, she wasn't pretty, he decided. She had depth and passion, traits he found far more interesting. "How do you know the comet's there?" he asked.

"It's a precise science," she explained. "Blind faith and magic have no place in science."

"This is the work of a gifted mind," Rowan assured her, perusing the calculations. "Keep working on it. Keep pulling back the curtain, little by little."

The three of them had no idea how strange they all were. Abigail and Michael Rowan behaved like slightly befuddled, scholarly colleagues. Helena regarded Rowan with the sort of reverent adoration reserved for fallen gods, but of course the clod didn't notice. Ironic, thought Jamie. Every man in the capital wanted Helena Cabot, but the one she wanted barely knew she was alive.

"Do you suppose I could see my quarters?" he asked, interrupting the comet discussion.

Rowan blinked behind glasses so thick they magnified his eyes. "Oh. Certainly. Right this way." With a shambling gait, he crossed the hallway and opened the door to a large but spartan chamber furnished with a bedstead, an armoire, a washstand and fireplace. Rowan frowned and scratched his head. "Odd. I thought I'd ruined this room along with the rest of the house."

"I sent Dolly over to clean it," Helena said.

"Oh. Thank you. Good of you." Rowan pointed to the window. "Look there. A view of both gardens."

Indeed, the high window looked down into the narrow row gardens behind the houses of Dumbarton Street. Senator Cabot's garden was adjacent to the one directly below the window, an arrangement Jamie might find quite convenient.

"Excellent. I'll take it."

"It's too perfect." Helena clasped her hands, beaming at everyone. "I just love it when things work out so neatly." She touched Rowan's arm. "Isn't that so? You need money, Mr. Calhoun needs a home and we need you to stay on as our neighbor. It's like doing a puzzle, and every single piece fits just right.''

''Those aren't the sort of puzzles that interest me,'' Rowan stated and left the room. Helena followed him, peppering him with conversation that he deflected with a shield of indifference.

Jamie found himself alone in the room with Abigail Cabot.

''Well,'' she said with a nervous flutter of her hands. ''That was simple enough, I suppose. We're going to be neighbors, then. How convenient for you.''

He scowled. Was he that obvious? ''Convenient in what way?''

''You shall have access to my sister every day. Most of the gentlemen who court her have to travel much farther.''

''Is that why you think I chose these lodgings? To court your sister?''

''You wouldn't be the first.''

The fact was, the idea hadn't crossed Jamie's mind. Helena Cabot was inordinately beautiful, but so was the *Venus de Milo* at the Louvre, and he didn't want to court *that*.

But let Miss Abigail make what she would of his motives. She'd find out his true objective soon enough.

''I'd best be going,'' he said. ''I'll be needing my things brought around.''

''Of course. Helena and I must be on our way as well. Dumbarton Street is an exceedingly pleasant place to live, but it thrives as much on gossip as it does on politics.''

''So does Congress, I'm beginning to understand.''

He held the door for her. "Come. I'll escort you and your sister home." He grinned. "Gallant of me, isn't it? Going ten steps out of my way, solely for your sake."

He spoke briefly with Rowan about the arrangement, then stepped out into the crisp autumn day. Leaves tumbled along the neat brick walkways. A few hacks and cabs stood in the roadway, their wheels angled and blocked against the incline of the hill, horses indolently swishing their tails. Students sat clustered around enameled iron tables at a café down the block, and neatly attired servants went about their errands.

It seemed to Jamie a neighborhood of intimidating self-importance. He'd been to the courts of Europe, to Middle Eastern palaces and to places the people of Washington could not possibly imagine. Yet to him, staid Georgetown, with its brick streets and pastel-painted doorways, its brass knockers, gaslight sconces and wrought-iron garden gates, was more exotic than the palaces of Luxor. Certainly its residents were far more baffling.

He was about to bid the ladies a good day, when a bicycle messenger arrived, puffing with exertion from his climb up the hill from M Street. The youngster wore the deep blue livery of a naval orderly, and when he dismounted the cycle, he came to attention with a smart salute.

"Ensign Clarence Sutherland at your service," he said. "I have a message for Miss Cabot, from Lieutenant Butler."

Abigail Cabot was transformed by the expression that brightened her face. Accepting the envelope, the little wren turned into a songbird, her smile fulfilling the promise of her incredible eyes. She was foolishly moonstruck over Butler, and had absolutely no skill at concealing it. This was unfortunate, for she was going to be eaten alive. Jamie had done his best to warn her, but clearly she hadn't listened.

"Goodbye, Mr. Calhoun," she said with undue haste. "I'm sure we'll meet again. Come, Helena, let's go inside."

Jamie wondered if, for once, he'd read the situation wrong. Could Boyd Butler actually be pursuing Abigail? If so, Jamie would be amazed, and he'd be reluctantly impressed. It took a certain subtlety of taste to appreciate a woman like Abigail Cabot. Perhaps Jamie had underestimated the young naval officer, dismissing him as slow-witted, shallow and unimaginative. More likely to go for the ripe-peach beauty of the sister, Helena. She was a fine enough bundle, but it took more than a first-rate set of breasts to hold a man's interest beyond the bedchamber.

Which sister was Butler after? The question nagged at Jamie as he watched the two of them, the swan and the wren, step through the heavy, imposing door to their father's house.

And why did the answer matter to him?

Five

Filled with bittersweet joy, Abigail scarcely felt the floor beneath her feet as she went upstairs to the parlor. Clutching the envelope to her bosom, she resisted the urge to press it to her mouth.

A letter from Boyd Butler.

Helena hurried after her. "Honestly, Abigail, must you rush so? I haven't seen you move so quickly since those mussels made you sick at the Spanish ambassador's house."

As if Abigail needed to be reminded of that. Helena never meant to be insensitive, although she was often blunt. In fact, that very night it had been Helena who had rushed her from the room and found a spittoon before Abigail disgraced herself entirely.

She led the way into the comfortable morning room and took a seat on the dark green settee. Helena sat in a wing chair opposite her and folded her hands in her lap. "So what does the letter say?"

Abigail took a deep breath, sorting through her feelings. The prospect of a letter from Boyd Butler filled her with delight, even though she understood perfectly that it was Helena he wanted. Why didn't that fact make her miserable? Because, she realized, this courtship would make her father happy and her sister happy—and two out of three wasn't so bad.

Helena's curiosity about Boyd Butler seemed strange to Abigail, for ordinarily she treated all suitors with equal disdain. Perhaps this time things were different. Perhaps she truly did want to be courted.

In a way, Abigail felt she'd been granted a reprieve. No gentleman ever took an interest in her, and Butler's brief flare of attraction at the wedding—exhilarating as it was—had unsettled her. She didn't know how she would act if he pursued her. Watching him court Helena was safer than being the object of his desire. This way, Abigail didn't have to risk making a fool of herself. It wasn't the same as having a love affair of her very own, but in her own private way, she might find safety preferable.

Or so she told herself as she took her time breaking the seal and opening the envelope. She tried to ignore a twinge of annoyance at Helena, who picked up her petit point and worked a thread through the design. This was the start of a romance, for heaven's sake. Couldn't she have a little respect for the weightiness of the momentous occasion? Or at least savor it? Didn't she even want to be alone to dream about it?

But, as usual, Helena left the thinking to Abigail. It wouldn't do to point out that the letter was a private correspondence and that Abigail had no right to read it. She and Helena shared everything; they always had. Raised by a constantly changing parade of nurses and nannies, tutors and taskmasters, they had taken refuge in each other. Motherless, and with a father like Franklin Cabot, they'd learned to cling to one another.

She unfolded the message. His stationery bore the embossed gold seal of a naval officer. "He has a fine clear hand," she said, feeling a thrill ripple through her. This falling-in-love business was heady stuff, like an exotic virus. Even though she loved him from afar, she had not expected the sensation to be so...so physical. She took a peculiar delight in seeing his penmanship for the first time. It was personal and intimate, a glimpse at a facet of Boyd Butler that had been hidden from her until this moment.

"Of course he does," said Helena. "They train them to do that in the navy, don't they?"

He probably learned penmanship long before going into the navy, but Abigail didn't point that out. She took a deep breath and started reading.

"'My dear Miss Cabot'—" She stopped, feeling a flutter of her heart. She'd never been anyone's dear. The designation made her want to laugh and weep at the same time. Taking another deep, steadying breath, she went on. "'They say that Helena of Troy had a face that launched a thousand ships. Dare I say that Helena of Georgetown has a face that could launch the entire United States naval fleet?'"

As soon as she read her sister's name aloud, Abigail turned into a machine. An armored reptile, impervious to feeling. All along she'd known Lieutenant Butler wanted Helena, but until she actually read the name, saw it shaped by his concise handwriting, Abigail had been able to imagine the tender words were meant for her. Without changing her voice, she read on, but everything inside her turned to ice. This was a *love* letter to her sister. Not even meant for her eyes. "'I find myself preoccupied with thoughts of you. In the middle of muster drills or morning inspection, every other notion drains from my mind. Should you favor me with the merest fraction of my admiration of you, I would consider myself the most privileged of men.'''

As she recited the words, Abigail sneaked a glance now and then at her sister. In the diffuse light of the late-autumn morning, she was like a goddess from another world, a place devoid of ugliness or infirmity. The polished copper fall of her hair framed a porcelain-perfect face, which was now consciously arranged into an expression of polite interest. Yet her hands stayed busy, working the petit point as though with a will of their own.

Struggling to hold her sick disappointment at bay, Abigail finished reading, though the aching tenderness of Boyd's closing nearly undid her. "'You hold my heart, a crystal, within your slender hands....'" Her voice trailed off into the sunny silence of the morning room. She stared down at her own small, squarish hands until the words on the page blurred, then she blinked to clear her vision and looked up at her sister.

Helena clasped her hands in her lap. "How lovely," she said. "How heartfelt and delightful." She frowned at Abigail's expression. "Are you all right? You look a bit ill, dear."

"I'm fine." Abigail folded the pages with a reverence reserved for holy relics.

"Now, who did you say that was from?" Helena inquired, her brow puckered with a frown.

Abigail nearly crumpled the note as she put it back in the envelope. "Oh, for the love of heaven," she snapped. "Are you so inured to having men's hearts laid at your feet that you can't keep track of them all?

Perhaps we should keep a book like a star log, listing all your conquests. Or maybe a strategy map such as Father keeps in his study, only instead of voting blocks, we can mark off each—''

"Abigail, please." Helena took out a handkerchief and pressed it to her cheeks. "I didn't mean to be flip. Why are you so distraught? This isn't like you."

Abigail gritted her teeth and held herself very still. "Of course. And I didn't mean to— Actually, I did. My frankness is surely the least of my assets. Honestly, Helena, have you truly forgotten which man has pledged his soul to you?"

Helena bit her lip. "It was either Mr. Troy Barnes or Lieutenant Butler. Both inquired about...well, you know."

Abigail did know. Ever since Helena had come of age and shocked the polite world by not settling down to an advantageous marriage, her sister had received offers with the frequency of honeysuckle attracting bees in summer.

"It's from Lieutenant Butler." Abigail pushed the letter into Helena's lap. "Lieutenant Boyd Butler."

"Of course. The Annapolis man."

"The vice president's son."

"He dances like a prince."

"And writes like a poet." Abigail stood up, pacing in agitation. "You cannot dismiss him, Helena. Not this time. He's too...important." She had almost said "vulnerable," but that would have been too revealing, even to Helena. "You heard Father this morning. An alliance with the Butlers would mean everything to him."

"Yes, it would, but I'm trying to remember why I should concern myself with pleasing Papa."

"Helena."

"That was quite naughty of me, wasn't it?" Helena lapsed into a dreamy silence, seemingly preoccupied with something important and mysterious.

Abigail held in her exasperation. While she labored in quiet diligence to do the right thing, Helena wavered between daughterly affection and open rebellion. Yet, for both women, the results were the same. Their father was never cruel to them, but he treated them with a remote civility that had a subtle cruelty all its own.

"He wants a reply," Abigail said, her gaze falling to the letter in Helena's hand. "He asked—begged—for one directly."

Helena dropped the envelope on a side table and picked up her sewing again. "Of course. But I could never— Oh, you know me, Abigail. I have no head for such things. The words simply aren't in me. I need you, dear." She raised troubled eyes to Abigail. "Would you be so kind?"

Abigail turned to the window so her sister wouldn't see her face. She supposed she could refuse; perhaps she would. But no. If she didn't write the letter, Helena would dash off some blunt rejection, dictating it to one of her father's secretaries who might or might not accomplish the task with tact and discretion. Several years ago, she'd sent an unscrupulous servant to dismiss a suitor, and the story had appeared in the next day's *Post.*

Abigail couldn't bear to see Lieutenant Butler treated in such a manner. Though she had every right to resent him, she discovered that she could not. Being angry at him for falling in love with Helena was like being angry at the autumn leaves for falling from the dogwood trees that lined the brick streets of Georgetown.

"And what is it you'd like me to say?" she asked her sister.

"Tell him how delighted I was to hear from him. Tell him I share his feelings."

"But you don't," Abigail said. Then a stunning thought struck her. "Or do you?"

"Probably not. But as you said, this is important to Papa. Think how pleased he would be with me if I really did win the heart of Lieutenant Barnes."

"Butler." Abigail had thought of nothing else. Could she bear seeing him wed to her sister? "And what would you intend to do with his heart? Add it to your collection?"

"Abigail, you know me better than that. I'm thinking of Papa, and you should, too."

"Believe me, Helena, I am thinking of Father, too."

"Then will you do it? You'll send a letter?"

"I have to go to Foggy Bottom this afternoon."

"Then do it when you return. Please, Abigail. It would mean so much to me."

"Very well. But only if you tell me what to say."

Helena flung her petit point into the sewing basket and stood up. "Oh, how I wish I had your head for words and paragraphs! You'll say exactly the right thing, I know you will, Abigail. You always do." She gave her sister a fervent hug and hurried from the room.

Abigail sat alone, pondering her options. She didn't really have any. There was only one person capable of sending a reply, and being discreet about it.

Unbidden, a memory of the previous night crept

into her thoughts. It was something Jamie Calhoun had said to her. *Why do you think they call it falling in love? When you truly fall in love, you'll know it. You will weep with the knowledge.*

Abigail didn't weep, but she felt like doing so. Perhaps that was what Mr. Calhoun had been trying to explain.

But how could he have known?

Six

Professor Michael Rowan's face turned red with exertion as he held up his end of the steamer trunk. "What do you keep in here, Calhoun?" he grumbled. "Do you draft legislation on stone tablets?"

At the other end of the trunk, Jamie backed into his room, holding steady as Rowan half lowered and half dropped the trunk. Supporting it with his chest, Jamie set the thing end up and corner-walked it against the wall.

"Just the usual whatnot," he said in response to his landlord's question. "I was told to expect a long legislative session this fall, so I came prepared." Unlatching the trunk at the top and side, he swung open the two halves. Immediately, a stack of books toppled onto his feet. "I had to pack my things in a hurry."

"You're a Southern gentleman, a Calhoun," Rowan pointed out. Extracting a ripe apple from the pocket of his trousers, he took an enormous bite and spoke around the food. "Aren't you supposed to have servants for this sort of thing?"

Jamie didn't like the edge of censure in the professor's voice. "Oh, of course," he said. "But today I beat my darkies so hard they couldn't work."

Rowan finished chewing and sent him a sheepish grin. "I suppose you must get tired of being regarded as a lazy, overprivileged planter's son with nothing better to do than sit on the porch drinking mint juleps and getting rich."

"My friend, if I were a lazy, overprivileged planter's son, why would I have come to the capital to room with a cranky, judgmental Northerner who wears his waistcoat inside out and thinks a Southern drawl signifies a lesser life-form?"

Rowan blinked, then glanced down at his waist-coat. Setting aside the apple core, he retrieved a pair of wire-rimmed spectacles from atop his head and in-spected the seams. He switched the waistcoat, then dug into the pocket, pulling out a gold watch on a chain. "I've been looking all over for this," he ex-claimed with a short laugh. "Good God, can it really be after three o'clock? I haven't even had lunch yet."

Jamie didn't bother to remind him about the apple.

Rowan put away the watch. "I do apologize, Cal-houn."

"Accepted."

"Good. I really am a tolerant man," Rowan said. "And I've a few foibles of my own."

Jamie thought of the cluttered house, the uniden-tifiable inventions covering every floor and table, the kitchen pantry and icebox stuffed with experiments, the lavatory lined with beakers and glass tubing. He'd even discovered a plump white mouse living in a maze on the mantelpiece.

"I noticed," he said.

"There's the door," Rowan said as the brass

knocker banged. "I'll just see who it is." As he left, a laundry chit fell on the floor.

The chit was dated two years earlier. Jamie deposited it, along with the apple core, in the dustbin and wiped his hands on a towel. His own foibles included an insistence on neatness and order, but he would have to confine that preference to his own quarters and simply shut his eyes to the rest.

Hearing voices in the parlor below, he went to the foyer and looked down over the rail to see who the caller was. For a moment, he stood unnoticed, watching from the doorway. Abigail Cabot had come to call.

She wore the same plain brown frock she'd had on this morning, but her demeanor had been quite transformed. She'd been amusing, almost playful as she and her sister introduced him to Rowan, and when the letter arrived from Lieutenant Butler, she'd shone like the sun at high noon. Now she was a dark little bird, her gaze darting furtively as she murmured something to the professor. Jamie wondered what was amiss.

"Hello, Miss Abigail," he said, putting on his best smile and walking down the stairs to greet her. "I was just getting settled."

She glanced at him, her striking eyes full of woe. But she spoke cordially enough. "That's good, Mr. Calhoun. I hope you'll be very comfortable here."

"Come help me unpack."

"I'll do no such—"

"Of course you will." Ignoring propriety, he took her hand and drew her up the stairs to his chamber. She resisted, stumbling a little on the stair, but he simply slowed his pace and pulled her along. "Rowan was helping,'' he explained, ''but I have no confidence in his organizational skills.''

A wry smile touched her lips. ''It didn't take you long to notice that.'' She stooped and picked up an armload of books, carrying them to the shelves that lined one wall. As she put them away, ordering them by topic and author, her movements became slow and thoughtful. ''Plato's *Republic*,'' she said. ''I haven't seen a copy of that in years.''

''Most people I know have never seen it at all,'' Jamie said.

''*The Manual of Epictetus, Measure for Measure*, St. Thomas Aquinas, Rousseau, Francis Bacon's *Novum Organum*...'' She shelved more books, rattling off the titles with a growing incredulity that Jamie found faintly insulting.

''Why do you seem so surprised?'' he asked. ''Is it so astonishing that a man from the Chesapeake low country can read?''

''Not that he can, but that he actually does,'' she stated. ''Please forgive my bluntness, but the fact is, the legislators I've met from plantation society have never troubled themselves to study the issues in much depth.''

''No?''

''They're more interested in pushing legislation that enables them to carry on as though the South had never even lost the war.''

Jamie's purpose for joining Congress couldn't be more different, but he would have to be cautious about revealing it. ''Tell me, does everyone in the capital share your view? Does your father?''

She resumed her work with increasing agitation. ''If you must know, my father and I share little in the way of political views. I imagine you're going to go after his support for the Chesapeake railroad corridor, aren't you?''

He felt a cold dart of suspicion. "Why would you suppose that?''

"My father's been a senator all my life. I've learned a thing or two about politics. The congressmen from the South are after improved and expanded railroads to create even more prosperity. And how convenient for the government to have to pay for it rather than the rail companies, the landowners and those who use the service.''

"Miss Cabot, I didn't come here for my convenience.'' Jamie went about his business, organizing papers and correspondence on the desk in the corner. Going into politics was a bad idea, he decided, but it was too late for regrets. Getting himself elected had been absurdly easy. He was a Calhoun, through no fault of his own, and there had been a Calhoun in Congress ever since the Constitution had been ratified. However, if his fellow legislators regarded him as the knowing Miss Cabot did, he would have a harder time than he anticipated.

"Then why did you come here?'' she asked.

To atone, he thought. To fix something that can't be fixed. Redemption was too much to hope for. He looked at Miss Cabot, who waited for an answer.

"To represent my district,'' he said.

She brayed with laughter. "If your district is made up of wealthy white male landowners, I'll believe that. Oh, the Koran,'' she said, losing interest in the conversation as she paused to admire the morocco binding of the large tome. "Some of the most gifted astronomers in history come from Muslim people. And what's this one?''

Jamie said nothing, but calmly watched her flip open the large, illustrated book. Her jaw dropped, and her cheeks bloomed with color. Just for a moment, true fascination flashed in her eyes, then she slammed the book shut and thrust it onto the shelf.

"That's the *Kama Sutra* of Vatsayayana,'' Jamie said, delighted by her reaction. "A Hindu text on the art of love from the third century.'' He pulled the book from the shelf and flipped through the pages. What would it be like, he wondered, to show Abigail Cabot the delights depicted in the intricate woodcut illustrations? To press apart her thighs and stroke her, to watch those midnight eyes grow soft and misty with ecstasy?

Grinning at the fantasy, he replaced the book and selected another. "I also have *The Perfumed Garden,* a manual of Arab erotology. Would you like to borrow it, Miss Cabot?''

"You're disgusting.''

"And you're no scholar if you would dismiss a classic text—''

"I said you were disgusting, not the text.''

"Tell me,'' he said, "are you always this charming to your neighbors?''

"I am charming to no one at all.'' She shoved the volume into the shelf and resumed her work. "But I expect you've already noticed that about me.'' She dropped a heavy book, letting out a yelp as it landed on her right foot.

Jamie hastened to pick it up. "Are you all right? Is your foot—''

"I'm fine.'' She spoke with such venom that he

paused to look at her. Color stained her cheeks, but she ducked her head.

Possessed by the urge to touch her, Jamie smoothed his hand down her arm. She was sturdy and wiry, yet oddly vulnerable as she lifted her face to his. "You shouldn't be so familiar with me. It's not proper."

"I rarely concern myself with being proper." Her lips, he noticed, were lovely when not pursed in disapproval.

She must have sensed the turn of his thoughts, for she stepped back, showing great interest in the book. "This is in the original Greek," she observed in an obvious effort to deflect his attention from her.

"Is that what all those funny symbols mean?" Jamie feigned a baffled expression. "And here I thought it was an algebra text."

The color in her face intensified. "I've been unforgivably disagreeable, haven't I?"

"Disagreeable. But not unforgivably."

"I deserve your scorn."

"You deserve a spanking." He laughed at the shock on her face. "And I would delight in administering the punishment," he added. "However, you're doing such a good job organizing my books that I'll give you a reprieve. Carry on. And try if you can to refrain from making any further remarks about my poor benighted intellect."

A yellowed card slipped from between the pages of Xenophon's *On Horsemanship* and drifted to the tabletop. She picked it up and studied it. "A photograph," she said. "Is it yours?"

He took it from her, feeling an immediate twist in his gut—a reluctance to open a private part of his life to this woman. "Actually, yes."

"Who is it?" Leaning toward him, she studied the small image of amber shadows and pale light. The portrait showed a striking light-skinned Negro man of middle years, small of stature, his patrician African features composed into a calm expression. He wore the silk jacket and cap of a professional jockey, and between his slender hands, he held a winner's cup.

"The best Thoroughbred jockey in the country. That picture was made at Saratoga Springs." Filled with bittersweet pride, he propped the photograph on the shelf at eye level, then turned to her. "His name is—was—Noah Calhoun. He was my half brother."

To her credit, she did not dive for her smelling salts, but regarded him with a clarity of understanding he found both surprising and gratifying. "I see. What happened to him, Mr. Calhoun?"

He wondered how much to tell her. That he had practically been raised by Noah, seventeen years his senior? That Noah had been more of a father to him than his own? That Noah was the reason Jamie had gone into public service?

Jamie and Noah had gone to the Middle East on an adventure, to see the world and acquire horses for Albion's breeding program. Oh, how he wished he could turn back time, leave Noah safe with his wife, Patsy, at their farm on King's Creek. But Jamie had insisted he come. What had happened to Noah on that ill-fated journey would haunt Jamie for the rest of his life.

"He died overseas," he said, deciding not to elaborate. He didn't want to share that painful episode, least of all with this strange little woman whose probing eyes seemed to see too much of him already.

"I'm terribly sorry. You must miss him."

"I do." To change the subject, he said, "On to more agreeable matters. What did your lieutenant have to say?"

Her face fell, and he realized the matter wasn't agreeable at all. "He wishes to take up a correspondence."

"But isn't that what you—"

"With my sister." She aligned the books on the shelf with obsessive precision. "As I told you last night, this comes as no surprise to me. But it's troubling...."

"What is troubling about it?"

"She asked me to write the reply for her. My sister isn't fond of writing."

Ah. He saw the whole picture now. He understood why she was upset and distracted, maybe even faintly resentful of her sister. "I'd wager you excel at it."

She shrugged. "It wouldn't be the first time I wrote something in her stead."

"You could always refuse to do it."

"Yes, but—" She bit her lip.

"So why don't you refuse?"

"I don't want the lieutenant to get his feelings hurt. He's a decent, sincere man."

Jamie resisted the urge to snap at her, to tell her to quit idolizing a dolt who valued beauty over substance. He studied her for a few moments, wondering at the passion that shone in her midnight eyes, and summoned patience. No need to alienate a potential ally. "I suppose there's nothing wrong with taking care of your sister's correspondence. Just make sure you understand the risks."

"What risks?"

"Bitterness and pain, to name a couple." He

smiled as he said it, but a peculiar authority rang in his voice.

"I know that." Yet she looked a little rattled. "I understand the risks. I know you can't force someone to love someone else. And believe me, Mr. Calhoun, I'm aware of my own limitations."

Jamie resisted the urge to pat her on the shoulder. "Look, why don't you go down to the study and work on it. I'll finish up here."

She stepped back. "All right. I promised Professor Rowan I'd do some computations for him as well." She checked the perfectly aligned books one more time, her gaze lingering on the exotic *Kama Sutra* and *Perfumed Garden*. The color crept into her cheeks again.

Jamie couldn't resist teasing her a little. He stroked a wicked finger over the agitated pulse in her throat. "Good lawmaking and good lovemaking are not incompatible, you know. In fact, one sometimes leads to the other."

She smacked his hand away. "I have work to do."

He grinned broadly as she left the room. He had not expected to be so royally entertained during his sojourn in the capital. He had not expected to be entertained at all, and only the memory of Noah kept him focused on his goal. He intended to introduce the legislation that would protect Noah's legacy, see that his agenda passed before returning to his freewheeling ways.

But Franklin Cabot's daughters turned out to be a surprise. Helena was as lovely as a song, but she didn't interest him half so much as the other. Prickly, ill-tempered and plainspoken, Abigail would never be the belle of anyone's ball. Yet she embodied the most intriguing combination of idealism and irascibility he had ever encountered.

He put up his ivory dresser set and razor case, his clock and a few personal items, but found himself distracted by the thought that Abigail was downstairs in Rowan's study, probably doing something far more interesting than stacking shirt collars.

The professor's study occupied the parlor and most of the dining room on the main floor. Books, magazines and manuscripts cluttered every available surface and were stacked in floor-to-ceiling shelves. Gadgets and machines abounded, as they did all through the house: mechanical enlarging machines, a Royal Typing Machine, a few other contraptions Jamie didn't recognize. He suspected a number of the inventions worked in theory only. But the professor's study was like a child's nursery, untidy and filled with playthings to amuse an inquisitive mind.

Abigail sat at the cluttered desk, an ornate fountain pen in one hand and a look of terrible despair on her face. She had not heard him come in, and watching her in this unguarded moment had a profound effect on him. Suddenly she was not merely a diversion and a necessary link to a powerful senator. She was a woman with feelings and secrets and dreams of her own.

Not that those secrets and dreams were any of his business, but he grew more curious about her by the moment. She was so damn interesting to him, from the carelessly scraped-together bun of her hair, to the hem of her outmoded brown dress. Watching her was like watching an industrious bird building a nest, fussing over each little twig and thread. In the strangest

way, he wanted to be part of her world—not because
she made it seem so inviting, but precisely because
she seemed so put off by him.

He trod noisily on the bottom stair to alert her, and
strode into the room as she looked up from her writing.

"Still toiling away?" he asked.

She spread her hand on the page, the protective
gesture both childish and testy. "I didn't realize I was
being timed."

"You're not. But I bored myself with my unpack-
ing, so I came to ask if you would take a walk with
me."

"No, thank you." Her reply was as swift and de-
cisive as the stroke of her pen at the top of the page.

"Do I offend you that deeply?" he asked, putting
on a wounded look. He turned to a piecrust table by
the window and examined a brass orrery. Spying her
reflection in the bay window, he was startled when
she slipped a few pages under the ink blotter on the
desk.

They were probably trade secrets or private notes
on Rowan's inventions, Jamie speculated. Though
tempted to catch her out, he stopped himself. Let the
woman have her secrets. God knew, he had his, and
he needed to make an ally of her father.

"Where has the professor gone?" he asked without
turning.

"To the laboratory, to work on subdividing his arc
lamp."

Jamie pretended to understand this. Nodding
sagely, he gave her a chance to pull the blotter back
in place. "I only asked you to go for a walk, not a
ride in a closed carriage." Such rides created endless

scandal in the city. Many a young lady's reputation had been tainted by forbidden, private rides.

"I'm not fond of taking walks," she said. "I'm not fond of company."

"Why not?"

"I seem to have little to say."

He considered the pages hidden under the ink blotter, but didn't mention them. Walking over to her, he offered a smile that worked like a charm on most women. "Then you need not say a word. I'll do all the talking."

She stared at him, clearly unmoved by the smile. "Such a blessing."

Remembering her reaction when he'd touched her before, he stroked his hand across her back, then let it linger at the nape of her neck. "I can be entertaining if you'll give me a chance."

She jerked away, as he'd known she would. "And why should I do that? Why should I give you a chance?"

He propped his hip at the edge of the desk, knowing his nearness would rattle her. "Because you've never met someone who has seen the pyramids of Egypt."

"Oh, and you have." She scooted her chair back to distance herself from him.

He edged forward an inch. "And the Taj Mahal." Another inch. "The Vatican and Versailles."

She lifted her eyebrows. "I've always wanted to visit the Vat—"

A door slammed in the lower hallway. "Hello?" called Helena's voice.

"—ican," she finished, lurching up from the chair and staggering a little.

He cursed under his breath. He'd been so close to cracking through her façade.

"In the study." Abigail flashed a look at Jamie. "Helena would probably love to take a walk with you."

He tucked his thumb into the waistband of his trousers and drummed his fingers. "I didn't invite Helena."

Her gaze drifted to his hand, then she seemed to realize what she was staring at, and looked away. "You should."

"Why?"

She exhaled an exasperated sigh. "Because it's a rare opportunity. Everyone wants Helena."

"Wants me for what?" Bright as a just-minted penny, Helena stepped into the room. Strolling over to the mantel, she took a handful of pumpkin seeds from her apron pocket and fed them to the mouse.

"Mr. Calhoun wishes to take a walk, and I told him he should ask you to go with him."

"I'd be happy to, wouldn't I, Mr. Socrates?" The mouse's pink nose quivered at her. Helena's warm smile created a perfect dimple in her cheek. "In fact, we can post the letter together." Dusting off her hands, she glanced at the desk. "Is it ready yet?"

"Almost."

"This is so good of you." With a decided lack of self-consciousness, Helena explained. "Abigail has a brilliant facility with words. She looks after all my correspondence for me."

"How fortunate for you. Your sister's a regular Cyrano de Georgetown."

Scowling, Abigail sifted a bit of blotting sand over the letter.

"Papa will be so pleased, won't he?" Helena said. "This was a tremendous idea you had, Abigail."

"It wasn't my— Never mind." Abigail regarded her sister with exasperation.

Jamie perked up at the mention of Senator Cabot. Yes, this might actually work. It made sense that the head of Railroad and Finance should want to form an alliance with the vice president. Cabot wanted his daughter to marry a Butler, and Jamie knew without asking that the senator didn't care which girl walked down the aisle.

"I must invent affection where I feel none," Helena said with a martyrlike sigh. "Papa expects it."

Fascinating, thought Jamie. She was indifferent— both to Butler and to the fact that her sister was smitten with him.

Abigail tapped the excess sand into a jar on the desk. "You hardly know Lieutenant Butler. How can you be certain whether or not this might grow into genuine affection?"

"That's a very good point, Abigail. I shall try very hard. Did you write him a lovely letter?"

Abigail pinched her lips together and made no reply.

The oak box contraption on the wall let out a crackle, then a screech. Jamie nearly jumped out of his skin. He swung toward the thing, assuming a combative stance, reaching for a pistol that was not there. He hadn't carried a side arm since he'd fled a revolution in Andorra, but now he wished he had one. The machine rumbled ominously, and a hammer beat against a pair of bells. The whole room rattled with the sound, as though a dozen angry ghosts had slipped into the coffin-shaped device and were spitting curses at the mere mortals gathered in the study.

"I'll get it." With an expression of pure delight, Helena went to the contraption and leaned into the machine, almost embracing it, her generous breasts brushing against the large conical structure at the top.

"Yes, it's Helena Cabot," she shouted into the shrieking cone.

Jamie had supposed the woman to be rather limited in her intellectual powers, but now he suspected she was insane as well. Abigail did not appear at all perturbed by her sister's behavior. In fact, she got up to join her, leaving the letter forgotten on the desk. A thin, alien voice announced something about a connection, then a disjointed phrase crackled through the cone.

"You'd better not be touching anything in my study." The machine emitted a broken male voice. "And you'd better not be feeding Socrates. He's on a special diet."

"What the hell is that?" Jamie demanded. The faint, disembodied sound gave him the shivers.

Abigail laughed. "It's Professor Rowan. Don't you recognize his voice?"

"I'm calling to say I shan't be back for supper," the black horn announced.

She was right. The phantom voice was Rowan's.

"Where the devil is he?" Jamie edged toward the tall wooden box, looked down into the cone. "You said he was at the laboratory."

"It's true," said Abigail. "Professor Rowan is over at the college, perhaps a half mile away. He's transmitting his voice to us through the device."

Both women burst into laughter. "I confess I

thought the same thing you're probably thinking the first time I saw a telephone work,'' said Helena.

''This is a telephone?''

''Indeed it is,'' Abigail explained, indicating the apparatus on the wall.

''I've heard of them,'' Jamie said, feeling a twinge of awe at the whole process. It was amazing to think of Rowan far away, his voice sounding here in this very room. ''Never seen one before. Is it useful?''

Pinch-faced Abigail shocked him with a smile that sparkled with a contagious enthusiasm. ''Last week, we telephoned the White House. The president's chief adviser was so frightened he swore there was a poltergeist in the Oval Office.''

''But it's Mr. Calhoun's first day here,'' Helena contradicted, yelling into the mouthpiece. ''Surely you won't neglect your guest.''

''He's not a guest, he's a boarder,'' said the voice. ''And a grown man besides. He can feed himself.''

''I'll give him the message.'' Helena's face flushed with delight the whole time she spoke to the cone. She really was taken with the eccentric professor, Jamie reflected. Oh, wouldn't her father love that.

Jamie bent down to address the mouthpiece. ''Don't worry on my account,'' he shouted.

''Ah, there you are, Calhoun. I wasn't worried. I am ending this transmission now. Don't disturb anything in the study.''

He was a real charmer, Jamie thought. What an odd company he had joined, two spinster sisters and their weird, slovenly neighbor.

Abigail yelled some incomprehensible technical phrases into the device, and the professor answered in kind. With chalk on slate, she made some notations.

The transmission ended and a servant appeared, looking a bit fearful, twisting her hands into the fabric of her apron. ''The very devil's in that thing, I swear to heaven. Your father has sent me to tell you to join him for afternoon tea.''

''And so we shall,'' Helena said. ''Thank you, Dolly.'' She and the maid started down the stairs. Predictably, Helena had forgotten her promise to walk with Jamie.

He stepped close to Abigail, barring her exit. The clean, no-nonsense aroma of plain soap failed to mask her subtle feminine scent. Bending close to her ear, he said, ''I've not had my tea yet.''

''The professor keeps his in a jar,'' she said tersely. ''Right next to the arsenic. He has a hired man to look after things. Have you met Gerald Meeks yet?''

''Actually, I was hoping—''

''I know what you were hoping, sir. In case you haven't noticed, I'm not a fool.'' She pushed past him and started down the stairs. ''I'm sure you'll manage to make the acquaintance of my father in due time. But don't expect me to make it easy for you.''

He chuckled, holding her shawl for her and cupping his hands over her shoulders for a moment. An unmistakable heat leaped between them. He could tell by the flare of alarm in her eyes just before she looked away that she felt it, too.

''Indeed, Miss Cabot,'' he said. ''With you, nothing is easy.''

After seeing her out, he returned to the study, circling the telephone transmitter with a mixture of wonder and distrust. Strange indeed, but it captured his imagination. If they could speak to someone a half mile away, why not two miles? Or ten or a hundred? He would speak with the professor about it. There was investment potential in this newfangled invention.

As he was leaving the room, he happened to glance at the desk where Abigail had been working. Picking up one of the pages, he saw $m1 = Ho + 5 \log (delta) + 2.5n \log (r)$ followed by a long calculation, in writing so neat it resembled print. No doubt about it, the woman was bizarre.

Beneath her formula lay the letter she'd prepared in her sister's name, a short, dispassionate note to Lieutenant Boyd Butler.

Dear Lieutenant, Your letter was most welcome and I await your future missives...

It sounded as bland and indifferent as Helena's attitude toward the man. Like a lamb to the slaughter, Helena Cabot was being offered up to accommodate her father's political agenda. Both sisters seemed preoccupied with pleasing their father, and both saw the vice president's son as the way to do it.

Pondering the situation, he drummed his fingers on the surface of the desk. A corner of white paper stuck out from under the blotter, and he remembered the hidden pages.

Jamie decided to investigate. He might have been a good man once upon a time, but that had been long ago. The mishaps that had befallen him, the deeds he'd done or been forced to do, changed all that. He felt no qualms about helping himself to the neatly penned pages. No qualms about pouring himself a glass of whiskey and lighting a cigar. No qualms about sitting down by the window to read Abigail Cabot's private correspondence.

My dear Lieutenant Butler...

He read at first with mild, perhaps faintly malicious curiosity. But as he continued, realizing what this was, he settled back and absorbed every single word.

These were not trade secrets or notes on Rowan's devices, as Jamie had suspected. What he held in his hand was something far more compelling.

These were the secrets of her heart.

It was a searing love letter to that human hitching post, Boyd Butler. She must have sat down to pen the letter for her sister, and the truth had come pouring out of her. No wonder she'd hidden it away.

When your letter arrived, I experienced a second sunrise.... Simply knowing that you are somewhere in the world brings warmth to the coldest autumn day. My joy at having a letter from you has only been surpassed by the ecstasy of dancing in your arms....

A stark and scorching envy burned through Jamie. To love like this, to be the object of this depth of devotion—it was the stuff of dreams. He had not thought it possible.

He called for more whiskey, and it was brought by a servant who was nearly as sloppy and disagreeable as Rowan himself. Jamie recalled that his name was Meeks, the man-of-all-work and the only employee who had not stomped away from Rowan in disgust.

"Leave the decanter," Jamie advised him, then returned to his reading.

Abigail Cabot, he realized, wrote the same way she did everything else. With clarity, precision and an honesty that bordered on the poetic, she let Butler know exactly the effect his stupid letter had had on her. And it was no innocent, maidenly flutter of the heart.

When I think of you, my heart sings with sweetness, and I can only count the days until we meet again. Your words have touched the deepest part of me, probing my sleeping passions to wakeful attention…. The very thought of you…

Someone, somewhere, must have told her that it wasn't proper for a woman to describe the sort of heat generated by the very thought of him, but Abigail Cabot wrote it anyway.

Although Jamie didn't know Miss Cabot well, one thing had been clear from the start—she was a gifted woman. Yet she was hopelessly blind, her judgment severely impaired when it came to matters of the heart. Her deep sincerity lashed at him, finding a tenderness that should have been hardened by scar tissue.

You light my world with the brilliance of the moon on a cloudless night. You are cherished as a treasure beyond price…

He knocked back the whiskey and poured another glass. The stinging elixir worked fast, muddling his thoughts and darkening his mood. She was like some goddamn female Walt Whitman, for Christ's sake.

And she was in love with Boyd Butler, a man only slightly more evolved than a Boston fern. A man who fancied himself in love with her sister. A man who would have no idea what Abigail meant by "the dark forest of my imagination" or "a consuming, sweet ache in the very center of my being."

What struck Jamie hardest was the passion that leaped from the pages. She offered no sugary declaration but a confession with dark edges, physical yearning and a longing of the heart that coaxed a reaction even from Jamie. Hell, by the time he finished reading, *he* was half in love with her. And he didn't even believe in love.

He hadn't believed in love since a woman's betrayal had nearly cost him the ultimate price. On that ill-fated trip he'd made with Noah, he had been filled with a young man's heedless abandon. In the tiny, old-fashioned principality of Khayrat, he had lost his heart—and the last of his good sense—to a native princess. She was called Layla; the haunting name spilled like a liquid song on his tongue. Even now, he could still smell her scent of jasmine, could still see the smoky surrender in her black eyes. He'd flung himself into the affair, never pausing to consider the consequences—until it was too late. Until Noah had died in his place. What he'd learned from that episode was that love meant pain and danger and even death, not the soaring joy described with such naive exuberance in Abigail's letter.

Stricken by the reminder of a love so pure and so passionate, he finished reading and drank more whiskey. She had signed the thing not with her name but with a heartfelt grace note: *From your one true love.* Abigail's words moved him unexpectedly, awakening

a terrible yearning he thought he had overcome. An-
gered by the emptiness inside him, he stood and wandered about the room, offering a few grains of millet
to Rowan's white mouse. "What does it all mean,
Socrates?" he asked the bright-eyed rodent. "And
what shall we do about it? Can we change this smart
misfit of a girl into an object of desire?"

The mouse twitched its nose and burrowed into its
nest.

"Will there be anything more, sir?" asked Gerald
Meeks, coming up from the kitchen.

In the bottom of his fifth glass of whiskey, Jamie
found a sense of humor. Unfortunately he also un-
earthed a maliciousness that came from a part of him
he didn't much like.

"As a matter of fact, there is," he said.

There was only one thing to do upon learning a
person's deepest, darkest secret. Use it to advantage.
He scooped up the private pages, folded them and
secured the little packet with a blob of sealing wax.
On the outside, he wrote "Lieutenant Boyd Butler,
U.S. Navy, Annapolis." Then he handed the pur-
loined letter to the servant. "Take this to Lieutenant
Butler right away."

Seven

Abigail flipped the brass knocker a third time and waited, tapping her foot. She cast a glance over her shoulder. The sun was setting over Dumbarton Street, its dying colors riding low across the copper-roofed houses at the top of the hill. The deep indigo sky in the east had already given birth to Venus and the reddish star Antares, the heart of Scorpius and always the first to greet her this time of year.

The tang of autumn air evoked a sense of nostalgia for her schoolgirl days when she'd been allowed to attend classes at the university, quiet and unobtrusive as a piece of furniture in the back of the lecture hall. Those days were gone, tumbled away like leaves dropping from trees.

Across the way, Mrs. Vandivert's parlor curtain shifted, and Abigail waved. She always did, but the nosy woman never acknowledged the greeting. Calling unchaperoned on a neighbor simply wasn't done, except by Abigail and Helena. The whole neighborhood had been hearing about the senator's wayward daughters for years.

"Lightning has not struck us down yet," she said, pushing open the door. "Hello?" she called.

No reply.

"Professor Rowan?"

Silence. He must still be at work, then.

"Mr. Calhoun?"

More silence. And then a hollow *thunk*.

Frowning, Abigail lifted her skirts and headed upstairs to the parlor. Truth be told, she felt more at home in this house than she did in her father's. The Cabot residence was a monument to past glories, filled with French antiques, Irish crystal and English porcelain, all lovingly tended by a small army of servants. The professor's house, by contrast, was crammed with utilitarian furnishings and modern conveniences, completely lacking in pretensions. For some reason, the scientific clutter didn't offend her natural bent for precision and order. She might be clumsy and untidy, but here, at least, it didn't seem to matter.

"Hello," she said again as she reached the landing. "Is anyone—oh." She found herself face-to-face with Mr. Calhoun. Face-to-chest, actually. He was too tall by half, she thought, not for the first time. But at the moment he looked…different.

His hair was unkempt, his cravat hanging loose around the open neck of his shirt. The shirt gaped open to reveal his bare chest. She was quite certain she'd never seen a man's bare chest before, even a veiled glimpse of it, and the sight had a curious effect on her. An unfamiliar heat rolled through her, and she was hard-pressed to draw her eyes from that place.

But she managed to, noting with a flick of her gaze that he held an unclipped cigar between the fingers of his left hand, a white mouse perched on his shoulder and a crooked grin on his face. "Come in, my dear," he said expansively. "Socrates and I were just getting lonely for company, weren't we, my pet?" With startling gentleness, he stroked the mouse with one finger.

Her throat felt dry; she swallowed two times before finding her voice. "Are you quite all right, Mr. Calhoun?"

"I am quite drunk, Miss Cabble—Cab...ab." He laughed. "Abby. You won't mind if I call you Abby."

"I won't?"

He went into the study and released little Socrates to his glass-front maze, watching the mouse scamper down the length of his arm. "Please come in. I'm sorry I didn't hear you knock. Must've drifted off." He studied the cigar in his hand with some surprise, as though he'd forgotten he was holding it. Setting it in an ashtray, he picked up a decanter and held it to the sinking light of the window. "Whiskey?"

"It appears you've all but finished it off," she said. "But no, thank you. I'm not fond of strong spirits."

"Spoken like a true lady." He upended the bottle, letting the last of it slide down his throat.

Heavens, what was wrong with her? Simply watching his throat reminded her of an illustration she'd spotted in his *Kama Sutra,* and that caused a new spasm of heat to pulse through her.

"The Calhouns are a family of hard-drinking men," he explained, putting the empty bottle on a side table.

"Congratulations."

"Oh, believe me, I wasn't boasting. Truth be told,

drinking never did any of us a lick of good. Cousin
Hunter of California gave it up entirely, and it made
him a new man.''

"Do you think you should give it up entirely? Become a new man?''

He snorted. ''Why would I want to do that? It's all
I can do to try to become an old man.''

"Your lofty ambitions impress me,'' she said.
''Perhaps you should drink faster. You'll expire and
we'll be shed of you.''

"It's a pity you cannot get paid for sarcasm, Abby
my love. You excel at it.''

She hated the way he called her *Abby my love* with
all the sincerity of a trained actor in a melodrama.
''Do I? It's nothing to be proud of.''

"Voltaire made a career of it. Mr. Mark Twain is
getting rich off it, too.''

She felt a little agitated, being alone with him in
the darkening parlor, seeing him so casually attired,
so insolently drunk. ''Actually, I came on an errand.
I forgot to post the letter I wrote earlier.''

"Not to worry.'' He waved a negligent hand. ''I
posted it for you. Sent Meeks off a good two hours
ago.''

She smiled. ''Why, that was very thoughtful.'' She
walked over to the desk. ''I'll just get my other papers
and—'' Her smile pulled into a frown. ''That's odd.
I left something under the blotter and now it's gone.''

"I told you. I posted it.''

She didn't understand. She'd written the lieutenant
a light, amusing and wholly inconclusive note on behalf of Helena. So where was the other letter, the one
meant for her eyes only? The one she never should

have written in the first place, the one that expressed all her secret dreams?

An icy thud of dread pounded in her stomach. Bracing her hands on the edge of the desk, she slowly turned. "Do you mean to tell me you posted the letter that was under the blotter?"

He rubbed his jaw thoughtfully. "You mean, the long, heartfelt one filled with tender declarations and passionate propositions? Yes, that's the one. You're welcome, by the way."

The blood drained from her face. "You read it?"

"Indeed I did." He grinned with infuriating satisfaction. "Who could have imagined you harbor such passion and fire, Abby? Butler will be amazed. I know I was."

Terror shrieked through her. She nearly stumbled in her rush toward the door. "We have to get it back."

He grabbed her arm. "Too late. He probably has it clasped against his heart by now."

She yanked her arm away from him. "That letter wasn't meant for anyone's eyes but my own." Fury reverberated through her words. "Not Lieutenant Butler's, and certainly not yours."

"But you started it out with 'My dear Lieutenant Butler.' Or was it 'Dearest'? Anyway, I quickly ascertained that it was for him, and that the shorter version was a failed first draft—a very boring first draft, I might add—so I put that one in the incinerator."

He was lying; he must be. Only the lowest of cads would have sent her private letter. But one look at his smug face told her otherwise. "Why in the name of all that is decent would you do such a despicable thing?"

"You just answered your own question, darling. I am not decent at all."

Moving slowly, like a soldier wounded in battle, she lowered herself to a chair. The phrases of secret admiration she had penned burned through her memory. She'd poured her heart out in that letter and this horrible man had read it, then handed it off to Lieutenant Butler.

"Are you all right?" asked the awful Mr. Calhoun. "You look a bit peaked all of a sudden."

"Forgive me," she snapped. "It's just that I've never had anyone do something so openly cruel to me before."

"I've done nothing cruel. You told me yourself you're eternally in love with the man. He, being a bit molasses-witted, fancies himself smitten with your sister, who, of course, has no genuine interest in him. So he must learn to love the right sister, and what better way than to snare him with your charming letter?"

"It wasn't my letter."

"You wrote it." With each phrase he spoke, he came closer to her, until he had his hands braced on the arms of her chair, his face level with hers. He had the most remarkable eyes, with awful secrets frozen in their depths. And his lips were so full and shapely, damp with carnal promises.

She forced her gaze away. "Yes, I foolishly wrote it, but he expected to hear from Helena."

"She would have bored even him."

Stalked, cornered and helpless, she felt her temples pound and struggled not to focus on the hard lines of his face. "And what part do you play in all of this intrigue?"

"Taking action on behalf of my fellow citizens is a congressman's duty." Then he startled her by going down on one knee and taking her hand in his. He smelled of whiskey and cigars and for some strange reason she could not bring herself to look away.

"Abby," he said, all sobriety and earnestness. "I like you. I've liked you from the first moment I met you. I like your twit of a sister, and I even confess to a grudging appreciation for the vice president's son. The three of you need some sorting out, that's all."

"And you've appointed yourself the one to do that."

"You weren't doing a very good job of it on your own."

"But it was our business."

"And it still is. Trust me, Abby. I know how these things work. Butler will reply to the letter—Christ, how could he not, given what you said to him?—and the two of you will carry on a correspondence. Eventually he'll speak to your father, who will crow with delight over the whole business, and everyone will live happily ever after."

Abigail couldn't help herself. It was all so absurd and so hopeless that there was nothing to do but laugh. She held Mr. Calhoun's hands and laughed until she no longer felt the tears burning behind her eyes.

Then a terrible notion occurred to her. "I never signed my name to that letter."

He looked up at the ceiling. "I believe you signed it 'your one true love.'"

"Then he'll assume it's from Helena," she said.

"The important thing is that he'll come to love the author of the letter. Even a potted palm knows that.

You must have faith in yourself. And maybe even a little trust in the dear lieutenant's judgment.''

"How on earth do you think this could work? I cannot will him to love me.''

"Don't be so sure of that. The human heart has a way of holding on for as long as it takes, until it has been fulfilled." He stood, insolently touching her cheek. "And your heart, my dear, is probably the most stubborn ever wrought.''

"For a cynic, you certainly have a deep belief in the power of love.''

"No. In the logic of strategy. There's no magic in love. It's simply a game. And you play it exceedingly well. That letter was a stroke of brilliance.''

She got out of the chair and pushed past him. This was a fiasco of the first order. In writing, she was as graceful and desirable as a princess, but in person she was a bashful, clumsy cipher. The one would not be mistaken for the other for very long.

"For heaven's sake,'' she said, "that was not a move on a chessboard. That was something that came from the deepest, most honest part of me.''

"Oh, honey,'' he said softly, turning her to face him and lifting her chin with two fingers. "I know.''

He spoke to her as though she were a different person from the Abigail the rest of the world saw. As though she were someone delightful and desirable, someone he cared for. But that was impossible. He hardly knew her, and he cared only for himself and his twisted little pranks.

She pulled herself away from his persuasive touch. "I only pray now that you haven't created a complete fiasco.''

"Impossible. Everybody wins. Butler gets a

woman who adores him, your father gets his dynastic alliance, your sister gets her freedom and you get your Prince Charming.''

''And what do you get?''

''The satisfaction of performing a public service.''

She couldn't help it. She laughed again. ''You are horrible and unforgivable, Mr. Calhoun. You deserve a horsewhipping for what you have done.''

''You wouldn't be the first to say that.'' He winked. ''Coming from you, the punishment might be diverting.''

''I'm curious, Mr. Calhoun. Why are you so horrible?''

He spent a moment in sincere thought. Walking away, he propped one elbow on the mantelpiece and stared down at Socrates, busily spinning in his treadmill. ''I don't believe I was born that way. In fact, I distinctly recall my mother saying what a fine baby I was, as fat and happy as a spring possum. I exhibited only average horribleness as a small boy. I think I came into my own as a horrible person when I was sent away to boarding school.''

''Why were you sent away?''

''It was the thing to do. My parents sent me away to a military school in the North.''

An image formed in her mind of a towheaded youngster aboard a gritty train headed to a destination he feared. ''It must have been so lonely for you.''

He shrugged. ''I was allowed to come home twice a year, at Christmas and for a few weeks in summer. I didn't think much of the Yankees, and I reckon the feeling was mutual. I wanted to go home, so I did all sorts of things in order to be sent down. But they kept me—God knows why—and I suppose I stayed horrible. I got smarter. I learned at an early age what love is and what it is not. Experience has only proven me right.''

''*Your* experience. And what is that, pray tell?''

He glared across the room at her. Then he struck a match, holding the flame to a lamp. A nimbus of diffuse whiteness glowed, illuminating the room. The new light outlined the bitter set of his mouth. ''Nothing I would share with a young lady.''

''Oh, really?'' Resentment prickled over her like a rash. ''But it's fine for you to meddle in my most private affairs.''

''You left your love letter on Rowan's desk.''

''Under the blotter.''

''It doesn't matter. It's in Butler's hands now.''

She shuddered at the thought. ''There's a special place in hell for people like you.''

He smiled and even laughed a little. ''Believe me, my dear, I would consider hell an improvement.''

She rose and went to the stairs, pausing at the top. She burned to know what had turned Jamie Calhoun into what he was, why he preferred hell to his own life. Or was that just the whiskey speaking?

Shadows flickered on the faded carpet runner as the cloak of evening fell. ''I must be going,'' she said. ''Thanks to you, I shall have to figure out a way to explain the mistake to Lieutenant Butler.''

''There was no mistake. Unless you lied about your feelings.''

''I didn't lie.'' The whisper escaped her before she could stop it.

He followed her out of the room, planted himself in front of her and barred the head of the stairs with an arm across the railing. His arm was bared to the elbow by a rolled-back sleeve, giving him the look of a common laborer. He was, she thought, quite a muscular man, wildly different from the slender, pampered gentlemen of her customary social circle.

She scowled the thought away. "Excuse me," she said.

"Don't go." He stood close to her, his body warmth reaching unexpected places in her.

Rattled by her response to him, she laughed without humor. "From any other man, I would consider that a romantic confession."

"You'll only make a mess of things if you try to tell Butler you wrote that letter by mistake."

"Things are already a mess, thanks to you."

"Abby." He descended two steps so his face was even with hers. In the shadowy hallway, he looked mysterious, corrupt, sensual...fascinating. "Let events unfold as they were meant to do. What you said in that letter—your honesty, your passion—it's a rare thing. You probably don't even realize how rare. I'll tell you what Butler is feeling right now, having read what you wrote."

He brushed his thumb over her wrist, his touch so bold that she didn't think quickly enough to pull away. "He's feeling ten feet tall, Abby."

"I don't know what you mean."

"To be the object of a love like that... It's a gift beyond price. Believe that, Abby. Believe in your own heart. God knows, Butler does. Don't take it away from him."

"How do you know what he's feeling?"

He leaned forward, and she noted with a shock that he was closer to her than any man had ever been. If she tilted her head the least little bit, they would be kissing, she thought wildly.

"Because, Abby," he said, "I felt that way myself, once, long ago."

Eight

Someone had taken a ball-peen hammer to his head. Lying in the dark in the middle of the night, Jamie could only conclude that some manner of assassin had broken into the house and stood over him, pounding at his unprotected head with a deadly rhythm.

He dragged his eyes open, blinking at darkness. His mouth felt like the bottom of a cave. A cave filled with bat guano.

God. What had he done?

He lurched to his feet and staggered across the room, banging his shin on something. Swearing, he groped his way to the washstand and found the basin filled with water. He bathed his face and rinsed his mouth and slowly began to feel human again.

He used to find entertainment in a glass or two of whiskey. During his lost years overseas, he'd found that and more in a taste of absinthe, heated by a match under a tiny glass spoon. But as time went on, he learned the limits of drinking. No amount of liquor could make him forget the things he yearned to erase from his mind—Layla's betrayal and the nightmare of his imprisonment. The botched escape and the sacrifice Noah had made for him.

Bracing the heels of his hands on the edge of the stand, he cast off his bitter regrets and glared into the darkness. Tonight's intemperance had been brought on by something quite different. He should not have done what he did. It was underhanded, dishonorable, manipulative.

Of course, he thought ruefully, that was why the people of Virginia had elected him to Congress.

He thought about Noah again and the reason he'd run for office in the first place, and renewed his conviction. Noah was gone, and now the home he had built for his family was in jeopardy. Jamie had to safeguard Noah's legacy. To do that, he needed Cabot's support. Cabot had two daughters. They were fair game when the stakes were this high. If Jamie took a hand in getting one of them married off to young Butler, he'd surely win the sponsorship of the two most powerful men in Congress.

The pounding in his head subsided to a dull thud. Finding his watch on the windowsill, he brushed aside the curtain and held it to the light to check the time. It was two forty-five in the morning.

Moonlight cast a milky translucence over the rooftops of Georgetown. The night was empty and still, giving him the impression he was the only person astir in the world.

Then a movement caught his eye. A flicker, no more. The wind blowing a shadow across his field of vision.

But no.

Fully alert now, he dropped the watch and pulled open the door to the balcony. Cold air struck his bare chest, arms, feet. He hadn't bothered removing his trousers before collapsing in bed. From the iron rail of the balcony, he located the source of the movement.

An intruder lurked on the roof of Senator Cabot's house.

Jamie acted before he thought. He hoisted himself up and over the rail, ignoring the cold. Edging to the corner of the town houses, he balanced himself on a brick corbel projecting from the building. He knew better than to look down. Reaching out, he leaped across the narrow gap between the houses, landing with a metallic *bong* on the iron fire stair that slanted along the side of the building. He paused, not letting himself breathe, to make sure the burglar hadn't heard.

When he was halfway to the top, it occurred to him that he had no weapon but his bare hands.

That had never stopped him before, and it didn't now.

The intruder moved across the roof. Jamie could hear but couldn't see him. He had a labored, lumbering gait as though he carried a burden of some sort. Senator Cabot's silver service or jewelry, perhaps.

Jamie boosted himself to the roof, knowing he'd have to work fast to maintain the element of surprise. He was running as soon as his feet touched the tarred and pebbled surface, and in three strides, he tackled the burglar.

They hit the surface of the roof in a pile of grappling limbs. Air rushed out of his quarry's lungs. A pair of fists beat at him, and a strangled scream tore through the night. He wrestled his opponent flat. A knee came up sharply, but he twisted to one side, avoiding the blow.

"Get off me, you great oaf. I can hardly breathe."

He rolled away and sat up, gape-mouthed with amazement. "Abby?"

She brushed herself off, tucking a long robe carefully over her legs and feet. "Are you still drunk?"

"After this?" He picked himself up, offered a hand. "I think not. Are you still angry at me?"

"Oh, anger doesn't begin to describe it."

"Everything will be fine, I promise you."

She hesitated, her gaze focusing on his bare chest. Her wide-eyed curiosity drew an unexpected reaction from him. Impatient, he grabbed her hand. As he pulled her up, she stumbled and lurched. He caught her against him, and for a long moment savored the closeness, the smell of her hair, her skin.

"You're nearly as graceful as I am," he commented.

Planting her hands against his chest, she pushed back and moved toward a dark, rounded hole in the middle of the roof.

"Abby, you're limping," he said. "Did I hurt you?"

She froze. The moonlight outlined her silhouette as she turned toward him. "You didn't hurt me. Not just now, anyway. What on earth were you thinking?"

"I was going to save the day by capturing a burglar on the roof."

Her shoulders trembled and he could tell she was holding in laughter. "You must be freezing, you great fool."

"I think I've gone numb by now."

"Here." She stooped, then handed him a long, fringed shawl. "Put this on."

Under other circumstances, he might have balked at donning a woman's angora shawl, but he was grateful for it at the moment. He wrapped it around his chest, but it kept sliding down.

"Here, let me." She stepped forward and draped the thing over his shoulders, then tied it loosely in front. "That's better. I suppose you're wondering why you found me on the roof in the middle of the night."

"I am."

She said no more but led the way to the far edge of the roof. When Jamie recognized the domed structure, he let out a short, incredulous laugh. "You have an observatory."

"Indeed I do."

"Your sister mentioned your interest in astronomy, but I had no idea you would be this...well equipped."

"You expected me to be a dabbler, then. A dilettante. Switching from embroidery to chinoiserie to painting on glass, and oh, when I have a moment or two, I might take a peek at the stars."

"I can tell by your hostility you've been asked that before. Don't lump me in with your critics, Abby. I don't belong there."

"Why not?"

He had a peculiar urge to touch her, but held his fists clenched into the shawl. "Because I know you."

"You've only just met me."

"You're easy to know."

"For those who have read my private correspondence, yes, I suppose I am."

That again. He'd done the right thing with the letter. She simply didn't understand that yet. "Let's not revisit that argument now."

"Afraid you'll lose?"

"Afraid we'll both die of boredom. And now you've intrigued me. I must see what has you wide awake and skulking around at three in the morning."

"Sweet heaven, is it that late?" She ducked into the opening of the observatory dome. He followed her, slamming his forehead against the top of the door.

At the curse that came out of him, she turned in the gloom. "What is that word you just said? I've not heard it before."

"It's Catalan," he lied, though it was actually low German. "If I translated it, I could be arrested for indecency."

"Oh. Never mind, then. Keep your head low and come over here."

The light inside the dome was bluish, as though they were under clear water. A telescope was positioned atop an iron pedestal that swiveled by means of a foot pedal. With a lens a good eight inches across, the base sprouting calibrated attachments, it was an impressive instrument, its size dwarfing the busy woman in front of it.

She motioned him over to a low stool. "Sit here. Have you ever looked through a telescope before?"

"No. A ship's glass, though."

"I think you'll like this." She bent her head and positioned herself at the eyepiece, making a slight adjustment with her hand on a small brass knob. "You mustn't touch anything. Take a look."

Bending low, he closed one eye as though he were

sighting down a rifle barrel and looked into the round lens.

Blackness.

He lifted his head. "What is it I'm supposed to see?"

"If you were viewing it correctly you wouldn't have to ask."

"Do you practice at being annoying or does it just come to you naturally?"

"Try again. Your head is at the wrong angle." She startled him by taking his head between her hands. With her palms over his ears, she held his gaze in position.

"This is very strange, Abby. I've had women grab me before, but never like this."

"Keep looking."

He tried again, this time making a subtle adjustment of the angle of his gaze. The blackness resolved to a field of stars. They seemed to leap to life the moment he focused on them. He held in the sharpness of his indrawn breath, afraid to move.

"You see?" she whispered. "That's the Hyades cluster, between the moon and Aldebaran."

He was able to discern a V-shaped constellation. "Yes, yes, I see it."

She guided him through several other viewings, and he was surprised to find himself enjoying the experience. He'd looked at the stars from the deck of a ship, the ramparts of a fortress and even from between the bars of a prison cell, but this was the first time he'd made order from the chaotic splendor of the night sky.

After a while, she led him away from the telescope,

out onto the roof. "How keen is your vision, Mr. Calhoun?" she asked.

"Keen enough, I suppose. Why?"

"There's a special event tonight, one that can best be appreciated with the naked eye. Look, it's starting." She turned him toward the northwest. He saw a peculiar hazy glow, and a distant movement, stars exploding in a rain of fire.

Amazed, he turned to her. "What is that?"

Even in the silvery blue darkness, he could sense her smile.

"It's a meteor shower. Fairly rare in October, but it seems we're lucky this year. We're seeing a meteor storm." She spoke with the hushed reverence most women reserved for prayer.

"It's incredible. Like magic."

"Not really. Earth is passing through a condensed stream of particles from a comet, and as the dust flies through the atmosphere, the particles heat up, creating the glow we're seeing. All those bright meteors and meteoroids are from the parent comet."

"Is that the comet you're looking for?"

"Heavens, no. That was discovered and named by a Vatican astronomer named Giacomo half a century ago. When I spot my comet, I will be the first to see it."

"How do you know where to look?"

She laughed. "It's complicated. Just call it magic."

He forgot the chill of the night and the fact that he was wearing a lady's shawl as he relaxed and watched the display. The heavens had caught fire and were falling to earth. And yet to most people it seemed like an ordinary night, made for sleeping with the drapes drawn tight. As he watched, a certain feeling clutched at him. He was reminded of the way he felt the first time he'd seen the Matterhorn or the Great Pyramids or the *Mona Lisa*. He was looking at something so much larger than himself, so much more profound, that he felt like a different person.

"I'm amazed, Abby," he said at last. "Truly amazed. You are a wonder."

"Not in the least. It's the universe that inspires wonder."

"But it took you coming out here in the middle of the night to see it. Who could have imagined that this was all going on?"

"Trust me, it's not that rare. The Leonids and Geminids will soon be on display. All things are visible if you know where and when to look. But you have to be patient and you have to look deep. Most people lack that patience."

"And a powerful telescope," he added. He was awash with the need to enfold her in his arms, to press his lips to her hair. But he didn't. She had a fragile heart, he reminded himself, and she had entrusted it to another.

The moments slipped by. Unaware of his rampant thoughts, Abigail made copious notes and calculations using an array of instruments, most of which he did not recognize. By the time a rose-colored thread of dawn spun across the horizon, she had created pages of notes and tables.

In a house across the way, lights blazed to life as the servants started their day. Abigail scowled at the glowing windows.

"What's the matter?" Jamie asked.

"It's frustrating. The lights of the city impede the view."

He thought for a moment. "What if I were to take you to a place that is completely dark?"

"Then I'd show you things you never dreamed of," she said.

Her comment sparked an erotic thought of showing *her* a thing or two.

Jamie knew she'd like to go to the coast country, where the landscape of his boyhood was still as wild and dark as a primeval forest. Her sense of wonder pleased him, and inspiring wonder in a woman was usually not so simple. He caught himself staring at her as she bent over a leather-bound book, filling it with mysterious symbols. Most would deem her a plain woman, small and pale and earnest, but Jamie recognized delicacy in the lines of her face, in the smoothness of her skin. Everything he discovered about her was fresh and new, unexpected. She must have sensed his gaze, for she looked up.

"I think we are going to be very good friends, Abigail," he whispered, touching her arm with blatant suggestion just to get a rise out of her.

She slapped his hand away. "To what end, Mr. Calhoun? What in the world would it serve? And why would I want that? You've already humiliated me beyond endurance by posting that letter."

He didn't reply to the accusation. He was supposed to befriend Cabot's daughter, not insult her. He needed to become a friend of the family, a trusted ally. Quickly, he changed the subject. "Does your father approve of these nighttime adventures of yours?"

Her shoulders stiffened. "He thinks my interest is eccentric but harmless."

"I would assume he'd be proud of a daughter who was a gifted scientist."

"Then clearly you don't know my father."

The bitterness in her voice startled him. "Are you saying he disapproves?"

"I'm saying he's a man with high expectations. And thus far, both my sister and I have fallen short of those expectations."

"Does that bother you?"

She hesitated, staring down at the pebbled rooftop. "Every day."

The melancholy in her voice touched him. "Why?" he asked, shoving aside the tender sentiment. "Why does his approval matter so much?"

"I often wonder the same thing. I suppose it has to do with my mother."

"I don't understand."

She turned her face up to the sky. "She died the day I was born, so I don't have any idea what it would be like to have a mother. I know only that a piece of my heart is gone."

Her candor struck at him with velvet blows. He didn't want to think of Abigail Cabot as a person with feelings, but as a means to an end. Yet each moment he spent with her drew him, made him want to know her better.

She focused her gaze on a distant star and said, "All that one feels for a mother is, in my case, given to my father. Do you have a mother, Mr. Calhoun?"

"A rather lovely mother," he admitted, kicking himself for having turned the conversation to this.

"And do you love her?"

"Of course."

She touched her chest. "I have that love in me,

too. But with my mother gone, it belongs entirely to my father. It's in his safekeeping.''

Jamie did not know the senator well, but he had a sneaking suspicion that Franklin Cabot had no idea what to do with the love of a brilliant, passionate, troubled daughter like Abigail.

''I'm sure he feels blessed by your devotion.''

''He'd feel more blessed if Helena or I were to settle on a husband of his choosing.'' She glowered at him. ''After what you did, that's not likely.''

Taking a soft polishing cloth, she wiped the telescope that extended outside the dome with the attention of a groom tending a prize racehorse. Closing the panel of the dome, she went to the low door at the top of the stairs. She gave a little grimace as she walked.

''Are you hurt?'' he asked, grabbing her arm. ''Should I help you down?''

She jerked away from him. ''I don't need any help.''

He backed off, holding his palms out in mock surrender.

She rested her hand on the doorknob. ''Anyway, I should think you would have other matters on your mind today.''

''What's special about today?''

She studied him for a moment, her large, thoughtful eyes making him forget she was a plain woman. ''You shouldn't drink so much, Mr. Calhoun, and you shouldn't stay out so late. It muddles the mind. Today's the opening session of Congress.''

''Is it, now?'' He chuckled. ''Fancy that.'' He let his gaze drift over the extraordinary little woman who had shown him a shower of stars.

"What are you looking at?" she demanded.

"You. I've never met anyone like you, Abby. Look at us. You in your robe, I only half dressed in a borrowed shawl. The stage is set for a scandal of the first order."

"You're forgetting something."

"And what is that?"

"I have no interest in you. And clearly, you have no interest in me, else you would not have done what you did with my letter. And so we can hardly create a scandal."

The letter again. He'd been hoping she would quit stewing about it. "Believe me, Abby." He reached out, brushed her arm in a slow, suggestive caress. "I could indeed create a scandal with you."

Nine

With a gloved hand, Abigail stifled a yawn. Ordinarily her late-night sweepings of the sky didn't affect her this way, but she'd stayed on the roof far longer than usual last night. She'd only had time for a nap before getting up to dress for opening session.

She peeked over her hand at her father, who sat across from her in the canvas-hooded barouche.

"Late night?" he inquired. His tone was mild enough, but she knew his every nuance. A subtle censure edged his words.

The memory of being attacked by a half-naked Jamie Calhoun brought a flush to her cheeks. "I observed a most impressive meteor shower."

"A meteor shower." Looking like a freshly cut rose from a master gardener's hothouse, Helena took Abigail's hand. "That's lovely, dear. I don't blame you for staying up to watch that."

Abigail gave her sister's hand a squeeze. It was doubtful Helena knew a meteor shower from a bridal shower, but her loyalty was touching.

"I just hope you'll be able to keep yourself awake during opening session," her father said.

"Of course I shall," Abigail murmured. "I've been in attendance each year of my life and I've yet to fall asleep."

Helena laughed. "Remember when you were tiny, and you told President Grant he smelled of ginger beer?"

Abigail did remember. It had not struck her as funny then, and it failed to now. Nor was her father amused. He clasped his hands over the head of his cane and glared straight ahead.

The hickory and tulip poplar trees lining Pennsylvania Avenue swayed and dipped in a brisk breeze. The barouche rolled past granite rows of foreign legations and federal offices, mysterious behind wrought-iron gates. Men in black suits hurried about their business, while day maids walked along with baskets of bread or linens tucked under their arms. Dark-skinned servants and drivers shouted and whistled through the traffic of the broad, busy street.

"And remember when you were thirteen, and that horrid woman stood up and addressed Congress?" Helena continued. "She claimed she was running for president."

"Victoria Woodhull," Abigail reminded her. "I didn't think she was horrid at all."

"You made your position abundantly clear when you hung that banner from the observers' gallery," Father said.

Abigail did recall every moment of that awful day. Even now, she remembered how eager and earnest she'd been. How idealistic and misguided. She thought she was doing the right thing. If women had the vote, she reasoned, they would all vote for Father. All the women she knew thought he was wonderful.

He'd be so proud of her for winning him more votes. How could he disapprove of that?

She'd stayed up half the night working on the large cloth banner. The next morning she'd tucked it into an enormous carpetbag and smuggled it into the gallery above the senate chambers. Working in secret, she'd secured the banner high overhead so that every member of the Senate, the press corps and the administration could read her slogan: Votes for Women Now.

The only problem was, she hadn't anticipated her father's reaction. After everyone gaped in amazement at her grand political gesture, a rival senator from the opposing party had broken the dumbfounded silence. "I say, Mr. Calhoun, isn't that your daughter up there?"

That was the year he'd sent her to Miss Blanding's Lyceum. Reputed to be the finest school for young ladies in the nation, the fortresslike institution huddled on the banks of the Potomac, not far from Mount Vernon. Father had hoped Abigail would learn self-discipline and feminine modesty there. Instead, he'd inadvertently found her a place that promised to nurture her lifelong passion.

At Miss Blanding's, she attended a lecture by a visiting scholar. Professor Mitchell was a sweeper of the night sky, the most famous astronomer in the world. In addition to claiming every honor given any scientist, Maria Mitchell was a woman. The first female professor of astronomy, the first to be elected to the American Academy of Arts and Sciences, the first to discover a telescopic comet, she had begun her speech with something Abigail would always remember. "We especially need imagination in science," Professor Mitchell had said. "Question everything."

Listening to the lecture, Abigail had felt the curtain opening on a great mystery. Finally, here was someone who understood her girlhood years of stargazing. From that moment on, Abigail had a purpose in the world, and it wasn't in this world at all. It was uncounted astral units away, in space, where the mysteries of the universe hid, where the stars were conceived.

Other teachers had intrigued, provoked and inspired Abigail, but only this one had changed her life by making her believe she could be more than she was.

Abigail wrote Professor Mitchell a letter after the lecture, and received a reply filled with wisdom and encouragement. They struck up a correspondence and had been writing ever since. Perhaps that was where Abigail had found her facility with letter writing.

Her mood darkened at the thought. Her recent letter writing had produced a disaster, thanks to the horrid Jamie Calhoun. She should have confined her correspondence to her mentor, she thought as they pulled around to the elegant eastern entrance of the Capitol building. A beautifully planted enclosure of cherry and dogwood trees graced the manicured lawn, and the streets and sidewalks had been swept clean of fallen leaves.

Two Negro footmen attended them as their coach joined a long line of other conveyances. Hacks and hired hansom cabs, open carts and ornate carriages lined the roadway. Some senators, like Pishey Harris of Philadelphia, lived in the fashion of untitled royalty, flaunting their wealth like a coat of arms. Others were simple men of the land, Minnesotans or Cali-fornians walking to the legislature under their own steam. A crisp scent of expectancy, a sense of new-ness and possibility, hung in the air. A mood of re-union lightened the day as legislators, their staffs and supporters streamed toward the building, eager to get to work. The idealistic vigor of the young congress-men combined with the settled authority of the elders to create a governing body that exuded power and energy.

While stepping to the curb, Abigail nearly stum-bled, but an attentive footman caught her just in time. She glanced at her father to see him watching with a pained expression on his face. Her heart sank. The day had scarcely begun and already she'd displeased him. He said nothing, but turned to greet his asso-ciates.

Men greatly outnumbered women, for only the wealthiest and most aristocratic of congressmen brought their families to the Capitol. That was why Father always insisted Abigail and Helena attend opening day.

Then, above the babble of voices, above the whips and whistles of drivers, came a clatter of hooves ap-proaching at a fast gallop.

People turned to look, some stepping hastily out of the roadway. Abigail joined everyone else in staring gape-mouthed at the arriving congressman. He rode a horse, not just any horse but a swift, muscular animal with a gleaming chestnut hide and long black mane. Its head had the fine noble shape of Arab breeding. It whistled and tossed its regal head, front hooves restless as the rider kept it barely in check. Autumn light glinted off the glossy hide like sunshine off a mirror. The force of the horse's energy caused the waiting footmen and grooms to shrink back against the chiseled granite wall surrounding the lawn.

The rider wore a suit that managed to be both flamboyant and fashionable, as though a cowboy had found his way into a Savile Row tailor shop. With skill and easy confidence, he dismounted the magnificent horse.

The rider caught the eye of a groom, motioning the lad forward. He placed the reins in one hand, tucked a gold coin in the other. "His name is Sultan, and you will treat him like visiting royalty," the congressman instructed. "Do so and he'll give you no trouble at all."

The groom bowed smartly and led the horse toward the Fourth Street livery stables. After surrendering his mount, the newcomer straightened his collar, brushed off his sleeves and faced the broad steps of the Capitol building.

"Who is that?" someone asked.

"He is a god that walks the earth," a woman nearby whispered.

Abigail rolled her eyes. "That's Mr. James Calhoun. A freshman congressman from Virginia."

He caught her eye and winked.

Pretending not to see, she turned to follow her father and sister into the building.

When she was very small, she used to feel like Alice in Wonderland when she entered the gleaming halls of the Capitol. The enormous white-domed rotunda dwarfed and overwhelmed her, giving her the sensation that she'd fallen down a rabbit hole and wound up in a strange new world of marble and gold, populated with creatures as alien as talking caterpillars and mad hatters.

Big-city lawyers clad in expensive suits walked around with legal briefs clutched in their hands. Inquisitive tourists looked on, and some of them appeared far more interesting than the Americans. Abigail noticed a group of elegant Frenchmen studying the inscriptions carved into the walls. Children chattering in Spanish fidgeted with boredom as their guide droned on. Most fascinating of all was a group from the Middle East, which included an important-looking, bearded man in a turban. He was accompanied by a woman so completely swathed in silken veils and surrounded by attendants that she was practically invisible to passersby.

Abigail would have liked to linger in the rotunda, but her sister pulled her along. They reached the long hallway leading to the chambers. Her father, who knew better than any man in the Senate the proper way to make an appearance, positioned himself between his two daughters. "Ladies?" He cocked out his elbows in invitation. "Shall we?"

Filled with pride and affection, Abigail fitted her hand into the crook of her father's arm. She lived for moments like this, shining moments when the whole world saw that she had a father who loved her.

He smiled a hearty winner's smile as he advanced down the busy, crowded hallway. "Keep your eyes straight ahead," he warned, clearly sensing her urge to scan the crowd. He gripped her arm with a firm imperative.

Abigail prayed that if people noticed her burning blush, they would assume it was merely the flush of excitement inspired by the first day of the fall session.

She prayed that when she wished her father a good day and turned toward the gallery steps, he wouldn't see the thin sheen of foolish tears in her eyes as she remembered her stumble on the west staircase last year. She nearly took all three of them down with her then.

When she and Helena were halfway up the stairs, she felt a prickle of awareness and glanced back. There, at the end of the hall leading to the house chambers, stood Jamie Calhoun, watching her with a bemused expression she didn't trust. He saw too much of her, this insolent, flamboyant man. She'd known him only a short time, and already he'd betrayed her. She would do well to steer clear of him.

Putting one foot in front of the other, she continued up the stairs to the observation gallery. But even though she didn't turn back to look at him, she sensed his gaze on her, and remembered the liberties he'd taken with her, mocking her even as he heated her senses with his touch.

The man was a danger to her. Not in any physical sense, but in a way she feared far more—he threatened her safety and the things she held to be true.

Helena had been asleep for the past half hour, and Abigail teetered on the brink. Seated above the crimson and gilt senate chamber, they'd observed the opening ceremony with all proper respect, but then the speeches began. Endless, tedious recitations, self-congratulatory oration, incomprehensible rhetoric and overblown statements of ambition for the deeds that could be accomplished by this particular legislature. The newly elected senators were the worst of the lot. Young Troy Barnes of the state of New York had been pontificating about his divine mission for a good forty minutes. Abigail wondered if he realized he'd been elected by voters, not God.

She sneaked a sideways glance at her sister. Over the years, Helena had perfected the art of looking alert when she was actually sound asleep. Her posture was impeccable, her face shadowed by the brim of a fashionable hat, her hands folded demurely in her lap. Only Abigail knew she was blissfully napping.

With the voice of a bullwhip, Senator Barnes gave no indication that he would yield the floor anytime soon. Abigail scanned the ladies' gallery, seeking an unobtrusive way to escape. The fashionable women of the capital appeared to be preoccupied with gossiping behind their hands. In the gallery across the way, a handful of diplomats and foreign ministers in formal gold-trimmed uniforms, a few newsmen and tourists watched the proceedings.

As Barnes blustered on, Abigail stood and crept from the gallery to the central passageway between the chambers of the Congress. Aides and pages moved through the halls, bearing messages and looking busy.

Her feet tingled as the blood started to circulate in her legs. Concentrating on walking gracefully behind the gallery, she judged that she probably had a good hour before the vice president would declare the day's session over.

Lieutenant Butler had not come to the opening ceremonies, and she was not certain how she felt about that. She dreaded seeing him, yet she yearned to at the same time. She pictured him reading the letter never meant for his eyes. He'd think the words came from Helena. At some point, Abigail would have to tell him the truth. She'd have to look him in the eye and watch as his confusion turned to hurt and inevitably to anger, and finally, to cold dislike.

As she passed behind the upper gallery of the house chambers, two newsmen burst out of the room and headed toward the wire service office in the basement. Curious as to the cause of their agitation, she entered the gallery and took a seat in the rear.

Unlike the gentleman's-club atmosphere of the Senate, the House of Representatives was loud, crowded and undisciplined. Men in homespun clothing sat around, spitting and smoking like spectators at a sporting match. It didn't surprise her in the least to see Jamie Calhoun at the podium, his collar undone and his hair falling over his forehead in maddeningly attractive fashion. What surprised her was the topic of his impassioned speech.

"...why I came to Washington, gentlemen. Not to build railroads but to protect the smallholders who would be turned off their land by the railroad expansion," he shouted over the buzz of the crowd. "What value is the iron road to a farmer who has no harvest to ship?"

A portly man across the aisle from Abigail shook his head in disbelief. "Man's got a death wish," he muttered.

His badge identified him as Timothy Doyle of the *Washington Post.*

"Why do you say that?" Abigail whispered.

"He's opposing the Chesapeake railroad expansion. The fool might as well oppose free enterprise." Doyle rubbed his jowls, frowning in concentration. "It's a puzzle, isn't it? Why would a man from plantation society oppose the railroads? They've been hand in glove for decades. What does Calhoun hope to achieve?''

"I'm sure I don't know." Abigail listened to the speech with growing amazement. In so many respects, Mr. James Calhoun was not what he seemed.

They returned to Georgetown at suppertime. Abigail's father was full of bluster and self-confidence, Helena with praise for a new object of interest—Senator Troy Barnes.

Their father frowned at her as they entered the foyer. "I thought you'd settled on Boyd Butler."

"Of course I did, Papa, every bit as much as you did. I replied to his letter right away, didn't I, Abigail?"

"You certainly did," Abigail said, feeling a cold chill at the memory of the passionate letter.

"I was very prompt about it." Helena handed her hat and shawl to Dolly, then turned to their father with a winning smile. "Ah, don't look so cross," she scolded. "I'm certainly allowed to admire more than one man at a time, aren't I? Senator Barnes danced with me twice at the wedding. He's a wonderful man from a fine New York family."

"You mustn't let him misinterpret that admiration."

Arguing back and forth, they headed upstairs. Only Abigail had noticed the notes and letters stacked in a silver tray on the table in the foyer. With a heart full of dread, she picked up the top letter, passed her thumb over the embossed seal of the Naval Academy.

With shaking hands, she raised the letter to her lips and shut her eyes, filled with panic and horror and joy. Lieutenant Butler had responded.

Part Two

In the midst of great joy, do not promise anyone anything. In the midst of great anger, do not answer anyone's letter.

—Chinese proverb

Ten

"I finally figured out why my father was so keen to send me up to Washington," Jamie said, holding his whiskey bottle aloft. Empty. The perfect end to his first day in the legislature.

Bent over one of his inventions, Michael Rowan tinkered with an apparatus of long tubes that dripped a dark liquid into a beaker.

"And why is that?" Rowan asked without taking his attention from the machine.

"Because he never forgave me for not returning home from my grand tour of Europe all those years ago. This is my punishment, surely."

"I take it you had a trying day."

"That would be putting it mildly. Christ. Where did those men learn to preach and pontificate? I was hardly able to make a dent in my cause."

"I think you'll find patience is a virtue in Congress." Rowan tipped the liquid from the beaker into a pair of marginally clean tumblers and handed one to Jamie. "Cheers."

"What's this?"

"A plum brandy, I believe." At Jamie's startled

look, he indicated the apparatus on the table. "It's a fast-action still. My own design."

Amazing. So few of Rowan's machines actually worked. Jamie lifted his glass. "Cheers."

Rowan had been busy, too, that much was clear to Jamie. He'd managed to add a layer of clutter to the mess already littering the parlor. On a slate hanging on the wall, he'd begun writing a long formula in what appeared to be hieroglyphics. The writing filled the slate board and spilled over onto the wall itself, all the way to the floor.

"So why didn't you return home from your grand tour?"

Jamie already regretted letting that slip. But the fact was, he'd taken an unexpected liking to the slovenly Rowan and didn't mind giving him a glimpse of his past. "Given a choice between hobnobbing in the courts and capitals of Europe or tending horses on a tidewater plantation, I chose the obvious."

"I've never understood tourism. Where is the value in standing by and watching others live their lives?"

Jamie took a sip of the brandy, finding it pleasant and mellow. "That's an odd question coming from someone who makes his living writing formulas and equations all day."

Rowan leaned back from the table. "That's the way I make sense of the world. And things beyond the world—" he added, then seemed eager to deflect the topic. "So your father wanted you in the legislature as some sort of revenge?"

"Punishment for all the fine wines and absinthe I drank, all the women I bedded. I reckon my father always resented that." He spoke lightly, but the fact was, the tension between Jamie and his father had been evident for years. Yet Jamie's decision to serve in the legislature had not come about due to pressure from his father. He had run for Congress as an act of contrition.

"You've had quite an adventure," Rowan said, fiddling with the homemade wine filter. "We'd all like to try our hand at absinthe and loose women. How did your family manage to lure you back to your native land?"

Jamie gripped the thick glass tumbler hard. "They sent my brother, Noah, to remind me of my responsibilities. But instead of boarding the next steamer home, I persuaded him to come with me on one last horse-buying trip to the Middle East."

Rowan tinkered with a flange on the still. "And was it a success?"

Jamie slammed back the brandy in three gulps, grimacing as the liquor burned his throat. "It was," he said, "my greatest failure."

He went to the window at the rear of the house and looked out. Shadows gathered in the garden below, an unkempt tangle of overgrown hedges, weeds and a spent kitchen garden with a few turnips and gourds rotting into the soil. By contrast, the adjacent garden of Senator Cabot was as perfectly groomed as a poodle, with clipped box hedges, firethorns and late-blooming roses arranged symmetrically in the small space.

A movement caught his eye, and he stepped closer to the window. In the tiny arbor, beneath a pair of arching yew trees, sat Abigail Cabot, her head bowed and her fists clenched around some papers in her lap.

He set down his glass, murmured "Excuse me" and let himself out the back. A brick wall with a concrete top separated the two gardens, but that hardly slowed him. He'd scaled higher walls than this—sometimes in a hail of bullets, in front of a pack of guard dogs, and once when a horse trader in Carthage had charged at him with a scimitar.

He hoisted himself up and over, landing on the carpet of grass in Senator Cabot's garden. Abigail shot to her feet and the pages in her lap drifted to the ground.

"What on earth are you doing?" she demanded.

"Paying a visit to my neighbor." He bowed in mock formality. When he straightened, he saw with a lurch of his gut that she'd been crying. Her nose was red, her cheeks wet, her eyes swimming with tears.

"You have a bad habit of barging in uninvited. Visitors are generally encouraged to call at the front door," she pointed out.

"If I'd known it would cause you this much distress, I would most certainly have done so." He took out a clean handkerchief and thrust it at her.

She made no response to his joking tone, but took the handkerchief and loudly blew her nose. Christ. Her tears made him want to move mountains, slay dragons, walk across hot coals—anything to make her stop hurting. Except none of those things would help; Abigail was more complicated than that.

Hoping to distract her from her troubles, he pretended to admire the silver gazing ball set on a pedestal near the arbor. The curve of the ball exaggerated the endless arch of the sky and made Abigail appear ten feet tall. "Did you enjoy your visit to the Capitol this morning?"

"My sister and I accompany our father with pride every year."

Interesting that she hadn't answered his question.

"I understand you made quite an impression with your introductory speech," she added. "Most new congressmen would be reluctant to publicly oppose the railroad companies."

"That's the whole reason I ran for Congress."

"Because you oppose the railroad companies."

"Here in Virginia, they're driving good people off their land and spending public money for private gain."

By now, her tears had dried entirely and she watched him with a round-eyed fascination that made him feel an inch taller than normal. He had an inexplicable urge to stroke his finger over the agitated pulse in her throat, to ask her what it was that made her sad.

"That's a very unusual position for a man like you," she said.

"I'm fond of unusual positions," he couldn't resist saying with an insolent grin.

She sniffed, tucking his handkerchief into her sash. "What a pity you have to be so crude. After realizing you came here to fight for the common man, I was thinking about revising my opinion of you. But I don't know if I can do that."

He tried not to sound too patronizing as he said, "You're a bright young lady, full of intelligence. I have faith in you, Miss Cabot. You can learn. Of course, in between sessions, I'll busy myself in the manner you seem so ready to condemn me of." He could tell, by the look on her face, that he'd managed to remind her of his seduction of Caroline Fortenay.

With a shrug, he bent to retrieve the papers she had dropped.

"Please," she said with a helpless cry, "you needn't bother—"

"Lieutenant Butler," he said, reading the signature. "My, my, he didn't waste a moment in replying to your letter, did he?"

"Give me that."

Jamie held the papers high overhead, well out of her reach. "Sweetheart, if I hadn't posted your long missive, you never would have received a response at all. I think I deserve some of the credit here. I think I—"

He broke off, focusing on a few phrases in the letter. By the sinking light, he made out the gist of it. "'When I read your letter, I found the other half of my soul,'" he read aloud. "'Your heartfelt words give me a reason to believe in life and all its joyful possibilities....'"

Jamie looked into her horror-struck face, and with a start, realized what he was witnessing. Two naive, basically decent people falling in love, their words heavy with the weight of sincere sentiment. In her eyes he saw the pain and wonder of a dawning new love. In Butler's response, he read the shining hope of a golden future. It was something Jamie didn't believe in anymore, but that didn't matter to Abigail. She was obviously new to this. She didn't understand what was at risk. She loved with a fullness of heart and a totality of faith that left no room for doubt.

"How it must amuse you," she said, "to toy with people as though they were game pieces on a chessboard."

"Butler wrote a love letter. You replied. I merely

performed the transaction. Do you hold the horse trader liable for the horse throwing a shoe?''

"It's dishonest," she said. "He thinks my reply was from Helena. This has already gone too far. I must send a wire immediately, informing him of the misunderstanding.'' Snatching the pages from his hand, she started for the house.

He planted himself in her path. "I wouldn't."

"You're in luck, then. You don't have to. I shall do this myself."

"Do what?''

"Inform him that there's been a mistake."

"Miss Cabot, brutal honesty has its place, but the occasional white lie does wonders for a fragile heart."

Her face softened. "I don't want to hurt him."

He pressed his advantage. "No, you don't. He's just had a letter from you declaring him the keeper of all your dreams.'' It was strange, the way he could remember word for word what she had written. "And look at the reply.'' He grabbed the page and read, "'With each phrase of your letter, my heart soared higher.'''

"He is so very sensitive," she agreed, snatching it back.

"And he's fortunate that you recognize his sensitivity. Really, Abby. A wire message?''

She returned to the arbor and sank down to the bench again. "I must figure out the best way to manage this.'' She stared at the final page of the lengthy letter. "He intends to continue this correspondence as a formal courtship."

"Your father will be overjoyed. You know that."

"Not when he discovers that Lieutenant Butler's

love for Helena is based on a letter from me.'' Abigail buried her face in her hands.

''You're making this much more difficult than it has to be. As soon as Butler discovers who wrote the letter, he'll transfer his affection to you.''

She dropped her hands and stared at him for a moment before bursting into laughter. Jamie loved the sound of her laughter, but not when it was edged with despair. ''Don't be absurd, Mr. Calhoun. It's Helena he wants, Helena he pictures as he pens all these adoring phrases.''

Jamie hesitated. If this didn't work out the way he'd planned, Abigail was going to get her heart broken. But he had to make her believe she could win Butler for herself. ''Read his words again, Abby. He's in love with the author of that tender prose, not with a pretty face.''

She scowled, and he realized he'd said the wrong thing.

''I refuse to go on with this deception,'' she stated.

''Don't call it a deception. Those letters—yours to Butler and his to you—are possibly the most honest things I've ever read.'' He did not add his assessment that they were wrongheaded and bordering on foolish.

''I refuse to—''

''A Butler, Abby. America's royal family. Think how proud and happy your father would be.'' Seeing a soft glow of hope in her face, he realized he'd found her most vulnerable spot. She lived and breathed for the old man.

''Helena already asked me to reply to him again,'' she admitted.

''Of course she did,'' Jamie said with an excess of patience. ''She knows how much your father values this association." He plucked a small purple aster and tucked the tender blossom into the bodice of her shirt-waist. His finger trailed lightly across the tops of her breasts. This was an interesting game—keeping her attention while urging her to write love letters to another.

She moved away, but he pursued her. This was his shot, he told himself. He could become Abigail's mentor, engineer a courtship with the vice president's son, then reap the rewards of her grateful father's political favor. Today in the legislature, the lesson had been hammered into him. Nothing was accomplished without powerful support, and no support was available to newcomers unless they found a way into the inner circle of influence.

Abigail Cabot, gateway to possibility, he thought wryly. "Unfortunately, your sister will lose interest in Butler."

"How do you know that?"

Because he knew women like Helena Cabot all too well. "Tell me I'm wrong."

She stared down at her hands, confirming his hunch.

"It's up to you, Abby." Seeing her hands tense up, he pressed his point. "For your father's sake, you have to keep Butler's interest. You're a kindhearted girl. You can't risk breaking the poor man's heart by stopping the correspondence." He stepped even closer, surprised and unexpectedly moved by her warmth, her womanly scent. "It's what you want, Abby. Admit it, you do."

She shuddered and half closed her eyes. "It's all so hard to understand. Everything seems brand new to me. Even the merest thought of Lieutenant Butler inspires a host of embarrassing physical sensations, things I can't even begin to comprehend.''

God, thought Jamie, if Butler could see her now, he'd be a goner. The idea of making love to this complicated, dizzy-in-love creature was almost too tempting to resist.

"He'll be delighted to hear that. Why don't you tell him in your next letter? It's you he wants, Abby. He's falling in love with your words.''

She seemed to catch hold of herself then. "You are so wrong, Mr. Calhoun. Lieutenant Butler is a man of good sense and honest sentiment. He's not that stupid.''

"He's a navy man," Jamie pointed out.

"You don't amuse me.''

"Fine, then give the poor clod credit. If he's as brilliant as you claim, then he's in love with the author of the letters, not some painted doll at a party.'' He had her there. He could tell, could see it in the way her attention riveted on him. This was almost too easy. "Attracting a man like Butler is a simple matter, requiring a few good intentions and a little creativity. Between the two of us, we have plenty of both.''

"You cannot make a man love me any more than you can keep a flower from turning its face to the sun. Nature has endowed us with certain urges. That's why we speak of the magic of love.''

"I disagree. Love is a science, not unlike astronomy.''

She burst out with a sarcastic laugh. "Now you're being absurd again.''

"Not at all. Courtship is simple animal husbandry. There's no magic involved, only smoke and mirrors. Common sense and imagination. Let us make a bargain, Abby.'' He held her gaze with his, actually enjoying this. ''You'll help me win your father's support against the railroads, and I shall show you how to make yourself irresistible.''

''Me? Irresistible.'' She laughed again. ''Now *that* would be a challenge.''

He plucked the flower from her bodice and tucked it behind her ear. ''You're halfway there already.''

''And how did you become such an authority on matters of the heart?''

''Oh, honey,'' he said with a wicked grin, ''if I told you that, I'd be guilty of corrupting a lady's morals.''

Eleven

"I cannot believe I agreed to this insane bargain. I should know better than to put my trust in a man who rides a racehorse named Sultan to the legislature." At the crossroads of M Street and Virginia Avenue, Abigail regarded the dressmaker's shop with skepticism. The tradesman's shingle was a black silhouette in the shape of a spool of thread and the moniker Madame Broussard, Modes Modernes pour la Femme.

The shop window reflected Jamie Calhoun's grin. "In the first place, his name isn't really Sultan, it's Oscar, but I wanted to impress everyone. In the second place, he's a *retired* racehorse. Oscar was a champion in his day, but now he's my pet. He spends his days eating molasses oats and standing stud to an array of mares that would make a real sultan envious."

She pulled her mouth into a prune of disapproval, sniffed and looked away.

"Ah," said Jamie with a burst of exasperation, "there you go again, pretending displeasure. It ill becomes you."

"How do you know I'm pretending?"

He grinned even wider. "I read your letter to Butler. I was drunk at the time, but I'll never forget that you admitted to a sensual nature."

She clenched her fists at her sides to keep from touching her burning cheeks. "That doesn't mean I'm not offended by references to the mating habits of horses."

"Of course you're not offended. You are a woman of science. You'd never take offense at a natural process. That would be like taking offense at planetary motion." He put a proprietary hand at her waist. "Come along, then. Madame Broussard is waiting."

Abigail balked, pulling back.

"Now what's the matter?" he asked with a touch of annoyance.

"I'm trying to figure out what on earth I'm doing. I consider myself an independent woman, yet I find myself preoccupied with pleasing my father and trying to appeal to a man who doesn't even know I'm alive."

"You wouldn't be Abigail if you didn't constantly question yourself." He regarded her with uncanny understanding. "Think of it this way, what is the worst that can happen if you fail?"

"Humiliation, social ostracism, outright scorn—"

"Has the fear of failure ever stopped you from conducting a scientific experiment? Of course not. Look, you agreed to this. Next time Butler sees you, his eyes will fall out of his head."

"I'm making a terrible mistake," she insisted. "I don't know what I was thinking." But that was a lie, of course. She did know. She wanted Boyd Butler; she'd been smitten with him ever since they had been paired up in dancing class as gawky adolescents. The trouble was, she had stayed gawky while Boyd Butler had grown into a god.

And like a shill buying medicine from a snake-oil salesman, she had agreed to Jamie Calhoun's program of self-improvement. One of the first lessons, he insisted, was to acknowledge that, like it or not, fashion mattered.

She glanced guiltily up and down the length of the busy street, lined with shops, cafés, reading rooms and taverns. "If anyone sees us going together to a dressmaker's, they'll assume we're having an affair."

"Which will only make you all the more fascinating in everyone's eyes." With insolent familiarity, he steered her toward the brass-trimmed door. Each time he touched her, inadvertently or not, a reaction sparked. She quickly squelched it by reminding herself he was an opportunistic, manipulative womanizer.

He escorted her into the studio of the famous modiste. Abigail had no idea how he'd managed to get an appointment. Helena had said that Madame Broussard had a lengthy waiting list of clients. Not that Abigail would have added her name to that list, but nearly every other lady in town was on it.

Rather than a shop, the Salon Broussard resembled a beautiful drawing room decorated with subdued elegance, with gilt furnishings, fringed drapes, new electrical lighting and stately old oil portraits of European aristocrats lining the walls. There was not a single garment or bolt of fabric in sight.

A maid welcomed them in French and Abigail was startled to hear Jamie Calhoun reply in kind. Despite his great height and almost overpowering masculinity, he didn't look out of place against the backdrop of pink wallpaper and lace curtains. He was a man who knew how to be comfortable in any surroundings, Abigail realized with a twinge of envy.

Madame Broussard arrived a few moments later, entering through an archway from a chamber behind the salon. She glided into the room as smoothly as a train on a track. Everything about her was elegant, and she appeared to be of an elegant age—perhaps fifty. She had the clean, simple grace of a classic sculpture—smooth skin with the milky quality of alabaster, dark hair pulled sleekly back from her face, a perfectly unadorned black gown that managed with its simplicity to remind Abigail of a modern painting in an art gallery.

With one glance at Jamie Calhoun, Madame Broussard came to animated life. She swept forward, bursting with rapid French phrases and smiles, and embraced Mr. Calhoun, kissing him on both cheeks, talking the whole time. Abigail watched the way the older woman touched him, holding his hands perhaps a beat too long. Going up on tiptoe, she leaned forward to kiss his mouth, and held herself there another beat while she shut her eyes and inhaled. Abigail caught herself inhaling, too, and was startled by a sudden pulse of heat like the one she had felt when she'd come across him in the White House garden. Perhaps this was why Jamie Calhoun didn't need an appointment.

Catching herself, she cleared her throat. Mr. Calhoun and the dressmaker broke apart. He introduced them, addressing Madame in French and Abigail in English, shifting back and forth between languages with effortless fluency.

Madame launched into a long recitation, all the

while circling Abigail, looking her up and down with a keen, assessing eye.

"How do you do, Madame Broussard?" Abigail said, feeling nervous.

"Enchantée." The woman reached out and pinched Abigail's upper arm. *Pinched* it as though she were a cow at the stockyards. She pinched a few other places as well until Abigail was certain she would die of mortification. Madame declared her current fashion to be *"exécrable,"* and Abigail deduced from her expression that this was not a good thing. Yet from the way Madame studied her, nodding occasionally, Abigail suspected the dressmaker had discovered some sort of hidden possibility that would need excavation.

Jamie Calhoun observed this initial inspection with a bemused, academic curiosity. The maid brought him a glass of ale.

"Don't you have anything better to do?" Abigail asked.

"What could be better than watching your transformation?"

"How do you know I'm going to be transformed at all?"

He translated this for Madame and the two of them laughed. The dressmaker put on a grave face and said something long and sincere.

Jamie nodded in agreement. "I expect a complete metamorphosis, like a tadpole into a toad."

Abigail glared at him. "How charming. You really do have a gift for flattery."

"Dear, you don't need flattery. You need Madame."

"You are a United States representative. You

should be spending your time legislating, not meddling in my life.''

''I legislated yesterday. You heard me address the House.''

I did. She pursed her lips to keep from admitting how much she'd admired his surprising oratory.

''There's nothing much on my agenda for the next few days,'' he said. ''I intend to devote them entirely to you.''

The way he looked at her as he spoke made her feel as though she'd been caressed. She had no time to ponder the sensation; Madame steered her into a rose-and-gilt room adjacent to the reception salon. The chamber was paneled with mirrors on every wall, floor to ceiling, many of them angled so Abigail couldn't avoid viewing herself from all sides, making it depressingly apparent that she was unattractive not just from the front but from every angle.

The modiste clapped her hands and called out orders in sharp French. Three assistants bustled forward, seemingly out of the woodwork, and they all started talking at once. Abigail had only a smattering of French and could scarcely follow the conversation, so she ceased trying to listen. They didn't seem to want to include her in the conversation, anyway. The Frenchwomen talked among themselves, surgeons engaged in a life-or-death operation.

Mr. Calhoun stood in the doorway, drinking his ale. One of the women unfolded a silk modesty screen.

''I really do think you should leave,'' Abigail called out.

''My colleagues in the House are playing golf or fishing today. Truly, I think I chose the better diversion.'' His disembodied voice came from the other side of the screen. "I hope your customary seamstress will not feel abandoned by your defection to Madame Broussard."

"Actually, I have no customary seamstress," she admitted.

"I know."

"How did you know that?"

"A wild guess." She heard the hiss and crackle of a struck match. A moment later, a curl of bluish cigar smoke rose above the screen.

Gazing into one of the many mirrors, she studied her workmanlike black-and-white shirtwaist and bit her lip. He was right, the rude scoundrel. She looked like a Puritan. Not that there was anything wrong with Puritans, but the son of the vice president would probably appreciate more style. Not long ago, Helena had tried to get her to wear a fashionable gown, but the result had been a multilayered disaster in pink-and-white taffeta that made Abigail look like a dark fairy from a child's nightmare. Since then, she had refused to give a thought to her mode of dress.

Through the privacy screen, Calhoun and Madame traded commentary in French like a burst of gunfire exchange in battle. The invading army of French-women descended on her, their busy hands loosening buttons, unfastening hooks and unlacing laces before she even knew what was happening. Madame kept poking, pinching, pointing. When they had Abigail stripped down to her petticoats, the dressmakers stepped back to consult one another.

Abigail found it all so sudden and surreal that she forgot to be embarrassed. Then, out came the bolts of fabric, and she was intrigued. These were not the candy-colored tulles and taffetas that made her look so ridiculous and pallid, but a peau de soie the color of a sunlit lake, an indigo satin shimmering with ebony and midnight iridescence, a raw silk in the shades of the dawn sky. Colors found in nature, not contrived in some laboratory.

Although no one asked her opinion, Abigail thought the fabrics were lovely. The cloth was held up over the screen for Calhoun's inspection, and he considered each with the gravity of a federal judge.

At a drafting table, the women swept aside a catalog of conventional gowns. Instead, they consulted a large collection of original drawings. Abigail gathered that they were the work of Madame herself. The dresses were unlike any she had ever seen. In contrast to the current mode of wasp waists, exaggerated bustles and pigeon-breasts, the modiste's designs depicted long, clean-lined sheaths that draped rather than bound and looked classical in the manner of ancient Greece. They would be considered radical, even scandalous, by Georgetown standards, except that in their own way, they were actually more modest than current styles.

As with the fabrics, no one consulted her. Apparently, after seeing the shirtwaist, they put absolutely no trust in her taste or judgment. One of the assistants took three of the sketches to Mr. Calhoun for another consultation.

"I honestly don't know why you're spending so much time with me," Abigail said, exasperated.

"Isn't it the duty of a congressman to see to the needs of his constituents?"

"I'm not your constituent. In the first place, I don't live in your congressional district."

"True. But I serve all our country's citizens."

"In the second place, I don't have the right to vote. No woman does."

"Also true, more's the pity."

She sniffed. "I suppose you favor women's suffrage."

"Universal suffrage," he said without missing a beat.

"I don't believe you. Why would a privileged white male landowner favor voting rights for women and people of color?"

"Well, call me ignorant, but last time I checked, the Fourteenth Amendment of the Constitution specified voting rights for all persons born or naturalized in the United States, not the people who happen to be white, male, wealthy, propertied and literate."

She imagined her father's blustering reaction to this. But the fact was, she liked Mr. Calhoun's iconoclasm. She also liked the fact that he had actually read the Constitution.

"A suggestion," she said.

"Yes?"

"When you're in a big congressional debate, don't mention your views about universal suffrage. They'll eat you alive." Though she couldn't see his face, she added, "Now, don't bristle and get self-righteous with me."

"How do you know I'm bristling?"

She wasn't certain. For no reason she could fathom, she had an affinity with this man, could read his moods in the very air. "I just know. For the record, I happen to agree with you."

"What about your father? Does he favor universal suffrage?"

She laughed at his naïveté. "How long do you suppose he'd keep his seat if he admitted that? Look, Mr. Calhoun, disagreeing with my father is like stepping into a pile of manure. You can never do it without looking stupid and making a mess. And you'd have no one to blame but yourself.''

''Your advice is so...picturesque.''

''In Congress, you must temper your views in order to advance your issues. You may fancy yourself a sophisticate when it comes to ladies' fashions, Mr. Calhoun,'' she added before he could interrupt. ''But if you're half as smart as you think you are, you'll listen to me when it comes to politics.''

''I defer to the senator's daughter,'' he agreed.

The women swarmed over her again, chattering and plucking aggressively at her chemise.

''Mr. Calhoun,'' she called, ''I would like to know what is going on.''

''Relax. They're saying that you've been all but swallowed whole by your petticoats.'' He paused, and a puff of cigar smoke wafted upward. ''An idea not without its appeal.''

''I think you should go away,'' she said.

''Such cumbersome undergarments won't work with the new mode Madame plans for you.''

It was unorthodox, discussing undergarments with a man—and probably highly immoral.

She felt a firm tug, and her petticoats fell in a pool around her ankles, leaving her standing in nothing but her chemise and bloomers.

Horror washed over her, swift and deadly as a flash flood. ''No, please,'' she said, snatching at the lace and tulle petticoats. ''You mustn't—'' She broke off, knowing they wouldn't understand her words, but if they were human at all, they'd understand her pleading look. "Please," she whispered again with a white-knuckled grasp on the voluminous fabric.

Madame took a firm grip on her wrist and murmured something, a question. Then she forced open Abigail's fingers so the garments dropped. Everyone stared down at her feet.

The specially made boot was an ugly blight in the middle of a froth of lace. Shame burned through Abigail.

"Is everything all right?" called Mr. Calhoun.

"Ne vous fâchez pas," Madame Broussard called back. She rapped out an order in imperative French.

"Very well. I'll take myself off to City Tavern." The bell over the door jangled as he let himself out.

"Tiens," said Madame, stepping away from Abigail. "Now the real *travaille* begins. We work with what we have. It is how Michelangelo sculpted, no? He found the beauty inside the block of marble." Without missing a beat, she selected a long underskirt from a hanger on the wall and tied the garment around Abigail's waist. Abigail's discomfiture faded beneath a growing curiosity.

"I didn't think you could speak English."

"I can." She took the tape measure from around her neck. "I rarely do. But here, I have no choice, for you Americans refuse to master any tongue, even your own." Her busy hands never rested. "Many women do less than their capabilities allow. Why is that? I wonder." She shrugged. "Fear, sometimes. Bashfulness. Lack of confidence, *sans doute.*"

Abigail felt shaken. So few were aware of her secret disability, fewer still had actually seen the ugly but functional black shoe she wore. Since she had grown old enough to bathe and dress herself, no one had seen her affliction.

"I was born with a bad foot," she whispered to the Frenchwoman.

Madame paused in her measuring to pull down her lower lip, showing a decidedly imperfect set of teeth. "And I was born with a gap in my teeth." She went back to work, calling out measurements to her assistants. "But such a thing would not stop me from opening my mouth, eh?"

She continued working, completely focused on Abigail. "*Chérie,* I will make dresses more beautiful than you could imagine, but the finest gown in all creation will be made ugly by a poor attitude. I need your pledge that when you wear my gowns, you will wear an air of confidence like an invisible mantle. If you wear my dresses with an attitude of defeat, you might as well don a gunnysack."

After the fitting at the dressmaker's, Mr. Calhoun took her walking along the Great Mall. A morning rain shower had washed the paths and roadways clean, and groundskeepers swept autumn leaves into piles along the greenswards. The Smithsonian buildings gleamed in the weak afternoon sunlight. A flock of geese arrowed overhead, and a pack of apple-cheeked children played a game of chase across the lawn.

"Did Madame give you an indication of when your dresses will be ready?" he asked.

"No, but she promised them soon. I fear her prices will be hideously high. I was afraid to ask."

"You're probably correct. Her clients include Mrs.

Vandivert, the first lady and all of the president's daughters.''

"I've committed a shocking extravagance, then," she said.

"According to your sister, you'll be able to manage it quite well."

"What exactly did Helena tell you?"

"She claims you've hardly touched your clothing allowance in at least five years."

"It wasn't her business to tell you that."

"Actually, she didn't."

Abigail eyed him from beneath the brim of her bonnet. "She didn't?"

"No. Your sister's a twit but she knows better than to reveal such personal information."

"Then how did you—"

"I took a guess." His laughter was both gentle and knowing. "Everything I've seen you wear is approximately five years old."

She hesitated, then looked everywhere but at him, trying to decide exactly what she thought of him. Few men knew ladies' fashion well enough to judge the age of a garment, but then again, few men greeted Frenchwomen with the familiarity of former lovers. "You are a terrible, manipulative person."

"We established that the night we met."

"Doesn't it bother you that I hold this opinion?"

"Of course it does, Abby. I want your esteem."

She knew he only courted her good opinion for the sake of her father, and was vexed at herself for feeling drawn to him. "Well, you won't get it by playing with my life and pretending to care about me."

"Who says I'm pretending?"

"I say."

"Why would I do that?"

"To worm your way into my father's good graces."

"Guilty as charged," he admitted. "Is it working?"

"It might, actually. Father will be grateful to see me in some new clothing." That was something, at least. Occasionally, he made pointed references to the fact that she had a generous clothing allowance she never touched—except for things like telescopic equipment.

A whistle blew, then a rhythmic clanging drew her attention to a busy construction area. The Baltimore and Potomac Railroad was laying tracks north to south across the Mall. Abigail glanced at Mr. Calhoun to see him contemplating the torn-up blight. "I suppose you're wondering if he'll be grateful enough to lend his support to your cause," she said.

"I do want your father to notice my kindnesses to you." He mocked her earlier tone. "Is that so bad?"

"It's politics, I suppose. In fact, I'm enjoying the attention. I've never had my own personal sycophant before." She ducked her head to hide a secret thrill. Half of her wished he was truly interested in her, the other half clung loyally to the dream of Lieutenant Butler.

"No need to be sarcastic," said Mr. Calhoun. "Currying favor is the key to success in Washington. In fact, I've devised a plan to present my case to your father."

"And what is that?"

"Your entire family will spend the Thanksgiving holiday as guests at Albion Plantation."

She eyed him warily. "We will?"

"Helena and I have already discussed it. Professor Rowan will join us, too."

The plan didn't sit well with Abigail, but she was fast learning that her opinion didn't count for much with this man. Setting her jaw, she continued walking with her eyes straight ahead. She nearly collided with a speeding child who crossed their path, chasing a hoop with a stick. As Mr. Calhoun put a steadying hand beneath her elbow, the boy neither slowed his headlong pursuit nor acknowledged the sedate pedestrians.

"There's something admirable in that," Abigail commented with a laugh. "In going after something with such single-minded determination."

"He'll probably grow up to be president," said Mr. Calhoun.

The shouts and whistles of draymen, the clop of horses' hooves and a babel of foreign tongues filled the air. A cluster of well-dressed ladies, out for their daily constitutional, passed by. Abigail recognized the wives of Senator Moreland and the secretary of war among them. The ladies' greeting was restrained as they swept past, then they huddled together to whisper about the encounter.

"Are we creating a scandal, walking without an escort?" he inquired.

"Does that matter to you?"

"What do you think?" He laughed and took her hand, his thumb rubbing over her wrist. "Abby, believe me, if you and I ever create a scandal, it'll be caused by more than a walk in the park."

Twelve

Daily letters arrived from Annapolis, their admiration and ardor increasing and intensifying. Abigail found herself barely able to eat or sleep, and often paced the floor until the wee hours. Close to despair, she sought out Helena in her room and found her seated at the dressing table.

"Abigail, I didn't hear you come in." Helena quickly shut a box on the table and shoved it aside. "Is everything all right?"

Abigail held out Lieutenant Butler's precious letters. Like hers to him, they were filled with hopes and dreams, declarations of affection, promises that made her heart soar. But they couldn't go on like this. The daily letters had come to mean everything to her, and she suspected hers had the same effect on him. "We have to stop this, Helena. It's gone too far."

Helena frowned at the papers. "Oh, the lieutenant's letters. Are they terribly boring?"

"I've read each one to you. Do you think they're boring?"

"No, they're rather lovely."

"What we're doing is simply wrong," Abigail

said. "He's replying to letters from me, but he thinks they're from you."

Helena picked up a silver-backed brush and drew it through her coppery hair. "You're so good to do this, Abigail. It's working out so well. Papa's simply thrilled with the way the courtship is going."

Abigail held on to the bedpost, needing support. "Suppose Lieutenant Butler were to...suppose he lost interest in you."

"No man has ever lost interest in me," Helena said without vanity. It was the simple truth, and they both knew it.

"But if he did, would it bother you?"

She gave a hollow laugh. "I should admire the man for aiming higher."

"Never speak of yourself that way," Abigail said, alarmed.

Helena crossed the room and hugged Abigail. "Don't worry about me. You must answer his letters, dear. Say whatever you will to the man. You're such a brilliant wordsmith. Just keep reminding yourself how much it means to Papa."

Almost against her will, Abigail found herself writing to Lieutenant Butler with pathetic regularity, and awaiting his replies like a child on Christmas morning. She was as bad as Jamie Calhoun. Worse, because she was not taking part in this deception for political gain, but for personal pleasure.

Yet each time she resolved to stop, to inform Lieutenant Butler that she no longer wished to carry on their correspondence, she would read back over his letters.

Something precious and, dare I say, permanent is happening between us, my darling Miss Cabot... My regard for you is as constant as the moon, as ceaseless as the tides....

Oh, how could she resist such persuasion? Yet how could she go on?

Troubled by guilt, she made her way to the rooftop one night, intending to formulate a plan to extricate herself from her dilemma.

She wasn't surprised to see Jamie Calhoun waiting for her, relaxing on one of the wooden chairs set up for viewing the sky. He'd taken to meeting her on the roof at night, sitting and talking to her while she studied the sky and recorded her observations.

"There you are, my stargazer," he said expansively. He held a snifter of brandy in one hand, a sheet of paper in the other, and a candle to read by flickered in the breeze. "I was just reading Sir Galahad's latest letter."

"Give me that." She snatched it away. "Honestly, can you allow me no privacy whatsoever?"

"We agreed that you'd share the letters," he reminded her. "It helps me to plan strategy."

"You needn't bother. I'm going to stop writing to Lieutenant Butler," Abigail informed him, tucking the letter into her pocket.

"You've got him on the line, ready to reel in. Why would you let him go now?" His breath made light puffs of mist in the chilly air.

"Because he thinks I'm my sister."

"Nonsense. He thinks you're his destiny. Didn't you read the letter? You must keep at it." He indicated the telescope, its round eye poking out of the observatory dome. "How long have you been sweeping the sky for a comet?"

"More than two years."

"Would you abandon the vigil now?"

"Of course not."

"You mustn't abandon your correspondence with Butler, either. He's all but declared his heart."

In spite of herself, she shuddered with anticipation. "But it's dishonest. I'm misleading him."

"You're afraid, Abby."

"He'll find me lacking."

"Lacking what?"

"My sister's beauty."

"He would be right, then. You do lack your sister's beauty."

She bristled. "Kind of you to point that out."

"Abby, you have your own appeal. If you tried to mimic your sister, it would simply be odd."

She frowned, uncertain. He hadn't called her beautiful—that would have been a lie. Still, he'd complimented her. Hadn't he? And why did his admiration make her feel so strange inside? Why did it make her imagine his hands on her, his lips?

"It's not just the way I look," she said. "It's…all of me. I'm all wrong."

He gulped back the brandy. "Christ. How did you learn to doubt yourself at every turn?"

"A woman like me has plenty of opportunities, Mr. Calhoun. Don't you remember the night we met? I was so graceless, and you saw what Lieutenant Butler wrote about Helena in his second letter. When she dances, she moves like a summer cloud. I, on the other hand, move like a coal tumbrel backing into a dark alley."

He laughed.

"That's it." She marched toward the door to the attic steps. "I'm putting a stop to this right now."

"I'm not laughing at you. Well, I am, but not maliciously. Look, your skill at dancing is just that. A skill. It can be practiced, improved." Setting down the letter, he crossed the roof in a few strides, the gravel crunching beneath gleaming riding boots. He positioned himself in front of her and made a formal bow.

"May I?"

"No."

He maneuvered himself in front of the door, barring her escape. "You rejected me the last time I asked you to dance, too. I won't accept no from you this time." Without giving her a chance to reply, he slipped a hand around her waist, hugging her close. Then he captured her other hand. "One-two-three, one-two-three…"

Against her will, he pulled her into the steps of a slow waltz. Here in his arms, with no one but the stars to see her, Abigail wasn't plagued by her usual self-consciousness. For a few minutes, she allowed him to sweep her along, feeling the rhythm of their dance steps pulse through her.

She tried to fantasize about dancing with Lieutenant Butler. Yet for the life of her, she couldn't think of anyone but Jamie Calhoun. He embraced her with a firmness that brooked no protest, and despite the unorthodox situation, she liked the feeling of closeness and intimacy. She even—and Lord forgive her—liked feeling warmth in improper places.

The thought caused her to stumble, then pull herself up stiffly, breaking the flow of their movements.

She awaited a scolding, but instead, Mr. Calhoun simply stood gazing down at her. "I know what your problem is."

She gasped, certain he read the dilemma in her eyes. "What do you mean?"

"You don't know how to let go."

"Let go of what?"

"Of...I don't know how to describe it. Of yourself. Your inhibitions. If you simply surrender yourself to your partner's rhythm, it'll go much easier for you. Trust me, I know these things. Now. One-two-three, one-two-three..." Pulling her along, he started up again.

Abigail made a conscious effort to relax, to follow his lead. To her surprise, she did indeed find it a little easier.

"Was I right?" He grinned at her. "I was."

She tightened her mouth against a smile. "Perhaps. But I've often wondered, why does the woman always have to go backward?"

"Because men are too clumsy to do it. But you're not supposed to know that."

Something was on Helena's mind, Abigail could tell the moment she came down to breakfast the next morning. Helena's whole being seemed to glow with an inner light, yet it wasn't a calming force. She drummed her fingers on the table until their father scowled her into silence. She jiggled her foot until her knee hit the call bell on the table leg, summoning Dolly.

Finally, Father asked, "Good God, Helena. What is the matter?"

"I'm excited, is all," she said. "It's been so long since I've spent a holiday in the country."

"Who said anything about a holiday?" asked the senator.

"Oh, didn't we tell you?" Under the table, Helena grabbed Abigail's wrist and squeezed hard to warn her sister to keep silent. "We've had an invitation to the seashore."

Mr. Calhoun had set it up with diabolical precision. Knowing Helena would follow Professor Rowan anywhere, he'd included him in the plans. And Helena had a way of getting what she wanted.

"The Calhoun family would like us all to come," she said. "They have a place called Albion. A Thoroughbred farm. Please say we can go, Father. Please."

Abigail twisted her wrist free. She already knew she'd be given no say in this.

"It's important to your Senate position," Helena pointed out. "The Calhouns are rich."

"So are we," he said.

"You're up for reelection next year. A donation from the Calhouns would certainly help your campaign." She took a dainty sip of her coffee. "Mr. Calhoun's father plays golf with the chief justice of the Supreme Court. Did you know that?"

Abigail couldn't help but admire her sister's acumen. When it came to domestic drama or matters of politics, she was like a skilled river pilot at the tiller, navigating rocky shoals and hidden undercurrents.

Very well, Abigail thought. A visit to the seashore with the Calhouns. By now, she should be accustomed to being pushed around by Jamie Calhoun. Maybe too accustomed.

Thirteen

Jamie was unexpectedly nervous during the journey to Albion. In the roomy hired coach, he played host to four guests, Franklin Cabot and his daughters and Professor Michael Rowan. Jamie had engineered the whole thing in order to make a point with the senator. Yet instead of sensing victory, he felt weighted by the idea that much was at stake here.

Keeping his apprehension carefully tucked away, he said, ''There's your disputed land, Senator. That's what the railroad companies want to claim.'' He pointed out the broad flatlands of the low country farmers. They were poor, simple families of the land, sharecroppers and ex-slaves tending crops and raising livestock. The railroad company wanted to reclaim the central valley in order to increase its coverage of Virginia, sending the long fingers of commerce down to the very edge of the Chesapeake, where barges and seagoing vessels could complete the link across the sea.

Holding aside the leather flap of the wind shield, the senator rubbed his side-whiskers in thoughtful interest. He studied the fertile lowlands fed by innumerable estuaries, the rice and indigo fields etched into the landscape and the occasional shanty hunched in the middle of a field.

"An expensive proposition, as you can see," Jamie said, "given all the drainage and reclamation work it would take to lay tracks. What were the calculations per mile?"

Cabot lowered his bristly eyebrows. "Your point being?"

"I just wondered, sir, if it's to be so hugely profitable, why wouldn't a private railroad company pick up the expense?" Jamie felt Abigail's attention like the heat of an unseasonable sun. He knew she couldn't understand his opposition to the expansion. As a moneyed landowner, he ought to favor it. But he didn't. He couldn't. And his task was to convince her father to agree with him.

"That's precisely what my opponents in Congress are fond of asking me," Cabot replied to his question. "They fail to see the long-term benefits of railroad expansion in this state. For years, there's been a fever for westward expansion, but when it comes to looking after our own home state, we fail to invest. That must change."

Jamie nodded politely. "That's why I came to Washington," he said. "To change things." He indicated the broad, misty fields, some of them still studded with sheaves of corn. In the distance, a lone farmer wrestled with a plow tugged by a rangy mule while his children played in the turned-under chaff in his wake. Jamie couldn't have asked for a better picture to show the senator—this was the American way of life at its most fundamental level.

"He's your constituent every bit as much as the

railroad companies," Jamie said. "More so. The rail-
roads are run by industrialists from Pennsylvania and
New York. These lands are worked by Virginians.
Tell me the railroads will put it to better use."

Cabot leaned back against the leather seat, crossing
his gloved hands over his knees. "I admire your ambition, Calhoun. But I remind you that politics is a
tricky business. Alliances are fragile things, and they
change with the wind. You'll want to form yours with
delicacy and skill."

"Excellent advice, sir," Jamie said, struggling not
to mock the patronizing tone. "I'm fortunate to have
the benefit of your wisdom and experience."

Abigail stifled a choking sound beneath a lacy
handkerchief.

"I hope you're not allergic to the sea air," her
father said with a frown.

"No," she said, looking as though she wished to
sink beneath the seat cushions. "It's just a bit thick
in here."

Jamie wanted to choke her himself. "Never fear,
Miss Cabot," he said. "We're almost there."

His guests reacted to Albion as he hoped they
would—with gratifying admiration. The seaside home
of his boyhood had a haunting beauty all its own. The
house occupied a gentle rise, bathed in the mysterious
sea-light unique to the Chesapeake.

Live oaks arched in a graceful canopy over the
long, straight drive leading to the main house. On
either side, pastures rimmed by endless white fences
rolled out into the gentle hills and down to the sea.
Mares and yearlings browsing in the high fields lifted

their heads at the scent and sound of the approaching coach horses.

The driver pulled up in front of the house. The surface of the horseshoe drive, composed of crushed oyster shells, crunched under the iron-banded wheels of the coach.

Two footmen attended the new arrivals. Seamus and Will were both cordial and deferential as they secured the stair in place and handed the ladies down. Helena smiled in appreciation of their old-fashioned manners, and both attendants nearly dropped their jaws at the sight of her. Predictably, Abigail accepted minimal assistance exiting the coach.

Jamie watched her as she tipped back her head, one hand on the crown of her hat, holding it in place as she regarded Albion. He saw the reflection of the imposing house in her wide eyes—tall windows, slender columns flanking the entryway, the pediments fashioned in the classic lines of a Greek temple.

"So this is your family home," she said. "It's lovely."

Rowan scratched his full beard and studied the imported, hand-carved spindlework trim that stretched the entire length of the gleaming veranda. "I should be charging you a higher rent, Calhoun."

At that moment, the front doors swung open. There stood his parents, as proper and stiff as a pair of lawn jockeys. His father wore a beautifully tailored frock coat and trousers of superfine; his mother was predictably lovely in a gold satin gown. Both of them smiled a cordial welcome, and none of the guests seemed to notice the tiny details that were glaringly obvious to Jamie. Lines of discontent had been permanently etched in his mother's face, and a subtle glaze of a morning dram of whiskey shone in his father's eyes.

Jamie took a deep breath to steady himself. The weekend stretched endlessly before him.

"Jamie was always such a trial to us," Tabitha Calhoun announced to everyone, but her beautiful smile softened the comment until no one noticed it was a condemnation. "I can't tell you what a pleasant surprise it is to find him in such excellent company, now that he's gone up to Washington."

With the measured gait of a bridesmaid, she led the way into the formal parlor and invited the guests to sit down. Jamie's father clapped him on the shoulder. "Didn't I tell you a stint in the legislature would be just the thing?" He lowered his voice, adding, "Hated to see you eating yourself alive over Noah."

"Indeed," Jamie murmured, gritting his teeth. It wasn't so bad, he told himself. Yet when he glanced at Abigail, saw her watching him with those deep midnight eyes, he wondered if he'd made a mistake in bringing her here. Unlike everyone else, she seemed to understand him and his fierce desire to be a part of this place that had never wanted him. It was unsettling, having someone in his life who saw him so clearly. He wasn't sure he wanted that.

Over a lavish supper, Charles and Tabitha Calhoun regaled the Cabots with anecdotes about their home, their horses, their neighbors. They did themselves proud, entertaining the senator and his daughters. Jamie never should have doubted his parents' charm, which was always more potent when fueled by the urge to make an impression, and, in his father's case, by a nip from the silver flask he always kept close at hand.

He regarded his parents as one might regard a pair of not very interesting strangers. In his younger days, Charles had a reputation for recklessness and lack of ambition. Some thirty years earlier, he'd carried on with a married woman, and when she died, he'd been adrift until his cousin Hunter, then master of Albion, had put him in charge of a new enterprise that had the whole county gossiping.

While most plantations raised tobacco, cotton, indigo or rice, Albion bred racehorses with Irish Thoroughbred bloodlines. The venture had carried enormous risk, but eventually it had brought the Calhoun family enormous profits. It had also brought Charles Calhoun the prettiest, most well-heeled debutante in the region.

Tabitha Parks was equaled in wealth and beauty only by her sister, Priscilla. Tabby and Prissy, as they were known, had always seemed to Jamie to be women who didn't quite fit into the present world. His aunt and mother were born and bred to be plantation mistresses, but the War Between the States had changed their lives irrevocably. While they labored to embrace the new order of things, Jamie suspected they'd never quite adjusted to having servants and workers who were free to come and go as they pleased.

With Albion's status as the premier stud farm on the eastern seaboard, all should have been well. All *had* been well—for a time. Until Jamie had grown old enough to understand that for people like his father and mother, true happiness was no more expected, or likely, than snow on the Fourth of July.

Jamie knew his parents loved him in a remote, detached way. But they also regarded him with a certain objectivity, as they might one of their prize horses. They discussed his strengths and his limitations in endless detail. Their expectations for him had been enormous. He could not recall one time he'd been given praise or approval for anything but a perfect performance.

To his mother's oft-stated disappointment, he'd been an only child. When he was old enough to understand that this was regarded as a family tragedy, he took on the task of fixing it. With all the sincerity and the flawed logic of an eight-year-old boy, he'd set out to tell the world that he wasn't an only child at all. He had an older half brother, Noah Calhoun, then twenty-five and the most successful Thoroughbred jockey in the country. Jamie sent a letter about him to the *Chesapeake Review,* and on publication of the letter, the whole region seethed with the news.

Jamie had always worshiped Noah. It never occurred to him that his mother might not want to acknowledge the son Charles Calhoun had sired on a slave woman. The episode sent his mother to bed in a fit of melancholy that lasted three months.

The next year, they sent him far away from Albion. They enrolled him in a dank, venerable academy for boys up in Philadelphia and he only came home for a week at Christmas, and during the summer. From that time on, his boyhood consisted of a process of being sent away, when all he really wanted to do was come home and live close to the land, to grow things and breed racehorses and sit on the porch in the evening, waiting for the stars to come out.

"You're so very quiet, son," his mother remarked,

joining him on the broad front veranda after supper. "It's not like you."

He took her hand, slim and pampered as a queen's. "Just enjoying the view, Mother."

"I do love it when Albion puts on her autumn colors. The poplars turn such a beautiful shade of gold."

"You have a fine home," Senator Cabot said, strolling outside with his host.

A servant came forward with a teakwood humidor. Charles selected a cigar, then offered the box to Jamie and Cabot.

"You must find our little piece of Virginia quite provincial after the bustle of the capital city," Charles commented.

"That's the key to its charm," Cabot said. Taking a silver guillotine clip from his pocket, he trimmed the cigar with a swift and expert motion. "You're blessed in having such a place."

"A pity you can't stay longer," Tabitha said with a smile at Jamie. "But I understand, you have your duties in the capital."

"Yes, ma'am, I do." It always came to this, to a reminder that Jamie was really only a guest in this place. If he was a guest in his own home, a lodger in Rowan's town house, then where did he belong?

Fourteen

"Don't scream," said a voice as a large hand covered her mouth. "It's only me."

Abigail had been immersed in a delicious dream she wanted to remember forever, a misty fantasy of dancing gracefully to a beautiful waltz while everyone watched her with admiration. Rudely awakened, she couldn't have screamed if she'd tried. Shock and terror held her mute and immobile, until her eyes adjusted to the darkness and she recognized the intruder.

He removed his hand.

"What in heaven's name do you think you're doing?" she demanded. "What time is it? Is something the matter? What do—"

Jamie Calhoun's hand came down again, pressing at her lips. "To answer your questions, I've come to show you something. It is two o'clock in the morning. And nothing is the matter unless you decide to wake the whole household and make a scene."

She clawed his hand away and regarded the unmoving lump of covers on the bed across the room, where Helena slept. "What on earth do you want to show me?'' she asked, adjusting her voice to a whisper.

''Nothing on earth.'' He dumped a long cotton robe in her lap. ''Put that on and come with me.'' With a sulfurous hiss, a match leaped to life as he lit a lamp. Setting it aside, he held up the robe for her.

Trapped. Abigail was trapped. She couldn't get out of bed, certainly not in the light. ''I'll do nothing of the sort.''

''Don't be difficult,'' he said, shaking the robe. ''Come, you're wasting time.''

''Get out of here. You'll wake Helena.''

''Professor Rowan has already seen to that.''

Clutching the bedsheets to her chest, she peered across the guest room. ''She's gone?''

''Indeed.'' Strolling over to the other bed, he excavated the pillows that had been arranged to resemble a sleeping body. ''Your sister has an appetite for adventure. I assure you, Rowan will look after her.''

Abigail felt neither surprise nor alarm at her sister's disappearance. Without ever actually acknowledging it, Abigail had known for quite some time that Helena sometimes went off on undisclosed errands, and that no amount of scolding or worry would stop her. If Abigail studied the sky in search of their mother, then Helena sought to fill the emptiness with adventures in forbidden, earthbound places.

''Do not tell my father,'' she said.

''What do you take me for? Don't answer that,'' he added quickly. ''Just put the robe on. Where are your slippers?''

Apprehension clutched at her chest. ''Leave the lamp and wait for me outside.''

He chuckled. ''Abby, we've broken every possible

law of decency already. Save your modesty for Boyd Butler. He'll appreciate it so much more than I.''

Right now, she could think only of Jamie, of his nearness, his keen eyes studying her. "Leave, or I will not move from this bed.'' She hoped he couldn't detect the panic in her voice. Holding her breath, she glared at him until he departed. Only when she heard the click of the door did she scramble out of bed. She put on her shoes, not the slippers, because she could walk better that way. The robe actually belonged to Helena but that was fine. That meant the hem would drag along the floor, the better to conceal the ugly shoes.

She picked up the lamp, slipped out into the corridor where Jamie waited.

"All right," she said. "What was it you wished to show me?''

He took her hand in his and led the way down the corridor. The occasional floorboard creaked, but otherwise an almost eerie silence hung in the antique halls of Albion. It seemed very strange to Abigail, accustomed as she was to the noise and activity of a city that never quite settled into sleep.

At the end of the hall they encountered a narrow doorway and staircase. On the next floor, they passed through a room full of draped furniture. She guessed it had been a nursery or child's room.

"Was this your room?'' she asked.

"Long ago.'' He slowed his pace and scanned the walls, hung with framed pictures of horses and riders.

She indicated three low, cloth-draped bedsteads. "Were there other children in the house?''

"No one shared the room with me. This nursery

has housed a lot of Calhouns over the years. Some generations were more prolific than others.''

She tried to imagine him growing up here, under the critical eye of his handsome parents. It was a troubling picture. He'd told her little about his past but she sensed a certain detachment in his family, a lack of connection. "It must have been lonely for you, being up here all by yourself."

Dropping her hand, he slid aside a wooden panel, revealing another set of stairs, these even steeper and narrower than the previous ones. She wondered at his reluctance to speak of his childhood. Albion should have been such a magical place for a boy to grow up in.

"A hidden door," she said. "Very intriguing."

"Family legend has it that the first generation of Calhouns installed escape routes through the attic and the root cellar to protect them from pirate attacks."

Cobwebs and forgotten furniture crammed the space. The wooden spindles of chairs and tables resembled dried bones in a knacker's yard. A rustle, followed by a scrabbling sound, startled her and she pushed herself up against him, remembering too late that she wore only a thin nightgown and robe.

She'd never touched a man like this before, with her arms wrapped around him from behind as though he were saving her from drowning. The overwhelming impression was of...firmness. He felt like the trunk of a tree, but warmer, more giving.

Flustered, she let go and stepped back. "Pardon me," she said. "I heard a noise."

"You should hear them more often, then." He turned, grinning in a way that made her wonder if he knew how hard her heart was pounding. "It was only

a squirrel, maybe a possum. Watch your head here.''
At the gable end of the attic, he opened a low door,
and they emerged onto a flat area of the roof surrounded by a low railing.

"Put out the lamp," she said. The welcoming night
filled her with an enchantment that left no room for
any other feeling. After he did so, she turned slowly
in a circle with her face raised to the sky. "This is
absolutely perfect, Mr. Calhoun. I've always longed
to be in a place this dark and remote.''

"You should've come to Albion long ago. We're
in the middle of nowhere.''

The perfect clarity of the night thrilled her. She'd
rarely seen constellations with such acuity, nor had
she been able to pick out so many uncommon colors
and formations with her naked eye.

"In the spring, you get so many frogs you can't
hear yourself think.'' Jamie wandered to the railing
that faced the water. "It's quieter this time of year.''
He pointed to a tall, straight-trunked tree a good hundred feet tall. "See that old loblolly pine out there?
Years ago, my father's cousin Ryan built a viewing
platform so he could watch the shipping traffic in the
bay. Later he became a sea captain. He's retired now,
living in a fine old house on Cape Cod. I'd take you
up to the platform but the wood's probably rotten.''

"This will do." She inhaled the smell of seawater
and dry leaves and hay. "Albion is a wonderful place.
It's full of your family's history, isn't it?''

"I reckon so." He spoke with a mild nonchalance,
and again she wondered how she truly felt about this
place.

She tried to discern a shadowy hulk on the distant
horizon. "What's that?''

"The ruins of a neighboring plantation. It was called Bonterre, and it belonged to the Beaumonts. Burned by the Yankees during the war."

"How did Albion escape the burning?"

"The Union Army designated it a hospital and officers' quarters."

"That was fortunate, wasn't it?"

"Luck had nothing to do with it. Some said the Yankees showed mercy due to our strategic location, but it was more than that. The Calhoun family embraced abolition back in 1851, when Cousin Hunter gave the slaves of Albion their freedom. When my father took over the farm, he carried on the tradition of using paid labor. I'm told it didn't endear him to the neighbors."

"You must be proud to be a part of that tradition, then," she said. A curious excitement gripped her. In getting to know Jamie Calhoun and his family, she felt as though she were peeling away layers, moving closer to the man he truly was.

"So how will you make your mark, Mr. Calhoun?"

"Is it required that I do?"

"Maybe. It appears to be a tradition with the Calhouns."

"I admit, knowing why Albion was spared during the war was one of the factors that prompted my decision to run for Congress—the notion that sometimes it pays to play politics."

He took her hand and brought her to the middle of the roof. To her astonishment, she found a thick blanket spread upon the surface. Laid out on the blanket was a basket of apples, a round of cheese, a loaf of bread. "What is this?"

"If you don't recognize a picnic when you see one,

then we're going to have to work even harder than I thought." He took both her hands in his. "Sit."

Excruciatingly conscious of her inadequate garments, she sank down, praying the robe would keep her covered. He didn't seem to notice her discomfiture as he sat beside her and offered her an apple. Taking it from his hand felt like a forbidden intimacy. With an air of defiance, she bit into the cool, crunchy flesh of the apple.

"So it's dark enough for you here?"

"Indeed it is." She angled her face to the night sky. "What a blessing to have this place. Will it be yours one day?"

"Maybe. Never gave it much thought."

His indifference piqued her curiosity. "Don't you love your home?"

"A home is where you belong. I haven't lived here in years. My lodgings in Dumbarton Street are fine until my travels take me elsewhere."

"And where might that be?"

"Who knows? Mexico? California? China? Have you ever thought you might like to travel, maybe visit a place like California?"

She chewed her apple thoughtfully, focusing on Mars, which exhibited its faint rose-tinged nimbus. The distant places sounded mysterious and exciting. "Absolutely," she said. "Oh, I should like to travel far one day. I would so love to go to the observatory at the Vatican, or to see the stars from a high mountaintop."

"Traveling so far wouldn't bother you?"

She set down her apple core and pointed to the sky. "Of course not. I dream of things that are uncounted worlds away. California seems close by comparison.

What about you? Do you long to travel and see the world?''

"Already seen the world, or plenty of it, anyway. Too much, perhaps. I stayed away...a good long time."

She sensed a dark note in his voice and wondered what had befallen him on his adventures, but wasn't sure how to ask him. With his too-easy insouciance, he pulled an invisible curtain in place, shielding himself. "Tell me of your travels," she said.

"Not tonight. You've got every star in the sky looking down at you."

Abigail didn't press him. "You pleased your family enormously by going into the legislature."

"How do you know they were pleased?"

"Your mother said so. She said you returned home from abroad and shouldered the mantle of responsibility. That's interesting, to have your life turn out exactly as planned."

He laughed. "Is that what you think?"

"It appears to be so."

"Honey, if my life had turned out exactly as planned, I'd be married to a blond Richmond debutante and we'd have six kids by now."

"Perhaps you'll still—"

"Marry one day? I won't. Ever."

His vehemence startled her. She wondered why he took such a dim view of marriage, or if indeed that was the case. While they shared a long silence, the moon began its rise, diluting the darkness of the sky. Blue-toned light shimmered down upon the gardens and quiet bay.

She felt his light caress on her hand, then her shoulder, and she pulled back in alarm. "What do you think you're doing?"

"Proceeding with your plan, or have you forgotten? By the time Boyd Butler comes to call, you must be totally prepared for his courtship. That includes knowing how to act when a man touches you."

"A gentleman wouldn't."

"That's a fallacy made up by women who dislike being touched. You're not one of those, are you?"

"I, um, wouldn't know."

He rested his fingertips on the back of her hand, grinning when she recoiled. "It's not a poisonous spider, love." He put his hand back.

"Are you sure this is necessary?"

"Trust me, it is. Showing affection with a touch is the most natural thing in the world. Enjoying it is natural, too. Seduction is a marvelous thing, but it takes practice."

Moonlight and indigo shadowed his face, and she could see the gleam of his teeth as he smiled. She resented the fact that he seemed to know what she felt, yet she could not banish the warm ribbons of sensation. She wished he'd been wrong about her enjoyment of his touch, but the truth was, she found it far too pleasant.

Warmth started deep and low inside her and radiated outward in slow, subtle pulsations that touched fire to certain parts of her. She felt a sweet burn in places she knew of only due to furtive, forbidden perusals of Professor Rowan's dog-eared copy of the *Physick's Anatomy.*

"It's all right to close your eyes," he whispered.

She did so, and felt him shift closer to her on the blanket. His hand rested on her thigh, imparting a new kind of warmth. She was so filled with panic and yearning and excitement that she could scarcely breathe or even think. She remembered seeing him in the White House garden that night, sliding his hand beneath a woman's skirt, lowering his head to the cleft between her breasts, and now she knew exactly how that woman had felt.

"It's all right to hold on to me, too," he said.

She gripped his shirt, closing her fist into the soft fabric. Her knuckles grazed his chest and she felt that startling firmness again, that heat.

"You'll like this a lot better if you relax," he told her.

"You don't understand," she whispered. "I already like this far too much."

He pressed his hand possessively against her side, and she thought perhaps that his thumb had strayed inside her robe, but she didn't dare look. She felt dizzy, overheated with sensation. It was vexing indeed, to have to remind herself that her purpose tonight was not pleasure but instruction.

"Is that so?" he asked.

"Lieutenant Butler will think me depraved if I behave this way with him," she said, forcing her eyes open.

"If he does, then he's even more stupid than I thought."

"What do you mean?"

"A man dreams of this, Abby. Dreams of a woman who welcomes his touch, is crazed by it. He dreams of a woman who is bold enough to touch him, who laughs at false morality and—how did you say it in your last letter?—consigns herself to the fire of passion."

"I never should have let you read that."

"It's powerful stuff, Abby. Powerful and rare."

"Really?" she said, but she didn't hear his answer because inside the robe, his hand did something that drove every last coherent thought out of her head. The last thing she heard was a ragged, indrawn breath— his—and a soft, almost musical moan—hers.

Then their lips touched, brushing and recoiling, then coming together again.

Her first kiss. It wasn't what she had expected, not even close. She supposed she had envisioned a fairy-tale moment, a touch of the lips and the world would turn candy pink.

Instead, this was a dark passionate clash, generating a forbidden yearning. There was nothing remotely sweet about it, or about her fiery reaction. She moved as close to him as she could, until his arm gently pressed her back so that she lay beneath him. She wanted the aggressive weight of him, wanted it all, and acknowledging the desire gave her a strange and soaring joy.

Each moment of the kiss was more shocking and delicious than the last. He coaxed her mouth open with his, probing with his tongue in a manner so startlingly intimate that she nearly came out of her skin. When at last he eased up the pressure of his body and lifted his mouth from hers, she couldn't think, had no idea where she was. She blinked up at the majesty of the night sky. "Oh." The sound of amazement slipped from her, borne on a sigh. "Oh, Jamie…"

"Mmm?"

How could she be feeling such bliss in the arms of Jamie Calhoun, a cynic and a womanizer? She was no different from Caroline Fortenay or some other conquest. Forcing her thoughts to her true purpose, she asked, "Do you think this is what it will be like with Lieutenant Butler?"

His strong arms drew her up, then thrust her away. He moved back, the night air cool on the parts of her body he had been covering a moment ago. "Well done, love," he said curtly. "You know all you need to know about kissing."

She peered at him through the dimness, trying to recover from the dizzy heat of his embrace. "Heavens, you're angry at me."

"Nonsense. Why would I be angry?"

"Because I brought up Lieutenant Butler's name just now."

"Fine. That means I'm doing my job. This is about him. It's been about him from the start."

"That was my first kiss," she confessed.

"You're a quick study, then. You have nothing to worry about." His voice was terse, perhaps slightly strained as he wrapped up the remains of the picnic in the tablecloth. "You're a natural."

"Am I?" She touched the front of her robe. Somehow, it had come unbuttoned. She hastened to refasten it.

When he stood, he didn't bother offering a hand to help her up. Instead, he turned away, heading for the attic door. "Bring along that blanket, will you?" he said over his shoulder.

She came awkwardly to her feet, staggering a little until she regained her balance. Scooping up the blanket, she followed him, wondering at his brusque attitude. Had she done something wrong? Had she been too bold? Too timid? But he said she was a natural.

"Mr. Calhoun?"

"At this point, you could probably start calling me Jamie."

"I'd like that," she said. "Jamie—"

"Hush." He stopped walking and she bumped into him from behind.

"What is it?" she asked.

"I heard something." Setting down his bundle, he moved to the railing. Abigail followed, detecting the sound of voices. A man's rasping whisper, a woman's giggle. Abigail spotted them first, picking out two figures crossing the yard. Barefoot and carrying their shoes, Helena and Professor Rowan headed through the garden, presumably to sneak back into the house.

"I see I guessed correctly about the adventure," Jamie said, and went to relight the lamp.

Still flustered from the kiss, Abigail followed him down through the attic and nursery. Jamie escorted her to her chamber. Muted noises from inside indicated that Helena had already arrived.

"Good night, Abigail," he said.

"Good night." She turned to the door, then turned back. "Jamie?" She felt odd using his given name, but after what they'd done on the roof, it would have been odder still to call him Mr. Calhoun.

"Yes? What is it?"

"I...thank you." She wasn't quite sure what she was thanking him for. Showing her the stars? The picnic? Heavenly days, the kiss? There should probably be some other term for it. A mere kiss didn't begin to describe the long, languorous encounter on the roof. And was she actually grateful for that?

He settled the matter by flashing a grin and saying, "You're welcome." Then, humming softly under his breath, he disappeared into the night shadows.

* * *

Abigail pushed opened the door and stepped into the bedroom. Moonlight spilled through the tall windows. Standing on the round hearth rug, Helena gasped, then clapped her hand over her mouth.

"It's only me," Abigail said.

"You frightened me half to death. Were you out viewing the stars?" Helena didn't wait for an answer. "Of course you were."

Abigail hated that she was so predictable. But, in fact, she *was* predictable. Helena was used to her sister's midnight comings and goings.

"Where were you?" she asked. "You're soaking wet. And what's that smell? Seawater?"

Helena grabbed a towel and rubbed her hair. "You mustn't tell Papa."

Fondness and exasperation tugged at her. "When have I ever told Father?"

She dropped the towel. In the eerie moonlight, she resembled a fairy, delicate and otherworldly. "I went swimming. With Michael."

"With—oh. Professor Rowan."

"Yes."

"But you don't know how to swim."

Helena laughed. "I do now."

"Wasn't it cold?"

"Yes. But after a while, I didn't notice."

"Well, you'd best hang your wet clothes on a chair so they'll be dry by morning."

Helena started brushing her hair with long, slow strokes. "My clothes aren't wet."

It took Abigail a moment to realize what she was saying. "Dear Lord. You swam in the nude?"

Helena giggled. "It was glorious. So natural and

elemental. Michael says among the aboriginal peoples of—''

"I can't believe you swam naked with a man."

"It would have been dangerous to swim without him."

Abigail told herself she shouldn't be surprised. Doing outrageous things was Helena's specialty.

"I certainly wasn't going to do it alone," Helena added. "Michael said—"

"And did Michael say your reputation didn't matter one whit?"

"My reputation." With practiced fingers, Helena braided her hair and climbed into bed. "It has been in tatters ever since I ran away from finishing school. Miss Madeira said I'd never marry well. I think she put a curse on me." She pulled the covers over her knees. "Thank heavens."

Abigail sat on the end of the bed and tried to hold in her anger. Helena had forced her to cultivate Lieutenant Butler's suit, yet she thought nothing of gallivanting with Professor Rowan.

"Anyway," Helena went on, "my carefree days are nearly over. Papa will be so happy when I finally settle down with—with…" She frowned, thinking. "Lieutenant Butler, is it?"

A chill rippled through Abigail. How could her sister encourage one man while cavorting with another? The lieutenant would be devastated if he ever found out. Abigail renewed her conviction to protect him from being hurt by Helena's carelessness.

"Actually, there's only one aspect of marriage that interests me," Helena said. "And now, well…" Helena yawned and stretched, then snuggled down into the covers. "I've discovered that my interest can be fulfilled without benefit of matrimony."

Abigail shifted to her knees. "Good heavens. Are you saying what I fear you're saying?"

Helena laughed, her mirth liquid with delight.

"You are," Abigail whispered. "You...you... didn't?" She couldn't even put words to it. "With Professor Rowan."

"Ever since he moved to Dumbarton Street, he's pretended to ignore me, so I decided to force the issue. Seduction is remarkably easy, Abigail. You should try it sometime."

Abigail stared at her sister, who smiled sleepily at the ceiling, as though she were in some other world. Helena didn't look different, or did she? "You could conceive a child," Abigail whispered. "Have you even thought of that?"

"If it happens, I'd have to get married in a great hurry, wouldn't I?"

Abigail couldn't help herself. She had to ask the next question. "So is this going to cause you to change your mind about Lieutenant Butler?"

"Papa would never forgive me if I rejected the vice president's son. Besides, Michael doesn't want to marry me. I don't even think he loves me." Helena laughed. "You're staring at me as though I'd grown antlers."

Abigail considered chastising her sister for loose morals and worse, but she knew it wouldn't matter. "So was the discovery worth the sacrifice of your virginity?"

"Virginity is a commodity prized only by those who have no idea what else to want in a wife." She grinned. "And the answer to your question is yes.

Absolutely, unequivocally, yes, it was worth it.'' She settled deep into the bed, hugging her pillow. "It is the most wonderful thing in the world, Abigail. That's what they never want young women to find out. It's truly wonderful.'' She sent her sister a last, glowing smile before closing her eyes. "It is like soaring.''

Fifteen

"I'll be damned. They've done it, haven't they?" Jamie asked Abigail the next day as they started off on their tour of Albion's breeding farm. He indicated Helena and Professor Rowan walking close together, furtive hands brushing as they pretended to listen to Jeffries, the breeding master, talk of Thoroughbred bloodlines.

Abigail forced herself to stare straight ahead at the little man and listen to his earnest assertions about his craft. "I have no idea what you're talking about."

Jamie chuckled, the sound as low and intimately modulated as a lover's whisper. A warm smell of oats and horse filled the stables as Jeffries led the way down a long aisle flanked by stalls.

"Then I'll be more explicit." Leaning down, Jamie whispered a phrase in her ear. Though she had never heard such a thing before, she had no doubt as to its meaning.

"Stop." She shoved away from him in a fury. "You are unbelievably crude."

"Believe it. I am crude."

"And what you accuse my sister of—"

"I'm not accusing her of anything. Besides, your blush confirms my suspicions."

"If I'm blushing, it's because your disgusting suppositions and your language offend me."

"You shouldn't be offended, but please, don't stop blushing. It's very becoming."

"Don't try to distract me with insincere flattery."

"Dear girl, a bluebottle fly could distract you. That's what I like about you, Abby. You notice everything."

She had no idea whether or not to feel complimented, and was rescued from responding when they reached the end of the stables and emerged into the coach yard. The elder Mr. Calhoun drove up in a small open buggy, her father at his side. Relaxed and jovial, they were framed by nodding oaks and the deepening sky of late autumn. Father looked wonderful today, Abigail thought. In his tweeds and tall boots, he resembled a country gentleman. He truly seemed to be enjoying the visit, and his pleasure in Jamie's home gratified her.

"Hello, Father," she said. "Hello, Mr. Calhoun. We were just admiring your farm. It's a remarkable place. You must be very proud of it."

"Indeed I am, Miss Cabot."

"Hello, Abigail," her father called. "Helena, do come along and join us in the buggy. You'll get too fatigued by all this walking."

Abigail felt Jamie's stare jabbing into her, but she ignored him. Father naturally spent more attention and worry on Helena. It had always been so. And it had always been warranted. Abigail was safe, predictable, easy to manage. Helena was none of those things.

"Coming, Papa." Helena tucked her hand into the crook of Professor Rowan's arm. "Good morning, Mr. Calhoun."

Jamie's father was as taken with Helena as the rest of the world, his pleasure evident when she gifted him with that dazzling smile. Professor Rowan handed her into the buggy and took a seat beside her. In her split riding skirt, Helena looked as dashing and countrified as their father. She'd insisted on making Abigail wear a split skirt as well, excavating it from an old cedar chest in the guest room, even though Abigail swore she had no need of riding togs. For her own private reasons, she favored fashions that denied a woman even had feet. But like the rest of the world, she did Helena's bidding. Fortunately, the hem of the split skirt brushed the ground, concealing her shoes.

"Miss Abigail and I will finish our tour on foot." Jamie rubbed the buggy horse's velvet muzzle. "We'll give poor old Lord Byron less of a burden that way."

"As you wish." Charles slapped the reins. "We're off to inspect the mile oval."

As the buggy rolled toward the seaside racetrack, Jamie absently rubbed Abigail's arm, seeming not even to notice he was touching her, reminding her of the previous night. "Does your father always do that?"

She stepped away from him, out of his reach. "Do what?"

He shook his head. "You know what. I suspect it's been this way for years."

"What way?"

"Don't play stupid, Abigail. It ill becomes you, and the whole world knows better, anyway."

She flinched and went over to the paddock fence, pretending great fascination with whatever Jeffries was doing with a glossy-coated, balky mare. She was less upset by her father's dismissal of her than she was by the fact that Jamie had noticed.

She gripped the peeled cedar rail of the paddock, concentrating hard and praying he wouldn't push her for a reply. Mercifully, he did not. He came and stood beside her, his warm presence causing her thoughts to shift once again to the moment on the roof the night before.

She couldn't seem to drive the memory of what they'd done from her mind. His touch, his kiss, had confused and overwhelmed her, and here in the broad light of day, things were no different. She still felt confused and overwhelmed. How could something as simple as a touch set off such a complicated reaction? And what was a kiss, after all, but another sort of touch? The inexplicable touching of mouth to mouth. Flesh and blood warmed by the flush of life, nothing more. Magic had flared between them, a spell so powerful she could feel its lingering effects even now. She shuddered with a delicious, forbidden pleasure at the mere thought of it. And this was with a man she didn't even love, didn't even much like. A man who didn't care for her. How much more powerful would it be with Lieutenant Butler, whom she adored?

"What are you thinking?" Jamie asked.

"Why do you suppose I'm thinking anything at all?"

"Because you're Abigail. You're always thinking. And whatever it is you're thinking about right now has brought a bloom of roses to your cheeks. It's quite lovely, as a matter of fact."

She sniffed. "If you must know, I was thinking of Lieutenant Butler."

He didn't move or speak, but a perceptible frost chilled the air.

"Do you disapprove?" she couldn't resist asking.

"Not if you're telling the truth," he fired back.

The breeder and two grooms had managed to halter the mare. She seemed agitated, switching her tail and flaring her nostrils, her noble head tossing as she tried to throw off the halter.

"What are they doing to that poor creature?" Abigail asked.

"Just watch."

An eerie equine whistle shrilled through the air, coming from the shed adjacent to the paddock. Then there was a series of whinnies, and a wild thump of hooves hammering the wooden gate. Jeffries shouted an order. The grooms freed the mare and cleared the area, leaping to the paddock rails and vaulting over. At the same moment, something streaked from the shed, so swift and unexpected that it took Abigail a moment to realize it was a powerful, angry-looking horse.

After the initial charge, he stopped short, forelegs splayed in a challenging stance. He dropped his head, bright eyes never leaving the mare, who trotted back and forth at the fence. Then the new horse burst into motion again, rearing up, hooves tearing at the air.

The mare increased her speed, half-crazed panic glinting in her eyes.

"This is cruel," Abigail said. "The poor creature's frightened half to death. Why don't the grooms do something?"

"Sometimes they use a teaser to bring the mare to

readiness.'' As he spoke, he never took his eyes off Abigail. ''In this case, it's not needed. They've already done their job. Now it's the stallion's turn to do his.''

The new horse lowered his head and charged, nostrils flaring, a vicious intent burning in his eyes. Abigail pressed a fist to her mouth to keep from crying out in alarm.

He'll kill her, she thought, wanting to squeeze her eyes shut but unable to look away.

The stallion came at the mare with eyes on fire and mouth wide open for the attack. At the last second, the mare swiveled and met him, biting back with a far more accurate and controlled fury, causing the stallion to squeal in pain.

''Daisy's our best breeding mare. She always makes them suffer,'' Jamie murmured.

''Then why don't you stop this? It's barbaric.'' A thick ooze of blood streamed over the stallion's flank.

''Because it's a natural process. In the end, no matter how much abuse she heaps on him, she always gives him what he wants. And he'll suffer any pain to get it.''

Abigail knew Jamie was perfectly aware of how disturbing and offensive this ''lesson'' was. He was probably also quite well aware of her sick fascination with the entire event.

The sentiment appeared to be shared in a different way by the breeder and grooms, who slapped each other on the back and swapped coppers to place bets on various aspects of the encounter.

Steam rose from the big bodies of the horses, and sweat mingled with the blood of the stallion. They performed an elaborate dance that had the primal rhythm of ancient ritual. She sidled close, raised her tail, and he subjected her to such an intimate inspection that all the words of outrage were burned from Abigail's throat. After what seemed like a long time, the mating took place, a violent coupling as brutal as it was compelling. Abigail watched with a mixture of horror, amazement and a peculiar heat. She suspected that the heat was a form of lust. It embarrassed her to feel lust and to realize it came from watching horses mate.

The violent ritual went on for some minutes, then the stallion made a deep grunting sound and ceased his attack. The mare hung her head, sides fanning in and out. She looked defeated, spent, and so did the stallion, still covering her. Sand and dust rose in little clouds around them.

Finally the stallion moved away. The two horses ignored each other entirely, tails twitching, bodies running with moisture. The air was filled with a rich odor of sweat and blood and something she could not identify, but could feel in her bones.

"I imagine you don't see that every day," Jamie said.

"Are you trying to shock me?"

"Yes."

"Then it worked."

"Good."

"Why did you want to shock me? And why is it a good thing?"

"It's always useful for a person to see new things. No one ever said mating was pretty. A hurricane isn't pretty, but you can't deny its power."

"That doesn't mean I want to witness a hurricane, either," she retorted.

"Maybe you should consider it," he shot back. "You spend your time stargazing and studying pretty things. Well, the world is not all crystal and velvet. You're hiding, Abby, with your eyes to the sky. You're hiding from life, from grit and reality." He laughed at the expression on her face. "Have I said something I shouldn't?"

No one had ever spoken to her like this. No one had ever criticized her for being interested in beauty and science.

She pushed away from the cedar fence and stomped down the lane. She had no idea where it led, but away was good enough for her. Hearing his boots crunching on gravel, she knew when he caught up with her. She stared straight ahead.

"I didn't realize you'd be averse to witnessing an act of nature," he said. "You being a scientist and all."

He was right, curse him. What could she say? *I'm not that sort of scientist?*

"You didn't show me that in the interest of science," she accused. "But to embarrass me."

"And it worked."

"How proud you must be."

"Look, you claim you want Boyd Butler to sweep you away into marital bliss. I thought that meant you were interested in all aspects of mating."

"What do mating horses have to do with my attraction to Lieutenant Butler?"

"Love isn't always all perfume and magic. It has a physical side, one that has nothing to do with tender feelings, fluttering hearts, sentimental poetry."

"Are you hoping I'll find it all so off-putting that I'll grow disillusioned with Lieutenant Butler?"

"Of course not. My purpose is to make your romance of letters become a romance in fact. But I don't believe in self-deception. You should know what you're getting yourself into."

"Lieutenant Butler is not an animal. He would never—"

"Trust me, love. He would. Does that frighten you?"

What frightened her now was that she could only think of Jamie's hands on her, Jamie making love to her. But of course, she excused herself, he was the only man who had ever touched her. So far. "Should it?"

"No."

"Good. Because unlike you, I believe in the magic of love. It is what elevates us above the beasts."

"But we still mate in a manner not so very different from a mare in heat and a hot-blooded stallion."

Abigail thought about what she'd just witnessed. Did a man and woman actually sweat and bite with such wild abandon? Such intense, single-minded purpose? She was surprised that she didn't feel more disturbed by the spectacle. Or maybe that was not so surprising. It was a natural event, and even Helena had nothing bad to say about it. Abigail reminded herself to stay loyal to Lieutenant Butler, particularly now that Helena had taken up with the professor.

"This way." Jamie steered her toward another long, low building with a fenced yard at one end.

"Now what? The mating habits of ring-necked pheasants? Hampshire pigs?"

"This is a bit different. Do you ride?"

"Ride what?"

"Horses, you goose. Well, one horse at a time."

"No."

"You don't ride?"

"No."

"Have you ever?"

"No."

He looked so stunned that she laughed in spite of herself. "The whole world didn't grow up in a place like this. Many people go through their whole lives without riding a horse. I know I intend to."

"Not if I have anything to say about it."

"You don't."

"Fine. Do as you're told and I won't say a word."

"I will not—"

"You will. It's part of your training. Every woman who aspires to marry is in training."

She sniffed, resenting his cynical humor. But despite his infuriating qualities, Jamie never bored her. That was something. She wasn't sure what, but something.

He brought her to the stables. In the yard, a tall boy worked with a horse that clearly didn't want to cooperate. The horse trotted back and forth, snorting and tossing its head.

"Welcome home," the groom said when they approached.

"Good to see you, Julius. What have you got there?"

"New three-year-old. Your father bought him for riding, but he's got a mind of his own."

"We'll see about that." Bracing a hand on the fence, Jamie vaulted over. "Most folks think this sort of thing is beneath them," he said to Abigail over his shoulder, "but there's a practical value in styling one's own mount."

"Surely you don't intend that I take my first ride on an untrained horse," she said.

"Of course not. What do you take me for? That's Miss Abigail Cabot, by the way," he told Julius. "She's visiting from the city. We're going to teach her to ride."

She greeted the boy with a smile. He and Jamie shook hands, then Jamie reached out and tousled his hair. "Don't let the beast get the better of you, son. Your daddy never did."

Julius showed Abigail into the stables, where a few horses poked their heads out. Jamie stopped in front of a stall and made a clicking sound with his tongue, then opened the door. "You'll ride Patrick."

Abigail subjected Patrick to a narrow-eyed assessment. He was small and rather homely compared to the other horses she had seen at Albion. He had a coat of nondescript brown, a mulish shape to his head and splayed hooves like dinner plates.

"You wouldn't be judging this critter by his looks, would you?" Jamie asked.

"Of course not," she said, chagrined that skepticism showed in her eyes.

"He's obedient, reliable and loyal. Everything you could want in a horse...or a wife."

"I don't want a wife and I'm not entirely sure of the horse."

He clipped a rope to the horse's halter and handed her the lead. "Off you go."

"I have no idea what to do."

"He'll follow you. But you have to go somewhere rather than standing there like a ninny." He gestured at Julius, who waited at the end of the breezeway, where she assumed he would saddle the horse. "Trust me, it works every time. I'll be out in the paddock with the new gelding.''

It was slightly intimidating to walk with a thousand-pound beast plodding behind her, but she was determined to master this. She insisted that Julius teach her to do the saddling, and he was pleased to oblige. She liked the boy instantly. He was perhaps thirteen, remarkably poised and quite possibly the handsomest boy she had ever seen, with his café-au-lait skin, slender, long-fingered hands and a slight build.

As he showed her each step of the process, Julius was more patient and polite than Jamie had been. So, for that matter, was Patrick the horse.

"Don't be afraid to touch him," the groom advised her. "It's always a good idea to get used to touching him."

She gingerly patted his neck.

"A horse needs a hard touch, ma'am. He can hardly feel that."

It took an act of will, but she learned to pat the horse with an aggression the creature seemed to like. She learned to put the headgear and reins on properly and to feed him the bit, ruining her gloves in the process. Abigail didn't care; she wiped her hands and rubbed the horse's nose and admired his long-lashed eyes—definitely the homely thing's most attractive feature.

"Mounting is tricky in skirts." Julius pulled the block alongside Patrick. "You'll be riding astride. Sidesaddle's too hard first time out."

Abigail balked, stepping back to eye the horse. "I don't think I can do this."

"Sure you can, Abby," Jamie called out from the

other end of the center aisle. He had managed to sub-
due and saddle the other horse all on his own.

"It's impossible," she called back.

"Suppose I said that about finding a comet."

Abigail stopped arguing when she realized that she
wanted to learn to ride. It was exciting in a way she
couldn't describe. "All right, Julius. What do I do?"

"First step is to get on." He demonstrated, swing-
ing his leg over the horse's back. She didn't like the
look of the difficult move at all.

Nevertheless, she was determined. Standing on the
block, she brought her other leg up, staggering a little
and nearly unbalancing herself. Julius put out a
steadying hand and instructed her to grasp the rim of
the saddle. On the third try, she managed to lift her
leg up and over, but that was only the beginning of
the ordeal. She failed to clear the saddle and slipped
back down. Then she swung her leg too high and fast,
and sprawled forward, banging her chin on the arch
of the horse's bony neck. Gritting her teeth with pain
and frustration, she dragged herself up. Good heavens. She sat astride the horse.

"I did it," she said.

"You did." Julius went around to the right side to
fit her foot into the stirrup. She nearly howled with
humiliation when he discovered the special shoe and
said, "This ain't going to fit in the stirrup."

"Then show me how to get off," she said, knowing
she was just inches from tears.

"Ma'am, I can't do that."

"Why not?"

"Because you're going to learn to ride. Wait
here." Julius disappeared into the tack room. She
could hear him rummaging around, whistling between

his teeth. How could he whistle when she wanted to curl up and die?

Except she didn't want to. She hated her foot, hated the misshapen shoe she had to wear. But she had realized something, sitting on the horse's back. Her bad foot didn't matter when Patrick had four good hooves to stand on.

Out in the yard, Jamie rode back and forth on the handsome new horse. Despite the chilly November day, man and beast gleamed with sweat. They were wearing each other out, but maybe that was the point.

After a few minutes, Julius emerged from the tack room with a pair of stirrup loops. "These are used for hunting, so the opening's bigger." He held them up for her to see.

She waited in silence as he attached the new loops.

"A perfect fit," he said. "Ma'am, you are ready to ride."

"Julius."

"Yes, ma'am?"

"Could you pull the hem of my skirt down? You know, to—"

"Yes, ma'am." He made sure the fabric draped over her feet. He was so matter-of-fact about it that she forgot to be embarrassed. What a pleasant young man he was, she reflected.

"Hang on now, ma'am," he said, then unhooked the horse from the cross ties and led him out to the paddock.

"Oh." Abigail clutched at the lip of the saddle, struggling to keep her seat. The lumbering, swaying movement of the horse made her feel as though she might fall at any moment.

"Just sit up straight," Julius advised. "Look between the horse's ears. Gravity will do the rest."

Abigail wanted to ask Julius how he knew about gravity, but she was too busy holding on. Her wild look of panic caught Jamie's eye, but he merely grinned and waved. "You look splendid, Miss Cabot," he said jovially. "Simply splendid!"

The liar. She was a terrible rider, fearful and clumsy. Julius and the horse had endless patience, and eventually she managed to exert a small amount of control over the reins. Within the generous oval of the paddock, she could compel the horse where she wanted him.

She kept her seat and steered him this way and that, even taking him up to a trot by prodding him with her heels. Abigail knew there was nothing elegant about her riding, but she didn't care. She was riding a horse. For the first time in her life, she moved with a normal gait, just like anyone else in the world.

Jamie had pushed her into doing this. How could he know what her soul yearned for when she didn't even know that herself? Perhaps he was magic. Or diabolical.

When Julius finally brought her from the paddock to the bridle trail, she had the most foolish grin on her face. Waiting for her astride the dun gelding, Jamie grinned back. She would never tell him so, but he looked as dashing as a painting in a museum.

"Where are we going?" she asked.

"It's a surprise. Your horse will follow mine." He headed down a broad, sandy path that followed a meandering creek. Gradually, the terrain changed and flattened into rich bottomland dotted with the small farms she recognized from the journey by coach. The surprise turned out to be a visit to one of the farms.

At their approach, a bluetick coonhound set up a racket in front of a snug house made of cedar planks. The remnants of a garden straggled along the side of the house, and in the distance lay a long, low barn and fenced paddock. In the yard, Jamie shushed the dog as he dismounted, then helped Abigail down. To her relief, he didn't appear to notice her foot at all, but seemed focused on the little house with its thin ribbon of smoke twisting from the chimney.

"Jasper!" yelled a woman's voice. "I swear, you're the loudest dog the good Lord ever saw fit to make." She stepped out onto the porch, a tall black woman wearing a man's dungarees and a flowered apron, a wooden spoon in her hand. When she spied Jamie, her face lit up with a smile. "Well, now, look who came to call. So can you come in a spell, or are you too citified these days?"

He took the porch stairs two at a time and swept the woman into his arms. "How've you been, honey?"

Abigail had never heard such warmth in his voice, and she was intrigued. She waited at the bottom step until Jamie turned to her.

"Abby, this is Patsy Calhoun, my sister-in-law. Patsy, this is Abigail Cabot, my…" His voice drifted off. He didn't seem to know what Abigail was to him any more than she knew what he was to her.

"How do you do?" she said, mounting to the porch and holding out her hand.

Patsy looked from her to Jamie and back again, lifting an inquisitive brow. "Your lady friend?"

"No." Both Abigail and Jamie protested with one voice.

Patsy lifted her eyebrow even higher. "I see," she said. "I do indeed. Best get inside, then. I got a chess pie in the oven."

Abigail passed a most unusual and pleasant afternoon in the simple, sturdy cabin of Noah Calhoun's widow. Jamie seemed a different person with Patsy. He was relaxed and jovial, and not a sarcastic word passed his lips. This, Abigail realized, studying his face by the light of Patsy's cozy fire, was the essence of a home. No wonder he was so committed to protecting the farms along the creek.

They arrived at the plantation house an hour before supper. Abigail dismounted on her own and gave a happy sigh, even pausing to press her cheek against her homely horse for a moment.

"You owe me an apology," said Jamie.

"For what?"

"For saying you didn't want to go riding."

"I didn't think I would like it."

He sent her a rakish wink. "Next time I tell you you're going to like something, trust me."

Sixteen

❡

"Try it. You'll like it."

"But it's alive."

"It's just lying there waiting to be eaten. I promise, it won't fight back."

"And that makes it permissible to eat it?"

"Abby, live oysters are a delicacy. People of quality eat them all the time."

"People of quality also hunt foxes and club them to death. That doesn't mean I would participate in such a thing," she stated with a sniff.

"Leave the poor girl alone, son," his father said from the head of the supper table. "It's a poor host who forces unwanted food on his guest."

Jamie never took his eyes off Abigail. "Oh, she wants it. I can tell she wants it."

"Truly," his mother said, "autumn is the best time for bay oysters."

"I couldn't agree with you more, dear," her husband said.

"Charles's grandfather started the oyster beds a half century ago," she explained to Senator Cabot, who happily sucked down an oyster followed by a swig of stout dark beer.

At the other end of the table, Helena and Rowan ate their share while flashing each other private looks and secretive smiles. Jamie couldn't believe the senator hadn't guessed his elder daughter was engaged in a love affair with the professor, but Franklin Cabot had glaring blind spots when it came to his daughters.

At the moment, the younger one was studying the oyster on her plate with a mixture of curiosity and revulsion. Something about her always made Jamie want to smile. She was that rarest of creatures, a woman devoid of pretense. For that reason alone, he liked her rather well. It had been a long, long time since he had found himself able to like a woman.

"Just one," he coaxed, convinced she would thank him. "It's just a little swallow, my dear."

She glowered at him. "I am not your dear."

"No one is," he agreed. "It's just an expression. Eat the oyster, Miss Cabot."

"I will not."

"My mother's cook went to considerable trouble to gather and shuck them for supper."

"If she's the cook, why didn't she cook them?" Abigail pushed her plate at him. "You should have it instead."

He pushed it back. "Eat the damn oyster."

"I will not."

"Coward."

"Bully."

"And you call yourself a woman of science. You won't even—"

"Must you argue about everything, Abigail?" Mr. Cabot asked.

Glaring at Jamie, she picked up the half shell. "Very well, but only to silence Mr. Calhoun."

Jamie knew very well that wasn't the reason she capitulated. Interesting and unfortunate, he thought, how quick she was to obey her father.

Holding the thing perfectly level in front of her face, she squeezed a lemon wedge into the shell.

"It moved," she screeched, dropping the oyster to her plate.

Jamie picked it up again. "That was your hand, goose." He leaned across the table, touching the edge of the shell to her lower lip. "Stop being a baby."

She nearly went cross-eyed, looking down at the oyster in front of her. Jamie bit the inside of his cheek. He couldn't remember the last time a woman had made him want to laugh. Yet it happened all the time when Abigail was around.

"Just eat it right from the shell," he advised. "Pretend it's a spoonful of delicious soup."

Taking a deep breath, she shut her eyes and opened her lips. Jamie tipped the oyster into her mouth. Her eyes flew open, blazing with alarm.

"Too late, dear," he whispered. "You'll have to swallow it now. It would be rude to, well, you know."

She screwed up her face and gulped hard.

"Oysters are a proven aphrodisiac," he pointed out, still whispering so the others wouldn't hear.

She made a small choking noise, reached for her glass of wine and took a deep drink. Finally, she pressed a napkin to her lips and seemed to regain a modicum of control.

"I just thought you'd want to know that."

"Why?"

"You're out to trap a husband. Feeding him oysters is not a terrible idea."

She flicked her gaze to her father, who ignored her, as usual. The senator was fully engaged in conversation with Jamie's parents and oblivious to both his daughters.

"I am not out to trap anyone," Abigail maintained in a low voice.

"Sorry. Poor choice of words."

"Perhaps the terrible idea is in trying to get Lieutenant Butler's attention at all."

"Believe me, you already have it. What did he call you in his last letter? The dainty repository of all life's hopes and dreams. Yes, I believe that was it. The man does know how to turn a sincere phrase, I'll say that for him."

"What the devil are you two whispering about?" Jamie's father asked, not unpleasantly. His mood was well lubricated by a good amount of stout.

"Just plotting the overthrow of the government, sir," Jamie said, winking at Abigail.

"I should never have let you see his letters," she said through clenched teeth.

"How else will I know what he expects? He's on the hook, Abby. You just have to land him."

"That's the part I'm afraid of. When he discovers that I'm the letter writer, not Helena, he'll probably run screaming into the woods."

Where the devil did she get such a low opinion of herself? he wondered, exasperated. Why did she care so much what people thought? Why did her father's opinion rule her?

Perhaps Jamie could understand that. He knew his parents regarded him with a negligent affection that was almost an afterthought. Every possible maternal instinct had been bred out of his mother, who had been taught that no woman of quality raised her own children, but gave them immediately to a wet nurse and then a nanny.

Jamie's earliest memory was not of his mother at all, but of a dark, fleshy arm tucked protectively around him, a gentle round face framed by a home-spun kerchief. Her name was Igee, and from the day of his birth, she'd seen to his care and training. One day, not long after he'd published his brother Noah's name in the *Chesapeake Review,* Igee had hurried into the schoolroom where his tutor, Master Whittaker, had been drilling him on his sums. Igee's face had shone like a full moon as she beamed at Jamie. "That'll be enough of lessons now," she said. "The child needs a bath and a change of clothes, because he's going to eat supper with the grown folk today."

Jamie had been buffed and scrubbed like a show horse on fair day. Igee cleaned and trimmed his hair and fingernails; she scoured behind his ears and put him in his Sunday best, shoes and all. He still remembered the way she planted him in front of the tall, freestanding mirror in his mother's boudoir, her chubby hands pressing his shoulders.

"Don't you look a sight, honey," Igee declared. "Don't you look a picture."

"Do I?"

She straightened his little neckcloth. "You the prettiest thing I ever did see. You so pretty, I could eat you up." Her laughter and his giggles rang as fresh as a dream in his memory.

Jamie's supper with the grown folk turned out to be his final one for a long time, though he hadn't known it that day. He'd minded every manner that had been drilled into him. He said please and thank you and he ate what was set before him. He never spoke a word except that which he was invited to say, and he remembered not to kick the table leg with his foot.

At the end of the meal, his father had folded his hands on the table, cleared his throat and said, "You're nearly grown now, son."

Jamie was proud to hear his father declare him nearly grown. But even so, he wondered why his mother looked so serious, why he could hear Igee crying softly in the next room.

"Tomorrow you'll be going away to St. Swithin's School. It's in Philadelphia, son. They'll give you a fine education there."

It had been Noah who'd accompanied him, trying to pretend Jamie was going on a great adventure, not stepping into a nightmare that would haunt him for years.

Pulling himself back to the moment and to the woman sitting across from him, he put on his most dazzling smile. "Nobody's going to run screaming from you, Abby, honey," he said.

She was still green around the gills from the oyster. She started to say something, then pressed her fist to her mouth and fled the table.

Seventeen

Abigail needed a breath of fresh air. She left through the back of the house, passing the gun room, the still-room, the pantry and storerooms that smelled of molasses and drying herbs. The cook's boy directed her to the door, which opened out onto a screened porch. Beyond that, she found a kitchen garden at the rear of the house, where a few hardy vegetables struggled through the chill autumn weather. Following a path downhill between an arch of ancient rosebushes, she emerged into a more formal garden of lush smooth lawns littered with fallen leaves and bordered by espaliered fruit trees contorted into unnatural shapes.

She'd survived the ordeal of the oysters, but in more important matters she was filled with doubt. What had begun as a harmless, almost playful flirtation of letters had somehow careened out of control. Her correspondence with Lieutenant Butler had fast escalated to a romance of deception.

Abigail used to pride herself on her honesty. Now she engaged in falsehoods on a daily basis. For a person who had never been good at lying, she was learning from a master—Jamie Calhoun.

He pretended to be a man of simple needs—the desire to serve his country—but she was coming to realize that he possessed hidden complexities she could only begin to imagine. And why should she imagine them at all? He was nothing to her, a mere device, someone to consult about the baffling rituals of courtship, much like an encyclopedia or an oracle, perhaps. He would probably enjoy being considered an oracle.

At the bottom of the garden, not far from the wind-bitten shoreline, she spied a low wrought-iron fence forming a rectangular border around a cemetery plot.

Dried yellow grasses waved in the cold sea breeze, and thorny bushes struggled along the fence, bulbous crimson rose hips showing through the dying foliage. For the most part, the markers sat low in the grass and lacked ornamentation save for a cross or brief verse carved into the stone.

Drawn by curiosity, she entered the fenced area and walked between the sad monuments, scoured and pitted by the salt air. Carved into the headstones were the names of Calhouns through the ages, the earliest being Samuel Calhoun of Bristol, England, 1684. *He Was Seven Years a Sea Captain and Fathered Seven Sons and Seven Daughters...* No wonder the plot was so large.

She was half-afraid to visit the newer-looking graves, for she didn't like to think of Albion as a place of tragedy. Silly, she told herself. People died. It was all part of the mysterious circle of life.

Instinctively her sharp eyes flicked to the sky, but it was too early yet for stars. At Albion, Mrs. Calhoun had explained, they served supper early so they could talk late into the night.

"You all right, miss?"

Abigail twirled around, grasping the wrought-iron fence for balance. "Julius. You startled me."

The boy made no apology but came into the cemetery through the iron gate.

"I enjoyed the riding today," she said. "And I owe you a great deal of thanks. You're a fine teacher for a timid rider, Julius."

His slightly bashful smile further endeared him to her. "Glad to hear it, ma'am."

Abigail faced the rows of stone monuments. "I suppose you think this is a strange occupation, wandering amidst the headstones."

He hooked his thumbs into the pockets of his trousers. "I reckon. But I don't reckon the dead mind." He walked over to one of the less timeworn graves. "Lacey Beaumont Calhoun," he said, picking up a spray of purple asters. "She gets fresh flowers on her grave every Sunday, even in winter."

Beloved mother, cherished wife.... Abigail could see that she had died back in 1852 at the age of twenty-six. Yet her grave was tended like a shrine, years later.

"Someone must miss her very much," she said.

"Reckon so."

Sensing a deeper truth, she said, "I wonder who that could be. Do you know, Julius?"

"Some of the old folks used to whisper about it," he said. "They say my granddaddy tends her grave because he loved her and could never have her. On account of she was married to his cousin."

It sounded terribly tragic to Abigail, like an opera by Herr Wagner she'd gone to see at Ford's Theater last summer. Unrequited love, illicit desire, dying young—it had all happened to the Calhoun family.

Maybe that was the reason Jamie shied from emotional involvement, the reason he was so cynical about romance and indifferent about Albion.

"And who is your granddaddy?" she asked, confused.

"Mr. Charles Calhoun," said Julius matter-of-factly.

She shut her mouth to stifle a gasp. Charles Calhoun—Jamie's father—was this boy's grandfather.

Julius moved on to the newest monument of all, a squat fieldstone with a polished brass plaque, the earth around it covered by fallen leaves.

"And this here's for my daddy," the boy whispered, folding himself into a sitting position on the grass and brushing dry leaves from the base of the grave. "It's where he should be, anyways, but he ain't here. This marker's just for remembering." Taking out a small, hand-carved figure of a running horse, he set the token atop the stone. "Hi, Daddy," he said.

Abigail's throat stung with tears as she read the inscription on the brass plaque: *Noah Calhoun. Son of Charles Calhoun. Champion rider, beloved husband and father.*

So Julius was Jamie's nephew, she realized with a jolt.

"You must miss your father terribly," she said.

Julius nodded.

"I met your mother today," she told him. "Your uncle Jamie took me to the place on King's Creek."

"I aim to work it myself, soon's I turn sixteen."

Abigail felt a tingle of insight. The bottomlands around King's Creek would disappear if the proposed railroad expansion went through. The people there would be put off their land.

"He was starting up a horse farm of his own," Julius continued. "Would have turned it into the best in the state. Mama sent me back to Albion on account of..." He eyed her from beneath lowered lashes. "Well, here at Albion, they look after me real good."

Look after him, she thought in a fury, as though he were a piece of property, as his ancestors undoubtedly had been.

"What happened to your father, Julius?" she asked.

"He went on a horse-buying trip overseas. He and Uncle Jamie bought horses in Ireland, Spain, Morocco, Tunisia." Julius's eyes shone. "They always sent us special treasures. A silk scarf for my mama, a set of brass bells for me. Daddy said I'd get to go with him one day. But on the last trip, Uncle Jamie came home alone. He was real skinny, had a mess of whiskers and he smelled funny. Told my mama that Daddy died on the other side of the world. He was a real good man, my daddy, and I purely miss him."

A strong wind, redolent of the marshy air, rolled in from the east. Abigail watched a raft of sandpipers take flight to the east, and she stood in contemplative silence, aching for the boy whose father lay forgotten in some unknown land.

At last, she was beginning to understand Jamie Calhoun. He'd always maintained that he'd got himself elected to Congress simply because he was bored and it was what men of his class did to show their commitment to civic duty.

She knew better now.

Eighteen

Senator Cabot was sound asleep even before the side-wheeler *Larissa* cleared Chesapeake Bay and churned into the mouth of the Potomac River. The travelers had decided to return to town by the water route. Jamie had made his point about the railroad issue on the coach trip, so for now he chose comfort over utility. Helena and Professor Rowan were off somewhere as usual, undoubtedly misbehaving and loving every minute of it.

Abigail stood at the figured wrought-iron rail, watching the pattern of early-evening stars coming out over the bay. Emerging from one of the grand saloons of the riverboat, Jamie joined her at the rail but she hardly spared him a glance.

"Are you in a temper?" he asked her.

"What if I am?"

"Then I'd feel compelled to tease you out of it."

"Don't bother. It won't work."

"Why not?"

"You're the cause of it, that's why."

He laughed. "You'll have to do better than that. Your spirits are low, and I am the cause?"

"It's silly, isn't it? Makes you seem more important than you are. But since you asked, the answer is yes, I'm cross with you."

"Why? I thought a weekend in the country would please you. Didn't I bring you to a place so dark you could see all the stars?"

"Yes."

"And didn't I teach you to ride a horse?"

"Yes," she admitted again.

He moved close, pressing his shoulder to hers so that she couldn't ignore his warmth. "Didn't I teach you to kiss? Perhaps you need further study in that area."

"No." She sidled away from him. "I don't need anything more from you. Ever."

She could hear him counting under his breath. Then he said, "I've obviously missed something. Only yesterday we were the best of friends sharing a delightful holiday. You taught me about the stars and planets, and I taught you to ride and flirt."

"We're not friends, best or otherwise. A friend is someone who knows you. He shares himself, even the parts that are difficult to share. You keep too many secrets to be anyone's friend."

He spread his arms. "I've told you a great deal about myself. Brought you to Albion. Introduced you to my parents. Isn't that sharing?"

Somehow he cornered her again, pressing her between the rail and a wall of the upper saloon. She felt intimidated by his height, and uncomfortably aware of the undeniable tension between them. Yet the genuine bafflement in his face irritated her.

"You've told me—shown me—only the surface facts. I know as much about Galileo, and he's been dead for centuries. You've shown me nothing of what lies beneath the outer layer. I know you only as a man behind a handsome barrier of charm and urbane manners.''

He grinned at that. "You think me charming? Handsome? My, my—urbane? I never knew.''

"Don't get a big head about it. A handbag can be handsome. A Pekingese dog can be charming.'' In the light emanating from the saloon, she studied his eyes, noting their disturbing shade of gray. It was not a flat color, but a storm of hues from opaque coal to pale ice. "A muffin tin can be charming on the surface. But it has no more substantive virtue than a hollow shell.''

He threw back his head and guffawed. "A perfect observation.'' Then he grabbed her shoulders, and she was startled by a swift, unbidden reaction. "That's exactly it. I'm all surface charm, no substance beneath,'' he said, seeming not to notice her flushed face, the nervous way she gripped the rail.

Trying to slow her racing pulse, she studied those eyes again, searching the complicated facets of shadow and light. "That's what you want me to believe.''

"That's what is true. There's nothing more than you see before you now.'' He bent to an intimate angle, his lips dangerously close to hers.

Heavens, what was it about the man? About her? She lost all perspective when she was around him. Taking refuge in resentment, she pushed against his chest. "Don't insult my intelligence. You have a past. You have an inner life. Just because you refuse to speak of them doesn't mean they're nonexistent.''

He traced his finger over the pulse in her throat and

smiled when she flinched. He was taunting her by crowding close, touching her, reminding her of what they had done together under the stars. But he didn't kiss her now, only rubbed the pad of his thumb over her lower lip in a manner so outrageous that she froze.

"Believe me," he said, "I'm not that interesting."

She took a deep breath, then looked him in the eye to prove she wasn't afraid of him or intimidated by his nearness. "Why don't you let me be the judge of that?"

"I don't subject myself to anyone's judgment, honey. Not even yours."

Furious, she ducked under his arm, escaping the imprisoning posture. "Then we really don't have anything to talk about, do we?"

"All right. I confess, you have me confused. You wanted lessons in getting a man to notice you— namely, Boyd Butler III. Am I to understand you also want to be friends with me?"

"What if I did?"

"I'd tell you to aim higher." He moved close to her again, his presence as oppressive as the heavy atmosphere of the estuary. Taking her hands, he added, "You can do better."

"Maybe I can, maybe not. You won't reveal enough of yourself for me to see who you really are." In the silence that ensued, it occurred to her that he was like the stars that had been her passion for years. At first they seemed distant, mysterious, impossible to know. In time, she had come to know the stars as well as the dahlias in her garden. But unlike the stars, he was not revealing himself to her.

"Why do you stare at me like that?" he asked.

"I was thinking of the stars."

"Clearly I missed something."

"They used to be a great puzzle to me. But then I applied mathematics and logic, and I understand them now. I know their size and color and weight, their brightness and composition. And I know precisely where they are, even when they're invisible to me."

"You'll have to explain the relevance of that observation. Are you saying that if you study me using scientific methods, you'll come to know me?"

"Perhaps."

"As I said earlier, there's nothing—"

"Noah," she said, watching him closely. "Is he nothing?"

A dull red crept into his cheeks. "What about Noah?"

"Why don't you tell me? Tell me about your half brother."

His mouth hardened. "I suspect someone already has. Julius, I assume. He told you all there is to know."

"He told me what *he* knows. I'd rather hear the truth from your lips. I very much doubt your nephew can explain a man like you. Tell me, does your father keep him as a slave, or does he pay him a pittance for working at Albion?"

He shoved away from her on the deck. "You've got the wrong idea, Abby."

The intensity of his anger intrigued her. "Then enlighten me."

"I never liked being my mother's only son," Jamie said. "Never liked being the legitimate one."

"Why not?"

"I don't want to be the one they expect everything of."

That didn't surprise her. "Noah's mother was a slave?"

He nodded. "When my father was young and even more foolish than me, he had an adventure with a laundress at Albion. Our father was—is—a decent man, but he's careless. He's always had the bad judgment to love inappropriately. I think he did love Noah's mother, but it brought them nothing but grief."

"And a son."

"And a son," he admitted. "Eventually, my father gave Noah his name, although he failed to acknowledge his son until Noah was sixteen and didn't need him anymore."

"I don't think it's possible to ever stop needing a father," Abigail said.

Jamie dismissed the comment with a careless shrug of his shoulders. "Noah did fine without him. Which was just as well, because by then my father was too busy with his other love affairs."

Abigail remembered the fresh flowers on the headstone of Lacey Beaumont Calhoun, and a chill passed over her. Jamie seemed to be saying the Calhoun men were destined to suffer through tragic love affairs. She studied his face, searching the shadowed planes and angles for the boy he'd been, but finding only an impenetrable hardness. Had he known of his father's affairs? How had they affected him?

As though she'd asked her question aloud, he said, "So you see, when it comes to love, the men of my family are not inclined to loyalty."

"Loyalty isn't an inborn trait. Besides, you probably have more of Noah in you than your own father, and according to you, Noah was a good man. Julius knows that, too, but at his age I imagine he has questions. I know I did, about my mother. Yet my father would never speak of her.'' She refused to back down. ''You ought to be ashamed for not telling Julius more about the way his father died. You owe it to him, Jamie.''

He cut the air with his hand. ''You think that would help? You think Julius needs to know every detail of his father's death?''

''He deserves to know the truth.''

''Not this truth.''

''What happened?''

He hesitated. ''It's a long story, Abigail.''

''It's a long ride up the Potomac.''

Hands on hips, he gazed out at the dark water and a faraway look crept into his eyes. ''We were on a horse-buying trip in the Middle East, and there was trouble.'' Jamie swallowed, then spoke softly as though he'd forgotten she was there. ''I'll say no more—to you or to Julius. Suffice it to say I had a half brother who was twice the man I am. He died. It happens. It makes us curse God and doubt his existence when a good person dies before his time. But it happens far too often.''

She thought of her mother and couldn't dispute it. The bitterness in his voice was edged with a regret she'd felt all her life. Though the things he said were painful to hear, she didn't want to drop the subject. He was beginning to talk to her in a way he never had before.

Jamie folded his arms and faced the city lights, just coming into view from the deck. The Potomac formed a sweeping bay around which the capital was built. A mile-long wooden bridge connected Virginia and

Maryland; the Navy Yard, Arsenal and penitentiary stood sentry along the shore.

"Why do you say Noah was twice the man you are?" Abigail asked.

"Because he did things that mattered. Yeah, he was a jockey. He won more races than he lost, but there was more to him than that. He taught me to ride and shoot and fish. He taught me that laughter's a good way to deal with things and that to worship, all I needed to do was to look out at the world of nature."

Perhaps that was how Jamie had formed his reverence for the land, why he was willing to battle the powerful railroads to safeguard a part of Virginia.

"I wish I'd known your brother." She regarded Jamie with new eyes. "Noah's the reason you ran for the legislature and the reason you're committed to halting the railroad expansion."

"Your point being?"

"You don't want to be considered a good man, even though you are."

"Shouldn't you be saving all these admiring thoughts for your lieutenant?"

She scowled at him. "I'm capable of being friends with more than one sort of person."

"Trust me, I know. I've read your letters."

She hated herself for having let him. Why had she given him that glimpse of her heart? It was like the rabbit turning belly up to the wolf.

"You of all people shouldn't criticize me for having feelings of admiration. You encouraged me to do so," she reminded him. He made her inexpressibly sad, and the feeling surprised her. Why should she feel a thing on behalf of Jamie Calhoun? They had formed this alliance for the purpose of snaring her a husband and winning Jamie the support of a powerful senator. That left no room for caring.

"Well," she said, trying not to seem flustered, "one thing is certain, my father is impressed with you and your family."

"Then the holiday was a success. Abby, don't mistake me for a man with a conscience. I came here with an agenda, and I'll do what I have to do in order to accomplish it."

"Including befriending Senator Cabot's homely daughter?"

He laughed. "Touché, darling."

She opened her mouth to respond, but he caught her chin in his hand and closed it, running his thumb lightly along her jawline with insolent familiarity. "You're very close to winning your lieutenant," he said. "That's what you should think about rather than decrying my low character, which is what you were about to do."

She jerked away. "You think this is a game to be won or lost," she said. "I love him. Can you understand that?"

"Love." He gave an unpleasant laugh. "You think you love Butler because he poses no threat to your well-ordered little world. He demands nothing of you beyond the occasional poetic letter. So long as he stays out of your reach, you won't have to risk yourself."

She glared at him. "How dare you say these things?"

"Because no one else will. Face it, Abby, you're afraid of risk. Pining away for Boyd Butler is like loving a star. You don't have to put yourself in the position of being vulnerable. Have you ever wondered what would happen if you dared to take a chance?''

"I take risks," she retorted. Why couldn't he see that? Why didn't he understand the ridicule she'd endured because of her clumsiness, her love of the stars? "Didn't I learn to ride a horse?"

"Then risk your heart," he snapped.

"As you've risked yours?" she demanded.

He ignored—or avoided—the question. ''You want to win your father's esteem, but nothing you've ever done in your life has garnered more than passing admiration from him. When you stop trying so hard, you might succeed.''

"Or fail."

They argued back and forth as the side-wheeler docked, then sat in stony silence all the way back to Georgetown. Helena chattered blithely away, while Professor Rowan listened with helpless admiration.

When they arrived at Dumbarton Street, Jamie insisted on helping the porters bring in the luggage, lingering to confer with Abigail's father on the brick walk between their two houses. Now that Father had seen for himself how wealthy the Calhouns were, he regarded Jamie with expansive approval and a growing openness to his position on the railroad issue.

Abigail checked the thought. She was becoming as cynical as Jamie.

As she watched him and her father talking together in a circle of misty gaslight, Abigail realized she was becoming increasingly confused by her feelings. Her goal was to attract Lieutenant Butler, yet when she drifted into daydreams, it was Jamie's face she saw, his laughing eyes and smiling mouth, his skilled hands reaching for her as he taught her to dance, to accept a man's compliment, to feel his kiss upon her cheek, her lips.

It was all so confusing, having pledged her heart to one man while being tutored by another. She wished she could talk to someone about it. To her dismay, she realized she wanted to tell Jamie Calhoun. He was infuriating, brutally frank, rude, licentious, sarcastic and disrespectful. He claimed he was only using her to maintain ties with her father. But he was the best friend she had.

He would mock her, telling her the feelings he provoked were the result of cunning and skill, not purehearted affection. According to Jamie, courtship was every bit as precise a science as astronomy. When its principles were applied properly, it was unfailingly effective.

Abigail had to acknowledge—in her mind if not in her heart—that she was the willing victim of a gifted practitioner, a mouse in a laboratory, as much an object of empirical study as Socrates in his glass maze.

Forgotten amid the noisy activity, she followed the small group into the lower foyer. Her father issued directives to the porters, then rang for Dolly to come help. Helena and the professor stood whispering together, their gazes locked in an intimate way that betrayed their secret—to Abigail, at least. The porters jostled past with the luggage, and she stepped out of the way, pressing herself back against the hall table.

Almost without thinking, she picked up a stack of cards and envelopes from the silver tray. The first was a note from Madame Broussard. The modiste had finished her dresses and was ready for the final fitting.

Most of the mail was for her father, and she set it

aside. Then she picked up the last envelope, opened it and gasped.

No one heard her. No one but Jamie, who seemed almost eerily aware of her moods. He thought nothing of intruding on her private thoughts.

"What is it?" he asked.

She didn't answer because she couldn't speak. But he must have read her thoughts in her wide eyes and blushing cheeks. With a wicked grin, he plucked the letter from her and scanned it. "My, my," he said. "The plot thickens. Prince Charming is coming to see his lady love."

Part Three

Nothing is so good as it seems beforehand.
                                    —George Eliot

Nineteen

The next day dawned a miserable charcoal gray, the skies leaking a cold mist. Undeterred by the inclement weather, Abigail held a broad black silk umbrella aloft and argued with Jamie all the way to the dress shop on M Street. "We must tell Lieutenant Butler not to come."

"Isn't that what you've wanted all along? For him to come courting?"

"Yes, but he's coming to court Helena."

Jamie dismissed the problem with an impatient wave of his hand. "When he sees you, he'll forget he ever met your sister."

"That's preposterous. No man can be that stupid."

"Trust me, any man can be that stupid. A glimpse of ankle, an inch of cleavage can reduce a scholar to a blithering idiot."

His graphic language made her blush, and she ducked her head. He had the unique ability to hurt her in subtle ways. She didn't know why she put up with it.

"This is what our entire association has been about, Abby," he said, apparently unaware of her mood.

"You challenged me to make you irresistible to Lieutenant Butler. Don't get cold feet now."

The day dimmed and the mist thickened. She could barely make out the terraced slopes of Georgetown leading down to the gentle curve of the Potomac. Far in the distance loomed the Navy Yard. The ghostly profile of the Arsenal on the riverbank to the south and east shimmered against the weeping sky. Sometimes Lieutenant Butler came down from Annapolis to conduct official business there. Unless she could find a way to stop him, he would soon have business right here in Georgetown.

"This is madness," she said, balking even as Jamie pulled her into the elegant shop. "You can't simply disguise me as my sister."

"Who said anything about a disguise?" asked Madame Broussard, bustling forward to greet them. "My purpose is to bring out your natural attributes, not hide them."

"But—"

The modiste ignored her as she drew her through the curtained doorway, leaving Jamie to fan the umbrella dry in front of the small stove in the salon. Madame scarcely stopped for breath as she issued instructions to her assistants in French. They brought out the dresses for the final alterations, but Abigail was too distraught to appreciate the fine jewel tones of the sumptuous fabrics, or the simple elegance of the accoutrements Madame's staff had ordered—hats and shawls, beaded reticules and lovely swanskin fans.

Though her understanding of French was only adequate, Abigail realized the dressmakers were once again discussing the woeful extent of her imperfections in great detail. She knew very well what her defects were, and did not need to hear them enumerated in rapid, euphonious French.

She marched to the door. "I'm going home now," she announced. "Madame, thank you for your time. The dresses are lovely. But no matter how attractive the dress, I will still have..." She paused, translating what she had overheard. "'Unfortunate hair and sallow skin.'"

The modiste planted herself in Abigail's path. "I am blunt. I do not apologize, and you are a fool to take offense. I merely speak the truth. You do have unfortunate hair. It is too long and badly cut. Whoever styles your hair does not know you, or care what you look like."

"I do my own hair," Abigail said.

"Ah. *Voilà.* You see? Solange will take care of the hair for you, *toute de suite.*" She summoned one of her assistants, a tall, thin girl with bony cheekbones and solemn eyes. "She is an artist with the scissors."

"I don't care to have my hair cut."

Madame refused to budge. "You have no sense of style. Surely you cannot deny that."

"I never pretended to be stylish."

"Like most American women, you do not understand style. It does not mean parading yourself around in the latest fashion, but simply presenting your very best self to the world. Contrary to your belief, this has absolutely nothing to do with physical attributes. Mademoiselle, it must be said. You have no self-confidence, and you need that far more than you need my dresses. It makes all the difference in the world. Did your mother never tell you—"

"My mother died on the day of my birth."

The dressmaker's businesslike façade never faltered. "For that, I am deeply sorry. *Tiens,* in the matter of style, I will play the part of the mother."

"Thank you, but I don't need—"

"Of course you do. Everyone needs a mother. I cannot give you all your mother could, but I will do my best to see that you make use of your advantages rather than hiding them. *Sacre bleu,* those eyes are stunning, yet you keep your gaze averted and let your hair fall over them. You have a face filled with intelligence and character, but you keep your brow knit with worry all the time. You wear this Gothic prison of a dress in the most terrible shade of pea green imaginable. This is all easily changed, and your attitude will change as well. A woman with great style faces the world differently. You'll see."

Abigail fidgeted through each step of the fitting and flatly refused to let Solange near her with the scissors. They wanted to change everything about her. But if they did that, how would she know who she was anymore?

Face it, Abby, you're afraid of risk. Jamie's words infested her thoughts. Perhaps he was right, but that didn't mean she could do anything about it.

"Madame, I'm sorry, but I cannot be what you want me to be."

"Taisez-vous." Madame Broussard lost patience with her. "You leave me with no choice. We must call at your home tomorrow for the final fitting." That decided, the dressmaker escorted her to the front of the salon, where Jamie waited. "I will bring my assistants around in the morning," she explained to him. "Perhaps Mademoiselle will be more amenable to a fitting at home."

"Perfect," said Jamie.

"Out of the question," said Abigail.

"Until tomorrow, then," said Madame Broussard.

"I have other plans—"

"Don't be a baby," Jamie said as he accompanied her back to Dumbarton Street. "Cowardice doesn't become you."

"Lying to a naval officer is not like me," she pointed out. "It's probably illegal, treason or something. Yet you've made me do it."

He roared with laughter. "Abby, if I had the power to *make* you do something, why the hell would I make you love another man?"

Lying awake that night, Abigail turned his remark over and over in her mind, but couldn't quite deduce what he'd meant by it. Nothing, probably. He prided himself on being an unsentimental man who regarded love and romance as baseless illusions. If she confessed that sometimes she felt her friendship with him deepening, he would probably laugh even harder.

As she and Dolly worked side by side in the kitchen the next morning, laying out the breakfast tea, Abigail had a mad urge to confess all to the housekeeper who had run the Cabot household single-handedly for two decades.

"I've done an awful, awful thing, Dolly," she blurted out, hugging the Wedgwood teapot to her chest.

"Have you, now?" Dolly never paused in rolling out the biscuit dough. Her generous arms jiggled with the motion.

"Yes. I am horrible," she said. "I've always been

horrible. And I'm beginning to think I shall always be horrible.''

"I'd argue with that," Dolly said, "but I gave up arguing with you years ago. Would you like to tell me about this horrible thing?''

"It's a very great secret, and I shouldn't even be telling you, but it's just so awful that I can scarcely live with myself.''

"This would be the correspondence you're carrying on with Lieutenant Butler, wouldn't it?" Weary wisdom shone from her round, pleasant face.

Abigail nearly dropped the teapot. "You know? Who else knows?''

Dolly cut a half-dozen sharp circles out of the dough. "Just myself, dearie, no need to worry.''

"I've made a mess of things, haven't I?''

"Heavens, no. Your sister needs a husband to look after her, and why not the lieutenant? You've done your part in keeping his interest trained on Miss Helena. I do love the girl dearly, and she's as lovely as the summer sun, but after the first flush of romance, a man looks for more than a pretty face. It's a fact that she's not the most brilliant conversationalist. And that, mind you, is what makes a marriage." She smiled in fond remembrance. "My husband of blessed memory used to listen to me for hours on end. He let me talk on and on...''

So Dolly didn't understand everything. Only Jamie Calhoun knew Abigail had carried on the correspondence not because she sought a suitor for Helena but because she herself was in love with Lieutenant Butler.

"I must send him an urgent message," she said, panic coming on strong again. "I will tell him that he must never visit or even think of Miss Cabot ever again. Yes, that is precisely what I—''

"Abigail." Her father came into the kitchen, beaming with stellar radiance. "My dear girl, why didn't you tell me?"

Startled, she set down the teapot and smoothed her hands down over her apron. Father never looked at her like this, never called her his dear girl. Then she noticed the letter in his hand, and her stomach turned over. The seal of Annapolis was embossed at the top of the page. Good heavens. Lieutenant Butler had written to Father.

Abigail swallowed hard, finding her voice. "Sir, I can explain. I—"

"You needn't, Abigail. I understand completely, and I can't tell you how much it means to me. I'm so proud of you."

"See? I told you there was no need to worry." Dolly wiped her floury hands with a tea towel and put the kettle on.

"I didn't realize you had a letter from him, Father," Abigail said. Oh, this was bad. This had gone too far. She felt as though she were drowning in quicksand.

"Mr. Calhoun told me what you've been doing."

"He did?" I'll kill him, she thought. I will shoot him point-blank in the heart.

"Yes, he said you've been the active party in this courtship between Lieutenant Butler and your sister. He claims it's all your doing. My clever, clever girl. What would I do without you?"

She nearly melted from the warmth emanating from him, she teetered on the verge of realizing a cherished dream, something she had wanted since be-

fore she was even old enough to know what it was
or why she wanted it.

True, she dreamed of a romance with Boyd Butler,
but in her heart, she was greedy for even more than
that.

Father's rare smile had a magical effect on her, for
instead of rushing to instruct Lieutenant Butler not to
call on them, she heard herself say, "Father, I'm so
glad you're pleased."

"It's not just me," he said. "The entire nation
owes you a debt of thanks."

Even in her desperation, she laughed incredulously.
Finding the humor in an outrageous situation was a
skill she'd learned from Jamie Calhoun. "Isn't that a
bit extreme?"

"Not in the least. The support of the vice president
is critical to my agenda in the Senate. He was wa-
vering, falling into the camp of the anti-Reformists.
But once we're related by marriage, he'll stand with
me on the issues that matter so greatly to our nation."

Marriage. The very thought made her mouth go
dry. Deep within her fear and confusion, she also
faced silent questions about her father. Which did he
want, marriage for his daughter or a political alliance
for himself? She didn't like to think of him stooping
to tricks like any politician.

He swept away her doubts by making the uncommon gesture of embracing her, kissing her cheek. He
smelled of bay rum and peppermint, evoking the
sweetest moments of her childhood.

His delight and confidence in her, his show of affection, caused the entire world to change color.
"Your mother would be as proud as I am to see you

looking after your elder sister's welfare. How I wish she had lived to see this day.''

''I wish she'd lived, period,'' Abigail said, touching her cheek where he had kissed her. Unable to abide the stifling kitchen any longer, she excused herself and hurried upstairs. It was Helena she needed to speak with about this, not Dolly or Father.

Helena was the one who would determine the outcome of this fiasco, after all.

Abigail pushed open the door to her sister's room. With a hasty motion, Helena slid a sheet of foolscap paper under the skirt of the dressing table with an almost furtive movement. Taking up her hairbrush, she counted the strokes. ''Forty-seven, forty-eight, forty-nine...'' Then Helena caught her eye in the mirror. ''Yes?'' she asked. ''What is it, Abigail?''

''Breakfast will be ready soon.''

''Excellent. I'll join you shortly.''

Abigail hesitated, unsure of what she wanted to say. Helena kept raking at her hair, counting under her breath.

''Helena, are you angry about something?'' Abigail asked.

''No, of course not.'' Dropping the brush, she stood and paced the small area behind the dressing table. ''Actually, I am. Michael—I mean, Professor Rowan has been absolutely beastly to me ever since we returned from our weekend in the country, and I'm thoroughly exasperated with him. What should I do, Abigail? I don't know what to do.''

''You're asking me?'' Abigail couldn't help herself. She laughed. ''We are a sorry lot, we two, aren't we? I don't mean to make light of this but I can't advise you on matters of the heart, Helena. I'm far more confused than you are.''

Helena sank down on the end of the bed. ''How I wish Mama were alive. She'd know what to do.''

Helena was right—a mother advised her daughters on tender affairs, but lacking a mother, the sisters had blundered their way into a sticky web of intrigue and forbidden adventure. They had wandered into places better avoided, places a mother would guide them away from.

''Do you remember anything about her?'' Abigail asked, hungry for the least little detail. It was not the first time she'd asked, but Helena usually avoided speaking of their mother. ''Anything at all?''

Helena released a long, sad sigh. ''I always thought that was impossible, for I was only three when she died. But sometimes—no, it's silly.'' She picked at the tapestry counterpane that lay over the bed.

''What?'' Intrigued, Abigail sat down beside her. ''Tell me. You must tell me.''

''All right, but you must promise not to laugh. The fact is, Abigail, sometimes I think I can hear Mama's voice, singing a little song.'' She hummed off-key, but even so, Abigail felt an eerie familiarity with the tune. She could not remember ever hearing it, yet a tingling awareness shot down her spine.

''Of course,'' Helena went on, ''that could have been one of the nurses or nannies Papa hired.''

''No. It was our mother. I'm sure of it.''

''How can you be sure?''

''I just know.''

''So do I,'' Helena agreed. ''When she sang, she used to touch me, here.'' She reached out, the back of her hand grazing Abigail's cheek. ''And there was…a smell. Flowers, but something more. A breath of flowers and something warm and soft. I cannot really describe it, but the memory of that perfume is very powerful.''

Abigail studied her sister with both compassion and envy. Compassion, because Helena had been old enough when their mother died to feel the loss. And envy, because Helena remembered anything at all.

Father never spoke of their mother except in the most general terms, so what little Abigail knew was gleaned from gazing at formal portraits, an entry or two scribbled in a social diary. Beatrice Gavin had been a famous debutante in her day, and she'd married the most eligible man in Washington. She'd been stunningly beautiful. Helena looked exactly like her. People were always remarking on it, and the resemblance shone from the photographs and from the gilt-framed portrait in the winter parlor.

''That's lovely,'' Abigail said wistfully. ''Thank you for telling me.''

''It's not much, I'm afraid.'' Helena peered at Abigail. ''Is something the matter? You look worried.''

Abigail took a deep breath. ''Lieutenant Butler is coming to call this afternoon.''

Helena went to the dressing table and resumed brushing her hair. ''Who? Butler…oh, him. The one who's been writing you all those letters. He danced with me at Nancy Wilkes's wedding.''

Part of Abigail wanted to shake the willful forgetfulness from her sister. How could Helena fail to remember Lieutenant Butler, surely the finest young man in the navy, possibly in the universe?

Yet another part softened with relief. It seemed Jamie Calhoun was right after all. If the impossible did

happen, and Abigail did manage to win the lieutenant's favor, Helena would not begrudge her the attention. She shifted on the edge of the bed. "I have a
confession to make."

Helena slowed the strokes of her hairbrush. "You
never do anything wrong. What could you possibly
have to confess?"

"You might recall that the day after the wedding
Lieutenant Butler wrote, hoping to strike up a correspondence."

"I do remember." Helena smiled. "And you were
kind enough to send a letter back to him, and Papa
was so pleased with everything. You're always so
good about that, Abigail."

"Yes, well, I'm afraid I was not so good this time.
Or maybe I was a little too good at it."

Helena's forehead puckered and she cocked her
head to one side. "What do you mean? Didn't you
say the correspondence went well?"

"I did." Abigail dug her hands into her knees.
"But I'm afraid I didn't quite...make it clear that you
considered this a passing flirtation. In fact, I suppose
you could say I encouraged him to believe his passion
was reciprocated."

"Why on earth would you do a thing like that?"

Abigail's cheeks burned. She stared at the floor and
secretly thought, Because I love him. I couldn't bear
to see him hurt.

"I did it for Papa," she stated, settling for a half
truth. "Mr. Calhoun started it, actually, by posting a
letter that—well, it said far too much."

Helena smiled fondly. "Ah, Abigail. When most
people put in two cents' worth of effort, you put in
four."

"I never meant for anyone to see that letter. I'd never have mailed such a personal note."

"Why would Mr. Calhoun do a thing like that?"

"He's a careless, manipulative man with a perverse sense of humor. He thought it would be a good way to impress Father by helping to attract the perfect suitor. Of course, I should have stopped it cold."

"And you didn't. You continued this romance of letters between me and Lieutenant Barnes."

"Butler."

"And now he's coming to see you in person."

"Yes. Er, no. He's coming to see *you*, Helena, remember?"

"Oh, Abigail."

"There's more."

"More?"

She nodded miserably. "The correspondence grew very...intense. Our feelings—that is, your feelings for each other have deepened."

"But that is wonderful! Father will be so—"

"Proud. He is. He already told me. But it gets worse. Lieutenant Butler's already written to Father as well."

"Then why do you look so glum, Abigail?"

"Because he's coming to propose to you."

Helena's face went ashen. "Good God. Oh, Abigail. How could you?" She drew the brush through her hair in nervous strokes, the coppery locks taking on a rich gleam.

Abigail felt miserable. "It's not my finest moment, is it?"

The strokes slowed to a thoughtful pace, and Helena said, "Well, perhaps you've gone too far with this, but it might work out. Are you certain of his intentions?''

With a shaking hand, Abigail took a folded note from the pocket of her apron. ''His writing is so touching and beautiful. Listen to this. 'Your letter is a treasure more precious than gold. I carry it tucked in a place next to my heart, letting its very essence flow into me. I beg you, write again, dearest angel, and it will be as springtime after gray winter....' How could I not reply to that, Helena?''

She swiveled around on the low stool. ''Abigail.''

''Yes?''

''You outdo yourself in all things. You always have. Even when it comes to getting into trouble, you surpass the experts.''

''Do I?''

''You never do anything halfway.''

''I don't.'' Her stomach rolled with anger and misery and shame.

''So what do you suppose is going to happen when he comes to call?''

''Actually, I thought you would meet with him.''

''Perhaps I shall, then. And I'll hear what he has to say, and Papa will still be pleased. But this deception must stop.''

''I agree.'' How on earth had she let this happen? ''You can tell him—''

''No, you must tell him. You got yourself into this mess, you can get yourself out of it.''

''You're the one who told me to write to him in the first place,'' Abigail protested.

''I certainly didn't mean for you to take things this far,'' Helena said.

Abigail glared at her sister, feeling a terrible shift

in the foundation of their relationship. They had col-
luded for years, been allies through many adventures.
This was playing out like a bad farce, except it involved people who weren't play-acting at all. This
would change lives.

"You're right, of course. There's only one possible
way to deal with this. I must tell Lieutenant Butler
the truth, and suffer the consequences." Grasping the
bedpost, she stood up and forced a smile. "They say
confession is good for the soul. After this, my soul
will be very healthy indeed."

Twenty

Helena Cabot slapped the brass doorknocker of Michael Rowan's house three times, then barged in before anyone answered her summons. She was in no mood to be kept waiting. She hadn't even been able to eat her breakfast, fretting about the impending visit, and had worked herself into a state of extreme agitation.

She had a matter of importance to discuss with Michael, but first she sought out Jamie Calhoun. She found him in the downstairs parlor, bent over his work. Papers littered the desk in front of him. No one but Helena could detect the change in his expression. She had an unusual sensitivity to nuance and mood, and she could tell instantly he would have preferred the other Miss Cabot.

"I swear, we have the prettiest neighbors in Georgetown," he said in a jovial voice, its rich Tidewater accent flowing smoothly through the words.

"You are in a world of trouble, sir," she said.

"I beg your pardon."

"That won't be necessary. But you should be on your knees, begging Abigail's forgiveness."

"And for which transgression would that be? There are so many to choose from."

"You made a fool of her, encouraging her to carry on a courtship with Boyd Butler in my name. You've made fools of us all."

"Love does that. Which is why I avoid it at all costs. But you're forgetting one thing, Miss Helena."

"What's that?"

"Abby's happy. She's enjoying this."

Helena considered her sister's mood this autumn, and she had to admit he was right. The scoundrel. Since invading Abigail's life, he had made a difference. Lately she hummed while toiling over her calculations, and her eyes, which had always been beautiful, sparkled with a special light. Once, Helena had even caught her practicing curtsies and dance steps in front of her bedroom mirror when she thought no one was watching. She'd fluttered an invisible fan and laughed into the mirror. Abigail had never been happier. Still, that new happiness was founded on lies and manipulation.

"She's not happy now." Helena hesitated. "Lieutenant Barnes—"

"Butler," he corrected her.

"—is coming to see me, and Papa expects me to marry him. You've made a mess of things, and she'll humiliate herself in front of the man who's been the dupe in all of this. But I don't suppose you care one whit about that."

He corked the inkwell on the desk, leaned back in his chair and clasped his hands behind his head. All Virginia insolence and privilege, he folded his arms and sent her a slow smile. "Sure I care, my dear. I've encouraged Abigail to find a new way to view herself, a healthier way. She's taken her head out of the stars for once. She faces the world with a smile. How bad is that?''

''Good glory,'' she said, peering at him. ''You love her.''

Calhoun threw back his head and guffawed, but his mirth didn't last as she fixed him with a lethal glare. Sobering, he said, ''Sorry, but you're wrong. I don't love like that. It's not something I want or need.''

He was clearly lying, even to himself, but like all men, including Michael, he was as dense as an unexplored wilderness.

Yet Helena had no inclination to probe into the secrets of Jamie Calhoun's heart. It was her sister who concerned her. ''Here is what you must do. You will stand with Abigail when she tells the lieutenant that you cooked up this silly romance just to impress Papa. And now *I* shall have to entertain a marriage proposal.''

''That should be entertaining indeed.''

''Mr. Calhoun, you will admit your part in the deception and apologize to them both. And then you will leave this place, never to return.''

He waited calmly through her diatribe, then asked, ''Are you finished?''

''For the moment.''

''I can see you care about your sister, but you're smothering her. Not to mention blinding yourself to her true feelings.''

''But I—''

He held up a hand. ''You said you were finished. Look, any fool can see the way it stands for the Cabot women. The smart one and the pretty one. It's probably been said so often that you and Abigail have come to believe it. Such an oversimplification should be an insult to you both.''

She found herself listening to him as the knowledge tingled through her. The rogue was correct, in this at least. "Go and find my sister, Mr. Calhoun, and we'll think about forgiving you. I must go find Michael now.''

Michael met her on the landing halfway up the stairs. He said nothing, but pressed her against the wall and kissed her swiftly and hard. Almost against her will, her fists grasped the front of his wrinkled shirt as she drank him in—the heat and lust, the explosion of emotion that flared between them each time they were together.

She was breathless by the time he eased up, and she nearly forgot her purpose. He stared wickedly down at her. "Miss Cabot," he said with mock formality. "What a surprise. May I offer you a cup of tea? A glass of cider? An hour or two of illicit sexual relations?''

"You are naughty, and I do like that about you.''

"I'm worse than naughty. I'm ruining your reputation.''

"Which I invited you to do." She slipped from his embrace and continued up the stairs. "But I've just remembered something. I'm cross with you.''

She nearly laughed at the flicker of panic in his eyes. Their love was new; they were unsure of each other and he had still not quite assimilated the fact that she wanted him and no other. He considered himself a lowly academic, and an unlikely match for Miss Helena Cabot. That was one of many reasons it was so delicious being his lover.

He buried his face in the curve of her neck. "Good. I'm cross with you, too."

She yearned to melt into mindless passion with him, to let the world fall away, but this morning that was impossible. The world was closing in.

"I must speak to you," she said, "about our future."

The expression on his face caused her heart to speed up in alarm. "If you'd like to visit tonight—"

"I don't mean tonight. I mean the rest of our lives."

"Don't be tedious, Helena."

She flinched at his mocking tone. "When two people love each other, it's natural to consider the future."

He paced like a caged bear. "Helena, you know better than that. You've got it wrong. I don't love you in that way. I never will."

Her heart sank to the floor, but she didn't move a muscle. "You don't mean that."

"It's what I've told you from the start, my pet. We're ill suited, mismatched entirely—the penniless scholar and the society belle. You could never be happy, defying your father. His disapproval would sour even the sweetest of romances."

His perception startled her. Perhaps he wasn't as absent-minded—or endearing—as she'd thought. Everyone believed she belonged with someone who had the looks and status of a Boyd Butler or a Troy Barnes. But Michael had taught her to seek the soul beneath the surface.

A terrible, wonderful notion had lately occurred to her, and it was time to tell him. "What if I'm with child?"

He froze, and then seemed to thaw himself out with the anger burning in his eyes. "Ah, pet. Don't try to snare me in that old trap. It won't work. You wouldn't want it to, anyway. I'm not cut out to be anyone's husband, let alone a father. I told you that from the start, too."

"But—"

"Anyway, you're not with child." He spoke with a certainty she wished she could share. "You should be with a man the senator approves of, someone like Senator Barnes—"

"Or Boyd Butler? He's coming to court me today." She couldn't keep the tremor from her voice when she added, "Tell me to reject him and I will. I swear. Just say the word."

"I should have told you it would end this way, but I thought you knew." He crossed his arms in a stance that emanated anger.

She didn't bat an eyelash, though his words struck hard, inflicting an emotional pain that took her breath away. Michael would never marry her, not even now that she'd told him her suspicion about the baby. All her life she'd rebelled against convention, but if a new life truly grew inside her, it changed the path she must walk. Perhaps she would have to accept the lieutenant after all. Perhaps she would have to do the right thing, even if it meant surrendering her soul, sentencing herself to a life of bleak servitude.

"I did know," she lied.

"That's good. You have a lot more sense than people give you credit for." He drew her against him just for a moment. But in that moment she remembered the hours of ecstasy she'd found in his arms, the sense that at long last she'd discovered her place in the world.

"Michael," she whispered. "I wish—"

"No, you don't," he interrupted. "Helena, you and I—we're only good at one thing." He pulled back, dropped a kiss on her forehead. "Go pretty yourself up, if that wouldn't be gilding the lily. Find a man who'll give you the world."

"What would I ever do with that?" she asked, moistening her lips to give him a brazen suggestion of what he was giving up. An inner voice screamed in protest, but he would never know. "I'll see myself out. Oh dear, that would make *two* things I'm good at."

She found Mr. Calhoun in the foyer downstairs, watching expectantly out the window.

"All settled with the professor?" he asked jovially.

She took a long, deep breath to steady herself. "As far as he's concerned."

Outside in the street, a whistle sounded. A delivery van and a hansom cab rolled up to the curb. Blinking back tears, Helena was amazed when she saw who exited the cab.

"That's Madame Broussard," she said.

"You recognize her?"

"Everyone on the continent recognizes her. She's the most famous dressmaker in America. But she told me she couldn't schedule a fitting for months!"

"This is for your sister."

"*Abigail?* I've been trying for years to interest her in fashion, but she never listens to me." She turned to him, and understanding dawned. Perhaps he knew Abigail better than anyone at all; perhaps she was doing Abigail a disservice, assuming her sister was content with her observatory and her telescope and her star charts. "You did this, didn't you?"

"I'm here to serve the people of Virginia."

"Good glory." Although she wanted to collapse in pain and confusion, her heartbreak would have to wait. Brushing past him, she hurried outside. "You might just be smarter than I thought."

Like a candidate awaiting election results, Jamie Calhoun paced the sitting room on the main floor of the Cabot household. Beyond a closed door, Madame Broussard spoke in her bossy voice. He heard the sisters exclaiming, occasionally even giggling. That was a good sign. Maybe this would work out after all.

Helena had almost ruined the plan and forced Jamie to reveal Abigail's secret admiration for the lieutenant. It had been a near thing, but Jamie convinced her to allow the visit to proceed. In fact, Helena just might be the key to making it work, for her troubled love affair with Rowan made her an unlikely match for anyone—except the professor.

Jamie tried to figure out why the success of Abigail's romance had become so important to him. Why must he be so relentless in getting Boyd Butler to fall in love with the little wren who'd worshiped him from afar for so many years?

At first, Jamie's sole purpose had been to ingratiate himself to the most powerful senator in Congress. But as he came to know Abigail, to understand her hopes and dreams, his ambitions had broadened. He wanted to see her happy. He had no idea why.

Good glory, you love her. Helena had made the pronouncement with naive conviction. It was laughable, and he had laughed. Yet even in the midst of his self-mockery, he'd felt an unexpected stab of yearning. There were empty, windswept places inside him, scoured by distrust and betrayal. When he was young and foolish, he had loved without caution, at a cost he could never, ever repay.

No, his commitment to Abigail Cabot came from a different place inside him. He wanted to help Abigail win her heart's desire. Success would never fill the emptiness, but Jamie had stopped hoping for that long ago. Redemption was not a piece of legislative business, nor was it a woman's contentment. But it was all he could expect.

The sounds of women dressing and laughing, perfuming themselves and doing their hair brought back memories of a distant place and time, when a golden haze of happiness had surrounded him, when he'd given his soul to an Arab princess, never thinking of the consequences until it was too late.

The noise in the adjacent room reached a crescendo, and at last the door opened. Every bone, muscle and nerve in his body tensed.

Madame came out first, an officious look on her face, a measuring tape draped around her neck. "She was a challenge," Madame said in French. "And she tested all my skills, not to mention my patience." Then she winked at him. "But I prevailed, of course, I always do. We shall see ourselves out." Accompanied by her assistants, she sent him a regal nod and led the way down the stairs.

Then came Helena, dabbing tears from her flawless cheeks.

Jamie's heart sank. Apparently Madame's best efforts weren't enough.

"Don't look at me like that," Helena whispered. "These are tears of happiness, you dolt."

Then, on a waft of floral perfume, Abigail stepped into the room, and Jamie could have sworn he felt the earth shift.

He'd always suspected her intense, unusual looks had been camouflaged by frowsy hair and weedy garments. He'd hoped Madame's skill would be like that of the gem cutter's art with a rough jewel, finding the hidden facets of beauty and fire. But never, not in his wildest flights of fancy, had he anticipated a transformation as dramatic as the one he witnessed now.

Madame Broussard had waved a magic wand and brought all of Abigail's unseen beauties to the surface, making use of every possible attribute. The careless brown braid was now a shining coronet atop her head. A vibrant wine-colored dress infused her skin with radiance, and Madame had done something to her eyes and mouth, adding lush color to her lips and bringing out the deep midnight glow of her eyes.

My God. She had a neck. And it was a lovely neck, rising from an artful décolletage. She had a waist, too, and shoulders of the sort that made him ache to touch her, to see if she was as velvety soft as she looked.

But the biggest change of all was in her face. She wore an expression of self-confidence, barely tinged with amazement.

"I won't say a word," he announced as he held out a hand, palm up.

"Why not?" She placed her hand in his, and he had to resist the urge to lift it to his lips. Her eyes had always been incredible, but now they looked even more compelling, those wide, intense eyes that saw stars. God, he could drown in them.

"Because if I were to say anything now, it would
be so insufficient and self-congratulatory that you'd
smack me."

"I would?"

"Yes. I have the urge to take credit for this."

"Fine. Then I'll accept your silence."

Butler is done for, thought Jamie. He's calf's-foot
jelly. Even a navy man would not be too dense to see
what Abigail Cabot was. Jamie would pound Butler
silly if he failed to fall to his knees before this
woman.

"Oh, look," Helena exclaimed, standing at the
window and holding the drape aside. "He's here."
She turned to regard her sister with nervous eyes.
"Oh, Abigail, he has a coach-and-four. And he's in
dress uniform. Come see. Don't you want to come
see?"

The glow faded from her face, draining away along
with her self-confidence. "I can't."

"But you wrote all of those letters just to get him
to come courting."

Abigail smiled a bit sadly, a bit mysteriously.
Standing in the doorway of the sitting room, she resembled a Pre-Raphaelite portrait, dappled by shadow
and light. The way her gaze lingered on Jamie made
him chafe as though the room had grown too warm.

"It can't work," she said softly, "even though, for
a time, it was fun to pretend."

"He's coming because of the letters." Helena
dropped the curtain in irritation and turned to her sister. "The moment I open my mouth, he'll know I
couldn't have written those brilliant, poetic letters. It's
your job to tell him the truth, not mine. We discussed
the matter this morning. Now that you're wearing a

new dress, you have no excuse for being bashful about it.''

''You're wrong, I—''

''Am I? We'll see about that.'' She marched to the door.

''Helena? What are you going to do?''

''What do you think? It's rude to keep the gentleman waiting.''

Twenty-One

Despite the lively fire crackling in the hearth, Helena shivered. The tips of her fingers were icy as she ran her hands down the front of her dress to straighten the folds. Only this morning she'd been prepared to defy her own father for the sake of true love, but Michael had spared her that folly. His cruel denial had frosted her heart, numbing her to the hurt she refused to feel. She'd been a ninny to fall in love with him in the first place.

The only man she could ever rely on was Papa, and starting now, she would attempt to change that. She *had* to, for despite what Michael believed, she had someone else's life to consider.

It was time to grow up, she told herself, squaring her shoulders. And her first act of maturity would be to marry the man her father had chosen.

When she walked into the formal drawing room where Lieutenant Butler waited, she expected to feel a soul-cleansing surge of purpose. Instead, panic flooded her. She must have betrayed herself with a sound, for he turned abruptly from his post in front of the fire.

In his crisp dress uniform, shoulders draped in gold braid, the man was as handsome as a war memorial statue. Even before he spoke, he worshiped her with his gaze. "My dear Miss Cabot. Every hour apart was a lifetime."

Crossing the room, he held out a perfectly symmetrical bouquet of gardenias and pink carnations. She accepted the offering with a tremulous smile, setting it on a side table.

The lieutenant did not seem to notice how horribly cold it was in the room. With an expert motion of his fingers, he took out a pocket watch and flipped it open. "Your father has requested a rendezvous at four o'clock," he informed her. "That gives us thirty-four minutes, by my reckoning."

No wonder Abigail liked him, Helena thought. He was as obsessed with numbers and precision as she.

"And then we can tell him of our plans right away," he added.

She sank down on a chair. "Plans?"

"The ones you outlined in your last letter."

"You'll have to remind me."

A small frown marred his noble brow. "The Christmas wedding. The honeymoon in South America."

"She would pick South America, wouldn't she?" Helena murmured. "There's to be a complete solar eclipse in the southern hemisphere. She'd be eager to see it."

"I beg your pardon."

Helena waved a hand. "Never mind. Let's get on with it. Shall I ring for tea?"

"Dearest, is something wrong?"

Her heart was screaming. Couldn't he hear it? Couldn't Michael?

"What could possibly be wrong?" she asked, fighting a burst of bitter, inappropriate laughter.

"Before we prevail upon your father, I must say how happy you've made me. The night we met, my hopes soared. But I didn't dare believe a love like ours could flourish as it has. Then your letters began to arrive, and I came to believe we were destined to be together."

This man, she realized, was nothing—*nothing*—like Michael. The lieutenant was impeccably neat, unfailingly earnest and utterly unaware of what she was feeling or thinking. She shouldn't want him to be like Michael, to be sensual and crude and brilliant. But she did, oh, she did.

"What made you believe that?" she asked.

"Your letters, of course."

"The letters."

"I memorized them, my darling. 'If I am nothing else in this life,'" he recited, "'I am the keeper of your soul. You have given me reason to believe in things even beyond heaven.'"

"She said that?"

"She?" He scowled. "You wrote it. Don't you remember? I never knew I could be loved like that."

The awareness that had been nagging at her strengthened into certainty. "Good glory. She loves you."

"What?" His perfect composure seemed to be fraying at the edges.

"I didn't realize— I thought she was merely writing the letters at my request, and nurturing this match to please our father. But she is in love with you. Not Mr. Calhoun, as I supposed, but you." She frowned, trying to adjust her thoughts to this new information.

"What a pickle. Mr. Calhoun loves her but she loves you. Now, I like my sister better than I like Calhoun, so I shall give her what she wants. And that, apparently, is you, Lieutenant."

"I'm afraid I don't understand." His forehead creased with worry.

"I didn't either, until just now." Oh, Abigail, she thought. Why didn't you tell me?

Because Abigail was simply being Abigail. The obedient sister, accustomed to stepping back and allowing Helena to take first pick of everything—including husbands. Helena would have kicked herself if she could have figured out how. She, who always prided herself on her keen insights about people, had been completely blind to her sister's desire.

"Darling Helena." Crossing the room, he went down on one knee before her and took both her hands in his. "Are you quite well?"

She studied his earnest face. She thought about her own need, and knew that if she went through with marrying him, he would be a steady and loyal husband and father, for he truly was a good man.

Yet she couldn't do that to Abigail, not even for the sake of Papa. Yet now Helena was faced with the task of explaining the situation to this man.

Upright and honest, Lieutenant Butler was surely not the sort to take deception lightly. For Abigail's sake, she must make him understand where all the passion in those letters was coming from.

"Tell me when you fell in love, Lieutenant. Tell me the exact moment."

"It was the first moment I saw you."

"It was not," she snapped. "Love at first sight is a romantic notion but quite false."

"No, I swear, I thought you were the most beautiful thing I'd ever seen—"

"Nonsense. If everyone fell in love with something they admired for its beauty, we would all be pledging ourselves to the Washington Monument and the azalea bushes in our neighbors' gardens. When did your admiration change to love?"

"I suppose it was..." He hesitated, and his expression softened with fondness. "When you said I was as constant in your heart as the polestar. I felt valued and strong. It was extraordinary, overwhelming."

Helena hesitated one last time. She was in real trouble, and marrying the lieutenant could solve that. But nothing, she realized, was worth stealing the man Abigail loved. Helena would find some other way out of her own troubles.

"I never wrote that," she said.

He frowned. "I have the letter—"

Taking a deep breath, she prepared to do one of the few selfless acts of her life. "The woman you love wrote those words," she told the lieutenant.

"Indeed you did, my darling. And so I've come today to—"

"Oh, Lieutenant Butler, do hear me out. I am guilty of the most desperate deception." Finally Helena felt liberated, lighter than air. To hell with Michael, thinking he could leave her in the keeping of another man. She clasped her hands in glee and laughed at the confusion on the lieutenant's sculpted face. "And it's all going to work out so marvelously well. I have such a particular talent for pairing people up in ways that make sense."

"I don't understand."

"Of course you don't. You're a man. Get up off your knees. We have much to discuss. Your life is about to change, sir."

Twenty-Two

"Go away."

Jamie stood on the stoop of the small arbor behind the Cabots' house, while Abigail sat on a banquette beneath twin arched yew trees, denuded of life this late in the season.

Even though she kept her back turned to him, she could see his reflection in the large silver gazing ball set atop a pedestal nearby. Distorted by the shining curve of the ball, he appeared larger than life, vaguely threatening. He stepped closer, and she felt the phantom heat of his stare between her shoulder blades.

"I'd like to be alone," she stated. "Is there any possible way to get you to go away?"

"Of course not. You're not supposed to be hiding out here. This was not the way things were supposed to turn out," he said.

"I should have known better than to listen to you." She watched a lone yellow leaf float to the ground.

"It's not like you to abandon a project," he pointed out. "You haven't even done your part yet. This was supposed to be a day of triumph for you. This was supposed to be the day you revealed yourself to Boyd

Butler, just as you revealed your heart to him in those letters.''

She cringed, thinking of her own stupidity. Turning, she sneaked a glance at Jamie, and for once his cocky grin was gone. Good. He deserved to feel like a failure for a change.

"No good ever came of a lie," she said. "I've always known that. Your mad schemes and my own stupid longing impaired my judgment. While we were so busy painting me up like a puppeteer's marionette, we forgot one key element. We forgot to consider what Lieutenant Butler wants.''

"That's not true." He paced back and forth. "We worked hard for this, Abby. The dress fittings, the dancing lessons. You learned to ride a horse and eat raw oysters. You learned to laugh, not be laughed at. Damn it, I taught you to kiss.''

The reminder stung with unexpected intensity. "Oh, you did, didn't you, Jamie? You taught me everything a young lady needs to know about love and romance, except what to do when it doesn't work out.''

"Abby—''

"He fell in love with Helena. He came to see her, not me. Now, please," she said. "Leave me. I'd like to be alone.''

With a frustrated gesture, he shoved a splayed hand backward through his hair. "You've been alone so much that you don't know any other way to be. At least talk to me.''

"I've talked far too much to you. That's why I'm in such terrible trouble. I beg you, if you have even the smallest bit of compassion left, please leave me. And don't come back.''

"You surprise me," he said. "For a person who has the tenacity to search the whole universe for stars, you're surrendering a simple matter very easily."

"I'm giving up on a lost cause I never should have taken up in the first place. I suggest you do the same."

Making a sound of impatience, he sat on the bench beside her and captured her hands in his. "Did you even bother looking at yourself, Abby?"

She pulled her hands away and brushed them over the rich silk of the skirt Madame Broussard had created. "A pretty dress is not going to turn me into my sister."

"Nor would you want it to."

"It won't make me beautiful, either."

She expected him to dispute that, but he smiled sadly and said, "True. Only you can do that. What will it take to make you believe it?" He didn't let her answer, but stood up and stepped behind her. A moment later, he put something cool and metallic around her neck.

"What's this?" she demanded, touching it.

"A little something I had made for you. Sort of a...commencement gift, to commemorate the completion of your education." He positioned her in front of the silver gazing ball.

Abigail gasped, staring at the distorted image. Her hand shook as she passed her fingers over the exquisite necklace. "Dear heaven. Are these..."

"Diamonds," he said easily. "There's really no point in pretending any other stone is equal to a diamond, is there?"

She leaned forward to admire the design. "The

stones are set in the shape of the constellation Andromeda.''

''The Chained Princess. She was in the sky the
night we met.''

Abigail couldn't believe he'd noticed that, much
less remembered it. ''I don't know what to say.''

'' 'Thank you' would be appropriate.'' Jamie took
her by the shoulders, giving her no choice but to face
him. The late-afternoon sun accentuated the gold of
his hair, the silver of his eyes. How could someone
with a face like his ever understand what it was like
to be plain? Yet she felt like a different person when
she was with him, as though she were as golden and
graceful and attractive as he.

''I'll go find your lieutenant,'' he said, apparently
growing impatient with her long silence.

Alarm flared through her. ''You'll do nothing of
the sort. He's with Helena now.''

''Are you saying you won't even greet the man?
After pouring your heart out to him, you won't even
do him the courtesy of saying hello?''

''Believe me, he won't notice. Jamie, we tried
something that didn't work. You should learn to accept defeat with grace.''

He spread his arms with elaborate innocence. ''I
only wanted to see you happy.''

''And to win my father's vote.''

''Well, that, too, but your happiness does matter to
me. Please believe that.''

She didn't want to feel what she was feeling. His
words sounded as though they came straight from the
heart, but he would only laugh at such a notion. And
even though his incredible gift lay upon her throat,

growing warm from her skin, she knew it was meant as a sop to his conscience.

"I can't accept this necklace," she said.

"You have no choice. You're the only woman on the planet who understands what it is," he said with brusque impatience, and then he was gone.

In the empty silence following his departure, she felt more bereft than ever, drowning in her own transgressions. She had done a terrible thing; she had gambled and lost, and now she was suffering the consequences. It was the law of cause and effect. She understood this law intimately. She should have had more respect for it, but she'd allowed her head to be turned by foolish dreams.

An unexpected tear plopped onto the back of her hand. Sweet heaven, she was weeping. How humiliating. On top of everything else, she was weeping, and couldn't seem to make herself stop. She tried to rationalize the sadness away, to tell herself that her troubles were over—the lieutenant would marry her sister and Father would be delighted and life would go on. But there was no reasoning with the sort of hurt she felt. It rolled through her in a great dark wave, touching the lonely places that yearned for something that could never be.

A rustle of dry leaves, followed by a masculine clearing of the throat, alerted her that Jamie Calhoun had returned. The cad. He probably felt guilty, as well he should.

"I told you to go away," she said, keeping her back turned and her head down. She didn't want him to see her like this. "I meant for you to stay away."

"Well, then, it's a bit awkward, because in your recent letter you begged me to come to you."

Abigail froze. Fine hairs on the nape of her neck stood on end. Dear God, it was him. Boyd Butler.

She couldn't think of a word to say. Squeezing her eyes shut, she prayed to every deity she knew to make the earth open up and swallow her whole. But no one heard her prayers. She remained seated in a sodden mess on the garden bench. With a furtive hand, she reached up and brushed the tears from her cheeks.

Then she forced herself to stand up and face him. In formal dress, his cocked hat tucked beneath his right arm, sword at his side, his epaulets glittering and his mustache perfectly groomed, he resembled a lead soldier in a display case. Only the small bouquet of flowers he held out to her contended with his military bearing.

But when he saw her face, his composure faltered a little. "I'm sorry," Lieutenant Butler fumbled. "I was looking for Abigail Cabot."

Abigail pondered the irony of the moment. Here she was, face-to-face with the man she'd vowed to love until the stars fell from the heavens, the man to whom she'd penned excruciatingly personal letters, crammed with every tender emotion she had ever felt. And he hadn't even recognized her.

In spite of her misery, she managed a short laugh. Her hand crept to the new necklace, feeling the sharp constellation that lay against her throat. "I'm not sure whether I should feel offended on behalf of the old Abigail, or flattered on behalf of the new."

He blinked, widening his eyes. "Miss Abigail! I didn't rec—er, you're looking exceptionally—um, that is—"

"Don't go any further," she said, deciding to rescue him. "I accept the compliment."

A dull red flush crept upward from beneath his starched collar. Shuffling his feet, he held out the bouquet.

She had no choice but to take it. And then she had no choice but to sneeze. Flinging the bouquet aside, she groped for a handkerchief, found none, and then sneezed again into the end of her sash. "I'm sorry," she said, blinking watery eyes. "I have a bad reaction to certain varieties of flowers." When her vision cleared, she gazed into his handsome, earnest face. "But, Lieutenant, that's not the apology you came to hear, is it? I scarcely know where to begin."

"Then let me begin it. When I first heard of your deception," he said, "I was all for storming back to Annapolis and shipping out to patrol the Canary Islands. But your sister prevailed upon me to reconsider."

"So you're here at my sister's suggestion?"

"I am here of my own accord. This is between you and me," he said. "And I will not leave until we sort this out."

"There's nothing to sort," she said, but couldn't go on, for her voice was afflicted with the most humiliating quaver.

"I'm not marrying your sister," he stated. "I want you to know that."

Her first thought was that their father would be bitterly disappointed, and her second thought was that she would take the blame. "Lieutenant Butler, I am so utterly ashamed and filled with regret for all that happened."

"Please don't say that, Miss Cabot, my…dear." He held his fists clenched, white-knuckled, at his sides. "You mustn't regret one word of those letters.

Ever since you started writing to me, they have been my whole world.''

She was sure she'd heard him wrong. ''I don't understand.''

''You do understand me, better than anyone ever has. Each time I received a letter from you, I felt as though I'd received a gift from heaven.''

A cautious hope glimmered. ''Really?''

He nodded, but maintained his stiff, military posture. ''I want to tell you about the moment I fell in love,'' he said. ''It was when I read something in a letter from a remarkable young lady. She told me I was the other half of her soul. No one had ever said such a thing to me or made me feel so adored and valued.''

''But how do you feel now that you know those were my words, not Helena's?''

''Miss Abigail, I fell in love with the person who wrote the letters, the person who kept me in a state of perpetual joy waiting for each new delivery.''

Abigail felt a sudden rush of bashfulness. She wanted to believe what she was hearing, but did she dare?

After a few seconds of being tongue-tied, she remembered something Jamie had taught her in one of the many lessons on social conversation. If she could imagine writing the words, then she could say them aloud. Closing her eyes, she pictured her pen moving along the page and said, ''I cannot begin to find a way to express my regrets that I took part in this deception. Lieutenant Butler, I beg your pardon. Please know that I'll understand if you simply disappear, never to return.''

''I don't want to disappear, Miss Abigail. I want to

know you, better and better with each passing day. To know the woman whose letters touched my heart and filled my days with meaning.''

Panic and joy bloomed inside her. Was he saying what she thought he was saying? Could Jamie have been right after all?

She couldn't be sure. He was so formal, standing there, revealing the depths of his heart with soldierly deliberation. Jamie would be touching her at this point, she thought. He'd grab her by the shoulders or perhaps even kiss her— She stopped the thought in its tracks. It was disloyal even to think of Jamie when Lieutenant Butler was addressing her.

''I only regret that you didn't feel comfortable explaining yourself to me right from the start.''

''Your feelings changed very quickly, Lieutenant. You thought you were coming here to see my sister.''

''I came to see the woman who told me she experienced a second sunrise when she received my letter. The woman who wrote that I am her polestar, guiding her heart.''

Dear heaven. He had memorized her letters, just as she'd memorized his.

''This isn't quick,'' he said. ''It isn't sudden. I've had weeks to think about it.'' Keeping his hat beneath his arm, he sank down on one knee before her.

She nearly exploded with giddy panic as reality closed in. Could he love her as he claimed to love the writer of the letters? What would he think when he discovered she had a physical imperfection? She'd imagined this moment a thousand times, but she'd never remembered to consider everything that was at stake.

This wasn't happening, she thought wildly. Dreams

simply didn't come true, not like this, not for her. He took her hand, holding it with the reverence he might afford a holy relic. She braced herself, expecting to be swept away in the same currents of awareness that engulfed her when Jamie touched her, but at the moment she was too numb with shock to feel a thing.

"My dear Miss Abigail," he said, "I have an important question to ask you."

She had no voice. That faculty deserted her along with the ability to breathe or even think. She swallowed hard and managed to croak, "What sort of question?"

"The most important one of all."

Twenty-Three

Franklin Cabot lifted his wineglass and beamed at Abigail in a way that was completely new to her. In the past, he'd been kindly and even tolerant, regarding her with duty-bound affection and sometimes even admiration when warranted. Now he afforded her the genuine respect and attention she had hoped for all her life.

She raised her glass to answer his salute, and Helena did likewise, the three of them sharing a celebratory supper in the wake of Lieutenant Butler's departure.

"To my extremely clever daughter," the senator said. Disbelief tinged his expression of delight. "Soon to be a bride. I'm so very proud of you, my dear."

Setting her glass precisely between the saltcellar and the finger bowl, Abigail tried to cherish her triumph. Things were working out as planned, after all. At last she had found the way to her father's heart.

"And to my even more clever sister," she added, looking in Helena's direction. "None of this would have happened without you."

Helena gave a careless smile and set down her wine

without tasting it. "'Twas you who wrote the letters."

"But he came to see you in the first place." Abigail could never guess at what Helena had said to Lieutenant Butler. But she did know her sister was capable of being extremely persuasive when she wished to be. Abigail wasn't sure how she felt about the idea that her sister had persuaded the lieutenant that he loved her. Wasn't it more romantic when a man fell in love almost against his will?

But it was silly to quibble over such a minor detail in the face of her triumph.

"The two of you are a remarkable team," Father declared. "You should have put your heads together years ago, by God."

"And don't forget Mr. Calhoun's part in this," Abigail said with a sudden surge of loyalty. After all, she'd promised to champion his cause with her father.

"Indeed," Father said. "He did you more good than a year of finishing school." Grinning, he put down his wine, then set to eating his thickly sliced ham and the buttered squash Dolly prepared in abundance each fall.

Abigail was afraid to pinch herself for fear that this wasn't actually happening. She, Abigail Beatrice Cabot, was going to marry Boyd Butler III. First, she'd loved him from afar with the hero worship of a calf-eyed girl, then with the unwavering fervor of a woman grown, and finally, now she would love him with all the fullness of a wife's heart. What's more, she'd pleased her father, putting the perfect sheen on her happiness.

"I do have you to thank, Helena," she said, pick-

ing at her food, hardly tasting it. "If not for you, he
never would have—"

"Enough of thanking me and applauding my clev-
erness." Helena laughed, though a bitter edge sharpened her mirth. "It's all worked out just famously.
You loved the man, I didn't, and now he's wound up
with the proper sister. Eventually, you and the lieutenant would have discovered your mutual tendre,
with or without anyone's help. Love finds its own
way," she added, her voice softening. "No one can
control that, no matter how much she might wish it."

Abigail wondered if Helena was thinking of Michael Rowan. Did she regret loving him, or did she
revel in it?

"Mr. Calhoun would certainly disagree with you
there," she pointed out. As she spoke, she cut her
ham precisely into ninths. "He believes love is a
game of strategy. He urged me to set about winning
Lieutenant Butler with a systematic approach. Do you
believe that, Father? Do you believe love can be
brought about by logic and strategy?"

He smiled indulgently, and a gentle, faraway look
crept into his eyes. "I believe that for a lucky few,
love can grow from what is truly important in life—
honor, respect and recognition. Now, those are matters worth pursuing, wouldn't you say?"

"Of course."

"Speaking of pursuit." He bit into one of Dolly's
buckwheat biscuits. "Senator Troy Barnes has
stepped up his campaign to win you, Helena, and
once it gets out that Butler has settled on your sister,
he'll redouble his efforts."

"I hardly know the man." Helena laughed again,

but Abigail noticed her taut grip on the stem of her wineglass.

"By all accounts, he's an excellent young man with bright prospects. Family fortune is in banking, and he hails from one of the most beautiful places in the country—Saratoga Springs, New York."

"The city is known for its Thoroughbred race-track," Abigail said, and thought immediately of Jamie and the horses of Albion. Her hand stole up to touch the exquisite necklace, but she dropped it when she realized what she was doing. It seemed disloyal to be thinking of Jamie at a time like this.

Helena frowned. "Oh, Papa. Isn't it enough that you're marrying off one of us at last? Must you get greedy?"

"My dear, it's not that I'm greedy. I'm simply de-sirous of the same sort of happiness for you that your sister has found." He passed her the tray of biscuits and the talk turned to plans and politics. There would be a meeting of the two families, of course, and they would set a date. Father was happy to leave all the details to others. He'd achieved his objective—he'd settled the future of his younger daughter and was poised to forge the political alliance he needed.

After the meal, but before retiring to his study, he bade his daughters good-night. When Abigail kissed him lightly on the cheek and stepped back, he studied her with unusual intentness. "This betrothal certainly agrees with you."

"Does it?"

"You look quite…quite different."

She couldn't help smiling. "You can say it, Father. I used to look a frightful mess. Mr. Calhoun convinced me to order some new things for myself. He escorted me to the dressmaker's.''

''Indeed. She's a wonder worker.'' He kissed Helena and went to his study for his nightly cigar.

''I've never seen Papa so happy,'' Helena remarked. ''Or you either, for that matter. You are happy about this, aren't you, Abigail?''

She was having trouble sorting through all the emotions crowding her heart. ''I'm a bit overwhelmed. I can scarcely believe it's happening. Part of me hasn't even accepted that it's real yet, and another part fears it will disappear at any moment.''

Helena took her by the hand and headed for the front door. ''I have the most brilliant idea.''

''Now what?''

''We must inform the *Washington Post* of your engagement.''

''I'm sure between Father and the Butlers, word will get out in due time.''

''Where's the fun in that?'' Helena pulled her sister out into the blustery night. ''We shall send the news by way of the telephone.''

Abigail knew better than to argue with her sister. Besides, she was feeling particularly kindly toward Helena, who had been the catalyst in all of this. And in the back of Abigail's mind, almost unacknowledged, lived an ugly little kernel of fear that maybe this was all an illusion. The more people she told, the more real it would become.

In her usual brazen fashion, Helena slapped the brass knocker a time or two, then let herself in. ''Hello,'' she called, leading the way up the stairs. ''It's us. The Cabot sisters. We need to send a wire on the telephone.''

Professor Rowan met them at the top of the stairs. His wrinkled shirt open at the collar, his thick spectacles crooked on his face, he appeared even more distracted than usual. "Hello," he said. "We weren't expecting you." His bleary-eyed gaze drifted over Abigail. "You look funny. Did you change your hair?"

"She looks beautiful. An idiot can see that," Helena said.

"Just what is it you want?" he asked.

Helena planted her hands on her hips in a challenging posture. "Papa wants to marry me off to Troy Barnes," she said. "Does that upset you?"

He followed her into the parlor. "Should it?"

"Yes," she snapped.

He scratched his head. "I thought the prospect was Lieutenant Butler."

"That was this morning. He's Abigail's prospect now. My latest suitor is Senator Barnes. Do you care?"

He flinched, and she had the satisfaction of seeing her dart strike home. But he countered with one of his own. "The question is, do *you* care? You seem content to accept your father's choice, regardless of whom he chooses."

Jamie Calhoun came to the doorway, bracing his hand on the lintel, shifting his hip negligently to one side. "I thought I heard voices," he said. "And how are the little neighborhood peahens?"

He looked more unkempt than Rowan, which was an even greater shock since he was normally so fussy about his appearance. Shirt agape, neckcloth missing, uncuffed sleeves flapping loose, he resembled a pirate too long at sea. Somehow, disarray looked well on him.

"We have the most amazing news," Abigail said, taking his hand. Instantly a current of warmth connected them, catching her by surprise. In her excitement over Boyd Butler, she'd forgotten her powerful reaction to Jamie Calhoun.

The unexpected pang of yearning was followed by a flutter of panic. It was Boyd Butler she wanted, she told herself. He was all she'd ever wanted.

A sharp, mysterious odor emanated from Jamie. She quickly let go of his hand. Stepping back, she looked from him to Rowan and back again. "You're both drunk as lords," she accused.

"Having never actually met a lord," Rowan said, "I can neither confirm nor deny this."

"I can," Jamie said with exaggerated self-confidence. "I've met a good number of lords in my travels abroad, and I assure you, they are often quite drunk."

"As drunk as you are?" asked Rowan.

Helena pressed her lips together. Abigail could tell she was trying not to laugh.

"Probably not." Staggering to the cluttered sideboard, he lifted a clear bottle of colorless liquid. "I don't think they have tequila in Europe."

"Have what?" Abigail held the open bottle to her nose and sniffed it. Tears sprang to her eyes. "Good heavens. Is it kerosene?"

"Woman, bite your tongue." He tipped a little into a tumbler and held it out to her. "Marvelous stuff. You should try it."

"We came to send a message over the telephone."

"What for?"

"To tell the newspaper my stunning news."

"What's that?"

"Oh, Jamie." Impulsively, she kissed his cheek, feeling another tingle flash through her, but attributing the reaction to her excitement about Boyd. "You were right after all."

"I was?"

"Yes. It worked."

"It did?"

"Yes. When the lieutenant discovered I was the letter writer, he wasn't offended. Thanks to Helena, he was intrigued rather than angry."

"Helena has that effect on people," said Rowan. Regarding her in stunned amazement, he gave her a glass of liquor. Abigail surmised that he had been operating under the grim assumption that Helena would marry Boyd. Now, liberated from that notion but challenged by the new threat of Troy Barnes, he didn't seem to know what to do with himself. He drank his tequila in one gulp. With a gleam in her eye, Helena did the same. When he offered her another shot, she hastened to hold her glass out of reach. "One is more than enough, thank you," she said.

"It all happened just as you said it would," Abigail told Jamie. "He asked me to marry him. I said yes, he spoke with my father and now we are to make the announcement to the papers. Can you believe that?"

"Believe it? Honey, I predicted it." With a sharpness that surprised her, he added, "In fact, I insist on being the first to kiss the bride."

The very sound of the word *bride* filled her with giddiness. He gave her no time to ponder the sensation, but grabbed her around the waist and planted a long, hard kiss on her. His mouth was hot and tasted of the dark, mysterious substance he'd been drinking. Abigail's shock splintered her thoughts until he let her go as abruptly as he'd seized her. Dazed, she tried to make sense of the feelings seething through her.

With careless aplomb, Jamie shoved the glass of tequila into her hands. "Now you have something to drink to, so drink."

Neither Rowan nor Helena seemed to notice Jamie's shameless display. They were completely absorbed in one another.

"Well, what are you waiting for?" Jamie urged Abigail. "Bottoms up. Cheers and long life to the soon-to-be bride and all that."

"To all that." Lifting the glass with a shaking hand, she swallowed a healthy gulp of the liquid.

Her insides burst into spontaneous combustion. A fire roared in her ears. She opened her mouth to scream but no sound came out. Without moving, she seemed to soar skyward. It was a heady sensation, yet frightening, too. The room tilted, and she felt Jamie's hands on her as he guided her to a chair. At last the roaring subsided enough so she could hear again.

"Better?" he asked with a wicked grin.

"What is that? It should be outlawed."

Rowan held up the bottle. Only a little of the clear liquid remained. "Tequila is a sacred substance, fit for kings and gods," he said, overenunciating his words. "Since the pre-Hispanic era, Indians from the highlands of Jalisco, Mexico, have made liqueur from the agave plant."

"My cousin Blue, who is a doctor in San Francisco, sent me several bottles," Jamie added.

"Doesn't your cousin like you?" Abigail asked. "Does he wish to do you in?"

Helena took a sip straight from the bottle. Then she held it to the light and frowned. "There's something rolling around in here. A little swollen brown thing."

"That would be the worm," Rowan said.

"The agave worm," Jamie added. "It's usually found only in bottles of Mezcal, but this is very high-quality tequila."

"A worm?" Helena held the bottle close to her face, almost going cross-eyed as she studied it with disgust.

"Aztec priests started the custom," Rowan said. "Gives the drink an actual life spirit."

Jamie took the bottle and refilled Abigail's glass before she could stop him. To her horror, the worm flowed into her tumbler. "*El gusano* is prized as an aphrodisiac," he said. "It's meant to be eaten, my dear."

She studied the grublike thing, pale and grotesquely swollen in the bottom of her glass. "Why would any-one eat that?"

"Within the worm lies the key."

"The key to what?"

"To freedom, to enchantment, to a new world of wondrous experiences."

"It's a worm, not the Holy Grail."

"There's only one way to find out if I'm right," he said. "You have to try it."

She recalled that he was the one who'd made her eat a raw oyster. "Never," she said, shoving the glass into his hand.

"You don't know what you're missing." He drank the liquor, worm and all, making a big show of chewing it with exaggerated relish.

Helena and Abigail exchanged a look. Abigail

closed her eyes, inhaling fresh air through her nostrils. Helena headed for the nearest spittoon.

"So you wish to contact the *Washington Post,*" said Professor Rowan, ignoring their disgust. He seated himself by the tall wooden box on the wall and set to operating the telephonic device. The machine crackled to life, and the operator connected him with the telephone at the paper. A faint voice sounded at the other end. "Yes? This is Timothy Doyle, at the *Post.*"

"Can you hear me? It's Michael Rowan in Georgetown."

"Yes, indeed, Professor Rowan, I hear you quite clearly."

"Good. I have a bit of news for you to print. The vice president's son is going to marry Senator Cabot's daughter."

"You don't say? Boyd Butler and Helena Cabot?"

"No," Rowan said quickly. "Boyd Butler and Miss *Abigail* Cabot."

"The short, odd one? Very funny, Professor. I can hardly print that. It would be taken as a joke, and I don't do satire."

Jamie severed the connection with a swift flip of the lever. Abigail felt as cold and empty as an abandoned cave. Rowan's face went pale. He muttered an apology and shuffled away to check on Helena.

"Abby, I'm sorry," Jamie said.

A joke. The reporter was probably right. "You've nothing to apologize for," she said to Jamie. "I am a fraud, and soon everyone will know it." Ugly doubts etched themselves across her thoughts. "In all fairness, I should give Boyd a chance to back out. He was a bit confused today, a bit emotional. I should not have accepted so swiftly.'' She was inches from tears she refused to shed.

He took both her hands, frowning at their clammy chill. "Look, the world hasn't seen the new Abigail Cabot yet. When they do, careless reporters will eat their words like agave worms."

She studied him, that wickedly handsome face, those merry eyes. He was so sure of himself; he was so sure of her. No one had ever been so sure of her before. He believed in her in a way no one ever had in her life. He looked as though he cared, though she knew better. "I'll see to it that my father understands your part in this. I must, after all, give credit where credit is due."

"Abby—"

"I shouldn't want you to think me ungrateful." She stood up, swaying a little in the faint aftereffects of the tequila. "Truly, I am."

"Fine," he said. "That little remark you heard on the telephone is only the beginning. You're going to have to be strong."

"I can do that," she insisted.

"Society is a harsh place, Abby."

"But so is loneliness," she said softly.

Twenty-Four

With clocklike regularity, letters and floral arrangements arrived from Lieutenant Butler, who seemed to have forgotten Abigail's sensitivity to flowers. Like those fits of sneezing, doubts assailed her. But this had to be right, she told herself. Everyone was so pleased—her father and sister, the Butlers, the astonished local gentry who had once believed her a hopeless misfit. She even received a note of congratulations from the first lady, and an invitation to the opening gala of the brand-new National Aquarium.

Yet even as her excitement rose, so did her uncertainty. Everything was happening so quickly—too quickly. Boyd was going to be given a command at sea, and he wished to marry her before setting sail. That gave her only a few weeks to prepare, and she didn't know where to begin. She needed help. And there was only one person who could help her with this sort of thing. She marched next door to pay him a visit.

Frustrated by the surly Gerald Meeks, she barged past the servant and rushed into Jamie's room without knocking. He was unkempt, half dressed, unshaven and clearly in no mood for company. Legislative documents and a half-eaten pie littered his work area. "You are the last person I wish to see," he said with a glower.

"You got me into this, you must be the one to get me through it." She flipped the invitation onto the bed. Being anywhere near a gentleman's bed should have thrown her into paroxysms of horror, but she was too agitated to worry about decorum now.

He gave a dismissive wave of his hand. "You don't need my help. You've got Butler for that now."

"He wouldn't understand. It's you I want—er, you're the one who proposed this bargain in the first place."

"And you've accomplished what you set out to do."

"How can I explain this to you, Jamie? I still need you." The words came out softly, on an aching whisper. Abigail bit her lip.

He caught his breath with a hiss, but quickly assumed a mocking smile, read the invitation and gave a low whistle. "The National Aquarium, no less. Stingrays and electric eels. You must be ecstatic."

"I am, of course, but—" She kept feeling twinges of alarm at the rapidly unfolding events. "This is all happening in such a rush," she said. "I'm afraid I might be having second thoughts."

"I can't believe what I'm hearing." He paced the room. "Do you think Napoleon had second thoughts before embarking on his march through the Alps? What if Galileo had had second thoughts during his inquisition by the Vatican tribunal? What would he have said? 'Oh, well, perhaps I'm wrong after all and

the sun is nothing but a random star, circling the
earth...'''

Abigail couldn't help herself; she giggled. Even
when he was exasperated with her, Jamie could always make her laugh. In the frenzy of her new social
whirl, she'd nearly forgotten how.

"So, is your impending state of matrimony everything you thought it would be?" he asked.

She hesitated. He had dedicated himself to bringing
her and Boyd together, and she didn't want to dis-
appoint him.

In that brief hesitation, he must have read her
mood. "Don't get cold feet now," he said in a joking
tone. "I've won your father over to my cause, and
he'll secure the vice president's support. So there's a
lot at stake here."

She laughed again, relieved to be talking to someone who didn't study her, who didn't wonder what
on earth a Butler was doing with Senator Cabot's odd
daughter. "Only you can make me feel responsible
for the well-being of all the farmers of the Chesapeake lowlands."

"You are, my dear."

"And here I thought I was simply getting married."

"Nothing's simple," he muttered, then turned
quickly away, shuffling through the stack of printed
papers on his desk.

She watched him for a moment, curiously moved
by the stiff set of his shoulders, the weary deliberation
of his movements. "Can I ask you something?" Before he could deny her the chance, she said, "Why
are you so soured and cynical about love and marriage? What happened to you, Jamie?"

He froze, then she saw his shoulders relax. By the time he turned to her, his easy grin was in place. "Isn't it obvious? I've had my heart broken." He spoke so lightly that she couldn't tell whether or not he was serious. "But that's not the issue before us. The issue before us is getting you ready for your first public appearance with your beloved. Now, pay attention. We've got work to do."

Over the next hour, they discussed what she would wear, how she would comport herself, what she would do and whom she would see. He reviewed the art of curtsying, demonstrating his technique with the exactitude of a drill sergeant. Whistling a waltz, he helped her hone her dancing skills. Regarding the art of conversation, he cautioned her against laughing too loudly, speaking too softly and weighing in with her opinion too often. When he approached the art of fan-fluttering, she could no longer hold back, and collapsed with laughter on the bed.

The next thing she knew, he was beside her, and she could feel the warmth of him, could smell the starchy scent of his shirt, and when she turned her head, she found herself close enough to make out every facet of his remarkable eyes. They reminded her of stones trapped in ice—chilly, unfathomable.

A wave of emotion curled through her. She wasn't certain which one of them moved first, but their lips met, tasting, exploring. With soft demand, his tongue slipped into her mouth, and she shuddered delicately. Small shocks of dangerous, invisible heat darted through her, igniting fiery aches in secret places. The seductive spell held everything he had taught her about kissing, and more, because now she brought her own feelings into it, her own confusion and disquieting passion.

He ended the kiss before she was ready, pushing her back and standing up, turning to the window. In the half light, he looked dissolute, slightly angry.

''Jamie?'' she asked.

''You'll be fine,'' he said, as though she hadn't spoken at all. ''You're as ready as you'll ever be.''

Part Four

The art of living is more like wrestling than dancing.

—Marcus Aurelius

Twenty-Five

Jamie Calhoun arrived unfashionably early for the gala opening of the National Aquarium on Constitution Avenue, not far from the White House.

He didn't want to miss a single moment of the event, not because he was keen on looking at specimens of alligators and sharks, but because the event would be Abigail Cabot's first official outing as a society bride-to-be. At the opulent new facility, the first of its kind in the nation, she would appear on the arm of Boyd Butler, whose father would deliver a short address and preside over the cutting of the ribbon.

All the elite of the capital would be present to inspect her. Everyone was curious about the girl who would become daughter-in-law to the second-most important man in the land. Her last appearance in society had been less than successful, so the buzzards were circling now.

It was well known that Boyd Butler III expected to take up a career in politics, and some boldly suggested that a future run for the presidency would not be out of the question.

When Jamie considered this, he felt an amused incredulity. Abby—his Abby—as first lady. It boggled the mind. And yet he couldn't help thinking how appropriate it would be, and how healthy for the American people. The White House had its Dolly Madison and its Mary Todd Lincoln, first ladies who brought refinements to the office, but the White House had never seen the likes of Abigail Cabot.

Hell, no one had ever seen the likes of Abigail Cabot.

Jamie discovered something startling—he would miss her. He should be glad his dealings with the Cabots would soon be over. He *was* glad, he told himself. He didn't mind using people but he wasn't a sadist. He didn't enjoy hanging about and seeing everything falling apart in the aftermath of his manipulation. And it undoubtedly would, for that was the nature of romance and love. But he was, he confessed to himself, curious about the way Abigail would be received tonight.

"You're scowling, Congressman." Caroline Fortenay greeted him the moment he descended the marble stairs into the main gallery.

Willfully, Jamie smoothed out his brow. He felt like a different man than the one who had found her seductive, not so long ago. "I often do that when I think too much."

"And what were you thinking?"

Jamie studied the gleaming new gallery with pretended interest. A gilded ceiling arched over the length of the wide hall. Along each wall and down each artery, thick glass windows displayed exotic marine specimens. At one end of the marble gallery, strains of a Saint-Saëns melody shimmered in the air.

At the opposite end, white-coated waiters put the finishing touches on tables laden with food and drink.

"I was just trying to remember the last time I held a beautiful woman in my arms." His flattery rang with sincerity. "My dear madam, it's been far too long."

Actually, he recalled his seduction of the lively widow Fortenay quite well. With a grin, he remembered the rude interruption that had ultimately saved Mrs. Fortenay's virtue—a loud, wet sneeze from the shadows.

"Is it funny, then?" his companion asked. "Your long loneliness?"

"It is a personal tragedy," he said, retracting his smile. "I insist that you rescue me from it by honoring me with a dance, Mrs. Fortenay."

With a barely hooded suggestion on her face, she accepted his offer. "Since you addressed me as Mrs. Fortenay, I take it you haven't heard. I've found a new husband."

She'd wasted no time remarrying, Jamie reflected, torn between admiration and cynicism. "Ah, you shatter my heart," he said, watching her eyes light up as she drank in the flattery. "But congratulations are in order. To you, and most especially to the lucky groom."

Despite her newly wedded state, she sent out signals like a semaphore flagman—the flickering tongue moistening her lips, the smoldering looks, the inviting squeeze of her hand in his.

The flirtation left him curiously unmoved. Or worse, it wearied him. Illicit affairs no longer held much appeal; there was a sameness and a hollowness

to the intricate dance that made the effort seem pointless.

When he failed to respond, his partner pressed her
thumb into the muscle of his upper arm. "I believe I
need more than one dance with you, Congressman."

"Ma'am, you slay me with kindness. What have I
done to deserve it?"

She laughed, the sound brittle, like the breaking of
crystal. "You don't deserve it. According to my husband, you deserve to be dragged to death behind a
runaway horse—or train, I should think."

The graphic, violent image intrigued him. "And
your husband is...?"

Leading backward, she turned him to indicate a ro-
tund older man with a bald pate surrounded by a
fringe of wiry hair. Oversize jowls weighted his
cheeks, and his large nose blossomed with the rud-
diness of habitual overindulgence. "Horace Riordan.
President of the Chesapeake Union Railway Company," she said.

"I'm clearly not his favorite person," Jamie observed, catching Riordan's poisonous glower from
across the room.

"I am supposed to be charming you into dropping
your pursuit of anti-railroad legislation. If you succeed, we'll have no railroad corridor through the
Tidewater region."

"That would be the general idea, ma'am. Your
charm is working, by the way." The fact that she had
an agenda added interest to the game. He slipped his
hand suggestively down her back. "I find you charming indeed."

She arched her back with a subtle ripple of movement, pressing closer to him. "Then you'll drop the issue?"

Of course, he thought. Why let a few thousand subsistence farmers stand in the way of one's personal fortune?

Jamie put on the smile that had won him many a luxurious night during his travels. "Darling," he said, "I never mix politics and pleasure, but I will—" Leaning down, he whispered one of his most shocking diversions into her ear.

Even at close range, he saw the color deepening in her cheeks. He prayed he'd read her correctly, that she would be intrigued rather than offended, but the blush worried him. She drew back, and he braced himself for a slap.

"When?" she asked.

He glanced again at Horace Riordan. It would serve the greedy bastard right if Jamie seduced his brand-new wife. But of course, a man like that was probably used to having his women seduced right under his bulbous nose.

"When?" she repeated in a fierce whisper. "Tell me, do."

Before he could answer, a babble of speculation erupted. Jamie drew Caroline to the edge of the dance floor. Senator Franklin Cabot had arrived in the company of the vice president and his wife, and the three of them stood at the top of the wide marble staircase. Like visiting royalty, they paraded down into the sea of party guests. Then a fresh wave of anticipation rolled through the gathering, and a young couple appeared at the top of the stairs.

"That's Boyd Butler," said Caroline.

"Yes. So it appears."

"And that must be his fiancée with him."

"I imagine so." He edged away from his partner and somehow managed to keep his expression composed. Abigail was as lovely as a dream. The new Abigail. He had encouraged this, he thought. He'd wanted this for her.

"But it cannot be," Caroline said. "I read in the *Post* he was marrying Miss Abigail Cabot."

Following the disastrous telephone call to the *Washington Post,* Jamie had gone straight to the offices of the newspaper, found Timothy Doyle and stood over him, dictating the announcement until every last word rang with praise for Miss Cabot, her vivacious manner, her style and her wit.

It was one thing for people to read the item. It was yet another for them to see Abigail in person, to compare what they'd read in the paper to what they saw with their own eyes.

"Well?" Caroline prodded him. "Was the *Post* mistaken?"

"Not at all. Butler's engaged to Miss Abigail Cabot."

"Then who—" She broke off and pressed forward to get a better look. "Good Caesar. That *is* Abigail Cabot with him. She cleans up rather more nicely than I would have imagined."

Judging by the storm of whispers sweeping through the room, everyone present shared her amazement. "She used to be a perfect wretch," someone said. "Messy and plain and quite hopelessly gauche," another woman agreed. "Who would have thought she could be so transformed?"

Anyone who bothered to look at her, Jamie thought. But of course, no one had bothered.

Not even the man she planned to marry.

Along with everyone else in the room, Jamie watched the young couple's descent into the grand gallery. Abigail's large, wide-set eyes shone with a rare and special excitement, and her face bore the dazzling confidence of triumph. Her victory was two-fold. She had won the man of her dreams. But perhaps even more importantly, she had achieved the one thing that had eluded her all her life, the one thing she craved above all others. The approval of her father.

Jamie couldn't understand why that mattered so much to her. Why would she allow her worth to be measured by another person?

Beside him, Caroline and Mrs. Whitney, the navy secretary's wife, wondered aloud at what magic had transformed the senator's mousy daughter into a ravishing creature suitable for someone as exalted as the son of the vice president.

"I believe that's one of Madame Broussard's creations," Caroline said, craning her neck to get a look.

"She's outdone herself," said Mrs. Whitney. "That is the most cunning gown I've seen in ages."

Jamie could see the dress was pretty; its long lines and iridescent hues gave Abigail the illusion of a regal height.

"Yes, how clever," Caroline agreed. "The dress is perfectly suited for the occasion of the opening of the aquarium. The silk positively shimmers, doesn't it?"

Jamie had no idea how they could read so much into a dress, but this was an aspect of womanhood he had never understood.

"With that diamond necklace, it's absolutely brilliant," Mrs. Whitney concluded.

By God, she'd worn it. His parting gift to her.

Caroline ran a furtive hand down his arm. "There. We've all admired the vastly improved Miss Cabot," she said. Lifting on tiptoe, she reminded him of his outrageous proposition, adding her own creatively wicked twist. "Shall we? Quickly, while no one is watching."

But as she spoke, Jamie saw a disaster in the making. Inundated by dignitaries, Butler and Abigail still hadn't made it all the way down the stairs. Near the bottom of the steps, Butler turned away from his fiancée to greet a dark-skinned foreigner in a burnoose. It was probably not deliberate, but he gave Abigail's arm a tug. That was all it took to upset her balance on the wide, bowed-out marble staircase.

Swift instinct propelled Jamie forward, leaving Caroline complaining under her breath. He reached Abigail just in time to avert her fall, positioning himself on the stair below her, angling his shoulder so she could grab onto him for support. In the crush of the crowd, his rescue wasn't apparent, except to Abigail.

Relief washed the terror from her huge, beautiful eyes. "I nearly disgraced myself," she said. "Again."

"What's the matter?" asked Lieutenant Butler, turning back. "Oh, hello, Calhoun."

"See to Miss Cabot," Jamie warned in a whisper. "If you let her fall, I'll—"

"Oh, for heaven's sake, there was no harm done," she cut in, then aimed an adoring look at Butler. What a change this was from the Abigail he had first met—

gauche and carelessly put together, afraid of her own shadow.

"If you're quite through being gallant," said Caroline, shoving a path toward Jamie, "I should like some refreshments." She latched on to his arm and led the way to the long candlelit tables laden with a feast. Sybren van Zandt, the celebrated chef from the Netherlands who was all the rage among Washington hostesses, had created a fantasy meal for the occasion. The spread was contrived to resemble an undersea scene, with weathered nets and colorful arrangements of coral and shells, a sunken chest overflowing with a treasure of marzipan doubloons, a selection of seafood and sauces, and enough caviar, it appeared, to feed the Russian army.

Jamie grabbed two glasses of champagne from a passing waiter and offered one to Caroline, but she was busy inspecting the food. A moment later, her doddering husband decided to reclaim her, so Jamie quickly gulped down one glass of champagne, set it aside and started on the second. Standing back from the crowd, he tried to figure out why he was feeling out of sorts. This was the culmination of his project. He had set out to win Senator Cabot's favor and influence his vote, and he had done so. He should be feeling a sense of accomplishment. Instead he felt...irritated. Cheated, perhaps, though he could think of no reason for that.

His gaze kept wandering to Abigail, who looked flushed and nervous, yet freshly becoming as she clung to Boyd Butler's arm, moving along beside him like a leaf caught in a strong current. The lout all but ignored her, Jamie observed, as the social elite of Washington, D.C., welcomed them into their midst.

Abigail might as well have been another medal
pinned to his chest.

If his disregard bothered her, she gave no sign. She
kept a close eye on her father as if to be certain his
newfound esteem for her had not wavered. The senator was engaged in jovial conversation with the vice
president, and all appeared to be well in that quarter.

Jamie considered Franklin Cabot to be a complex
and baffling man. The match between Boyd Butler
and Abigail had been a dream come true for the senator. In gratitude, he had lent Jamie his support in
Congress and had convinced the vice president to protect the small farmers from the encroachment of the
railroads, but Jamie couldn't predict how long that
would last. He was still in favor; he knew that by the
fact that his association with the Cabots had garnered
him an invitation to this exclusive event.

As if she felt Jamie's stare, Abigail scanned the
room until her gaze locked with his. He grinned and
sent her a broad wink. At the same time, he felt a
swift and powerful surge of lust, remembering the
incident in his bedroom the other day. He'd nearly
seduced her...and she'd nearly surrendered.

She pretended not to see the wink, but something
in her face, some flash of yearning and confusion, told
him she was remembering their kiss, too. Butler had
begun moving along the table, sampling the hors
d'oeuvres and sweets. Now and then he would murmur something to Abigail but he seemed more focused on the food—smoked gravlax salmon and pick-
led herring, crab cakes and great tureens of chowders
and bisques.

Jamie positioned himself on the opposite side of
the table and moved along concurrently with Abigail.

"What do you think you're doing?" she asked in a low voice.

"Looking after you."

"I don't need a keeper." Realizing the conversation was attracting undue attention, she edged away from the crowd around the table.

He followed her to an isolated round table draped in white cloth. "I could have sworn you did a few moments ago on the stairs."

"A minor mishap, nothing more."

"What if I hadn't been there to catch you?"

"I would have plunged myself into ignominy. It would not have been pretty. But it wouldn't have been the first time, either."

"I know." He thought of the gawky creature at the wedding, and in some perverse way, he missed her. He missed her loud, brazen laugh, her artless enthusiasm for matters no proper lady would even know about. He missed her wry, caustic humor, her insatiable curiosity and her playful sense of the absurd. He missed—though no torture would ever drag this admission from him—dancing with her on the rooftop at two o'clock in the morning, and he missed teaching her how to kiss.

That Abigail had gone away somewhere, disappeared like a shadow burned away by the sun. In her place was a glittering creature who had found a treasure trove of self-assurance, making idle conversation with heads of state and railroad barons, flirting with men who had given the old Abigail no more notice than a carved newel post. And although she occasionally checked with her father, she grew bolder and more confident each time he nodded his head in approval.

"You know, Rowan mentioned that Jupiter and Saturn move into Taurus tonight," Jamie remarked. "Surely you're aware of that."

"Of course I am. The professor's free to use my telescope anytime he likes."

"You're missing the event."

Her gaze took in both her father and her fiancé, still loading his plate with delicacies from the buffet. "It cannot be helped."

"I see. We mustn't let a rare astral event get in the way of social obligations."

"Why are you being so beastly? Isn't this what you wanted for me?"

"Is it what you wanted?"

"Of course."

"Aren't you even the least bit curious about what you're missing at the observatory?"

"If I went to see it, I'd be missing this." She encompassed the beautiful hall with a sweep of her arm. "I never did thank you properly, Jamie."

"For what?"

"You know what. For changing my life."

He laughed. "You did that on your own."

"On my own, I hadn't the first idea how to get on in society."

"How can you keep the entire quadratic equation in your head yet not know how to discuss the weather with the war secretary's wife?"

"It's a puzzle, I confess. But I give you credit where credit is due. You are my Pygmalion."

It wouldn't have been the first time a woman called him a pig, but he hardly expected it from Abigail.

She laughed at his expression. "Clearly you're not familiar with the myth. Pygmalion was a sculptor who was disenchanted with all women. He wanted to create the ideal female, because he couldn't find one in real life. So he sculpted her out of ivory. But of course, the rest of the myth doesn't really fit us.''

''Why not?'' He rather liked the idea of fashioning a woman to his specifications.

''Well, Pygmalion became obsessed with his creation. He fell in love with it, adorning his sculpture with jewels and fine Tyrian cloth, and ultimately, he begged the goddess Aphrodite to bring the statue to life. His kiss breathed life into her, and he married her and—well, there are several interpretations of the myth's conclusion. In one version, they had a fine son and lived happily ever after. But in another, there were problems.''

''What sort of problems?''

''Once she took on a life of her own, he could no longer control her, and ultimately she did him in.''

''Is that what I have to look forward to?'' he inquired, capturing her hand and pondering its power to ruin him. ''Dying at your hands?''

''Undoubtedly.''

''At least it's for a patriotic cause.''

''Very funny.''

Balancing a plate of food in each hand, Boyd Butler joined them at the round table. ''There you are, my dear. I swear, I've heard more compliments about you than I have about the piranha exhibit.''

She favored him with a smile of delight, worshiping him with her eyes. ''That's a relief. I should not like to be eclipsed by a flesh-eating fish.''

A waiter arrived with a tray of crushed ice beneath a flotilla of raw oysters on the half shell.

''Look,'' Jamie said. ''Oysters. Your favorite.''

Her gaze flicked to Butler. Picking up an oyster, she handed it to her fiancé. Judging by her blush, Jamie knew she was remembering what he'd said about oysters being an aphrodisiac.

Butler sucked down the tidbit and grinned at her, and even Jamie could feel the glow of her happiness. A triumphal moment all around, he thought, grabbing another glass of champagne. But in creating his ivory woman, he'd overlooked one small detail. He had to release her to another man.

Which he was doing—willingly. He didn't want her. He had never wanted her, not in any romantic fashion. He was well beyond entanglements of the heart. He was far too urbane and sophisticated for that.

But still it galled him to see Butler's proprietary attitude toward her, to see her regarding him with the moon in her eyes.

"Your turn," he said, selecting a plump, cold oyster from the tray.

She blinked at him, startled and flushed.

"Go ahead, my dear," Butler said in amusement.

It was eerie, the way she obeyed him with the same unquestioning submission as she did her father. Jamie could tell she was thinking of her first experience with oysters as she took the delicacy from her fiancé's hand and swallowed it down. Only Jamie saw her panicked eyes widen as she struggled to hold in her disgust.

"Well done," Butler said. "Well done indeed."

He was amazingly like her father in his patronizing manner. She was trading one self-centered, condescending man for another. Couldn't she see that?

Didn't it bother her? Cutting short his speculation, Jamie excused himself with formal courtesy and went in search of more champagne.

The dedication ceremony began with a lengthy recitation of gratitude to the patrons whose generosity had contributed to the creation of the aquarium and an acknowledgment of the architects, designers and scientists whose brilliance had created it.

Vice President Butler was called to the dais to unveil the centerpiece of the aquarium, concealed behind a velvet drape. It was the largest tank ever built to house creatures of the sea in captivity, and it boasted dozens of species of plants and animals.

The piano played a salutation, the vice president made a brief speech, then surprised everyone by deferring the honor of the ribbon-cutting to his son in recognition of Butler's recent engagement.

Boyd Butler III and his bride-to-be.

Duty discharged, Jamie thought as he stood back, propped his shoulder against a pillar and watched from a distance. The two looked as proper as the wax bride and groom on the top tier of a wedding cake. Abigail kept darting glances at her father, who radiated pride and approval. Then she stepped behind Lieutenant Butler while he read, in smooth oratorio fashion, the dedication of the great national treasure.

Jamie studied the crowd, which included everyone from visiting foreign dignitaries to steel millionaires to cotton planters. Once she married Butler, this would be Abby's world, her friends and acquaintances. He didn't like the way they were watching her, hungry dinner guests waiting to be served. Perhaps that was extreme, the product of his disenchant-

ment with the whole affair. Perhaps these people
would cherish Abby's sensitive, brilliant, amusing
and earnest nature.

Perhaps the stars would fall to the earth.

These people didn't care that Abigail Cabot missed
having a mother, that flowers made her sneeze, that
she was looking for a comet, that children made her
laugh and sad songs made her cry. Jamie told himself
it didn't matter whether or not they cared. But it did.
Somewhere in the middle of all this, something had
happened to him. He had unknowingly stepped into
a sticky web of sentiment, and each time he made a
move to extricate himself, he became even more en-
tangled.

Butler reached the end of his speech, cut the ribbon
and drew the drapes aside to reveal the most impressive feature of the aquarium—a glass lagoon filled
with rare predatory sharks from the South Seas. A
Smithsonian official gave a brief overview of the exhibit, and when he finished, live food was released
into the tank.

A collective gasp went up from the crowd. Even
Jamie watched with a sort of grim fascination. The
sharks fell in a frenzy upon their prey, swarming over
the lesser creatures with a violent aggression, tearing
into the fish, denuding the bones with swift and ruth-
less efficiency. Women shrank from the sight but they
never did stop looking.

With her natural curiosity, Abigail stood close to
the tank, unafraid, her palm pressed to the glass. Yet
when she saw the violence of the feeding, she drew
back in horror. Clearly, this was not her brand of science. It lacked the mathematical order of the heavenly

bodies. Instead, this was a chaotic force of nature that probably made no sense to her. Offer the guests a chance to view a meteor shower or a feeding frenzy, and most would choose the latter. Since time began, people had been spectators at gladiator trials, bear baitings, cockfights. In London, aristocrats tipped the wardens of Bethlehem Hospital to bait the insane inmates. Blood lust was a human trait. Jamie had witnessed it more times than he could count and it was not pretty but very real.

Butler laughed like a schoolboy, leaning down to get a better view of a bloody fish head.

In a mercifully short period of time, the demonstration ended. But then an odd thing happened. The avid curiosity shifted its focus away from the aquarium and over to Butler and Abigail. People pushed forward, intent on making the acquaintance of Washington's most recent bride-to-be. Some did so out of courtesy, though most out of the need to ingratiate themselves with the fathers of the young couple.

As the spectators pressed close, all speaking at once and offering handshakes of congratulations to the happy couple, Abigail disappeared. Her short stature made it easy for her to drown in the middle of the aggressive crowd. Watching from the fringes of the group, Jamie had a cold premonition that all might not be well for the socially defenseless Abigail. Now that he'd handed her over to Butler, how would he be able to protect her?

Jamie turned away in time to see Helena arriving on the arm of Senator Troy Barnes of New York. He was upright as a cigar-store Indian, obscenely wealthy and hopelessly infatuated with her. Not that Helena cared. These days, she thought only of Michael Rowan. Since Abigail had freed her from her duty to marry well, Helena probably dreamed of a true love match between her and Rowan.

Like her sister, she was still naive enough to believe love was the key to all fulfillment. Like Jamie, Rowan knew some things weren't meant to be. A Georgetown professor with no fortune, nor even a pedigree, was no match for the daughter of Franklin Cabot. Enticed by a research grant and generous salary, Rowan would be leaving soon to teach at a college in Barnes's home district.

"What did you think of that?" asked Helena. She'd broken away from Barnes and approached Jamie with two glasses of champagne. "Did you enjoy the feeding frenzy?"

He tossed back the champagne in a gulp. "Which one?"

She sipped hers. "Grim, isn't it? I half expect to see my sister reduced to a skeleton once the crowd moves off."

"She'll be fine. She's stronger than she looks."

"Are you trying to convince me, Mr. Calhoun, or yourself? I think you feel guilty."

"Why would I feel guilty?"

"Because you have a conscience, much as you try to conceal it. I want you to know, if she suffers one single moment of hurt, I'll make you sorry you ever met the Cabot women."

He peered at her, looking for sharks' teeth. "Weren't you the one who convinced Butler that he was in love with Abigail?"

"Yes, but the romance is your fault, and I shall hold you responsible if anything goes wrong."

"This is the thanks I get for helping your sister snare the man of her dreams?"

"You're very sure about that," Helena said. "About the fact that Lieutenant Butler is the man of her dreams."

"He is. She told me herself."

"My sister is a brilliant woman. But sometimes she's blind to the things that are obvious."

"What's that supposed to mean?"

"At first I was certain she loved the lieutenant. Now I have my doubts. If she suffers, you'll pay the price."

He chuckled. "You'd have to get in line, Helena. After going against the railroad companies in Congress, I sense that my enemies have multiplied."

"Of course they have. The railroad interests believed my father's support was a foregone conclusion. No one expected that you'd become his chief adviser."

"For a while. So long as this engagement remains intact." He nodded in the direction of Abigail, who was speaking with her father. "See how she smiles. This is everything her heart desires. We should be enjoying this."

"But we aren't. The fact is, we're both worried about Abigail. Why is that?"

"Because we've had too much champagne. What is it about your father, anyway?"

"What about him?"

"He makes King Lear look like jolly old St. Nick."

"What an awful thing to say."

"He's eating her alive. And you, too, though perhaps to a lesser degree. Why do you and Abigail allow it?"

"He is our father." Her voice broke, and her face pinched with the same need he'd glimpsed in Abigail. "His esteem is everything to Abigail. The sun, the moon and the stars combined."

"Why is that?"

"You should ask her."

Jamie had no intention of doing so. He was through with Abigail and all the Cabots. His work was done. He would muddle through until the legislature recessed for the holidays, then he would probably find new lodgings well away from Dumbarton Street.

"I think I'll step out for a cigar, if you'll excuse me," he said.

He turned and headed toward the door.

"There you are, Mr. Calhoun," Caroline Fortenay Riordan said, intercepting him and blocking his exit. "I'd like you to meet some very special guests. They've come a long way to visit the capital. Halfway round the world, if you can believe that."

Pasting on a cordial smile, he stepped forward to greet them—and froze. He stared into golden, almond-shaped eyes, still as familiar to him as a recurring nightmare. Glossy lips, now parted in shock even deeper than his own. Midnight hair that shone with blue highlights. Though he knew it was as long as she was tall, she now wore it in the traditional coiled braid. Dusky olive-toned skin exuding the scent of jasmine. Oh, he remembered her all right. He remembered with razor-edged clarity.

Beside her stood the man he never thought he'd

see again, tall and elderly but still possessed of a dark power that seemed to emanate from beneath a jeweled turban.

"Prince Abdul Ali Pasha and Princess Layla of Khayrat," Caroline announced.

The princess blinked her dark-lashed eyes, and all the color drained from her beautiful face. "Jamie Calhoun. Allah be praised. I thought you were dead."

Twenty-Six

Escaping to the ladies' powder room, Abigail wondered why she wasn't enjoying herself more. The pressure of the crowd still clung to her like strong perfume even though she had the room to herself. Her status was still brand new, and she was so giddy with excitement she couldn't enjoy anything. Giddiness and excitement, she realized, were not necessarily pleasant sensations.

She wondered if sitting down on the upholstered banquette would wrinkle her dress. It was tempting; she felt as though she'd been standing for hours, and her bad foot ached.

With a furtive glance at the door, she decided to risk the wrinkles and sank with a grateful sigh to the low bench. Shutting her eyes, she relived the evening, from her grand entrance with Lieutenant Butler, his parents and her father, to the gruesome demonstration in the shark tank.

It had not gone perfectly. She shouldn't have expected it to. She should have watched her step on those marble stairs. As it was, she had needed Jamie Calhoun yet again to avert a fall. But she couldn't go back out there, not yet. Not when she could still hear the whispers echoing in her ears. She wasn't supposed to hear the remarks, but she knew perfectly well that she would be the object of speculation and criticism. She'd overheard someone say Lieutenant Butler was marrying her only for her fortune and her father.

But she refused to let the petty remarks dim her happiness. She was a different person from the awkward wallflower who had bumbled her way through Nancy Wilkes's wedding reception. Since that humiliating event, she'd been transformed from a sneezing, undistinguished blot on her father's reputation to the fiancée of America's most eligible bachelor.

The trouble was, she hadn't realized being gracious and charming took so much time and energy.

One of the most irritating aspects of the evening had to be Jamie Calhoun. He watched her every move with vigilant intensity, but not because he cared about her. She was simply the subject of a cynical social experiment conducted by a man who derived amusement from observing the hypocrisy of high society. But like a celestial body drawn by the gravitational influence of a greater force, she was helpless to resist. She reminded herself that the attraction shimmering in the air when she and Jamie were together was merely an illusion.

She glanced in the mirror. Just as her guise of a pretty, charming young lady was an illusion, his regard for her was as false as the special shoe she wore on her bad foot.

To her dismay, the door to the powder room opened and a silk-clad whirlwind burst into the room. To her relief, the whirlwind was Helena.

"You should have seen it, Abigail," her sister said,

skidding to a halt in front of the gilt-framed mirror
that covered one wall of the powder room.

"Seen what?"

"The look on his face was too delicious."

"Whose face?"

"Jamie Calhoun's. At last, we get a hint about his
mysterious past and the notorious secret he's kept for
so long," Helena declared, patting a coppery curl in
place.

Abigail frowned at her sister's reflection in the mirror. "What past? What secret?"

"Ah, you didn't hear, then. You were too busy
with all that pomp and ceremony. I shall miss you,
Abigail," she added with a wistful sigh. "I'm happy
for you, but we've always been so comfortable as
sisters until Lieutenant But—"

"What are you talking about?" She was losing patience with Helena's mercurial conversation.

"Jamie Calhoun."

A terrible panic seized her. Getting up from the
bench, she grasped her sister's arm. "What's wrong?
Did something happen to Jamie?"

Helena blinked at Abigail's white-knuckled grip on
her arm. "I didn't realize you cared so passionately
about him."

Abigail let go. "I certainly do not, but what happened? Did he hurt himself?" Although he'd seemed
fine a moment ago, her mind conjured up a host of
terrors—a riding accident or tavern brawl.

"It appears our Mr. Calhoun has a secret past. It
came to light this evening."

"Really?" She considered the night she'd discovered Caroline moaning with pleasure in Jamie's arms.

Had someone else discovered them? Dear heaven, perhaps Horace Riordan had challenged him to a duel.

"It was too dramatic," Helena recounted, turning this way and that to study herself from all angles. "In walked this foreign princess, ferociously gorgeous, and her husband the prince looking like something straight out of the *Arabian Nights,* lacking only a scimitar. She nearly fainted dead away when she saw Jamie."

"Who nearly fainted?"

"The princess. I tell you, I could hear her gasp as though she were drowning, and she whispered something in a foreign tongue. And then she said the most curious thing. In perfect boarding-school English, she said, 'I thought you were dead.' Right then, everyone realized your Mr. Calhoun must have had quite a notorious past. Even from a distance, I could tell theirs had been no casual friendship. The passion was positively boiling in the air. Mr. Doyle says he was to be executed, and he barely escaped with his life. Think of it, Abigail, they must have had the wildest of romances."

Of course he had a past, Abigail told herself. He didn't suddenly appear out of the mist, fully formed. Things had happened to him. A good many things. But never had she imagined it would be a love affair with a foreign princess.

"Well," she said, trying not to limp as she went toward the door, "I certainly have no business worrying about Mr. Calhoun's romantic background. Lieutenant Butler is waiting."

Abigail did her best to pretend she had no interest in Jamie's sordid past, but the moment she entered the gilded hall, she sought out the princess. It was impossible to miss her and the prince, the two of them fiercely exotic yet curiously old-fashioned and stiff as they made the rounds of introductions. The princess wore a gorgeous garment of blue silk that wrapped her in mystery. Pantaloons of the same fabric showed beneath the hem of the dress, and golden gauze cloth wrapped her shoulders. She had a pierced nose, eyes outlined in sleek black and scarlet lacquer paint on her fingernails.

Abigail found her uniquely terrifying, yet as mesmerizing as a cobra. She hoped her fear didn't show when Boyd introduced her to the dignitaries, and she sank into a studied curtsy. The princess murmured nothing more than a polite-sounding greeting, and the prince offered a regal nod, holding himself ramrod straight with the military bearing of a much younger man.

Jamie was nowhere to be seen. How typical of him to disappear the moment she discovered something of this magnitude.

The royal couple moved on to greet more people. Boyd and her father both kept pace with them as though they were part of the foreigners' entourage, leaving Abigail standing by herself.

She wasn't alone for long. Her pretty face wreathed in smiles, Nancy Wilkes embraced her lightly. ''Abigail, dear. I haven't seen you since my wedding. Who would have thought catching the bride's bouquet was more than a party game? Yet in your case, it worked. The moment you caught the bouquet, you turned around and met the man of your dreams. I declare, magic was at work that night.''

As she recalled, Abigail had rushed from the room

and encountered Jamie Calhoun, seducing the sister of the president. She only wished she could believe magic had been at work. Instead, she knew it was all calculated manipulation. Perhaps she should thank Jamie for taking the veil of self-deception from her eyes. Why believe in true love? Skill and cunning proved more reliable in her pursuit of Lieutenant Butler.

"How grand to see you, Nancy. I've missed our conversations."

Nancy had been a brilliant scholar at Miss Blanding's, and she and Abigail had often studied together. Nancy's keen interest in astronomy had made her a skilled computer of star charts.

"How are your observations going?" asked Abigail, linking arms with Nancy to make a promenade around the aquarium.

"What observations?"

"The stars, of course. You were always so keen on astronomy."

"I suppose I was, but honestly, I haven't had a moment to record a single thing. I haven't even looked at the celestial atlas you gave us as a wedding gift. Honestly, I've been so busy, I haven't had a thought of the night sky in ages."

Abigail was stunned. She couldn't imagine that. What on earth could keep a person so preoccupied that she forgot to look up at the stars? "Why not?"

A touch of mystery darkened her smile. "Marriage changes a woman's priorities. You'll find that out very soon. A married lady cannot trouble herself with astral projections and meteor showers."

"Why not?" she asked again.

"Who has time?" Nancy dropped her voice to a

whisper. "Believe me, I've found other uses for my time at night. During the day, I have to manage my husband's social schedule and his agenda of duties. And of course, the children will be along before we know it..."

Abigail could not fathom lacking the time to devote to her studies. Excusing herself, she hurried over to Boyd, who had gone to study a display of piranhas of the Amazon.

At the other end of the room, Jamie Calhoun had reappeared and become the center of attention; Doyle and Joseph Pulitzer of the *Post* crowded close as he conversed with the group of foreigners.

Her pulse fluttered as Boyd turned to smile at her, and she put aside her curiosity about Jamie. "Nancy Wilkes was just saying the most curious thing to me. She no longer pursues astronomy because her marriage keeps her too busy. Once we're wed, will I be that busy?"

"I hope so," he said. "I know I intend to be."

A sigh slipped from her before she could contain it. In a small voice, she asked, "Do you think I'll be able to continue my work in astronomy?"

He patted her hand. "If you insist, you shall have all the time you want. But it seems a shame that you'd want to spend your time gazing at stars when everything you could ever want or need is right here on earth."

Jamie didn't know or care who was watching as he faced Layla and her husband. Years and distance peeled away in painful layers, and he remembered the last time he'd seen her, standing frozen with shock while her father's palace guards had dragged him away. He remembered screaming her name until they beat him unconscious.

Layla's shock upon seeing him burgeoned into dewy-eyed joy. With a smile, he carried on as though nothing were amiss. "Will wonders never cease? Never thought I'd see Your Highnesses again."

The prince's translator repeated the phrase in murmured Arabic. Unlike Layla, he'd never mastered English.

"You always used to say you wanted to visit America," Jamie said to her. "And here you are at last." Leaning close enough to make her burly attendant nervous, he whispered, "How many men did you have to kill to get here, hmm?"

She gasped softly, and he remembered that sound in his ear as he made love to her. "What the hell are you doing here, Layla?" he demanded.

She motioned with her hand to keep her servant away. "I am part of a foreign legation. But your country is so strange. I have no place in your world."

"Then you should go back to your own."

He could feel her gaze trying to probe past his anger. He could hear her whisper as though they were alone in the bedchamber.

"Jamie," she said, "I still dream of you."

At that, he threw back his head and laughed loudly. "And I of you, Your Highness, but I was never fond of nightmares."

Twenty-Seven

The frenzy of wedding preparations took over Abigail's life. Between her father and Boyd's mother, the event had burgeoned into a national holiday. Every conversation concerned caterers or floral arrangements, every heated discussion involved guest lists or musicians.

Each night, Abigail collapsed into bed, too harried and exhausted even to work on her observations or calculations. Staring at the ceiling, she reflected that if she wasn't careful, the comet she was waiting for would arrive, unobserved, and she would miss it because she was too busy choosing the seed pearls for her bridal peignoir.

She told herself this should be the happiest time of her life. Her father was bursting with pride, her days were filled with plans and a childhood dream was about to come true. Yet a nagging sense of ennui still plagued her. She found herself preoccupied with inappropriate thoughts about Jamie and the foreign princess. Were they meeting? Had he taken up with her again? The thought of him holding another woman, kissing her as he'd kissed Abigail, made the world turn dark. She needed to stop brooding about him. She needed reassurance. She needed to know that she and Boyd were destined for happiness.

She asked him to call on her one cold night. She wanted to spend time alone with the two things she loved above all others—the night sky and her fiancé.

When corresponding by letter, they were at their most compatible, and his reply was both prompt and enthusiastic. *I send you a warm embrace across the miles that separate us, looking to the moment I can hold you in my arms at last. I will come at once.*

On the appointed night, Abigail took special care with her appearance, letting her hair curl softly around her face rather than scraping it carelessly into a crooked braid, and donned one of her new gowns, a flattering creation of deep blue merino that fell gracefully to the floor rather than binding and masking her figure. Studying herself in the mirror, she wondered why she hadn't understood how to make proper use of fashion until Madame Broussard had taught her. These were simple matters, she realized, things a mother might impart to her daughter. Abigail had missed out on them without even realizing the lack, and it made her wonder what other, more important omissions existed in her education.

As she stood at the window and watched Boyd arrive, she felt a surge of anticipation. This was what she needed, time alone with him, to show him what was important to her. This would bring her life back into balance.

Dolly let him in, but quickly disappeared to her own tidy room facing the rear garden. Boyd stood in the middle of the parlor, looking adorably nonplussed. "She's not staying to chaperon us?"

"Do we need one?" She almost wanted him to imply they did.

"Of course not. I wouldn't dishonor a single hair on your head, my dear Miss Abigail. But I must say, this is quite unorthodox, meeting at such a late hour."

"The stars don't observe proper calling hours," she said, leading the way up to the rooftop. She prayed he wouldn't watch her feet. When she'd mentioned her concern to Madame Broussard, the French-woman had said, "*Tiens,* a man does not look at a woman's feet, of all things."

Abigail hoped she was right.

It was cold on the roof, and their breath made ghostly puffs in the air as she showed him the domed chamber that housed the telescope, her pride and joy. "So here it is," she said. "I've spent more time with the stars than I have with society."

"We'll certainly change that soon enough," he said with a fond smile. "Dearest Abigail."

She heard a soft note of yearning in his voice, and she could almost picture the words as the salutation of one of his marvelous letters. "Yes?" she responded. Oh, kiss me, she urged him silently. Please kiss me.

"I had a message from Ambassador Dolittle from England. It seems he'll be out of the country for the wedding, and he wondered if we would be terribly offended if his son Malcolm came in his stead."

The last thing she wanted tonight was to discuss the wedding. "Did you know that I've bisected over a thousand stars with a micrometer?"

He smiled indulgently. "As a naval officer, I am conversant with astronomy, of course. If we were stranded in the middle of the Arctic Sea, I could find the way home with the stars.''

''Oh, I wish we could be lost at sea together,'' she said with a sudden burst of passion.

''Why?''

''Then we wouldn't have to think about wedding guests and travel plans and all the thousands of things that are keeping us apart.''

He laughed as though she had made a joke. ''Darling, those unending details all have the express purpose of getting us together.''

''I wish I could believe that. Lieutenant Butler— Boyd. This getting-married business is all quite rushed, isn't it?''

''I'm being shipped out to sea. There is nothing to be done. My family expects a wedding by Christmas, and it's our duty to deliver that.''

''So marrying me is your duty?''

He squared his shoulders. ''Nearly as sacred as the oath I took to serve my country.''

''Suppose I wanted to wait?'' Abigail ventured.

''That's impossible, of course.''

''Suppose I changed my mind?'' she asked, growing bolder.

''Well, in that case, there wouldn't be a wedding, would there?''

''Would it bother you terribly if there was no wedding?''

He patted her hand. ''Dear, everyone has a wedding sooner or later. Ours simply happens to be sooner.''

Heavens, it was like talking to a hearth plaque. She tried to interest him in the night sky, pointing out Betelgeuse, which appeared very red in the constellation of Orion. His polite admiration seemed distracted, and Abigail's heart constricted.

"Oh, Boyd," she said, her hand venturing out to take his. "I've been awful to you, haven't I?"

"I beg your pardon?"

"You're even more nervous than I am about all of this, and I never even noticed."

"Nonsense, my dear." He gave her hand a squeeze and then released it. "I'm not nervous in the least."

She moved closer to Boyd, feeling the hem of her skirt brush against his legs. Trying to recall the things Jamie had taught her concerning the proper way to invite a man's kiss, she gazed into his eyes and blinked slowly, then moistened her lips. She found herself distracted by his wide mustache, groomed to stiffness with a wax that smelled faintly of creosote.

He frowned at her. "Are you unwell?"

"No, not at all." *I was just wishing you would sweep me off my feet and kiss me senseless.*

"We'd best go inside. You'll catch a chill out here."

She laughed to cover her frustration. "I spend nearly every night under the stars, and I've yet to suffer any ill effects." Since he'd clearly missed her purpose a moment ago, she took his hands and moved in close, tipping back her head. He held himself very tall and stiff, his hands icy cold in hers and his gaze aimed at some point beyond her.

"Oh, where are you, Boyd?" she asked, studying the play of starlight on his face. She wanted to weep and kiss him all at once. Why was that?

"Pardon?"

"You are still such a mystery to me," she confessed. "There's so much I want to know about you.

I want to know what you think of life and nature. I want to find the poet inside the soldier. I want to know the man who wrote such sensitive letters.''

''You do know me, dear,'' he said. ''And you shall have all the time in the world to know me better.''

He was such a strong presence, she thought, standing in his shadow. But a tiny voice in the back of her mind whispered that he might be the wrong presence. Ah, but how could that be? She had wanted this for so long, worked so hard for it.

''Now, we really must be going,'' he said, crossing to the door and holding it open for her. ''I shall stay up late tonight and compose a poem for you. Perhaps that will calm your nerves a little.''

Abigail didn't respond. She was too preoccupied with grinding her teeth together.

He left her swiftly, and she stood in the foyer, staring out into the empty street, damp and aglow with gaslight. She felt a terrible realization pressing at her, something she had been denying for a very long time.

It built with a steady insistence, crowding out all thoughts save one. How foolish of her. In bringing Boyd out to view the stars with her, she'd tried to duplicate her experience with Jamie Calhoun. She should have known better. There was, after all, only one Jamie.

Twenty-Eight

Jamie strode out of the house and crossed in front of the coach horse, signaling to Butler's driver to wait. Butler opened the half door and stepped down into the street, his faultless uniform gleaming in the lamplight and his breath freezing in the night air.

"Mr. Calhoun, is something the matter?" he asked.

"I think you should come inside," Jamie said.

To his credit, Butler didn't hesitate, but followed Jamie into the house and up the stairs to the sitting room. Rowan had drunk himself into a stupor and had staggered off to bed hours ago. There was a lot of intemperance going on in this household lately, Jamie reflected.

He found himself seeking comfort far too often in the bottom of a glass, particularly since the opening of the aquarium.

Layla, for Christ's sake. She was the last person on earth he'd expected to encounter. And quite clearly, she'd been more surprised than he, since she'd witnessed his execution more than two years before. She used to lie in his arms and wish she could go to America. But that, like everything else she'd told him, was a lie. They'd arranged to meet in secret at the port of Almulla, but instead of Layla, he'd encountered a gang of palace guards armed with cold weapons and deadly intent.

Women were natural deceivers, but Jamie had found the one exception. She was his reason for dragging Boyd Butler into his house. Despite all his intentions, Jamie was plagued by concern for Abigail.

Her needs were simple and honest. She wanted so badly to be happy. Did Butler realize that?

The two men entered the sitting room, lit only by the subtle flicker of flames from the iron stove. Rowan claimed to have installed electrical lighting in the house, but it never seemed to work.

"Whiskey?" Jamie demanded, holding out a decanter.

"No, thank you," Butler said. "Mr. Calhoun, what is this about?"

"Your future wife," Jamie said, nearly gagging on the words. Setting down the bottle, he advanced on Butler, practically cornering him. "I wish to know your intentions toward Abigail."

Butler laughed, sounding more confused than amused. "I'm going to marry her, of course."

"How much time have you spent with Abigail? How well do you know her?"

Butler's military bearing sharpened with his temper. "What do you take me for? And for that matter, who are you to question my intentions regarding Abigail?"

"I'm a friend of the family," Jamie said, a bit startled to realize it was almost true. "Abigail is a special young lady. She has a guileless nature and a heart full of love."

"I know what is in her heart," Butler said, and Jamie realized he was referring to the letters. "Just what is it you expect from me?"

"I'm glad you asked." Jamie took another step toward him. "I expect you to cherish Abigail as though she were a national treasure. Better yet, worship her like a goddess."

"Sir, I am a gentleman. I know how to treat a wife."

"But what do you know about Abigail? Do you know she's looking for a comet?"

"A what?"

"Christ, she didn't tell you?"

"My fiancée has more important things on her mind."

What could be more important than her comet? Jamie wondered. Butler would never understand. "Look, you have to trust that I know what she wants. You'll encourage her to pursue her science."

The lieutenant smiled slightly, a patronizing expression Jamie wanted to pound off his face. "She won't be needing a vocation other than that of being my wife."

"Have you asked her that? Because if you do, you'll find out that she wants to visit the Vatican Observatory, and she wants to climb to a mountaintop and look at the night sky to her heart's content."

"Not that it's any of your affair, but my duties leave me no time for a wedding trip."

"Then make time, damn it." He couldn't seem to keep the words in. Although he couldn't stand the thought of her with another man, he also couldn't deprive her of the happiness she craved. "Are you prepared to do those things, Lieutenant? Because if you're not, I'll—"

"Sir, I am trained in hand-to-hand combat," Butler said. "You don't want to tangle with me."

Jamie was startled to realize he'd drawn back his fist, ready to strike. But at the lieutenant's words, he began to laugh loudly and bitterly. Given all he'd survived in Khayrat, he was hardly intimidated by a naval officer's threat. Besides, in his current state of mind, he might do real damage. "No, Lieutenant," he said, lowering his fist. "I don't."

Butler slowly released a long breath, as though he'd been holding it in. "Tell me something, Calhoun. Why do you care so much?"

"Because I—" He caught himself. "What matters is that *you* care."

"Believe me, Mr. Calhoun, you've nothing to worry about."

There was nothing left to say. Jamie realized he'd only cause Abigail hurt if he didn't back off. He accompanied Lieutenant Butler out to the coach and stood there for a long time after it rolled away. A futile anger filled him, and he didn't know why. Or perhaps he didn't want to examine the reason. He wanted it to be enough that he'd done his duty, found a decent man for Abigail. The steady, letter-writing Butler would not transport her to the heavens, but neither would he break her heart. There was much to be said for preserving one's heart.

Jamie took himself off to bed, but he couldn't sleep. He wondered why it troubled him so to surrender her to Butler. He supposed it was because she was the one good thing that had happened to him since losing Noah. In Abigail, Jamie found genuine goodness, and he felt cleansed just being with her. But their friendship could only be temporary. She would be much better off with bland, safe Lieutenant Butler.

Unable to sleep, Abigail crept downstairs in her nightgown. She donned her winter cloak, opened the door and slipped out into the night. The cold air struck her like a slap in the face, and she found it bracing, welcome, because she finally understood something she'd been avoiding for a long time.

What a ninny she'd been. The truth was staring her in the face, yet she'd willfully blinded herself to the desires in her heart. But no more. Now she knew it was time to trust her own judgment, not bend to the dictates of someone else's expectations. Tonight she would stop forcing herself to make the safe choice, the proper choice. Tonight she would take the only risk that made life worth living.

She didn't expect anyone to respond to her knock, and no one did, so she let herself in and made her way swiftly to Jamie's room. A pale wash of moonlight bathed the tall bed, and a sound of surprise and annoyance rose from beneath the covers.

Not so long ago, the idea of barging into a man's bedroom would have paralyzed her with horror. But true love, she discovered, was a source of great courage.

Stepping inside, she began speaking at once. "You haven't fulfilled your promise to me," she said, dismayed at the prissy note in her voice but determined to speak her piece. "You swore you would teach me to—Great Red Spot of Jupiter!" Her hands flew to her cheeks. For the first time since barging into his room, she noticed that he was naked, at least from the waist up. And she dared not look lower.

Cold moonlight through the window gave his skin the smooth sheen of a marble sculpture, and his expression was that of a stranger. He glowered at her as he reached for the decanter of water on the bedside table. "What the hell do you want?"

She kept her eyes averted, or tried to. But it was impossible not to stare. Muscles shaped his shoulders and chest with a powerful symmetry she simply couldn't help staring at. There was something about the combination of strength and smoothness that held her riveted.

"Well?" he demanded, drinking straight from the decanter. "Has a star fallen out of the sky? Did you spot another moon?"

"Why are you being so disagreeable?" she asked. Nervousness and uncertainty made her irritable. "I'll bet it's that Arabian princess at the aquarium."

"What about her?" He spoke with bland indifference, but he often used bland indifference to mask his deeper feelings. It was something she had learned about him.

"They say she was your lover many years ago." She knew Helena had only been guessing, but Helena's instincts were usually correct. "They say you were madly in love with her."

He laughed unpleasantly, then leaned over to light the lamp. Bathed in a golden glow, his bare skin was even more fascinating than ever. Despite his relaxed posture, he looked faintly intimidating. Abigail felt a spasm of warmth inside that reminded her of her purpose in coming here.

"You know better than to listen to gossip." He

laughed again. "You know I'm not the sort to lose my head over a woman."

"They say her family wanted you executed and you barely escaped with your life."

"They also say angels dance on the head of a pin. That doesn't mean it's true."

She knew she would get nowhere with this line of questioning. Besides, digging into his past was not her purpose at all tonight. She had a far more important agenda. She'd come to admit the terrible mistake she had made in agreeing to marry Lieutenant Butler.

But she hadn't realized how hard it would be to explain.

"Are you ill?" he asked, leaning back against a bank of pillows. Unlike her, he seemed completely unperturbed by the shocking impropriety of the circumstances. "You look strange."

"You're the second man this evening to ask me if I'm ill," she said. "I'm not. I came to tell you—" She hesitated. Words would never say what was in her heart. Her failed correspondence with the lieutenant was proof of that. And Jamie had a special talent for rendering a heartfelt declaration null and void. She simply didn't know how to tell this bitter man how she truly felt about him. He'd only laugh at her, tell her love was a trick of the light, as elusive and insubstantial as mist.

Very well, she would show him then. Taking a deep breath, she said again, "You haven't fulfilled your promise to me."

"Me? Break a promise? Never." He clutched at his heart, putting his hand over his bare chest.

"No need to be sarcastic. You did promise, didn't

you, that you would teach me all the aspects of conducting a romance?''

"And haven't I done so? You've got the poor sod eating out of your hand, Abby. What more do you want?''

She swallowed hard, marshaling her courage. "I know virtually nothing about physical love."

Just for a moment, he looked utterly confounded. Then he leaned back against the pillows and chuckled, his bronzed throat rippling with mirth. "You're a smart woman, Abby. I've seen you poring over Rowan's anatomy texts. And don't pretend you didn't study every page of the *Kama Sutra* when you thought I wasn't looking."

Oh, Lord. He'd noticed.

"It's not the same," she persisted. "I read books about riding a horse, but until I actually rode one, I had no idea how it was done." She stepped boldly forward, nearly touching the edge of the bed with her knees. "Think what a disappointing bride I'd be if I proved graceless and bashful on the wedding night."

"If you believe I'd think about that for one moment, you're insane," he said, waving his hand with impatience. "Go away, Abby. You don't want to be with me tonight, or any other night."

She sniffed. "You're afraid of what will happen if I stay."

He laughed again in that strange, cruel way. "I can't teach you about love, physical or otherwise. If it's whore's tricks you want—"

"What if I do?"

"Take your clothes off," he said.

He was trying to frighten and intimidate her into

running away, but this was Jamie, she reminded herself. She could never be afraid of him.

Resolutely, she dropped her cloak to the floor. Beneath it, she wore the dainty batiste nightgown Madame Broussard had created. Then the awful truth struck her, something she hadn't thought of until now. In fact, she hadn't thought much about her infirmity in weeks. Jamie had kept her too busy with dress fittings and mule-barge rides down the C&O Canal, with mock social engagements and riding lessons. He had, she realized, kept her too busy *living* to worry about her foot.

"Put out the light," she said.

"No." He folded his arms across his chest. "Love doesn't just happen in the dark. You've got to learn that." He crossed his arms over his chest, looking quite sure of himself. He expected her to flee and hide.

She resisted the urge. He'd once told her that she was afraid to take a risk. Now she was about to risk everything. How terrible could this be? she wondered. Surely no worse than the uncounted humiliations she'd suffered in the past. Women all over the world disrobed in front of men and survived the experience.

But most women didn't look like she did.

Taking a deep breath, she stepped out of her slippers, undid the row of pearlized buttons down the front of the gown. Finally she let the garment slide to the floor, leaving her clad in nothing but a thin shift. When she saw the way he stared at her, she battled an even stronger urge to flee and never come back. But deep down, she realized she didn't want to go. There was something compelling in his angry stare, something that made her yearn to stay, to touch him.

"Now what?" she asked.

Again, she glimpsed uncertainty—just a flicker—beneath his façade. But all too quickly, the cynicism returned. "Come to bed, and I'll show you."

She took a step toward him, lurching a little. And then she realized he was staring at her foot.

Abigail froze, wishing the floor would swallow her up. She didn't dare look at him as she backed away, groping for her cloak. But then he was there, standing before her, taking her in his arms.

"Oh, honey," he said, smiling down into her face. "Is this what had you so worried?"

With a decided lack of inhibition, he swept her up and laid her on the bed, still warm from his body heat. He slid his hand down her leg, cradling her foot.

She wasn't sure what startled her more, his reaction to her foot, or her reaction to the fact that he didn't have on a single stitch of clothing. Good heavens...

"Abby, love, don't look at me like that. I would never hurt you," he said. All his cruelty had dissolved into a new tenderness he'd never shown her before. "You needn't hide a single precious part of yourself, don't you know that?"

He didn't seem to expect an answer, which was just as well, for Abigail found herself speechless. When he pressed her back against the bed, she sank willingly beneath him, melting with shock and lust and wonder. He held her gaze with his as his fingers slowly untied the ribbon of her shift. Then he parted the fragile fabric, looked down at her and let a quiet hiss escape him. "On second thought, maybe you'd better hide this particular part of yourself." He lowered his head for a wickedly intimate kiss. "There is such a thing as too much beauty."

She shuddered with a flash of nervousness, of wildness.

"Are you sure you want to do this?" he asked.

"Very sure. But I don't know what to do."

"Yes, you do," he assured her.

Letting impulse take over, she ran her fingers through his hair and traced her hands over his back, lifting herself toward him for a kiss. But when she found a band of ridges across his back, she drew away with a frown. "What is this?" Moving to one side, she gasped. "Jamie, dear God. What are all these scars?"

"A reminder of youthful indiscretion," he said, reaching to extinguish the lamp. "It was so long ago, I barely remember it."

"You mean you refuse to speak of it."

"Love, there's no need."

Ah, but there was. He had been hurt, too, and she wanted to know all of his secrets. She wanted to know everything about him.

He skimmed his hand over her bare shoulder and ran it down her arm. "According to Arab lore, the universe consists of seven heavens, one above the other," he said. "The first is made of emeralds, and the second of red marigolds..." Between his whispered words, he paused to kiss her in places he had no business kissing—except that she wanted him to. She would die if he stopped.

"And the third?"

"Red hyacinth. The fourth of whitest silver, the fifth of gold, the sixth of pearl..." He traveled lower still, his hands leaving fire in their wake. "...and the seventh consists of brilliant light." His lips found hers, and he kissed her with excruciating slowness.

Then he lifted his mouth. "How am I doing, Madame Astronomer?"

Finally, somehow, she found her voice, though it was no more than a whisper. "Oh, I have to believe there are so many more, too many to count."

A flush spread over her body, and she felt the burn of a hunger she finally understood. It had to do with the things she felt when she danced with him under the stars or studied his forbidden books, or watched a stallion covering a mare. The urge inside her was natural and compelling, with a crude majesty all its own.

Her hands explored at will, moving over him with a mysterious knowledge she hadn't known she possessed.

He kissed her again and again, and their bodies strained so close that she began to believe the theory of spontaneous combustion might be true. His hands and mouth slid lower again, finding places of such shocking sensitivity that she could hardly breathe. His touch strayed everywhere, awakening every inch of her body, lingering at her knee, calf, ankle...her foot. She tried to tell him what she was feeling, but words had no place in this moment, and the sound that drifted from her was a wild, almost feral cry.

She learned that, for now, she needed no teacher but instinct. She simply touched his strong, scarred body, trying to show him what was in her heart, her hands drawing from him an unguarded response of delight. The contrasting smoothness and hardness of him was a wonder to her, and she surrendered to the knowing gentleness of his caress. When their bodies joined, she gasped and buried her face in his shoulder, overcome by the sweet pain and wonder of her first intimacy.

"Are you all right, love?" He whispered the soothing words in her ear, but she scarcely heard, because her heart beat so loudly in her head.

"I am now," she said. "Yes, I am." Guided by instinct alone, she moved beneath him, and the moonlight through the window outlined his shoulders, trembling slightly as he matched her movements with a slow rhythm. In his way, he was more magical than the night sky, looming over her, full of dreams and mysteries, endlessly seductive.

She had the strangest feeling that every moment she'd spent with him had been leading up to this, from the time he caught her in his arms at the Wilkes wedding, through all the laughter and teasing, the absurd lessons in deportment and dancing, the enticing ones in kissing and flirting. Everything seemed designed to bring her here to his arms, his bed. She shut her eyes, and the colors of the seven heavens spun through her mind, emerald and marigold and silver and finally, brilliant light. Then there were no colors or even a coherent thought, only a whirlwind of feelings rising on an updraft of emotion as he took her to the place where stars were born.

In the long moments afterward, neither of them moved. The only sound was that of their breathing, and after the interlude of silence, he lay beside her, tucking her against the curve of his body.

So this was what all the fuss was about, she reflected, finding it ever harder to think with any coherence. No wonder people never spoke of it. There simply weren't any words for this soaring joy.

Moonlight through the window illuminated Jamie's

face, and she thought perhaps he looked a bit stunned, and more vulnerable than she'd ever seen him.

"Is something the matter?" she whispered.

"I feel like a different man with you," he said.

She released a drowsy sigh of contentment, and because she couldn't resist, she slid her open hand across his chest, exploring. "I think I've just discovered a new heavenly body."

"You're better off spending your time on the roof, looking for comets."

"Jamie—"

"Abby—"

They both spoke at once, and she laughed a little nervously. "Something is happening to us. This time we've spent together has come to mean more to me than you could ever imagine." She saw him frown in the shadowy light, and hurried on before he could interrupt her. "You showed me so much, Jamie. You taught me to be my very best self. But now I realize I can only be my best when I'm with you. Because you see, another transfer of affection has occurred."

He stiffened, and she could tell he was bracing himself. "What do you mean?"

"Well, after discovering I was the letter writer, Boyd transferred his affection from Helena to me, just as you predicted. What you neglected to tell me is that our flirtation of letters was only that, a flirtation, shallow and lacking in substance."

He thrust her away and sat against the pillows. "Did the cad throw you over?"

"No, nothing like that. This is something *I've* discovered, because you taught me to listen to my own heart." Abigail floundered. She wasn't saying this well at all. "Heavens, can't you feel it, too? This—

what we did just now, what we are together—is no
flirtation, Jamie. It's very real. More real than anything I've ever felt.'' She held her breath, waiting for
his response.

He stood swiftly, not bothering to cover himself,
and tossed the nightgown at her. ''Go home, Abby.
The tutorial is over.''

''Don't you understand what I'm saying? I love
you.''

The words hung in the air like a forbidden curse.

Then Jamie spat a real curse and pulled on his trousers with insulting haste. ''You have no idea what
you're saying.'' He tugged Abigail's gown over her
head, stuck the slippers on her feet and pulled her up,
wrapping the cloak around her. ''You don't fall in
love over something like...what we just did.''

''It's not only that,'' she said. Why was it so hard
to make him understand what she now saw so clearly?
''We should have realized what was happening, right
from the start. We've been falling in love moment by
moment, day by day, from the first time we met.''

''This has never been about love, but mutual convenience. I wanted to make an ally of your father,
you wanted a romance with the vice president's son.
We both got what we wanted, didn't we? Christ, if
you reject the poor sod now, his father will turn right
back to the railroad companies, your father will drop
his support of my cause and I'll lose everything I
came here to accomplish. Worse than that, the people
of my district will lose. They'll be turned from their
homes, and then what?''

''So a railroad issue is keeping us apart?''

He chuckled. ''You know it's more than that,
Abby.''

"It doesn't have to be that way. If you'd only listen—"

"You don't love me," he snapped. "You have better judgment than that. Affection that switches on and off so quickly is not to be trusted."

"You're wrong. I do love you, and you love me. I know you do."

With a gentle shove, he pushed her toward the door. "No, you don't, and neither do I. And that's a damned lucky thing, because otherwise, this would be a very sad moment."

Twenty-Nine

The old Abigail would have given way to tears and hopelessness. She would have accepted defeat with a quiet shrug of her shoulders. She would have cried for hours, all alone, unwilling to upset her father and sister with her misery.

But what she discovered, after Jamie sent her from his bed, was that there were some things that hurt so deeply she couldn't cry. Weeping would merely trivialize the pain when in fact it was a magnificent wound. When a woman declared her love for a man, went to his bed and offered herself body, heart and soul, she was entitled to collapse when he rejected her.

Abigail did not collapse. Jamie's dismissal merely sharpened her determination to prove what she knew in her heart was true. Somehow, amidst all the tutoring and teasing, the verbal sparring and political maneuvering, she and Jamie had fallen in love.

He was going to be hoist by his own petard, as the saying went. He'd taught her to dig for the truth behind the façade, that words had a power all their own and that true love happened even against a person's will. He'd also taught her what heartbreak felt like. She wouldn't thank him for that, but neither would she surrender to it.

In a state of steely calm, she went to bed and stared at the ceiling. Many years ago, when she was only twelve, she had used silver-leaf paint to depict the night sky there, earnestly and inaccurately arranging the constellations of the zodiac overhead, hoping her father wouldn't notice and order the ceiling to be re-painted.

He'd never said a word about her project. She wasn't certain he'd even seen it, but something told her he had, long ago.

She slept with surprising soundness and dressed with care, leaving early the next morning before her father or sister arose. They wouldn't miss her. Often after her late-night sweepings of the sky, she stayed abed with the door shut. They would assume she was still asleep.

But, in fact, she had much to do, and planned her day with the attention to detail of a battle commander.

Stepping from a hansom cab at the corner of Tenth and D Streets, she caught the reflection in a broad shop window of a stylish young woman who carried herself with a certain panache. With a start, she realized the young woman was her.

Somewhere along the way, without really knowing it was happening, Abigail had learned to comport herself differently. When she walked down the street or entered a room, she didn't shuffle her feet or slump her shoulders as though afraid she might stumble and fall.

She held her head high and forgot to worry about her bad foot. She looked people in the eye and com-

manded attention. Despite what had transpired between her and Jamie Calhoun the previous night, she
kept her composure. Indeed, his rejection made her
all the more determined to find out what had turned
him so cold and cynical.

She felt the nip of winter in the air, and tucked her
hands into her knitted muff. When she walked into
the editorial offices of the *Washington Post,* a young
man came instantly to assist her.

"I would like to see Mr. Timothy Doyle, please."

"Right this way, ma'am." He led her through a
maze of long tables where clerks hunched over typing
machines. At one end stood a Linotype operator cast-
ing type with a loud, metallic chatter. Telegraph op-
erators sent and received wires at a furious rate. At
the end of the room, a row of desks lined one wall.
Doyle sat at a rickety oak desk littered with snippings,
photographs, invitations, magazines and menus.

He stood immediately, offering his hand in greeting. "Miss Cabot. Such an honor," he said. "Such
an honor. To what do I owe the pleasure?"

"This isn't a social call." Abigail still remembered
Doyle's reaction when he'd first heard she was going
to marry Lieutenant Butler. To remind him of that
incident, she allowed a touch of frost to glaze her
stare as she looked around the big open room and
raised her voice over the clack of machinery. "However, I prefer not to conduct business in a sweat-
shop."

"Of course. Shall we step into my private office?"

She nodded, and he held the door for her. "Please,
right this way." The office window offered a view of
a pleasant area of town houses and embassies. A line

of bare trees marked a cobbled path to a small city commons.

After they seated themselves, Abigail went straight to the point. "In your recent column, to which I confess an unhealthy fascination, you mentioned Princess Layla and her adventure with Jamie Calhoun."

Doyle leaned back, looking impressed. "I never mentioned Calhoun's name."

"Your innuendo was sufficient. I want you to tell me what part of it is true and what you made up in order to sell papers."

"Miss Cabot, I'm a journalist. I write of factual matters."

"Even when they humiliate visiting royalty?"

He subjected her to a narrow-eyed stare, but she refused to flinch. "What is it you really want to know?" he demanded, as direct and blunt as she.

Good. She wanted the truth, undisguised by sly insinuation. "Everything," she stated.

He chuckled. "You must have an appetite for scandal, ma'am."

"I have an appetite for the truth. Even if it's upsetting—or unflattering."

He regarded her sheepishly. "Will I ever live down that remark I made over the telephone?"

"Tell me what I came to know, and I'll consider letting you apologize."

He took out a thick file and set it on the table between them. "These are my sources from the original reports. About two years ago, there was a wire from a London correspondent about a scandal in the small principality of Khayrat. A royal princess was discovered to be carrying on with a westerner. She was sentenced to suffer the traditional punishment for her behavior.''

''What sort of punishment?''

''She was to have her nostrils slit.''

Abigail shuddered, picturing the beautiful princess, scarred and humiliated. ''Thank God she escaped the mutilation.''

''She didn't escape. I assume she traded information for mercy and identified her lover as Jamie Calhoun.''

Abigail's chest tightened with tension. ''What did he do?''

''Even after his arrest, he proclaimed the innocence of the princess. He alleged that, despite his attempts to compromise her honor, she had maintained her virtue. He begged punishment for himself. The princess's family obliged all too willingly. I doubt they were eager to see their daughter disfigured and dishonored. Calhoun was hauled away to prison and sentenced to die by beheading. There was an escape attempt, but he was recaptured.

''Witnesses said the prisoner was tortured to the point of insanity. A hood was tied over his face, and he was dragged to a public parade ground before a crowd of thousands, with platforms built for royalty and dignitaries. The princess was forced to watch.''

Abigail couldn't feel her fingertips. She had her hands clasped so tightly they'd gone numb. She could feel the color being leached from her face as he spoke, and she must have looked terrible, for he paused.

''Shall I go on? We couldn't even print the rest of the story. Decency forbade it.''

She was tempted to let him stop, but this was a part of Jamie's past. If there was any hope of healing his heart, she had to understand the events that had turned him hard and bitter.

"Don't spare me a single detail, Mr. Doyle," she said.

He clenched his fists as he spoke. "First they...cut off his hands, one at a time. Then they took his head. They say the princess's screams could be heard above the roar of the crowd until she fainted dead away. The accused man's body was left to be devoured by wild dogs." He exhaled with a shudder. "So Jamie Calhoun escaped. What we don't know is who was killed in his place."

Abigail sat silent, battling nausea and listening to the cold wind rattling the office window as she pictured the strange and violent scene.

Her blood chilled. Because unlike Doyle, she did know.

Intent on finding the rest of the answers, she went straight to the splendid row houses of Willard Square, where foreign legations and visitors often stayed. Doyle had given her the address of the residence where the Khayrati legation was staying. Outside, it resembled all the other staid greystones of the area, and she calmly gave her name and made her request to the guard posted there. Moments later, a man of enormous girth and height summoned her to follow him. Although his size was intimidating, his face was as round and mild as a summer moon.

Past wrought-iron gates and a stone archway, the house resembled the Alhambra in miniature. A courtyard tiled in intricate geometric designs surrounded a burbling fountain. Servants and officials moved quietly along the colonnaded archway at the periphery.

Abigail had the eerie impression that she'd stepped into another world, someplace foreign and exotic…and dangerous.

Her escort led her through the colonnade and up a flight of stairs. He spoke briefly to a robed serving woman who motioned Abigail inside. She found herself in a perfumed cave of red silk. As Abigail surrendered her wrap to the woman, the foreign princess stood to greet her.

Without the half veil, she was even more stunningly beautiful than Abigail had imagined. Her dark coloring and lush lips echoed the provocative images depicted in Jamie's books, and her watchful eyes held secrets the old Abigail would have been too timid to probe.

"We made each other's acquaintance at the aquarium," Abigail said after greeting her.

"Of course. I remember you, Miss Cabot." The princess spoke with a startlingly precise boarding-school accent as she gestured toward a grouping of ottomans and cushions around a low table. "Please be seated."

Abigail perched on the edge of an ottoman. The serving woman poured tea that smelled faintly of jasmine into a tiny cup. "I shall come straight to the point. I'm here to ask you about a matter of importance to me—Jamie Calhoun."

The princess's face and posture were a study in control as she sat down across from Abigail. "About his political troubles, you mean."

This took Abigail completely by surprise. "I don't understand. Political troubles?"

"With Mr. Horace Riordan and his railroad company."

Abigail regarded the woman with amazement. "I didn't realize you were so interested in the politics of my country."

"Everything about your country interests me, Miss Cabot. Here, a man's fortune is more important than life or death." She sent Abigail a mysterious smile. "A woman behind a veil is invisible to powerful men. The Americans believe I'm not only invisible, but deaf and mute and too stupid to understand English. They're all wrong. I was educated at St. Catherine's in Lincolnshire."

Though she spoke beautifully, there was a subtle undercurrent to her tone that Abigail disliked. "So you're smart enough to tell me of this, but you weren't smart enough to stop your countrymen from arresting Jamie and sentencing him to death."

At last, the princess's composure faltered. The color faded from her face, and her eyes darted wildly, like those of a trapped animal. She said something in her native tongue, and the serving woman left the room. "Someone has told you lies about me," the princess said.

"Then you can tell the truth, and set me straight. You can tell me what really happened."

"Why do you ask me about something so long past? Why not him?"

"Because he wouldn't tell me."

"Why should I tell you?"

Abigail should have expected this. She didn't quite know what to say. "He's a changed man because of what happened in your country. There are wounds that have never healed."

"And telling you will heal him?"

"I have no idea. But I know it wouldn't make

things worse. There's a part of him I don't understand, and...I want to. I need to.''

The princess sipped her tea, and her hand shook a little when she set down her cup. "I see."

"Do you?" The room was so quiet that Abigail could hear her own heart beating.

"Only as two women who love the same man can see." The princess began speaking in a low, slow, beguiling voice. "The Jamie Calhoun I met in my country was a very different man from the cynical stranger I saw at the aquarium. He was a romantic young man, with a huge appetite for life. The Khayrati people loved him. We loved his talent with horses, his merry ways. He was constantly in motion, always laughing, always talking of this or that.'' She gazed off into some unseen distance, her eyes clouded with remembrances Abigail could only imagine.

She pictured Jamie as that laughing young man, his edge of cynicism gone. Oh, how she wished she could have known him then.

"I loved him with all that I was," the princess said, her voice taking on a tone of confession. Most likely, Abigail realized, she had never spoken of what had happened. "But I had to let him go. Because, of course, a love affair with a *ferenghi* is forbidden, but more so because he was...too much for me. It is hard to explain. He had too much passion, strength, appetite for life. His expectations were too high. I never felt equal to that.''

"But that didn't keep you from carrying on a love affair with him.''

"Would it keep *you* from him?'' the princess countered.

"It would if I knew he'd be killed for loving me," Abigail shot back.

"The heart is a foolish organ," she whispered. "I had no thought of danger."

"Tell me what happened," Abigail said in a gentler tone. "Please, I must know."

"We arranged to meet at the seaport of Almulla. Jamie and his brother had finished with their horse buying and were ready to take ship for Gibraltar and then America. What we didn't know was that Prince Abdul Ali Pasha's spies knew of the plan."

"The prince who is now your husband."

She acknowledged this with a nod. "Jamie was arrested at Almulla, and we were questioned separately. I'll never know what it is Jamie said, or what they did to him."

Abigail winced, remembering the hard ridges of scars she'd discovered on his back. She couldn't bear to think of what he'd endured. And how could he have let another man take his place? She suspected that was why he was so haunted and driven.

"I never saw him again until the day—" The princess stopped and took another sip of tea. "The day of his execution. I was never to know the condemned man was not Jamie. From a distance, I could see only a wounded man dressed in bloody rags, with a sack tied over his head. The proclamation of death certified that the victim was James Calhoun." She set down her teacup with a nervous clatter. "I am not a terrible person. I watched a man die because of me. Do you think it left me unaffected?"

"You married the murderer."

"In my country, a woman is not free to choose."

Abigail let it go. The princess had told her enough,

and finally, Abigail understood. She'd seen into the shadows of mystery that darkened Jamie's heart. To save her beautiful face, Jamie had proclaimed her innocence, willingly trading his life for her beauty. Somehow, the life taken had been Noah's. This was why Jamie could not, would not let himself love anyone. This was why he had stopped believing in love altogether. Love had failed him entirely.

Thirty

Abigail wanted to go straight to Jamie, but when she returned to Dumbarton Street he was out, and had left no word of when he would return. It was just as well, she decided. She had a matter of honor to attend to.

The journey to Annapolis and the meeting with Boyd occupied all of the following day, and upon her return, she felt drained and peculiar, as though she had just been to a funeral. He'd accepted her decision with military decorum and a faint hint of relief. Apparently, in the matter of marriage, he had felt the pressure of duty as well.

And she hadn't even faced the most difficult part of the ordeal. That would occur when Father returned home. She made her way to Helena's room, needing her sister's understanding and moral support.

But Helena's room was empty save for the phantom scent of her favorite perfume hanging in the air. Restless from being confined to a hired coach all day, Abigail paced the room, pretending she could glide like an ice skater. In truth, she'd become less preoccupied with her infirmity of late, but maybe she was only fooling herself, and she was as clumsy as ever. The very thought caused her foot to catch on the edge of the rug, and she tripped, breaking her teeth-jarring fall with both hands splayed out in front of her. She managed to tip the skirted dressing table on its side, sending bottles and atomizers flying across the floor.

Hoping Dolly wouldn't come to investigate the noise, she sat back on her heels, muttering in frustration. Would she never learn?

An old cigar box had been hidden under the skirt of the table, and Abigail had managed to knock that over, too. She began stuffing the papers back into the box, but in a moment her movements slowed and her forehead creased with a frown.

The pages were covered with row upon row of an almost childlike scrawl, Helena's name, over and over again:

Miss Helena Cabot
Mrs. Michael Rowan
Mrs. Rowan...

Despite her own troubles, Abigail felt a rush of sympathy for her sister. Helena pretended her inability to read and write didn't matter in the least to her. Abigail used to offer to help, but Helena always shook her head, proclaiming that the cause was lost. "I am a grown woman. If I haven't learned by now, I never shall."

But this discovery proved that Helena, too, wished for things beyond her grasp.

Abigail was using the hearth broom to sweep up the bits of broken glass when Helena walked in the room, carrying a large wooden carton.

"Abigail? Dolly and I thought we heard—oh." She

stood in the doorway, surveying the skirted table lying on its side, the broken bottle...the box of papers.
A fevered shade of crimson rose to her cheeks. She
said nothing, but set the carton on the bed, crossed
the room and set the small table upright again.

"Helena, I'm so sorry," Abigail said. "I came
looking for you and overturned the table. It was an
accident."

"Of course it was." She spoke softly as she positioned the table against the wall beneath the hanging
mirror.

Abigail took a deep breath. "Helena, dearest, I
wish you'd let me help—"

"We've spoken of this before, Abigail. Nothing's
changed. I still have no head for learning, and I never
will."

"I've changed," Abigail said. "It wasn't easy, I'll
admit that, but I finally stopped letting my foot and
my shyness keep me from living my life. The only
difference was that I couldn't hide my problem under
the dressing table." She shoved the crate beneath the
table skirt. "I could help you. And what about Professor Rowan?"

"Michael is a brilliant man. He could never tolerate
a dunce like me."

"Give him a chance. He might surprise you."

"I gave him a chance. He's pretending the reason
he threw me over is that he lacks the money or status
for a Cabot. But the real reason is that he knows, in
time, he'll get bored with me."

Hearing a scrabbling sound in the crate on the bed,
Abigail peered inside. A busy pink nose twitched at
her. "He gave you Socrates?"

"It's the only thing he ever gave me." An ironic smile thinned Helena's lips. "Well, practically the only thing. You see, he accepted a post at a women's college in the North, and he'll be leaving soon. I imagine he'll be quite content, teaching at an institution with a thousand wealthy young women who'll treat him like a god."

Abigail blinked in surprise. "He's leaving?"

"He is."

"But I thought the two of you— Helena, you love him. You can't let him go."

"I already have." Her mouth flattened into a firm line. "My mind is made up. I'm going to marry Mr. Barnes."

"Senator Troy Barnes?"

"The very one."

"You hardly know the man."

"That's about to change, isn't it?" In a flutter of movement, Helena's slender hand strayed to her midsection, and then she busied herself making a place for Socrates on the windowsill.

A faint whistle sounded in the street outside. Two floors below, the front door swished open. Abigail hurried to the window, drew aside the lace curtain and felt a knot form in her stomach. "Father's home," she said.

She made certain every hair was in place, every fold of her gown straight and all traces of nervousness ruthlessly buried. Then she took a deep breath and knocked smartly at the door to her father's study.

"Yes, what is it?"

Stepping inside, she found her father at his massive

fruitwood desk, reading the *Post.* He set it aside and smiled at her, and for a moment Abigail simply stood there and savored that smile, knowing it would vanish into fury when she made her confession.

"May I speak to you a moment, Father?"

"Of course. I'm sure you've been busy with your plans. I can't tell you how pleased I am that the Butlers prefer a short engagement."

"That's what I need to speak to you about," she said, keeping her voice steady.

"Is there a problem with the date? Mrs. Butler wished it to be the day before Christmas especially, so I do hope—"

"Father." Her sharp interruption startled them both. "There is no easy way to tell you this. After much soul-searching, after much discomfort and regret, I've broken off the engagement with Lieutenant Butler."

A ruddy flush crept into his cheeks, and a rime of frost hardened his eyes. "What?"

"I can't marry him. I traveled to Annapolis today, and told him myself." She paused, remembering the stiff shock in Boyd's face, and the fact that beneath his surprise and dismay, she'd detected that flicker of relief. "Lieutenant Butler is a young man with many people who love him. He professed to be disappointed, but actually, I sensed he was a little relieved."

He pressed the palms of his hands on the green leather desk blotter. "Nonsense, girl, you can't cancel this wedding. You've got a case of the bride's jitters. Common enough, I'm told."

"It's not the jitters. Believe me, I know the difference. What I mistook for love was simply a powerful form of wishful thinking, Father.'' She looked him straight in the eye, expecting lightning to strike, but to her surprise it didn't. ''And a big part of my wishing had nothing to do with the lieutenant or even getting married. It had to do with pleasing you.''

''Pleasing me?'' He lifted his eyebrows, and at that moment she had a glimpse of the man he was when a rare uncertainty overtook him.

''You seem surprised that I would concern myself with that.''

''I never demanded that you please me. I never pressured you and your sister to marry well. Don't you think I heard the gossip, the speculation that something was the matter with you, or with my ability to provide a dowry? Yet I never forced you to choose a husband. *Damn it,* Abigail, I waited until you came to me, announcing your plans.''

She had never heard him curse before. The cold apprehension in her gut knotted even tighter. Yet she refused to back down. Lack of honesty had caused her no end of trouble, and now she was through with deception. ''Perhaps you never explicitly demanded that I marry, but I felt the pressure of your expectations nonetheless.''

''Did you?''

Taking a deep breath, she said, ''I agreed to the marriage with one aim in mind—to make you proud of me. And do you know what I find most distressing? It worked. The moment I behaved in a fashion that met your approval, you showered me with love and pride.''

''Of course I was proud of you. He's a Butler. He

could have any bride in the country, and he chose you.'' He turned to the oil portrait on the wall of the study. Beatrice Cabot gazed serenely from the canvas, forever young, forever beautiful. ''It seems you made a lot of assumptions without asking me.'' When he looked back at Abigail, his face was filled with a peculiar anguish. ''If I applauded the match, it was because I believed you would finally be happy, Abigail. That's all I've ever wanted for you.''

The chill inside her started to burn with anger and frustration. How many years, how much anguish had she wasted, trying to please him? *That's all I've ever wanted for you.* Could she truly be hearing those words from him?

This was the first time she could remember defying her father. Bracing herself for his rage, she kept expecting the world to come to an end, but amazingly it didn't. ''If ending this betrothal means I must forfeit your love, then so be it. I've done without it before.''

He froze, and his face turned white. He looked as though she'd shot him. ''My God. Is that what you think?'' Something in his manner held her silent with apprehension. ''Abigail, you could not be more wrong about me. From the instant you drew breath as the tiniest infant, you've owned every bit of my heart, you and your sister both.''

She felt her jaw drop. He was like a different man, sitting there, no longer remote and godlike, but confused and...real.

''I was pleased with your marriage plan because I thought, at last, you'd finally found a man who could

give you what I've failed to provide all your life—
true happiness.''

"Oh, no, Father—'' She stopped to make sense of
her thoughts, but the whole world had turned upside
down. Everything she'd believed about her father was
changing, becoming unfamiliar...but true in a way
she hadn't recognized until now. "I never knew. I
felt inadequate, my achievements as well as my troubles overlooked—''

"If I dismissed you, perhaps it's because you never
seemed to need me." He flexed his hands nervously
on the desk. Her father seemed less at ease with her
than he was with the United States Senate. "Can't
you understand that, Abigail? You were always
smarter, better, wiser than the rest of the world. When
you were a child, I couldn't even read you a bedtime
story. By the age of four, you were reading them to
yourself and to your sister. You never needed help
with your studies, for your learning surpassed mine
years ago."

Abigail didn't dare move. She forgot to breathe.
She wondered if all this time she had been missing
something or inadvertently fending off his love and
concern. She heard herself say, *Don't worry, I can do
it myself, Father* over and over again, never thinking
about what her words told him—that she didn't need
him, perhaps didn't even want him.

Regrets welled up inside her. What a terrible waste
of years and tears. Why couldn't she have let him see
her need? Why couldn't he have let her know his
heart?

"You had your stars and your dreams," her father
continued. "You already possessed things I couldn't

touch or imagine or begin to give you. I felt inadequate, and so, I suppose, I gave you nothing.''

''Father, no. That's not true.''

''Then I didn't give you enough. Not because I didn't love you but because I had no idea what it was you wanted or needed. With Helena, it was always clear. She needed guidance, wisdom, advice, control. You already possessed those things in abundance.'' His voice shook. ''Hard as it is to admit, you never needed me. I had nothing to add to your gifts.''

''But I thought—'' She swallowed and started again. ''I've always been the most imperfect of daughters. From the moment of my birth, I've been that way.''

''Dear God, you mean your foot?'' He stood and paced in agitation, his face florid. ''You can't possibly believe that.'' Turning his back on her, he faced the portrait again. The artist had captured her mother's deep, mysterious eyes, her almost-smiling mouth. ''When you were born, your mother declared that you were the child she'd dreamed of having. In her last moments, she held you in her arms and wept for joy. And I—'' He turned and faced her at last. ''I wept, too, Abigail. You were her last gift to me. How could I possibly regard you with anything but affection?''

It took several tries before she found her voice. ''If that's true, why did you always disapprove of my clumsiness?''

Confusion creased his brow. ''Disapprove? My girl, each time I saw you stumble or fall, I suffered the torments of the damned. I had no idea you took that as disapproval. Don't you know I'd give anything to spare you from the pain you've suffered all these years?''

She swayed, almost unable to speak, but she forced herself to say one last thing, the truest thing in her heart. ''Father, I only ever wanted one thing from you.''

''I realize that, finally.'' He sat down slowly and stared across the desk at her. ''Is it too late to offer it to you now?''

Thirty-One

The night was cold and the hour was late. His hair still damp from bathing, Jamie stood at the window of his room, staring at the house next door and flexing his raw knuckles. He'd tried to escape what he was feeling. He'd ridden Oscar long and hard into the countryside until both he and the horse nearly dropped from exhaustion. He'd joined a group of Georgetown canal lock tenders in their nightly pursuit of violent sports, but even several rounds of bare-knuckle boxing had failed to blot out his thoughts. The agony hung on the edges of his awareness, and when he stopped riding or stopped fighting, it all came flooding back.

Now, back in his room, he had no means of exhausting his mind into blankness. Next door, the lights had been extinguished, but he wondered if Abigail would appear on the roof to pursue her solitary search of the night sky. If she did, he knew he'd be tempted to join her, but he also knew he wouldn't let himself indulge the urge. It was too dangerous; it made no sense.

Ah, but she haunted him. He could still feel the silken warmth of her, could still savor the sweetness of her innocent offering. Could still hear the faint echo of her whispered *I love you.*

That declaration would stay with him for the rest of his life, a bittersweet reminder of an extraordinary friendship with a woman who believed he could be so much more than he was.

It was over now. They had separate paths to follow. Jamie gritted his teeth and shuddered, feeling the loss of her like a physical pain, sharper in its way than any torture he had suffered in a dank sandstone cell in a far-off land.

The empty house sighed and settled. Now that Rowan was gone, taking all his messy contraptions with him, Jamie had the place to himself. Not that he'd be keeping it long. He couldn't possibly stay on Dumbarton Street, so perilously close to temptation.

A knock sounded in the foyer below, and he started, then tightened the towel slung around his waist. It was Abigail. Who else would come to call at this late hour?

Frozen in place, he waited for her to go away. He shouldn't have been surprised when he heard the door swish open and footsteps on the stair.

Damn her. She seemed determined to chip away at him.

Feeling an instant physical reaction to her proximity, he pulled on a robe, then went to wait at the top of the stairs. He racked his brain for the words that would banish her, but the woman who emerged from the shadows was not Abigail.

"Caroline," he said. "What the hell are you doing here?"

The uncertain light of the fireplace spilled from the bedchamber. Her bold gaze coasted over him.

"I had to see you," she whispered. "No one must know. My driver is waiting at the end of the lane."

"Good." Grasping her shoulders, he turned her toward the stairs. "He can take you right back to wherever you came from."

She wrenched away and walked straight into his bedroom, dropping her cloak on a chair as she passed it. "I'm not leaving."

He ground his teeth in silent frustration. The last thing he needed was for the wife of Horace Riordan to take up residence in his bedroom.

"You have to drop your opposition to the railroad plan," she informed him. "I thought it only fair to warn you that my husband intends to see to it that it goes through."

"This isn't news to me, Caroline." She still amused him, he realized. He admired her cold nerve, her brazenness. He couldn't help but like the way she kept staring at him.

"Don't cross him, Jamie. That's what I came to tell you. Horace has a certain talent for making things difficult for those who oppose him."

"Oh, dear," he said softly. "A threat?"

"An offer," she said. "He's prepared to pay you a fortune to drop the issue."

Jamie laughed aloud. "Sweet Caroline, I didn't come to Washington to sell the families of my district down the river. God knows, my granddaddy made a practice of that."

''The railroad company will offer them the chance to move out of their poverty. They wouldn't have to live or die by the seasons. Think of it, Jamie. Those struggling families could move to the city, find steady work—''

''In sweatshops and unheated mills. Sounds like heaven on earth, Caroline.''

''They'd never have to wonder where their next meal was coming from, never again suffer through drought or frost. It's a stable life.''

''It's a filthy life. This is their own enterprise. They won't be bought for a wage or a promise of broth and bread, and you damn well know it, or you wouldn't be here.''

''That's not the only reason I came to see you,'' she said, her voice thrumming with a seductive promise.

Abigail was anxious to see Jamie, but she forced herself to wait until she knew everyone in the house was asleep. She didn't care how late it was; from the start, they'd made a practice of meeting at improper hours, and tonight would be no different. At last, everything was going to be fine. Now that she understood what lay buried in his past, she saw the future clearly.

Jamie had been right about so many things, and she was only now realizing it. He'd been right when he told her that she was hiding from the world, afraid to let her heart love fully. She discovered the truth of that the night she'd spent in his arms.

And he had been right when he told her what she should have known all along about her father. His respect mattered far less than the more difficult issue of learning to respect herself. She'd been so fearful about telling him she wasn't going to marry Boyd, yet it had turned into the most honest conversation she'd ever had with her father.

Jamie had also been right, so long ago, on the first night they met, when he claimed she didn't love Boyd, because true love couldn't be expressed by poetry on a page. It came from somewhere deep and mysterious, a place that wasn't always safe and comfortable.

The only thing Jamie had been wrong about was the fact that he didn't consider himself worthy of anyone's love.

She had much to discuss with him tonight.

Dumbarton Street lay quiet and deserted save for a closed hack at the end of the road. Soft gaslight played over the carriage horse, its head lowered in slumber. Holding her cloak around her, she hurried toward Jamie's house.

Even before she tested the door, she was startled to hear a murmur of voices upstairs, and then footsteps coming down toward her. She barely had time to shrink back into the shadows of the tiny walled yard before the door swished open and two people emerged. Her sharp eyes picked out a crimson-cloaked woman with slender hands and a pale, beguiling—and exceedingly familiar—face.

Caroline Fortenay Riordan looked every bit as beautiful as she had the night of Nancy Wilkes's wedding. And with Jamie, she acted every bit as bold, clinging to his arm, whispering his name. Abigail couldn't hear his murmured reply as he escorted her to the waiting hack at the end of the street. By now, she could only hear the terrible pounding of her own heart in her ears.

Every instinct roared at her to run and hide, to curl up into a ball of private pain, but she resisted. Despite the sudden frost sweeping over her emotions, she forced herself to wait until he returned. He stood talking to Caroline for a long time before handing her up into the coach as Abigail struggled for composure. Had she been wrong about him after all?

The slow clop of the horse's hooves against the brick surface of the street filled the night. Jamie returned to the house, stopping short when he saw Abigail waiting for him.

"Christ," he said. "You scared the hell out of me." He looked both annoyed and dissolute with his mussed hair, gaping robe, narrowed eyes. Hands pulled into fists.

Abigail's conviction faltered. Perhaps he was no different, after all, from the corrupt, bitter man he'd been when she first met him. "We should go inside," she said, disappointed to hear her voice waver. "We'll wake the neighborhood."

"An excellent idea. You go inside your house, and I'll go to mine." This was a stranger standing there, glaring down at her, issuing harsh imperatives.

"Jamie, I must speak with you," she persisted. "There's so much to say. I learned what happened to you in Khayrat, and the guilt you've borne for so long, and I—"

"Then there's nothing left to talk about." Grabbing her arm, he steered her toward her father's house. "You should have left well enough alone, Abby. You should have accepted me at face value. I needed your father's favor, you were a way to get that, and if I gave the impression you were anything more, then I did you a disservice.''

"I went to see Princess Layla," she said. "She told me what happened to you. But she didn't understand how you survived. I do, Jamie. Noah died in your place, didn't he? On that horse-buying trip you told me about. Tell me the rest, now. You owe me that.''

He flinched. "Noah and I were both arrested, but we figured out a way to escape. In the confusion of running through the city and finding the harbor, we were separated. I barely made it aboard because my injuries slowed me down.'' The whole time Jamie was speaking, he hadn't looked at her, and when he finally turned to her, his eyes were haunted. "I collapsed. By the time I regained consciousness, we were already at sea, and...Noah was already dead. Another trader saw the execution.''

Abigail pressed her fist to her mouth, remembering Doyle's description of the event.

"So," Jamie said, "do you still think I should tell Julius the truth about his father?''

"Of course not," she replied in a thick rasp, her throat half paralyzed with shock.

"I thought not. So there's your explanation of my dishonorable past. You know why I am the way I am, and why I'll never be the man you need me to be.''

"You already are," she said softly.

"Look, I made a mistake the other night. I let myself get carried away. But we're nothing together, Abby, no more than a stud to a mare.''

"I know better than that," she said, snapping in

her fear. ''I know what I felt when you made love to me, and I think I know what you felt when I surrendered everything to you. I *know,* Jamie. I—''

''Hush.'' He pressed two fingers to her lips. ''I took you to my bed, and a better man than I would feel responsible for you at this point. But you don't need me anymore, Abby. I made a mistake with you. By now you know me well enough to understand that I never make the same mistake twice.'' Stepping away from her, he raked a hand through his damp hair. ''I did love Layla,'' he softly admitted. ''She got the best part of me, and there is no more.''

Even though it was the middle of the night, Jamie dressed in haste. What Caroline had said was less important than what she hadn't. Something was afoot, and it couldn't be good for the people of Jamie's district. He had to go with his instinct on this one. He'd failed to do that once before, with tragic results, and he couldn't let it happen again.

And as for Abigail… He didn't want to think about her, but couldn't seem to stop himself. When he should have merely made use of her connections, he'd made the mistake of getting involved. Perhaps he was a bit like her mythological artist, Pygmalion. He'd proved to her that she could be the sort of woman who combined brains with self-confidence, panache with charm. The sort of woman even he couldn't resist. But he'd never take credit for her innocent, trusting heart and frankly sensual nature. Those things came from Abby and Abby alone, whether she knew it or not.

Her declaration of love had hit him like a hammer,

though he'd done his best to ignore it. He hadn't the heart for love, nor had he the stomach for the vulnerability, foolishness, responsibility...and the fulfillment.

The look on her face when he had shut the door on her would stay with him a long time. Where had his streak of emotional cruelty come from? Perhaps there was more of his father in him than he'd imagined. He told himself it was the least he could do to give Abigail her heart back. She had no business giving it to him anyway.

He hurried out of the house and made his way on foot to the livery where Oscar boarded. She'd survive, he told himself as he lit a lamp and set about saddling the horse. Before she knew it, Abigail would be married and settled. She would live a life of quiet decency, of safety and security, and who the hell was he to say that such a life wasn't worth living?

Thirty-Two

After that night, Jamie Calhoun never returned to Dumbarton Street, and Abigail discovered the true meaning of heartbreak. She drew herself through each day with sheer strength of will, and no one seemed to notice how quiet she'd grown, how introspective. No one seemed to realize that her outward cheerfulness masked a battered spirit.

Perhaps Jamie hadn't meant to teach her to bear up under unbearable pain, but he had shown her that appearances were everything, and illusion was a powerful tool.

She made use of that at breakfast one morning, when she joined her father and sister—late, as usual.

"You're spending more and more time on your comet hunt," her father commented, setting aside his *Post* and standing to help her into her chair.

"I keep thinking I'm going to see one soon," she said.

"Your patience is admirable," he said, pouring her morning tea.

Thanking him, she savored the warmth in his eyes.

This newfound bond of affection with her father filled a years-old emptiness. But the victory was bitter-sweet, for its price had been the sacrifice of a love she'd discovered too late. Still, she learned to appreciate the pleasant aspects of easy conversation with her father, and he learned to give more of himself. He shared stories and anecdotes of his courtship and marriage to her mother, and seemed surprised at how she and Helena treasured those glimpses of the past. Lately, he lingered with them over his morning coffee or evening port, more interested in his daughters than his duties.

"Helena," he said, "will you have coffee or tea?"

"What?" She blinked, clearly far away in her thoughts. "Oh, no thank you, Papa."

Helena, too, seemed different of late. She smiled less and rarely sang, making her plans and moving through each day with somber purpose.

"Are you quite well?" Abigail asked, feeling a pulse of concern for her sister.

"I am indeed," Helena said, though the brightness in her voice sounded forced. "Just...preoccupied with wedding plans."

"You're sure you want to marry Senator Barnes?" Father said, watching her intently. "Your sister agreed to a marriage for the wrong reasons, and I fear you might be doing the same."

Helena patted his hand. "Never worry about that, Papa. I've made my choice, and I'm content. Be proud of me." Her bright, beautiful smile almost masked her sadness. "I've finally learned to put youthful indiscretion behind me."

Her declaration seemed to reassure him, for he

went back to reading his paper. After a few moments, he frowned and cleared his throat.

"Bad news?" asked Abigail.

"Arsonists set fire to three barns and a home along King's Creek," he said.

"Dear God, was anyone hurt?"

He scanned the column. "Apparently not. The residents were warned, and the arsonists caught. There's a rumor that a railroad company is behind the crime, and will be subjected to an investigation."

Each night, after everyone else was asleep, Abigail went to her observatory alone to pursue her solitary search. As often as not, she devoted the time to thinking, trying to create a new dream of happiness now that all the old ones had slipped away. She probed the wounds of her memory for every last particle of knowledge of Jamie.

Had she ever really known him at all? Was he the dashing, romantic man who once traveled the world and fell in love with a fairy-tale princess? Or was he the world-weary politician, making use of people and then discarding them after they'd served their purpose?

She wanted to believe his cynicism was all an act, shielding a core of nobility and a heart that still remembered how to love. But now that he'd gone, she would never know for certain. All she knew was that she was a different person for having known him, even for a short time.

Why do you think they call it falling in love? When you truly fall in love, you'll know it. You will weep with the knowledge.

His words haunted her long after the night they'd met. It was the first lesson he'd taught her, but the last one she'd learned. She had known a love as intense as the brightest star, and a betrayal deeper than the blackest void in space.

Both love and betrayal, she thought on a cold December night as she sat shivering on the roof, had a peculiar majesty all their own. Jamie taught her that she would never find happiness in trying to please others if she didn't honor her own gifts. How simple life was when she stopped trying to do what was expected of her and followed her will.

Despite a broken heart, she drew strength from the memory of her love for Jamie, and focused as never before on her work. She mapped her sweeping searches with dead-on accuracy, but now she knew how to look for the magic, even in the midst of a mathematical calculation.

That was why she climbed to the roof each night, why she sat alone in the cold with her comet-sweeper aimed at the sky, a celestial chart in her lap and her sky log at hand.

The winter sky welcomed her searching, yet a persistent heartache lowered her spirits until she began to believe, after all these years, that perhaps there was no comet for her to discover. She should give it up, stop chasing stars and find something useful to do with herself. Yet a powerful force kept her coming to the roof, unable to stay away, even on a night as cold as the present one.

In the area of her search, she spied...something. A glimmer, quickly gone behind a high cloud, so startling that she nearly upset her equipment in her haste to read off the coordinates of the setting circle. As the possibility of discovery drew near, her outward calm masked an inner excitement that shimmered through her like a fever. She forced herself to hold still.

A few minutes before midnight, a light wind cleared the sky, and that faint glimmer teased her again. Now it was bright enough to see with the naked eye. A fuzzy beacon. She blinked, fearful that her eyes deceived her. At first she thought she might be seeing an asterism, but there it was, diffuse, lacking a tail, a distant and hazy object moving in the opposite direction of the earth, and outside the earth's orbit.

Her comet.

The head was so tenuous, she could see stars right through it, but that only added to the misty majesty of the object, riding a thin line of flame. The beauty of the distant heavenly body filled her senses to overflowing. Her heart rose almost painfully in her chest, and she had to remind herself to breathe. She nearly forgot to record the time and position, but training took over, and she quickly scribbled down the information. Even as she wrote, she never took her gaze away from the wonder in the sky.

Her comet. She always imagined that she would shout with excitement when she spied it, but instead, a feeling of quiet awe settled over her, a reverence that both humbled and uplifted her. Tonight, a comet had appeared in the night sky, and she was the first to see it.

Although she was alone, an almost overwhelming sense of well-being swept her senses. She felt alive as never before, whole and complete. "Oh, Mama, I did it," she whispered, surprising herself with the words. "I found a comet."

She felt an instant urge to go tearing downstairs, to hammer at the door of Jamie's house and tell him. But he was no longer there. A shadow of hurt marred the triumph. Jamie was her best friend, the only person who seemed to understand her lonely, late-night vigils. Now he was gone, and she didn't know if she'd ever see him again.

Her face was awash with tears and great sobs rolled up through her. She wiped impatiently at her cheeks, fearful of getting the eyepiece of the telescope wet, but for the longest time she couldn't stop weeping. Gale winds of emotion shuddered through her in unending waves.

She gave herself a stern lecture— Had Edmond Halley cried like a baby after correctly formulating astral motion? Had Maria Mitchell wept over her telescopic comet? Certainly not.

Abigail concentrated on practical matters. She had just made an extraordinary scientific discovery. She would have to send the customary telegram to the astronomical society, confirming the sighting. In the days to come, her discovery would have to be verified, but Abigail knew with unshakable faith what she had discovered. Scholarly journals and the popular press would report the find, and soon, ordinary people would spy it. Maybe even Jamie would look up one night and see her comet. A gold medal would be struck in her honor.

Would she become a celebrity like Professor

Mitchell? The notoriety didn't interest her, but winning credit for the discovery did.

Feeling the night breeze cool the tears on her cheeks, she leaned back, gazing at the sky. As always, thoughts of Jamie filled her heart. She'd always thought a broken heart would heal with time. Now she knew the hurt only went deeper with each passing day.

The thought added a bittersweet edge to her discovery. But that was all right, she decided. If she hadn't paid the price of her heart, perhaps this gift would never have been hers. She was the first person on earth to witness the comet, and the ache in her heart only made her sense of reverence more poignant. "I found it," she whispered to the empty night, to the stars and the wind.

"Comet Beatrice Cabot," she said aloud, tasting the name she'd chosen in honor of her mother.

Thirty-Three

At King's Creek, winter brought a stark, hushed beauty to the land. The low fields lay bare and etched by frost, and all along the creek, wind and cold leached the pigment from the reeds and grasses, creating an atmosphere of texture rather than color. After a two-hour ride from Albion and a soul-satisfying meal prepared by Noah's widow, Patsy, Jamie smoked a cheroot on the porch of his brother's place and waited for twilight.

He would always think of it as Noah's place, although his brother would never again work stock in the training ring, ride fence along the edge of the property or drive a plow behind one of the muscle-bound Shires that had been his wife's dowry.

Nor would Noah ever see the sight Jamie could see from his seat on the porch steps—a tall, strapping Julius bringing in the wood for his mother. He and Julius had spent the past week rebuilding one of the barns that had been burned in a clumsily idiotic attempt by the railroad company to intimidate residents along King's Creek. You'd be so proud of your boy, Noah, thought Jamie.

After a while, he lit a lantern, for it was growing too dim to see the book he'd been reading—*From the Earth to the Moon* by Jules Verne. Not long ago, he would have dismissed it as an improbable yarn, but now...thanks to Abigail Cabot's wild imagination and precise science, an outlandish story about members of a gun club planning a journey to the moon no longer seemed far-fetched. The chance of being shot into space from a cannon was not without its appeal.

Everything reminded him of her. The whisper of the wind through the bare trees was her voice speaking his name, the indigo sky at twilight was the color of her eyes, the phantom scent of winter evoked memories that didn't just ache, but stabbed.

This was not supposed to happen to him. He was supposed to be immune, impervious. But the fact was, there was a hole in his life, and that hole was the exact size of a small dynamo, a woman he had pushed away on purpose.

Tugging a shawl around her, Patsy came out on the porch. She looked distracted, not as pretty as she'd been when Noah had married her fifteen years before, but strong and wise in the way of a woman who had survived hard times. "Come back inside," she said. "It's cold as a frog's fingernails."

"I'll be along shortly." Jamie put aside his book and took out the newspaper he'd brought along to read then share with Julius. He turned to an article about the fall congressional session, his chest tight with satisfaction as he read the summary of the railroad legislation. The Senate vote had tied, and Vice

President Butler had cast an unexpected ballot, breaking the tie and favoring the farmers not the railroads.

As he scanned the pages of the *Post,* another item caught his eye. Timothy Doyle's byline under the headline Senator Cabot's Daughter to Wed in Gala Ceremony.

A frost swept over him, colder than the winter wind from the bay. The cheroot dropped from between numb fingers. He could hear the sounds of Patsy and Julius in the house behind him, the cozy clank of utensils as they put up the supper dishes. He told himself to join them, to forget the headline, or at least to admit he was pleased by it.

The marriage was his doing, after all. He had practically engineered the whole thing, and he'd done a damn good job of it. He'd shown Abigail how to be— how had she put it that night?—her best self. She'd become a woman who was far too good for the likes of him.

Or so he told himself. But he kept wondering if that was true, or if it was only an excuse. *I know what I felt when you made love to me, and I think I know what you felt when I surrendered everything to you.* Those were the last words she'd spoken to him, and they lingered and ached inside him. Because of her, he was a better man, and she'd understood that long before he did. Maybe that was why losing her had knocked him flat, because he could have made her happy.

Unable to resist probing the wound, he turned up the lamp and read the item in the paper.

Over two hundred guests will be in attendance at the nuptials of Senator Troy Barnes of New

York and Miss Helena Mae Cabot of Georgetown, daughter of Senator Franklin Rush
Cabot...

Jamie had to read the announcement twice before
he trusted his own eyes. The news story was about
Helena Cabot, not Abigail. *Not Abigail.*
He drowned slowly in the article. His senses filled
with the pounding of his own heart, the hiss of the
gas lamp, the clack of the wind in the reeds along the
creek. The nuptials belonged to Helena, not Abigail.
Not Abigail.
Almost as a postscript to the article, there was a
mention that the senator's other daughter recently discovered a comet, and that all the principal observa-
tories in Europe and the Americas were being noti-
fied.

Miss Cabot's comet will be visible for naked-
eye viewing over the next three weeks....

Jamie extinguished the lamp and tore like a mad-
man away from the house, turning his back on the
square of golden light in the kitchen window. Twilight had only just begun to yield to the first stars,
glimmering in the clear December sky. He found the
star called Vega, the reference point given, and studied the field for a comet. Minutes passed like hours.
He had only a vague idea of what to look for. Was it
the yellowish wink or the white, crescent-shaped nimbus? Finally, with his eyes watering and a crick in his
neck, he spotted a fuzzy, bluish glimmer and felt a
clutch of recognition.

"Is that it, Abby?" he said aloud. "Is that your comet?" Whether he had found it or not was unimportant. What mattered was that Abby had found it, just as she'd predicted.

He stood there, grinning like an idiot, his heart full. "Miss Cabot's comet," he said, and then the grin faded. *Miss* Cabot. Not Mrs. Butler.

Questions flashed through him. What had happened? Why hadn't she married Butler? She was supposed to be better off with him. That had been the whole point, hadn't it? But maybe...

The door to Noah's place slapped open with a bang of impatience. "You coming in for a piece of my chess pie?" Patsy yelled.

"Something came up," Jamie called to her. "I need to go."

"It's dark, fool."

"I'll take a lantern."

"You know better—"

"I have to." He was already running for his horse. "This can't wait."

Part Five

"It occurred to me when I was thirteen and wearing white gloves and Mary Janes and going to dancing school, that no one should have to dance backward all their lives."
—Jill Ruckelshaus

Thirty-Four

The bridal bouquet sailed past a dozen outstretched arms, but Abigail Beatrice Cabot remembered to duck out of the way. She was more than happy to see the tradition embraced by someone—anyone—other than herself. Sarah Generes let out a squeal of triumph, clutching the prize to her chest.

Wedding guests crowded the Long Room of Georgetown's City Tavern, but there was plenty of space for dancing to the lively music of a small ensemble. Catching Helena's hand as she passed by, Abigail gave an encouraging squeeze.

"You've made a lucky girl of Miss Sarah," she said. "See, she's holding the bouquet as though you'd sprinkled it with fairy dust."

Helena was quite possibly the most beautiful bride ever to grace the elite society of Georgetown, yet a private melancholy softened her smiling façade. "I wish her well, then. Perhaps she'll find a happy ending."

"Ah, Helena." Abigail kept hold of her hand and drew her to one of the tall windows with a wrought-iron balcony projecting out over M Street. "You were meant to be happy, and you will be, I just know it."

"And you always were the smart one, weren't you?" Helena asked. Her eyes suspiciously bright, she laughed softly. "Truly, Abigail, you've been such a comfort to me in so many ways."

"What are you doing, hiding from the guests?" Their father motioned them back into the Long Room. "Never let it be said my beautiful daughters are wallflowers!" His pleasure in the event seemed to pour from him in waves of enthusiasm. Cocking out both elbows, he escorted his daughters into the midst of the admiring crowd. "A senator's bride and a distinguished astronomer," he declared. "You make me proud, my girls."

Abigail felt a rush of love for him. Their new understanding of one another strengthened with each passing day. As for Boyd Butler, he'd gone to sea, and rumor had it he was carrying on a happy correspondence with the war secretary's pretty daughter.

Father gazed at Helena with fond melancholy. "I can't believe my firstborn daughter is leaving me."

"Papa, I'll always be your firstborn," Helena protested.

"That will never change," Abigail assured him. "Dance with the bride, Father. I believe I'll go join the Vandiverts for oysters and champagne." Disengaging her arm from his, she stepped back to send them onto the dance floor.

As she approached the banquet table, Abigail felt something catch the heel of her shoe. Pain shot up her leg. She clutched wildly at empty air, finding nothing to hold on to.

Mrs. Vandivert's face registered pure horror, but

not surprise. Abigail Cabot's clumsiness was legendary and probably always would be.

Then a miracle occurred. A pair of strong arms caught her from behind and propped her against someone warm and firm.

"Easy now, honey," he said in a Virginia drawl. "You don't want to become the main dish at the banquet."

Abigail's bones melted. *Jamie.*

She mouthed his name, but no sound came out. Turning in his arms, she gaped at his smiling face.

"I can't leave you alone for a moment," he whispered. "As soon as I turn my back, you get in trouble again."

"Is..." Her voice broke. "Is that so?"

"Dance with me, Abby love. I need an excuse to hold you close."

She followed in shocked obedience, and the aching familiarity of his embrace, his scent, his nearness, filled her. She drank in the longed-for sight of him, the feel of his arms around her, the subtle spice of his scent. Magic was at work tonight. He was an apparition from her sweetest dreams.

The weeks apart seemed to evaporate into thin air, and she danced in his arms as though he had never left her.

"You know what they say about fast women and blooded mares," he explained with a familiar, wicked wink. "Give them free rein, and they'll trample you every time."

He was as obnoxious—and endearing—as ever. Abigail knew her heart shone in her eyes when she said, "What are you doing here?"

"Isn't it obvious?"

"No." The urge to laugh pressed at her with the same insistence as the urge to cry.

"You're always so literal, Abby. Very well, we'll make a list. I came to humble myself before you, grovel at your feet, beg your forgiveness, declare my undying love and ask for your hand in marriage. Is that what you wanted to know?"

"Those are only words," she said, thick-throated with emotion. "How do I know you mean it this time?"

"Ah, you know, Abby. You knew before I did. You knew I could love you better than any man alive, but I didn't think I could." He shut his eyes briefly, then opened them to watch her intently. "That look on your face when you saw Caroline leaving my house— I feared that I could never love you without hurting you."

"The only way you hurt me is by staying away," she whispered, her heart lifting with every step they took. "I do like the sound of everything on your list, but the undying love will suffice."

"You have it, then," he said, and he wasn't smiling, but gazing at her with an intensity that surged through her like an intimate caress. "You have every bit of my heart, Abby. Always."

The dance set ended, but they held each other until another started up. "Damn," he said. "I need to kiss you. *Bad.* And then I need to—" Bending down, he whispered the rest in her ear.

She indicated the wrought-iron balcony leading to a secluded loggia.

"Lead the way, love. And *hurry.*"

She did her best to move discreetly toward the exit, but managed to step on his foot. "Ah, Jamie." She smiled at him through her tears. "How will you abide having a wife with such disgraceful dancing skills?"

"Wrong question, my wren. Dancing is for earth-bound creatures. I'll have a wife who can touch the stars."

Dear Reader,

Although I strive for historical accuracy in my novels, I didn't indicate the precise year *Halfway to Heaven* takes place. Like all dreams and fairy tales, this story is true at heart no matter when it takes place. I did drop hints at the time period to give you a taste of the wildly romantic Gilded Age. The advent of this period was 1873, when Mark Twain and Charles Dudley Warner published their book *The Gilded Age: A Tale of Today,* and the era continued until approximately the turn of the century.

In spring of 2002, please watch for a very special reissue of one of my favorite books. *The Lightkeeper* is a dramatic "Beauty-and-the-Beast" story of a grieving man and the woman who brings light and joy into his life.

And for those of you wondering what's to become of Abigail's sister, Helena, she has a very compelling story of her own, and will be the subject of a new novel to be published in October 2002.

Until then, happy reading,
Susan Wiggs
Box 4469
Rollingbay WA 98061-0469
www.susanwiggs.com